The story of Josephine Cox is as extraordinary as anything in her novels. Born in a cotton-mill house in Blackburn, she was one of ten children. Her parents, she says, brought out the worst in each other, and life was full of tragedy and hardship – but not without love and laughter. At the age of sixteen, Josephine met and married 'a caring and wonderful man', and had two sons. When the boys started school, she decided to go to college and eventually gained a place at Cambridge University, though was unable to take this up as it would have meant living away from home. However, she did go into teaching, while at the same time helping to renovate the derelict council house that was their home, coping with the problems caused by her mother's unhappy home life – and writing her first full-length novel. Not surprisingly, she then won the 'Superwoman of Great Britain' Award, for which her family had secretly entered her, and this coincided with the acceptance of her novel for publication.

Josephine gave up teaching in order to write full time. She says, 'I love writing, both recreating scenes and characters from my past, together with new storylines which mingle naturally with the old. I could never imagine a single day without writing, and it's been that way since as far back as I can remember.' Her previous novels of North Country life are all available from Headline and are immensely popular.

'Josephine Cox brings so much freshness to the plot, and the characters . . . Her fans will love this coming-of-age novel. So will many of the devotees of Catherine Cookson, desperate for a replacement' *Birmingham Post*

'Guaranteed to tug at the heartstrings of all hopeless romantics' *Sunday Post*

'Hailed quite rightly as a gifted writer in the tradition of Catherine Cookson . . .' *Manchester Evening News*

By Josephine Cox

THE EMMA GRADY TRILOGY
Outcast
Alley Urchin
Vagabonds

QUEENIE'S STORY
Her Father's Sins
Let Loose the Tigers

Angels Cry Sometimes
Take This Woman
Whistledown Woman
Don't Cry Alone
Jessica's Girl
Nobody's Darling
Born To Serve
More Than Riches
A Little Badness
Living A Lie
The Devil You Know
A Time For Us
Cradle of Thorns
Miss You Forever
Love Me Or Leave Me
Tomorrow The World
The Gilded Cage
Somewhere, Someday
Rainbow Days
Looking Back
Let It Shine
The Woman Who Left
Jinnie
Bad Boy Jack

JOSEPHINE COX

Bad Boy Jack

First published in hardback in 2002 by
HEADLINE BOOK PUBLISHING PLC

First published in paperback in 2003 by
HEADLINE BOOK PUBLISHING PLC

This edition published in paperback in 2017 by
HEADLINE PUBLISHING GROUP

3

Cataloguing in Publication Data is available from the British Library

ISBN 978 1 4722 4578 6

Typeset in Times by Avon DataSet Ltd, Bidford-on-Avon, Warwickshire

Printed and bound in the UK by Clays Ltd, St Ives plc

Headline's policy is to use papers that are natural, renewable and recyclable products and made from wood grown in well-managed forests and other controlled sources. The logging and manufacturing processes are expected to conform to the environmental regulations of the country of origin.

HEADLINE PUBLISHING GROUP
An Hachette UK Company
Carmelite House
50 Victoria Embankment
London EC4Y 0DZ

www.headline.co.uk
www.hachette.co.uk

This book is for the lovely Geraldine, whose smile and delightful nature I will never forget. Thank you for everything, Geraldine. You were one in a million.

A word of warning to every lonely, vulnerable person, man or woman: let me tell you about two friends of mine. I won't use their real names for obvious reasons, but they are both family women, currently unattached, smart and attractive.

One was conned by a man into signing for a car, which she now has to pay for.

The other: a very professional woman who has suffered many setbacks and who, like the first, was vulnerable, got cruelly tricked out of her savings and her home.

You might think they were silly, but you would be very, very wrong! These are two intelligent, likeable and capable women.

Their only fault was that they were too kind and trusting.

Nobody, not even the police, can find the rogue responsible.

What I say is this – May he rot in hell.

Contents

Part One

JANUARY 1895

GONE AWAY

Chapter One

Mary's heart was pounding as she hurried down the country lane. The biting wind whipped her long, loose hair and the driving sleet stung her face, but she didn't flinch. Instead she quickened her pace.

She had no idea where she was headed or whether she would find contentment when she got there. She had packed only the most necessary items; enough to see her over the first week, and though her purse was not bulging with money, it would feed her and rent a room for a fortnight. Other than that she had her hopes and dreams, which in themselves would fill the biggest heart.

She needed to re-evaluate her life, and for that she had to find a place far away from here; a place where she had never been before – a safe, quiet place where she could either curl up and smother herself in self-pity or, if she was brave enough, find a new life and forget what had happened here, in this street, in that house . . . all her dreams shattered.

Deep in her heart she knew she would never find the same powerful, all-consuming love that she had experienced with Robert, but she had already resigned herself to that. She might never find riches, or contentment, but that was of no matter.

Already she was filled with regrets, but she would learn to live with them. Whatever happened now, there would be no going back. Not for anything . . . *or anyone*.

At the corner of the lane, she stopped and glanced back. He was at the cottage window, watching her, holding a lamp in his hand. Their eyes met, and her heart leapt. Then she saw him turn away. She paused for a moment, but he did not reappear – then with new resolve she bowed her head to the wind and pushed on.

Nothing had changed.

Inside the house, Robert Sullivan made his way upstairs to the back bedroom. Inching wide the door, he stood there for what seemed an age, his broad shoulders resting against the frame, his emerald-green eyes marbled with pain as they probed the darkness of that tiny bedroom.

From the village street outside he heard the sound of a couple laughing; almost immediately the laughter changed to anger, the cutting voices shattering his quiet mood. Curiously, the verbal abuse then gave way to another sound, sharp and quick, like the crack of a whip, or a spiteful female hand slapping against a man's undefended cheek. A brief, brooding silence followed, until a burst of hearty laughter once more took its place.

He smiled knowingly. 'A lover's tiff,' he murmured cynically. In that one lonely moment, he envied them.

Gathering his thoughts, he returned his attention to the small, sleeping figures. Just now, with the hazy light from the lamp bathing their faces, his children appeared to be looking at him with accusing eyes, but of course they were not. Lowering his gaze he looked away; strange, unbearable emotions raging through him.

Bowing his head, he stepped away and closed the door softly. In that moment, he realised the enormity of what he must do, and almost changed his mind.

Inevitably, the moment passed and his resolve returned. Taking a deep breath he quietly assured himself, 'You have no choice.' His voice hardened. '*She has left you no choice!*'

In his tortured mind he could see her face; not beautiful, but incredibly pretty in a childish way. He thrust the image from his mind. He would never forgive her! *They* would never forgive her!

Making his way downstairs he crossed the hall and entered the living room, where he slumped into the armchair; his face bathed in the heat from the fire, his eyes closed and his mind alive with all manner of unquiet thoughts.

After a while he shifted his reluctant gaze to the photograph on the mantelpiece. The young, fair-haired woman was smiling, her brown eyes returning his gaze. Wanting to hate her, but unable to stifle the love he felt, he wisely looked away.

Disturbed now, he got out of the chair and collected the photograph into his strong, workworn fingers. He smiled, a forlorn kind of smile. 'I'll always love you,' he told her, his voice grated with emotion, 'in spite of what you did.' A moment of regret, then he kissed her cold uplifted face. 'Goodbye, Mary, my love. God keep you safe . . . wherever you may go.'

He had no way of knowing where she had gone. In fact, he never expected to see her again. No matter. Maybe it was for the best.

With his immediate concern for the morning, and the fate of the two innocents upstairs, he replaced the photograph, and for the next hour, busied himself in tidying the room. He put away the children's toys – little Nancy's rag doll with the round flat face and big blue eyes encircled with outrageously long eyelashes, and Jack's precious wooden train . . . a long, black, meticulously detailed replica with red wheels and a whistle that actually sounded like the real thing.

Robert proudly recalled how he himself had carved it from a piece of wood he and Jack had found in Yardacre Spinney.

After clearing the room, he made himself a nightcap . . . a mug of hot milk laced with a generous measure of brandy. Turning once more to pleasure in Mary's sweet smile, he raised his cup with a flourish, but he didn't speak. These past few days there had been too much of that . . . too many words with nothing meaningful!

Frowning, he downed the drink in one long breathless gulp. The liquid warmed his insides, helping him relax and settle his thoughts.

More contented now, he sat for a time, his long legs stretched out in front of him and his arms lazily dangling over the sides of the chair. Mentally going over the events of the last few days, he became enraged. With *her*! With himself. The heat and the brandy had started to affect his senses, he knew, and he sprang out of the chair, determined not to let events overwhelm him.

Taking his empty cup to the scullery he set it down on the draining-board and, leaning on his hands, he stared into the sink with unseeing eyes. *He hated her!* No! He loved her. *He wanted to kill her for what she had done!* Yet he wanted her back . . . if only to advise him as to what he should do. But she wasn't coming back and there was no use wishing.

Turning on the cold tap, he bent his head over the sink, closed his eyes and swilled the shockingly cold water over his face and neck. Thankfully, it seemed to sober his thoughts.

Returning to the living room, he glanced about. The dark sofa and two matching chairs were the worse for wear, and yet the dresser, long ago scarred by generations of users, had been polished to a mirror finish by Mary.

On the opposite wall, the oval wooden-framed mirror above the fireplace was whisker clean, and below it, straddling the mantel, the velvet cover was brushed smooth, its long silky tassels gently lifting in the rising heat from the fire. Green it was, and soft to the touch . . . he moved now to stroke his fingertips over its surface, but it didn't help to soothe him. He was foolish to think it ever would.

His favourite item in the room was the solitary picture that hung against the back wall. Large and bold, it depicted a lively scene in the marketplace, Mary's regular weekend haunt. Many was the time during the past year she had lived with him that she would return from a Saturday visit to Bedford Town, her face flushed with excitement at some bargain or other she had managed to secure.

He saw it all in his mind and his heart leapfrogged at the bittersweet memory. Emotion spilled over. In spite of all his resolve, it was more than he could bear.

A burst of rage erupted inside him. Grabbing the small chair he swung it into the dresser, slicing the smile from her face, and shattering her image into a million pieces. Tiny slivers of glass and small china ornaments exploded in all directions. He stared at the dismembered face for a moment, then, with an anguished cry, he brought his foot down on it, and ground her to pulp beneath his boot.

Exhausted, he surveyed the room through bloodshot eyes; oddly gratified to see that it was now a shambles. With a heavy heart and his features set like granite, he turned on his heel and made his way upstairs to his room, where he fell across his bed and drifted into a deep, fitful sleep.

In the room opposite, the young boy lay awake. Time and again he heard his father call out in his sleep, and guilt surged through his soul. He knew what was happening – that she had gone, and that he was to blame – and a feeling of terror gripped him. Things had got out of hand, and he no longer understood his own motives. Oh, if only their real mother had come back! If only she and his daddy could be together again, everything would be all right.

The boy shivered and turned restlessly in his bed. He would

not be able to sleep this night. How could he, when he had no idea what the morning might bring?

One thing was for certain. Whatever happened, he knew he would have to be brave . . . if only for his baby sister's sake.

Chapter Two

Nancy woke and leapt out of bed. Running to the window, her bare feet icy cold, she screamed with delight. 'Jack! Jack! Look at the snow!' Her voice shook with excitement, as she pressed her face to the window. 'COME AND LOOK!' A small, pretty child with the face of an angel and the heart of a lion, Nancy was coming up to three years of age. 'Three years old, going on ninety-three,' her father laughingly claimed, though these days he didn't laugh much, more was the pity.

Jack smiled at her from the far side of the room, where he was pulling up his trouser-braces. 'I know,' he answered with a boyish pride. 'I've already seen it.'

His sister's small face was etched with disappointment. 'Oh!' She had so much wanted to be the first to see the snow.

'It started while you were still fast asleep.' Returning his attention to fastening the top button of his one and only good shirt, he glanced at his image in the bit of mirror hanging on a nail; tall and slim of build, he was a quiet-natured soul, opposite in personality to the exuberant Nancy, and because of their unsettled situation, the seven-year-old boy had already adopted a protective role towards this darling little girl. 'I've been awake a long time, you see.'

Momentarily distracted by the falling snow, Nancy seemed

not to have heard, but then with her wondrous eyes following the large, fluffy snowflakes, she asked curiously, 'How long?'

Sighing, Jack rolled his chestnut-brown eyes. 'Don't really know.' He shrugged his shoulders. 'Three, maybe four hours.' He sighed again, 'All I know is, I've been awake a *l-o-n-g time*.' He dragged out the word to emphasise the dreary unending night he had endured.

'Can we make a snowman, Jack? Can we?' His sister's sapphire-blue eyes lit up.

Before Jack could reply, another voice intervened. 'Sorry, Nancy, there's no time.' Robert was at the door, washed and shaved, and ready to go. 'We'd best be off, before the snow sets in. Come on! Move yourselves!'

Shocked by the harshness in his voice, the children looked at him. Not surprisingly, it was Nancy who spoke. 'Where are we going, Daddy?'

Unprepared for his daughter's direct question, Robert quickly searched for a suitable answer. 'We need to find a new house.' It was a downright lie, and he hated himself for it.

'Why can't we stay here?' The little girl's lip trembled.

'Because we need to make a fresh start, *that's* why.' This time it was no lie. A fresh start was what they all needed – him, Mary, *and* the children, he thought. Through his torment he had convinced himself of that.

'Will it have an orchard and a spinney, and will it be the same as here?' Nancy's blue eyes filled with tears.

'I hope so, sweetheart.' His voice had softened a little.

Her brother was not so easily pacified. 'Will I have to go to a new school?' he asked sternly.

'Probably.' Taken aback by the fire in his son's eyes, Robert wondered how much the boy knew. An old head on young shoulders, Jack was a quiet child, deep and private, and it was not beyond the realms of possibility that he knew all there was to know. It was a daunting thought. 'Maybe you won't have to change schools,' he answered lamely. 'It all depends.'

Jack was hopeful. 'Do you mean we might come back here to Hilltops to live . . . if we can't find a house we like?'

'That's enough talk for now.' Backing up towards the door, Robert indicated that he was through discussing it. 'Move yourselves then, you two. If we hurry we might just catch the eight-thirty omnibus into town.'

'Daddy?'

'Now what?' He turned to face his son.

The boy smiled, a sly, infuriating smile, his voice little more than a whisper. 'I'm glad *she's* gone.'

Robert's features hardened. So, he *did* know after all, damn and bugger it! The boy had never warmed to Mary, and had taken every opportunity to come between them. 'Get a move on!' he ordered. He had calculated that with the thirty minute journey into town, it would be about quarter to nine when they arrived at their actual destination; five minutes added on to organise everything and, thankfully, the children would not have to wait in the cold for too long. He had to do it. *For their sakes more than his, he had to do it.* And may God forgive him.

Sensing that his father would not be drawn any further, Jack reconciled himself to whatever lay ahead. 'Come on,' he urged his sister. 'You'd best get dressed.' Collecting her clothes from the back of the chair where she had placed them the night before, he laid them on the bed; there was a long, frilly petticoat, some warm red stockings, and a soft, woolly dress, sage green in colour, with a black collar and belt.

Relieved that his daughter seemed to have accepted his answer, and that his son had at last fallen silent, Robert smiled from one to the other; though it was a sad smile that never reached his troubled green eyes. 'Good girl, Nancy, and you'd best get a quick wash, eh? We don't want folks thinking you're a pair of vagabonds.' Again, that sorry smile. 'Don't be long now.'

'I won't, Daddy.' She stole a moment to take a last look at the familiar world outside her window; the long, meandering fields now shrouded in snow and the swathes of forest that skirted the horizon; the small lake shimmering silver in the distance and the army of sparrows that sat huddled like soldiers in the branches of the tree just below her window. Because they visited the house every day, Nancy had named every one of them.

Hilltops had been the children's home now for the past eight months. Some three hundred years old, it had stood the test of time well. A pretty cottage in an old lane with few neighbouring houses, it had three bedrooms, a spacious living room and a tiny kitchen. Set in a small village in some of Bedfordshire's most beautiful countryside, it was a little isolated from the outside world, but that was what gave it its appeal.

Tearing herself away from the fairytale scene outside, the tiny girl skipped across the room and gave her father a hug. 'Mary will wash me.'

Her innocent remark turned his heart over. 'Not today, sweetheart,' he said gruffly.

A look of confusion coloured her features. 'But she *always* washes me!'

Helpless, Robert appealed to the boy. 'Will you see to it, son?' He threw him a warning glance. 'And don't let your tongue run away with you.'

Jack understood only too well. 'It's all right, Nancy.' He took his sister by the hand. 'I'll help you.'

Taking the moment, Robert returned to the living room where he hastily wrote a letter that the children were not privileged to see.

While Nancy changed from her nightie to her petticoat, Jack went down to the kitchen where he poured some warm water into a bowl; folding a clean towel over his shoulder, he carried bowl and cloth upstairs and helped Nancy wash the sleep from her eyes. He reluctantly assisted in brushing her long, corn-coloured hair, and afterwards held the dress while she put her arms through it. 'Do I look pretty?' Holding out the hem of her dress, she gave a twirl, her blue eyes shining mischievously.

Jack laughed. 'You look just like the doll in the music-box.'

Twirling again, Nancy got dizzy and fell laughing into his arms.

Cutting through their fun, Robert's voice called up to them, 'Are you two ready yet?'

Jack answered, 'In a minute.' He had so many pressing questions, yet he dared not voice any one of them.

When they came downstairs Robert was pacing the living room like a caged animal. 'There's toast and marmalade, and I've made you both a hot drink.' Leading Nancy to the table he sat her on a chair with a cushion and drew it up. 'We've about ten minutes before we need to leave.'

Jack didn't eat, while Nancy eagerly tucked into the hot toast, though she didn't drink much, which was just as well since she had only recently been trained from the baby potty.

While Robert went to fetch her hat and coat, she took it upon herself to pay a visit to the lavvy. 'See! I can go all on my own now,' she declared proudly, though her father had to free her knickers where they had caught up in her dress.

To Robert's relief, they caught the omnibus with a minute to spare; it was a mad dash down the country lanes to the main road, past the woodshed where his son Jack and he had spent many an hour chopping wood and carving, and where last winter they had built a rocking-horse for Nancy.

As they hurried by, the young lad couldn't help but wonder if they would ever see this place again.

Too young to entertain such thoughts, Nancy believed with all her heart that they really would come back, if only because the idea of leaving this place for ever was too terrible. In the past eight months she, like Jack, had come to love Hilltops. She loved it all . . . the shed where they watched their daddy build Jack's tree-house, and make the big flat tables for hammering to the trees so the birds could feed easily. Then there was the orchard with its many fruit trees, the rows of raspberry canes that spilled over with lush berries and splashes of colour in late summer and autumn; and oh, that magical spinney, where the children had spent many a happy hour playing hide and seek.

They were never lonely, even though they neither of them had many friends, save for the milkman's son, who sometimes played boyish games with Jack, like racing and conkering and things that Nancy was too young and small to join in. But he only visited once a week and was soon gone.

And now they themselves were going, and neither of them knew if or when they would ever come back.

Bedford Town at a quarter to nine on a Friday morning was a town just waking up. As the trio walked through the snowy marketplace, the sleepy traders trudged from cart to stall, shivering, carrying their wares and setting them out, ready for the rush they hoped would happen. All around them, horses trotted through the square, going about their business; big, handsome shire horses pulling the brewery drays, the milkman's old grey mare, ambling along with her eyes on the fat, juicy carrots now laid out on the market stalls, and even a donkey . . . with straw bags hanging from his withers and a hat with broad brim, seemingly to protect his long ears from the cold.

'Look, Nancy! Look at the coalman's hat!' Chuckling, Jack called his sister's attention to the flat cap atop the man's jolly round face, its wide, stiff peak piled high with coal dust. Before heaving a sackful of coal from the cart onto his back, the man would shake his head and the black dust would go everywhere, especially up his nose, at which he would sneeze and yell, and frighten the pigeons that had settled on the roofs close by. They took off in a mad rush, and returned a moment later, only to swoop off again when the horse appeared to have got a noseful and gave out a bellowing sneeze that shook the cart on its axle.

By the time Robert and the children arrived at the town hall, it was ten minutes to nine; just as Robert had planned. 'We'll wait here,' he told the youngsters. 'I'm sure it won't be long before they open.'

So they sat down and waited – a pathetic little group, huddled together on the grey steps of that huge formidable building, and all around them was the hustle and bustle of busy people, hurrying to the boulevard and the shops or their places of work, or merely browsing through the half laid-out stalls.

Concerned that he might be seen and afterwards remembered, Robert grew agitated. 'Are you sure your coat's done up properly?' he fussed, turning from a curious woman's stare to check Nancy's coat and satisfy himself that his little daughter would be warm until someone arrived. At the same time, he slipped the all-important letter inside her pocket. 'What about you, Jack? Are you all right, son?'

Jack nodded, but said nothing. Robert was not surprised. He had seen the accusing look in the boy's eyes and was shamed.

Another moment and a young woman arrived; small and homely with a bright red scarf tied round her shoulder-length dark hair and a long coat down to her boots. She appeared to be not much older than Robert, 'Well! Well! Waiting for me, are yer?' she said. She had the warm, colourful accent of a Bedfordshire local.

To Robert's immense relief, her ready smile told him that here was a woman he could trust. 'By! I hope you haven't caught your death o' cold, sitting on them steps.' Turning the key in the lock she threw open the big, panelled door. 'You'd best come inside.'

Once inside, she gestured for them to sit on the bench beside the office window. 'Before you tell me what business brings you 'ere, I'll get me hat and coat off, and see if I can't rustle up a hot drink for the young 'uns.' Laughing, she added with a cheeky wink, 'If I look hard enough, I might even be able to find a biscuit or two.' She asked Robert if he would like a drink but he gratefully declined, taking great care not to draw too much attention to himself, and all the while avoiding eye contact with her.

With the children seated on the bench and the woman gone to bring the drinks, Robert made his move. 'You two stay here a minute,' he suggested. 'I won't be long.'

'Where are you going?' Nancy didn't much like being left there. 'I want to come with you.'

'No, sweetheart. It's too cold for you to be wandering about, and anyway, that nice woman is bringing you a drink. Like I say . . . I won't be gone but a minute or two.'

He gave her a long, hard hug and kissed her tenderly on the forehead; he might have done the same for Jack, if it hadn't been for the hostile look he received.

Taking a deep breath he shook his head, 'For God's sake . . . don't look at me like that, son.'

Unmoved by his father's plea, Jack looked away.

Leaning towards him, Robert lowered his voice. 'Look after your sister, son,' he said. 'Whatever you might think, I *do* love you both.'

'No, you don't.' The look Jack gave him was shrivelling. Taking the infant into his arms, he assured her softly, 'Don't worry, sis. I'll look after you.' Taking hold of her hand, he led Nancy down the corridor, 'Let's go and find that nice woman, eh?'

Already he had turned his back on his father. It was a hard thing for Robert to accept, but he knew he had no one to blame but himself. Maybe there would come a day when Jack might understand and forgive. But not today. Today was the end of something precious.

Not once did Jack glance back at his father. Nor did Nancy; though she wanted to. Instead, there was something about what Jack was saying that frightened her. 'Don't tell them *anything*!' he urged. 'Just you keep quiet, Nancy. I'll take care of it.' He had no idea what might happen to them now, but of one thing the boy was certain . . . their daddy was not coming back. First their mammy had deserted them, then Mary, and now *him*. There was only Nancy and himself left now.

'When will Daddy be back?' Clutching his hand, Nancy looked up to him with tearful eyes.

Jack gave no answer. Instead, he quickened his pace and continued down that narrow gloomy corridor.

By the time the woman ushered the children into the tiny kitchen, Robert had already made his way out of the building.

Once outside, he hurried away. He dared not linger, nor look back. Instead he broke into a run and as he ran he sobbed, the tears rolling unheeded down his face.

Leaving the children behind like that was the cruellest and hardest thing he had ever done. Though it made what he was about to do now all that much easier.

Chapter Three

His mind unsettled, and his thoughts back there with the children, Robert had been wandering the streets of Bedford Town all day; the cold and wind tore at him, and the snow fell about his feet in folds, but he wasn't aware of any of that. Darkness began to close in, and still he did not realise that day had shifted into evening. All he knew was his own failure and the awful truth – that he had delivered his precious children into the hands of strangers. And why? Because he was too much of a coward to go on, *that* was why! He had given up.

He had loved his wife Mathilde so much. In the ten years they had been wed, and had had their two bairns, he had never once looked at another woman. Oh, he had had plenty of opportunities, but he wanted no other. Then, a year ago, he had been devastated when she walked out on him and the children. *I'm starting a new life*, she wrote in her letter. *I'm in love with someone else*. It was only later that he discovered she had gone off with the rentman, whose father had recently died and left him a string of properties. Mathilde, apparently, had leapt at the opportunity to better herself.

Because of the children, and because he loved her still, he had tracked her down and begged her to come home, but she would not be persuaded. '*This* is what I want!' She stood at the door of her fine house, wearing silk and pearls, and scoffed at his attempts to reason with her. 'This is my home now, Robert. I have servants at my beck and call and enough money to buy whatever I want.' She laughed in his face. 'What makes you think I'd swap all this for a cramped house in a back street, with never enough money left over for luxuries? You and the children must make your own way. God knows, I gave you the best years of my life. Now you can have a taste of it. I don't need you any more, Robert Sullivan, and the sooner you get that into your head, the better!' With that, she handed him back her wedding ring and slammed the door in his face.

Only his pride kept him from breaking it down.

Over the next few weeks he went about his work and wrote endless letters asking for her to come and see the children, if only for a short visit, as they were pining for her. But she never answered, and he wondered how he could ever have fallen in love with a woman so selfish and hard-hearted that she could abandon her own childer, and Nancy still practically a babe in arms.

The last time he had gone to the house, it was a night much like tonight . . . snowing heaven's hardest, with a wind that could slice the skin from your face. 'Gone away,' the servant told him. 'We have no idea when the master and mistress will be back.' And that was that. There was nothing more he could do.

After a bleak few months had come his meeting and falling in love with Mary – a joy he'd never thought to taste again – and the move to Hilltops where, instead of joy, something had gone wrong between them. Discord had wormed its way into their lives, destroying everything.

Tonight, his life seemed once again in tatters. And so he trudged the streets, thinking about and regretting the sequence of events that had brought them to this sorry state of affairs.

When after a time his thoughts began to clear, he remembered what he must do. With that in mind, he made his way to the railway station. It was time to put the second part of his plan into action.

In those first few hours when he had wandered aimlessly through the chilly streets, he had considered going back to get the bairns. But he had nothing to offer them any more, only his love – and that was small compensation for what they had lost, first their mother and then his beloved Mary.

Leaning over the railway bridge, he stared down through the swirling snow to the maze of track below; in his mind the faces of his children haunted him. They deserved more than he could ever give them. Better to let them be found a loving new home, with a mother who would cradle them in her arms and give them the guidance only a mother could; and a father who was strong enough to forge a life for them, even when his own life had collapsed about him.

Robert Sullivan saw himself for the coward he was, but right now, none of that seemed to matter.

He leaned further over the bridge, slowly edging forward, until the weight of his body balanced precariously over the parapet, his upper half dipping dangerously forward as his feet were lifted from the ground below. The bitter-cold breeze froze his face and split his lips, but he felt no pain or regret. *This* was his plan. *This* was what he wanted; what he deserved.

All he had to do was raise his hands and let go, and his troubles would be over.

'Hey, you!' The man had come up on Robert without him realising. 'Careful there, matey, or you'll be over the top an' no mistake!' Grabbing Robert by the arms, he hauled him back. 'Been out celebrating, 'ave yer?' Giving the other man a gentle shake, he sent him on his way. 'There've been times when I've had a few pints meself, and gone home three sheets to the wind,' he laughed. 'Go on! You'd best get off home, afore the missus comes looking for yer.'

Once he was satisfied that Robert was far enough from the bridge to be safe, he went away chuckling. 'The poor sod will cop it when he gets home, I'll be bound, and serves him right an' all . . . drunk as a skunk if yer ask me!' With the cuff of his sleeve he wiped the dewdrop from his nose and shivered in the cold night air. 'By! It's as well I came along when I did, or he'd have been over the top and done for.'

Blinded by the driving snow, Robert kept going until he had no idea where he was. After what seemed a lifetime, he saw the sign from the Nag's Head Inn, and realised that he had wandered back into the centre of town.

Just then, a family of four hurried by – two small children and their parents. Suddenly the parents were running and laughing, helpless under the bombardment of snowballs thrown by the children.

Their jollity cut through his feverish mind like a ray of light. In an instant his thoughts clarified and he knew what he must do. His resolve growing by the minute, he quickened his footsteps and headed back towards the town hall. 'The children!' he kept saying. 'Dear God! *The children!*'

Clumsily now, with the snow clinging to his shoes and slowing him down, he started to run. 'I'll get them back!' he began to gabble. 'We'll manage somehow. We'll make a life for the three of us . . . I'll tell Jack how sorry I am – what a coward I've been. I'll make it up to them, I swear to God.' He grew excited, shouting, his voice raised to the heavens. He was so eager now, to make amends. 'We'll be all right, me and my kids. We'll move away – start afresh.' He was laughing and crying; bursting with all he had to tell them.

A few minutes later he was running up the slippery steps to the town hall. When he realised the big, wooden-panelled door was closed against him, he grew frantic, banging his fists on the door, his voice echoing across the square. 'LET ME IN! I WANT MY KIDS!' But it was no use. There was no one there to hear him.

'I'll be back first thing!' he sobbed. 'You tell them that! And tell them I'll never leave my childer again!'

The sight of a police constable approaching warned Robert he would do well to make himself scarce. 'I'll be no good to them if I get locked up inside,' he reasoned. As it was, he would have some explaining to do when he came back on the morrow.

Incredibly weary now, he leaned on the door, his raw, battered face pressed hard against the wooden panelling, tears streaming down his cheeks. 'I'll be back for you, don't worry. Mark my words . . . first thing in the morning, I'll be waiting right here.'

As he walked away, he felt good – safe, somehow. True, his wife was no longer a part of his life, and he had no regrets on that score. But as for Mary? Oh God! He loved her so much it was like a physical ache inside him. Even after everything that had happened, he had never really thought she would leave, but he didn't blame her. How could he?

It was a bad state of affairs, but it was not the end of the world, He would learn to cope; he knew that now. Jack and Nancy were still here, and in deserting them, he had been no better than their mother. The children did not deserve that.

Now, for the first time in a long while, his depression lifted and he began to feel that life could be worth living after all.

Reluctant to go all the way back to Hilltops and feeling the need to celebrate, he remembered the Nag's Head Inn. 'Happen I'll take a room there for tonight,' he mused. 'That way I'll be on hand for Jack and Nancy in the morning.' He daren't even think where they might be spending the night but, late or not, if he had known where they were, nothing on earth would have kept him from going there.

Now that his sense of awareness was returning, he could feel the cold invade his bones. His teeth chattered and his stomach churned for the want of a bite to eat; nothing had passed his lips since yesterday. 'A hot meat pie and a pint of best bitter will do me for now,' he told himself. 'Then a warm bed to ease out the chill. Early to bed . . . early to rise.'

Drawing his coat about him he fought his way through the snow and heightening wind, back to the Nag's Head. The cheery lights from the window and the lively sound of men enjoying themselves, drew him there all the faster. The laughter gave him heart. He smiled wryly. 'Life isn't all that bad after all,' he muttered as he pushed open the door.

Almost instantly the stench of tobacco and stale sweat invaded his nostrils, but it was the laughter that touched him deepest . . . warm, human, invigorating laughter. It was a long time since he had heard that comforting sound.

'Evening, guv.' The landlord was a big fellow; Robert reckoned him to be in his late sixties. His small eyes and loose mouth were cradled in a mound of flesh and hair, and his broad bulbous nose had turned blue from swigging too much ale. 'By! Yer look frozen to the bone.' The man leaned over the bar, his trunk-like arms folded one over the other, and with a merry twinkle in his eye that gladdened Robert's heart, he asked, 'What's it to be then, squire?'

Robert didn't need asking twice. 'A pint of your best bitter,' he answered with a smile. 'I'll take it in there, if that's all right?' Rubbing his hands together to get the blood flowing, he gestured to the adjoining room. Through the open doorway he could see the deep, comfortable-looking armchairs and the wide open cheery fire; he could even feel the heat from where he stood.

The man told him he was welcome to use whatever facilities

he had to offer. 'I've a pot of thick beef stew on the simmer,' he told him, 'and the best meat pies you'll ever see this side of heaven.'

Robert licked his lips in anticipation. 'Make it two meat pies,' he answered, 'with a generous helping of gravy poured over. That should be enough to keep me going for now.' With his empty stomach playing tunes, he meant to keep his options open.

'One pint and two meat pies coming up.' Drawing the pint, the landlord slopped a trail of froth over the counter as he pushed it towards Robert. 'That'll be eightpence altogether.'

Taking out his wage-packet, Robert counted out the coins. The remaining money he folded into his waistcoat pocket.

'A word of friendly advice.' The landlord lowered his voice. 'I'd be a bit more careful with your money if I were you.' He glanced about. 'You can never be sure who might be watching . . . *if* you know what I mean?'

Robert understood exactly what he was implying and thanked him for the advice. 'I'm usually a bit more wary,' he confided, 'but I've a lot on my mind at the minute. Not thinking straight, you understand?' He patted his waistcoat pocket. 'Me and my two youngsters will be moving from the area soon,' he explained. 'Anybody who tries taking this from me will have his hands full, 'cause I need every penny, and more.' His face broke into a smile. 'Now that I intend making a new life for me and the children.'

'Good luck to you then.' The landlord nodded in approval. 'But mind what I say – keep your money out of sight.'

'I will. Thanks, mate.' With pint in hand Robert made his way into the snug. Being as there were others warming themselves at the fire, he could get no nearer than the small round table by the window, but it was of no matter, for the whole room was warm and cosy. He soon began to feel sleepy as the heat gradually thawed out his bones.

Comfortable in the knowledge that on the morrow he would have Jack and Nancy back in his charge, he sipped his ale and began making plans. It was good to have a purpose.

The ale gave him an inner glow, and the warmth from the fire gave him a thirst, and when the landlord arrived with his pies, he ordered another pint of ale. 'Then I'll need to have a word with you about a room for the night,' he said.

'Sorry, guv.' The man was apologetic. 'We've six rooms but they're all taken. At this time of year, especially in this weather, we have folks who come into town for one reason or another – travelling salesmen and such. When the weather changes like this, they tend to stay put till it clears. Our rates are reasonable, you see, and we serve a hearty breakfast, so once they've stayed with us they keep coming back.' He chuckled. 'We've a couple of rooms I wouldn't keep a dog in, but mind you keep that to yourself, or the missus will string me up from the highest tree. The rooms are all clean, mind. You'll not get bitten alive with fleas here, oh no!'

Robert tried again. 'All I need is a bed for the night. Are you sure there's nothing?'

The big man shook his head dolefully. 'If I could put you up, I would, but we've absolutely nothing. Sorry.'

'Then can you recommend another inn – somewhere like yourselves?'

'I'll have a word with my missus if you like. Ethel's more in the know than I am about things like that. You sit still and relax, while I fetch your ale.' And off he went, at a slow, laborious pace.

Disappointed but hopeful, Robert refused to be downhearted. Instead he did as the big man suggested; he sat back and relaxed, and bit deep into the first succulent meat pie. The exploding burst of rich juices thrilled his taste buds and made him slaver; this was the best pie he had ever tasted.

'Good, ain't they?' The voice was not too far from where he was seated. 'The landlord's missus might resemble a sow in farrow and she's got a tongue that would slice a loaf of bread, but by God there ain't nobody who can bake pies like Ethel Morton!'

Wiping the juice from his chin, Robert turned to see who was addressing him; it was one of the men from the next table. 'I'm inclined to agree about the *pie*,' Robert answered with a grin, 'but as I've never so much as clapped eyes on the lady in question, it wouldn't be right for me to voice an opinion, would it?'

The other man lowered his tone. 'Take it from me, sunshine. Once seen, Ethel Morton is never forgotten. But there's not a man in Bedford who wouldn't wed her if she were on the loose – for her meat pies if nowt else, ain't that right, Marlon?' He turned to his younger companion for moral support.

Nodding in agreement, the young man leaned forward to impart in a whisper, 'He's right. Ugly as sin Ethel is, but a man could forgive her *anything*, provided she woke him up of a morning with one o' them meat pies.' He rolled his eyes at Robert's supper. 'Best get it down you . . . afore me and Geordie here decide to tek a chunk out of it!'

His guffaw echoed across the room, only to die down on seeing the innkeeper enter with Robert's second pint of ale. 'All right, Daniel, are you?' he greeted the big man with a friendly grin.

Placing the pint of ale on the table, the big man stared him in the face. 'You seem to be finding something very funny, young Marlon,' he said sombrely. 'You wouldn't be having a laugh at my good wife's expense, would you?'

Seeing how the big man could flatten them with one mighty blow, both men protested vehemently. 'No, no! We were just talking to this fella here, that's all.' The younger of the two nodded hopefully in Robert's direction. 'We weren't even discussing his missus, ain't that right, mate?' Robert gave no indication one way or the other, for he had taken an instant dislike to this brash young sulk. Too devious by half, was Marlon.

'So? You've better things to talk about than my missus, eh?' There followed an ominous silence, while Daniel Morton looked accusingly from one to the other, before taking a step forward, to confide in a softer voice, 'That's a real pity, 'cause there's a lot I could tell you about my Ethel . . . such as how she's got breasts a man can lose himself in – drives a man *mad* with desire, she does, an' no mistake. By! You should see her when she does her belly-dance round the bed – especially when it's a full moon. She strips off slow-like . . .' licking his lips, he moved his arms over his body in evocative motions '. . . weaving and dipping, making a man gasp for it.' He gave a long, shuddering sigh. 'You've no idea.'

Marlon and Geordie gaped at each other, while Robert grinned to himself. 'Bloody hell!' The older of the two couldn't believe what he was hearing. 'No kidding?'

The big man shook his head. 'Forget your meat pies, Marlon,' he groaned. 'You'll need a cold wash from top to bottom when she's done wi' you!'

Leaving them open-mouthed with astonishment, he turned on his heel and ambled away. 'I never would have thought it!' the older fellow gasped. 'Ethel Morton . . . doing a belly-dance round the bed! By, it don't bear thinking about!'

Suddenly the sound of raucous laughter rocked the room. 'If you'll believe that, you'll believe *anything*!' The huge landlord was helpless in the doorway; laughing and squealing, he leaned on the door-jamb. 'If ever my missus tried to do a belly-dance, the bleedin' floor would collapse under her weight!' The frightening image was so vivid in his mind, he erupted in another fit of laughter, as did every other man in the room – including Robert and his companions.

'Mind if we sit at your table, mate?' the younger man asked

Robert. 'Only we can't feel the heat from back here.'

Robert had no objections to that, although he had first thought the men to be rough-looking and sly – particularly the younger one, Marlon. Still, he reasoned that if Daniel Morton knew them by name, they must be all right. And so they moved to his table and, as the evening wore on, they chatted and drank and, with every pint of ale, Robert was invited to join them until he was so relaxed and comfortable he began to open his heart to them. 'I heard you tell Dan that you wanted a room for the night,' said Marlon casually. 'Ain't you got no home to go to then?'

'Not from tomorrow, no,' Robert answered. 'I've dropped the keys through the rentman's letter-box, paid the last of the rent and packed my job in.'

'What kinda job was that then?'

'Offloading freight trains.'

'Hmh! Damned hard work, but they pay good money, so I'm told.'

'You were told right.'

'So why'd you pack it in? And what made you give up your house?'

For reasons known only to himself, Robert chose not to answer his questions in full. 'It was time, that's all.' Time to end it all. Time to give in and leave his kids to the mercy of others. For shameful, selfish reasons. How could he tell any man the truth – especially a stranger?

'Got a missus, have you?' Marlon persisted.

'Not any more, no.'

'A woman friend then?'

'Nope. She left yesterday.' He took another sup of ale.

'You've got kids though?'

Robert smiled at that. 'Two – a boy by the name of Jack, and a girl called Nancy. She's nearly three. The boy's some five years older.'

'If you ain't got no home, and no wife or woman – who's got the kids?' The older man, Geordie, was not as callous as the dark-haired fellow. He appeared to have a friendlier nature.

'They're being looked after. I'm to collect them in the morning, then we're on our way.' He didn't even notice when the dark-haired fellow ordered another round of drinks and pushed one under Robert's nose. Instead he grabbed the mug into his fist and took a long, soothing drink.

'What happened to your wife?' Curiosity overtook the younger man's deeper, more sinister interest.

After another swig or two, Robert felt more able to confide. 'She left me a year or so back – for somebody who could give her more money.' There was a hint of disgust in his voice that he could not disguise.

'And the woman?'

Robert suddenly felt the need to be cautious. 'I'd best go and see if the landlord's talked to his missus about me finding a place to stay the night.' Standing up, he shook his head as if to clear his mind. 'I need to stay in town . . . keep close by. I've important things to do in the morning – mustn't be late.'

The younger man persisted. 'I'm surprised a good-looking fella like yourself couldn't hang on to your women.' With a hostile glare he scrutinised Robert's handsome features and long, lean style. 'Seems to me you're the kind of bloke who lures other men's wives away . . . the same sort as lured *my* woman away from me.' He made as if to rise from his seat, but was stopped when Geordie put out a steadying hand.

'Leave it,' he said firmly, and so the other lapsed into a brooding silence. It wasn't long ago that he had been cheated on, and it still rankled. 'You can't blame every bloke you meet, just because your woman ran off with somebody else.'

'She was a bloody whore, that's why she ran off! One thing's for sure . . . it weren't *my* fault.' There was a violent rage in the younger man's voice and manner. He slapped his mate's hand away, with the harsh warning, 'Anyway, you mind your own damned business – if you know what's good for you!' And, knowing how he had lately become dangerously aggressive, his mate wisely backed off.

The landlord had some good news for Robert. 'The missus says there's a likely place along the river, where you might get fixed up. It's not as good as ours, o' course, but I'm told they do a reasonable bed and breakfast at fair rates. Go down as far as the second bridge, then cut off to your right. It's called the Bridge Inn – you can't miss it. Ask for Sarah.'

Thanking him, Robert bade him good night. 'Tell your missus I'm very grateful to her.'

Daniel acknowledged this, then gave him a word of advice. 'Mind you don't fall in the river, my friend. I mean, you've had a few pints an' all. If you ask me, you'd do well to call for a hansom cab.'

'No need for that,' Robert decided. 'A bit of fresh air and a walk along the river will do me good.' With that he gave a wave of his hand and was out of the pub and away.

'Time we were on our way an' all.' A minute or two later, Marlon ushered his mate outside. 'Look! There he is!' He drew Geordie's attention to Robert's shadowy figure as it headed for the main road. 'HEY!' His voice echoed through the air. 'Wait for us, mate!'

'What the devil d'you think you're playing at?' The older man restrained him. 'What do we want with *him?*'

'Don't tell me you didn't see his pay packet?'

'I saw it, same as you. So what?'

'Aw, come on, Geordie. You're not that bloody thick!'

'No, an' I'm not that bloody *desperate* neither.' Being a former family man, before a prison sentence had split him from his wife and kids, Geordie had certain sympathies. 'Seems to me that fella's got enough on his plate without us robbing him of his pay packet. Besides, you heard how he means to move on from these parts, and that few quid is his ticket out of here.'

The young man's answer was to sneer in his face, 'I hope you're not going soft in your old age?'

'Happen I am, and happen I'm not. All I'm saying is, there are plenty of other wasters whose pockets we can pick, without taking from our own kind.' He placed a reassuring hand on the young man's shoulder. 'Leave it, son. We don't need his money.'

The other shook him off. 'And I don't *need you*!' he snarled. 'Bugger off and leave me alone.' As he ran he called out, 'And don't get any funny ideas about turning me in, neither, or you'll wish you hadn't.'

'Don't be so bloody daft, man.' More afraid for his mate than for himself, Geordie took up the chase. 'Give it up, Marlon. *Come back 'ere!*' But the young scoundrel was already way ahead; fleeter of foot and with a black hatred in his heart that drove him on.

Robert was almost up to the main road when he was set upon. Taken unawares and still feeling the effects of the drink, he turned, unsure, when he thought he heard something behind him. Like a crazed animal his attacker sprang on him and began beating at him with fists and feet; relentlessly, as though he meant to stop only when Robert lay dead on the ground.

Bloodied and confused, Robert finally retaliated, his daily hard labours lending him strength and muscle that stood him in good stead. 'What the hell d'you want with *me*?' he shouted, spitting blood. Grasping the scoundrel by the shoulders, he pinned him tight to the wall. 'My wages – is that what you're after? Or is it like your mate said – you blame every other man for your woman running out on you? Wake up, man! You're not the first bloke to be dumped by a woman, and you'll not be the last – you can be sure o' that!'

Shaking him by the shoulders, he thrust him aside. 'Clear off, and think yourself lucky I don't give you the thrashing you deserve. The truth is, I know what you're feeling. God only knows, I've been there myself. I know how women can drive a man crazy if they've a mind to. So go on!' He dragged him towards the alley. 'Be off with you . . . before I change my mind!'

When Geordie pounded heavily round the corner, all he could see was Robert manhandling his mate, 'Oy! Leave him be!' he bawled. Lunging forward, he made as if to grab the young man out of Robert's reach, but the other was too quick for him. With a cry, Marlon flung himself at Robert, and soon the three of them were grappling.

Desperate to separate them, Geordie was knocked to the ground by the young man's flailing fists; at the same time, Robert was sent sprawling towards the kerb edge.

Suddenly the older man looked up and spotted the runaway carriage and four as it came careering towards them. Horrified, he roared out a warning, but it came too late. Already thrown off-balance, Robert was unable to right himself in time, for as he tried to stand up, the young man kicked him hard in the back, deliberately sending him straight into the path of the runaway horses. In an instant he was flung under their hooves, helpless to save himself.

The horrified screams of late revellers and passers-by filled the air as they came running to help. By this time Robert had been dragged down the street by the thundering hooves, which in turn threw him back beneath the carriage. Finally the carriage broke free and, panic-stricken, the horses galloped on.

Somehow they were eventually brought to a halt, after which the small crowd calmed and tethered them.

At the mouth of the alley, they sat the shocked driver on the kerb; he was cut and bruised but apart from one finger hanging by a thread where he had tried desperately to control the runaway horses, there was no visible damage. They broke loose,' he kept repeating. 'It was a dog . . . a rat mebbe. It ran across in front and they shied. I couldn't hold 'em.'

Tenderly they pulled Robert's mangled body from the mass of metal and timber. 'He's a goner, I'm afraid.' Broken and battered and washed head to toe in his own blood, Robert was unrecognisable.

When somebody cried that the police were on their way, Geordie and Marlon backed off and vanished, in fear for their lives. Seeing what they had done, the older man was filled with horror, but the other had no sense of compassion or remorse for the carnage he had caused. Instead he felt a warped sense of pride in himself; almost as though he had dispensed some kind of justice.

Soon the hospital conveyance came and took Robert away. 'There's still a fighting chance.' The medical attendant had detected a glimmer of life as they lifted the patient in.

His colleague shrugged dismissively. 'The poor devil's cut to ribbons,' he grunted. He had seen some bad things in his time, but this accident was the worst. 'If you ask me, we've already lost him.'

Chapter Four

Having left on the spur of the moment and already regretting her hasty decision, Mary had spent the night in a small Bedford hotel. She didn't sleep much. Instead she paced the floor, hoping Robert would love her enough to come looking for her, but he never did, and now she was washed, dressed and ready to leave for good.

'Thank you, miss.' The powdered and rouged, smiley-faced receptionist handed her a receipt. 'Looks like we're in for some more bad weather.' She picked at her nails, then at her nose, and now she was patting the underneath of her sagging chin. 'It drops when you're not looking,' she joked, cupping and waggling her ample bosom. 'Like everything else.'

In spite of her sorry mood, Mary had to smile, 'I don't suppose you know what time the first train leaves the station?'

'Can't say as I do.' The woman pursed her lips and seemed to be thinking. 'No, I've no idea. Sorry.'

Mary nodded resignedly. It's all right,' she answered. 'I'll make my way there and ask for myself.'

The woman eyed her up and down. 'I'd say you've got man trouble.'

'Really? Why do you say that?'

'Because I can tell, gal, that's why. I've had enough bleedin' man trouble myself, to recognise the signs. Bastards! They're all the same. Once they've got what they want, they don't need you no more. They're off to the next floozie what's willing to drop her drawers.'

'Ellen!' The manager's voice startled them both. 'Smarten up, girl, or you'll be back in the kitchen before you know it.'

'Yes, sir.' As he walked away, the receptionist leaned across the desk to confide in Mary. 'See that? You wouldn't think we were lovers right up to last week, would you?' Glancing towards the inner door to make sure he wasn't eavesdropping, she told Mary, 'Thick as thieves we were. Then I went and let him have his wicked way, and now he doesn't want to know. He keeps threatening to put me back to work in the kitchen – thinks I'm not good enough to be behind this desk. Hmh! I were good enough when he had me on the floor here, with me cami-knickers round me waist . . . randy sod!'

Mary liked her. 'You're right,' she admitted. 'I *have* got man trouble, but it's not like you think. He's a good man. Only there are problems I can't seem to deal with any more.'

The young woman's eyes opened like golf balls. 'What! Can't he get it up no more? Drinks, does he? Got brewer's droop?'

Mary chuckled. 'No, nothing like that.'

After a moment, they said goodbye and Mary went out to brave the elements. It was still icy cold. She followed the main road and kept going, until she arrived at the railway station. Windblown and bedraggled, she hurried directly to the ticket desk and enquired where the first train out of Bedford was headed. She wanted to go as far away from here as possible, she told the man behind the window.

'One minute, please.' Full of a cold, the clerk took out a grubby hankie and blew hard into it; then he coughed and sneezed and wiped a droplet from his nose with the flat of his hand. After a few more minutes of messing and fussing, he licked one finger with which he selected a timetable from the pile in front of him.

'Lytham St Annes. Let's see now . . . That's a good long way from here, and you'll be near to Blackpool, with all the seaside attractions – not that there'd be much call for 'em, this time o' year. Still, you've got the brand new Tower there – that's one thing . . .' Crinkling his eyes until they were mere slits, he perused the timetable through murky spectacles.

'The next train will take you to Rugby – it's due in ten minutes – then you must change for Preston, and from there, it's on to Lytham. It's something of a round trip, miss, but well worth it, I dare say.'

Toying with his pencil, he waited patiently for Mary to decide what to do. Because of her wanting to get far away from Bedford, he suspected she was running away from something. It was not the first time he'd been asked that very same question. He could always tell when the traveller didn't care which way he or she went, just as long as it was far enough away from the troubles that haunted him – or *her* as the case may be.

'I've never been to Lytham St Anne's,' Mary admitted. 'Whereabouts is it?'

'I see!' Her admittance had only confirmed his suspicions. 'Well now, it's a pretty place by the sea, not too far from Blackpool as I said, but without the hustle and bustle, if you know what I mean? If you're looking for peace and quiet, you'd like it well enough.'

Regarding Mary with discretion, he recognised the symptoms; traces of teardrops smudged on the face; a look of terrible loneliness, and guilt. Oh yes, there was always the guilt.

'What time did you say it leaves?' She wondered if Robert was on his way to persuade her to stay. But she didn't want that because *Jack* didn't want that.

'Let's see now.' Looking up, he pursed his lips. 'In eight minutes' time.'

Taking her purse from her bag, Mary asked, 'How much?'

'Will you be going all the way, miss?'

She nodded.

'Single or return? First, second or third class?'

'One way please. Third class.' She winced as the clerk fetched forth an almighty sneeze and proceeded to blow his nose with a harsh, trumpeting sound.

'As I said, it's a good long trip – a total of one hundred and fifty miles in all. Right – at a penny a mile for third class, that'll be twelve shillings and sixpence, please!'

Gasping in shock, Mary paid him, then went to the waiting room to shelter for the last minute or two. With its green-painted walls and four armchairs scattered round the fire, it was cosy enough, she thought. There was even a peg-rug in front of the hearth, 'just like home'. Rubbing her hands together she felt the blood returning. 'You've got no home now, gal,' she murmured with a sorry smile. Her heart and mind were drawn back to Hilltops, to Robert and the children, whom she had grown to love as her own, but her instincts told her to keep moving on, because things would never again be the same between them. How could they be?

Undoing the buttons on her long-coat, she sat by the roaring fire and mulled over the events of the past few months. If only we could have worked it out, she thought. Leaning back in the chair she began to doze. She had loved Robert from their first meeting and she loved him still; she would *always* love him. But she couldn't cope any more. Not with the way things were.

If it was up to her, she would have done something about it – something more drastic. In a way she blamed Robert, but on reflection it hadn't been easy for him either. No matter. It was all too late now. There were too many issues before her time that had not yet been resolved. Things were out of control. Things of the heart. Things painful, and lasting. Not of her making, but there all the same.

Of all the people involved, her heart went out to Robert. After all, it fell on *his* shoulders, and though it filled her with shame to desert him, she could think of no other way.

The sound of a train whistle drew her out of her reverie. Wrapping her coat about her she reluctantly left the warm glow of the fire, to face the bitter cold outside.

On the platform, more passengers appeared, seemingly out of nowhere. Others disembarked from the now stationary train, into a billowing trail of steam which gave them a ghostly appearance.

A few minutes for them all to clear a path, and she was climbing aboard. Cold and weary, she curled into a corner seat and fell deeply asleep. A guard had to wake her at Rugby and guide her on to the Preston express. Still groggy and losing confidence with every minute of this reckless journey, Mary sat down and waited for the huge train to start moving. At Preston, the final leg of her journey, she wearily climbed into a third-class carriage and sat down, dragging her carpet bag with her. By this time it began to weigh painfully heavy. A man with sallow features and shifty eyes sat opposite, unnerving her. Every time she looked up, he was looking back. Suddenly, a round, jolly woman bumbled into the carriage at the last minute and Mary felt more secure.

They passed two stations before Mary felt warm and comfortable. By the time they had arrived at the third station she was fast asleep again.

'Bitter-cold weather, don't you think?' The round woman had hoped to start up a conversation with the sallow-faced gentleman, but he turned his face to the window and said not a word in reply.

A few minutes later he left the carriage and never came back. 'Miserable git!' Taking over his seat, the woman smiled on Mary's sleeping face, 'By! You're a pretty thing, an' no mistake!'

Now, as the whistle blew and the train shuddered to a halt, the woman leaned over and gently covered Mary's exposed calf with the tail end of her coat. 'Can't leave you looking like that,' she commented with a tut. 'You never know what dirty old man might be lurking about.'

With that, she calmly collected Mary's large tapestry bag and disembarked with it, passing all and sundry as cool as you please.

Exhausted by the turmoil of the past two days Mary slept the entire journey, and only awoke when she was shaken by the conductor and told, 'This is the end of the line, miss. You're at Lytham St Anne's now.' It was then that she realised her travelling bag was gone. 'Oh, my God!' she panicked. 'Everything I own is in that bag!' The sky had darkened and it was evening again. She felt lost, lonely and terrified.

In the station office, the duty-officer was very sympathetic. He asked her for a description of the thief and once he had heard it, he sighed and groaned, and swore under his breath. 'She's a regular thief, I'm afraid,' he revealed. 'I'm sorry, lass, but you'll not get your belongings back. That there Mother Evans is too clever by half. The police have been trying to get their hands on her for years, but she's as tricky as a bag full o' monkeys.'

In the line of duty, he took Mary's name, but when he asked for an address to pass on to the authorities, she had none to give. 'I'm new to the area,' she explained. 'I'm looking for work and a place to live.'

'I see.' The duty-officer looked her up and down, and concluded that she seemed too nice a lady to be wandering the streets. 'There's a guest-house along the front called Bluebell House,' he told her. The landlord is a good sort. What with the season finished and more than half the rooms empty in Lytham, I wouldn't mind betting he'd let you stay there, without too much bother.'

Growing frustrated and still not over the shock of losing her bag, Mary reminded him, 'I can't pay for accommodation! At least not until I find work.'

The duty-officer understood. 'Paul Marshall is an obliging sort. I'm sure he'd let you stay until you found work. Besides, you've got a trustworthy face.' A pretty face, too, he thought, with those nutmeg-brown eyes and that long fair hair coiled into a bun. Taking out a pen and paper, he began scribbling on a pad. 'Here's his name and address.' Tearing off the page he handed it to her. 'At least go and see him. Tell him Alan sent you.'

Thanking him, Mary took the scrap of paper and headed off in the direction in which she was pointed. 'Straight down here and turn left on to the front,' she was told. 'You'll find the house directly opposite the sandbanks – name of *Bluebell House*, like I said.'

Mary soon found the address, but halfway up the front steps, she hesitated. Whatever will he think of me – a lone woman with no money nor belongings? she asked herself. The idea of going to a stranger with no money to pay her way, and the lame excuse of having had her bag pinched, was too shameful.

Just then, she glanced up to see a curtain twitch in the front room; it was just a glimpse but in that second or two, she saw an old woman's face staring back at her and none too kindly neither. Suddenly, the curtain dropped and all was still.

The fleeting incident panicked her. Quickly now before anyone else saw her, she turned and ran down the steps. She didn't stop until she was partway along the street, then she crossed the road and sat on a bench overlooking the beach; like her life, the sea looked pitifully bleak.

Back inside Bluebell House, the old woman was talking to her nephew, 'Some young woman was about to knock on the door,' she informed him. 'I didn't like the look of her, but it's all right. She'll not be bothering us now, 'cause when she saw me looking, she turned tail and ran off.'

'What young woman?' Paul Marshall had grown used to his aging aunt's curious ways. 'And why would she suddenly turn tail and run?' Having stoked the fire in her sitting room to a lovely, rosy glow, he replaced the poker in its stand.

'Well, *I* don't know, do I?' When she frowned as she did now, her wizened old features seemed to disappear behind the wrinkles.

Frustrated, Paul ran his hands through his thick shock of brown hair. 'Oh, Aunt Agatha!' There were times when he didn't know how to deal with her. 'You weren't scowling at her through the window, were you?' She had done it before and lost him precious customers.

'Hmh!' Looking hurt, the old woman eased herself into the armchair. 'If I *were* scowling – and I'm not saying as I were – it's only 'cause I were looking after your interests.' Her bottom lip trembled. 'I don't know why I bother, for all the thanks I get.'

Taking a moment to consider her familiar antics, the man scratched the back of his neck as he did when frustrated. 'What am I to do with you, eh?'

She gave a cheeky grin. 'I expect you'll have to have me put down.'

He gave out a bellow of a laugh, saying mischievously, 'Happen that won't be such a bad idea.' She was always making that sort of comment, but he had come to see it for what it really was – a show of bravado; a way of trying to make him feel guilty for chastising her. 'If you carry on frightening away my customers, you'll ruin my business, you do know that, don't you?'

'I've told you before, Paul Marshall, you don't need a business, not while you've got me.' She feigned weariness. 'Since your poor Uncle Josh passed on, I've more money than I know what to do with. You can have it all if you like, so long as you close this guest-house and make it a proper home, just for the two of us.'

Discreetly now, she took stock of her nephew and was proud. He was a good man; a homely sort, with kind, dark blue eyes, and that broad, strong build of a man who had worked hard since he left school. 'You're thirty-eight years old,' she chided. 'You've worked on the docks as a lad; you've loaded goods at the packing houses and driven a horse and heavy load along the towpath, till your hands bled from the rope burns.'

'It's what a man does,' he answered simply. 'He works and earns, and saves for the family he hopes to have one day.'

While she took stock of him he regarded her intently; the small, extraordinarily pretty features set in that cruelly shrivelled skin. The eyes were vivid brown, like two small raisins set in batter, the mouth full and moist, like that of a young girl's. Sadly, old age had taken away the glow of youth, until now, a body could only imagine what an amazing beauty she must once have been.

'But you haven't *got* a family!' she snorted. 'If you hadn't spent your entire life working every hour God sent, you might have met the girl who'd have given you the family you crave. So you've no one else to blame but yerself!'

'You could be right.' It was a fact that he had not yet found the right woman. 'But there's time enough yet.'

'Not if you work from morning till night in this place! Never any time for socialising. Always organising – decorating, mending and making, and other such things. Work! Work! Work! How will *that* find you a family, eh? Tell me that.'

'Aunt Aggie, we've been through all this before. I've work to do. You just settle down, eh? Emily's just arrived to collect the laundry and do a couple of things for me.' Emily was their general help, and the backbone of the small hotel. 'I'll get her to fetch you a bedtime drink.'

As always, the old woman would not leave it be. 'I don't *want* any tea, thank you, and stop trying to change the subject! All I'm asking is that you let me make your life easier. I've got the money. You don't need to run a guest house. Take it easy. Look after your old aunt and do as you please in between,' She shook her head with disbelief. 'By! Any other man would chop off his right arm for what I'm offering you.'

He didn't doubt that, but, 'Look, I know you mean well, and I am grateful, but I worked long and hard for too many years, to get the money for this place. It was no easy achievement, I can tell you. But it's mine now, bought and paid for. These past four years I've managed to build up a list of good-paying, decent folk who come here time and again, because I provide clean, comfortable accommodation and good wholesome food on the table. Whatever you might think, I'm proud of that.'

When it seemed she was lost for words, he crossed the room and stooped before her. 'I won't turn you out if that's what you're worried about.' He grinned. 'But if you don't stop nagging me, I might put you in the cellar and lock the door behind you.' He took her hand in his. 'It's really kind of you, Aunt Agatha, but I don't want your money.'

'But that's plain daft! It'll all be yours one day anyroad.'

He shrugged his shoulders. 'In that case, I'll use it to decorate this place,' he teased. 'I might even have it extended so I can take in more guests. Or happen I'll buy a second guest house, or even open a string of 'em right across the country.' He pretended to be in deep thought. 'I could set up in one o' them new amusement arcades that's growing popular round these parts. Yes, why not?' He winked. 'You'd like to think that's where your money'd gone, wouldn't you?'

She laughed out loud, a full, hearty chuckle for an old woman of eighty. 'I'll haunt you if you do! You're a tormenting bugger!' she chided him. 'I ought to smack yer arse.'

Now it was his turn to laugh heartily. 'Hmh! You should be so lucky!'

The room echoed with their laughter. 'I'd turn you out,' he threatened, 'only who would I have to make me laugh then, eh?'

She gave him a playful shove. 'Go on with you. And you can send Emily in with that drink, if you like.'

'Right away,' he said, and kissing her soundly on the cheek he told her to behave herself. 'I daren't even think what you were like when you were twenty.'

'Well, I liked the boys and I liked a laugh. Trouble was, I had a mother who thought young ladies should be seen and not heard,' she replied with a wink. 'It were just as well she didn't know what I got up to behind her back.'

He chuckled. 'I can imagine!'

He was still chuckling as he went out the door.

Emily already had the milk on the stove when he walked into the basement kitchen. 'I thought she'd want a drink round about now,' she said when Paul asked if the milk was for his aunt. 'She'd rather have a drop o' gin, but she'll have to settle for cocoa.'

Paul smiled at the truth of it. 'She's in one of her impossible moods tonight,' he confided.

Emily returned his smile. 'That's when I like her best of all.' A widow in her fifties with no children, Emily was a darling woman; round and small, she had the tired face of someone who has known hardship, but she was always cheery and could play old Agatha at her own game when she had a mind to. 'I'll take her in some of that jam sponge cake I made last night,' she told Paul. 'She has a weakness for it, and it shouldn't lay too heavy on her stomach neither.'

As he went to leave the kitchen, Paul was stopped short by Emily's next remark. 'Why anyone should be sitting out on a bench in the dark, in the middle of winter, is beyond me. The poor woman must be out of her mind.' She gestured up at the window, where the legs of people passing by could now and then be seen.

Returning to her side, Paul wanted to know, 'What woman? Where?'

Emily poured the hot milk over the cocoa and stirred vigorously. 'A young woman – out there, across the road. I did stop and ask if she was all right, but she didn't seem to want to talk.' Placing the cup of cocoa on a tray, she took out the mountainous sponge cake and began slicing. 'Pretty young thing . . . been crying, I reckon. I asked her again if she were all right, but she didn't want no interference, so I left her alone.'

Placing the slice of cake on a plate she set it against the cocoa, before collecting the tray into her fat little hands and remarking thoughtfully, 'Sometimes a body needs to be left alone. I were the same when I lost my husband. Y'see, sometimes there are things nobody else can help you with.'

Curious now, Paul followed her upstairs into the sitting room, where his Aunt Agatha was sitting with her eyes closed, enjoying the music emanating from the wind-up gramophone. She was quietly singing, and tapping the floor with the head of her cane, in time to the waltz.

Emily set the tray on the side table nearest her. Time for your nightcap,' she shouted. She drew the table right up to the old lady and tapped her on the shoulder. 'Here's your cocoa, and I've brought you a slice of cake to go with it.'

Turning off the gramophone, Paul had a question for his aunt. 'What did that young woman look like?'

Momentarily confused, she stared at him. 'What woman?'

'The one you frightened off.'

Indignant, she sat bolt upright, looking from one to the other. 'I never frightened *nobody* off!'

Emily laughed comfortably at that 'Give over,' she said, 'You've frightened off at least six poor devils that *I* know of.'

Agatha snorted. 'Only because they weren't suitable!'

'Oh, I see.' After two years of waiting on her hand and foot,

Emily was used to the old lady by now. 'And who says they're not suitable?'

'I do. And it's none of your business. You're just the hired help. Washing and ironing and doing the cleaning, that's your business. Suitable women in this house is *my* business – oh, and Paul's, of course.' She glanced at her nephew, who was both amused and annoyed by their banter.

'Oh, is that right?' bridled Emily. 'Well, I'd better stop baking cakes and curling your hair then, hadn't I, eh? And what about when I have to cut your toenails 'cause you can't reach 'em? I'd best stop that an' all!'

'That's enough, you two.' Paul stepped forward. 'There's some poor woman probably freezing out there in the cold and here's you two arguing.' Addressing himself to Emily he instructed, 'Go on, lass. Describe the woman to my aunt.'

In as much detail as she could recall, Emily did as she was asked. 'She was a pretty thing – in her late twenties, I'd say. I reckon she were taller than me.'

Agatha laughed out loud. '*Everybody's* taller than you! They ran outta legs when you were made.'

When she received a warning glance from Paul, she hastily asked Emily to 'get on with it then'.

After glaring at the old woman, who was quietly sniggering, Emily continued, 'Well, she had her face turned away most of the time, and she were sitting down, so I couldn't see her properly. But she had pretty hair, I could see that – fair hair in a bun that were tumbling down. And she had a quiet, pleasant manner about her.'

Paul turned to his aunt. 'Is that the same woman?'

Still sulking, she took her time in answering. 'It could be, I suppose.'

'*Is it?*' Not before time he was running out of patience.

'Well, yes.' She shrugged her shoulders peevishly. 'It sounds as if it could be . . . and there's no need to get on your high horse with me, young man!'

There were times when Paul was so exasperated he forgot how much she made him laugh. Turning on his heels, he hurried to the door.

'Where are you going?' Aggie called out.

'I think we owe someone an apology, don't you?'

'It might not be the same woman.'

'It doesn't matter. Whoever it is, if they've been out there for any length of time, especially in this weather, they'll be chilled to the marrow. Besides, Emily said she seemed upset.' When neither of them replied, he addressed his aunt in a stern voice. 'By the way, apart from your own quarters, this house, and who comes into it, is *not* your business. It's mine. You need to remember that.'

That said, he went out and closed the door, but he could hear the squabbling that broke out. 'Now see what you've done!' came Aggie's shrill voice. 'Why did you have to go and tell him about that woman? Why couldn't you just mind your own business and leave well alone?'

'What about *you* then?' came the retort. 'Why don't you stop trying to lead his life for him? He's a grown man with heavy responsibilities. He built this place up long before you came along. He's doing very nicely, thank you – and there's no way he's gonna let you take over!'

'Right – that's quite enough from you. You will leave now. You're sacked!'

'Oh no, I'm not. Not until Mr Marshall says I am,' Emily said smartly. 'He took me on and he'll get rid of me when he's good and ready.'

Groaning, Paul shook his head. 'What in God's name have I let myself in for, with them two?'

As he hurried to get his coat and another with it, the bickering went on at full blast behind him. It only stopped when he slammed the front door. As he went down the street at a quickening pace, he could see the two of them in his mind's eye, already on their way to the front window, to see what was happening.

True enough, Aunt Agatha had hobbled to the bay, her stick in one hand, the lifted curtain in the other. 'What does he want to fetch her in for anyway?' With her nose pressed to the window, she was well and truly miffed. 'She could be *anybody*. A tart off the street even!'

Emily still hadn't got over the old woman poking fun at her little short legs. 'Oh, and what about *you*?' she said immediately.

Giving her the evil eye, Aggie demanded: 'And what precisely d'you mean by that, woman?'

'I mean he took *you* in off the street, didn't he, and you're no tart.' She grinned cheekily. 'Not that I know of, anyway.'

'He did *not* take me in off the street!' The old lady's cheeks were flushed with indignation.

'As good as. When your Josh passed on, you sold the house and planted yourself here. Paul, being the good man he is, didn't have the heart to turn you away, even though you're taking up precious room he could be using for his customers.'

Agatha gave her a warning. 'You had better mind what you're saying. Besides, I'd pay him whatever sum he might care to name, only he won't even hear of it.' She gave a sly little grin. 'As for me being a tart, I can tell you, I had my moments, although they're long gone now, more's the pity.'

'You old devil!' Emily loved these harmless set-tos between them, even though there were times when she could quite happily have strangled the old bugger.

'What I'm saying, Emily, my dear, is that this woman, if it *is* the same one who came to the front door – well, she wasn't even carrying a handbag and certainly not a suitcase. So you tell me what she's doing wandering the streets on a night like this, and why did she find her way here, to this particular house? Paul obviously doesn't know who she is.'

'This is a guest house. Mebbe she was looking for a room?' Emily said sarkily.

'I don't think so. If she meant to buy a week's board and lodging, she'd have had a portmanteau. Even if she was looking for a room just for the one night, I'd have thought she'd have some sort of a bag. Besides, what made her run off like that?'

'*You* did!'

'Rubbish!' Peering out of the window, the old woman cursed when she realised she had lost sight of her nephew. 'I'm sure I don't know what to think,' she went on, 'but he's bound to bring her back with him, so we'll soon know the truth of it, I expect.'

Having seen all they could for the time being, and having exhausted themselves, the two women retired to the fire, where they sat and ate cake, laughing, and telling naughty tales of men and youth gone by.

Outside, Paul could find no sign of the woman Peggy had described. He walked up and down the promenade, but she wasn't sitting on any bench that he could see, nor was she anywhere along the streets leading from the promenade.

Lost in thought and feeling curiously sad, he stood a moment looking out to sea. From what Emily had said, the young woman must have been really distressed. He reached his gaze as far out to sea as the moonlight would allow. 'I hope to God she didn't do anything foolish,' he whispered.

Disheartened and frozen to the bone, he headed for home. He wondered if she might have sought lodgings elsewhere, or whether she had gone back where she'd come from . . . wherever that was. Head down against the wind, he turned into his street. When he looked up to climb the steps he saw her there; wet and bedraggled, loitering on the threshold of Bluebell House as if afraid to knock.

Taking the steps two at a time he apologised when she swung round like a startled bird. 'I'm sorry,' he told her. 'I didn't mean to frighten you like that.' Something about her touched him deeply.

Mary smiled, then sneezed. 'Do you know the man of the house?' she asked nervously, her teeth chattering. 'I need to speak with him.'

'Then you'll need to see *me*,' he answered cheerfully, 'because I'm the man of the house.'

'Oh, I'm sorry . . . only I . . .' Acutely embarrassed, she wasn't sure how to begin.

'Let's not talk out here in the cold.' Taking the coat from under his arm he opened it wide. 'Here.' He had taken the coat with him on the off-chance he might find her on that bench, and now, having managed to keep it relatively dry, he swept it round her shoulders. 'We can talk inside.'

Locating the key in his coat pocket, he quickly unlocked the door. With another word of encouragement he gently ushered her into the warmth of the hall.

She made no objection; instead she smiled shyly at him, grateful that she was off the streets and out of the cold. 'Why did you have a spare coat with you?' Her curiosity got the better of her.

He smiled. 'Time enough to explain that,' he answered. 'First, let's get you dried out, before you catch your death of cold.'

Once she was inside, Paul slid her own damp coat from her shoulders, concerned to find that her clothes underneath were soaked and clinging to her skin. When she began sneezing again, he took her by the arm. 'There's a fire in the sitting room,' he said, leading her along the passage.

'I'm sorry to barge in on you like this.' Mary had expected the proprietor to be an older man, but this one was no older than what – his mid-thirties? And so pleasant into the bargain. 'I ought to explain why I'm here,' she told him. 'I really do need to tell you why . . .' She hesitated, a feeling of shame coming over her.

Paul was adamant. 'First things first.' He was intrigued by her, yet all that concerned him at that moment was for her to be warm and comfortable.

Inside the sitting room, Emily and Agatha were still reminiscing. When the door opened to admit Paul and the young woman, the old lady's face bristled with hostility, while Emily was instantly concerned about the state of their visitor. 'Good Lord!' She leapt out of her chair by the fire, where she had been enjoying a chat before going off-duty and home to her beloved cats. 'You poor thing, you're soaked to the skin!'

Embarrassed at so much attention, Mary thought she had best explain why she was here, before things went any further. Turning to Paul, she thanked him for taking her in. 'My name is Mary Honeywell, Mr Marshall, and I'm at my wit's end. You see, I had my carpet bag stolen on the train. It had my purse inside and all my things. I'm sorry, but I was told you might be able to help me.'

Agatha was quick to retort, 'Had your purse stolen? Huh! That's a likely tale! And besides, why *should* we help you? We don't even know who you are!'

Paul instantly reprimanded her. 'That'll do! Can't you see this lady is distressed enough, without you going at her like a dog at a bone?' All the same he had been taken aback when she called him by his name. Leading her to Emily's welcoming arms, he asked, 'How did you know my name?'

Ignoring Paul's warning, Agatha intervened again. 'That's exactly what *I* was wondering. And who gave her this address?' She regarded Mary as though she was some sort of a criminal. 'It *was* you who came to the door earlier, wasn't it? I saw you through the window, hanging about outside, looking very suspicious if you ask me.'

Mary had already recognised the old woman as being the face at the window; it was because of her that she had run off. And now, when she sounded so hateful, it made Mary doubly nervous. 'I . . . well . . .' Swallowing hard, she made a supreme effort to calm herself. 'It happened just like I said. A woman robbed me on the train and when I got off, I went straight to the duty officer here, who said he would inform the police, only I couldn't give him an address, because I hadn't yet got one. You see, I'm new to the area.'

The words tumbled out in a frantic rush. 'I had no money and nowhere to go, and he very kindly gave me Mr Marshall's name and this address. He said you would know him – his name is Alan – and that he was sure I might be allowed to stay on here, until I got myself a job and could repay everything.' She looked from one to the other. 'I'm sorry. I'd just as soon leave now than cause any trouble.'

'You'll do no such thing.' Furious with his aunt, Paul gave her a warning glance, before addressing Emily. 'Take Miss Honeywell upstairs, please and help her out of these wet clothes.'

'Right away, Mr Marshall.' Taking Mary by the arm, Emily turned her towards the door, chattering away in her broad Lancastrian accent, and endearing herself to Mary without even trying. 'Robbed, eh?' Tut-tutting, she confided, 'I've heard as how them rascals ride all day on the trains, watching and waiting for folks to drop off to sleep afore they steal their bags and purses. By! They want 'anging, the lot of 'em!'

'See that our visitor has everything she needs, will you Emily?' Paul called out as they left the room. 'Oh, and she can have the first-floor front room. We don't have a booking for that one until the end of March.' He told Mary, 'It's the best in the house – warmer, too. And it has a great view of the promenade.'

The minute the two of them were out of the room and on their way upstairs, Paul closed the door and rounding on Agatha told his aunt exactly what he thought of her spiteful behaviour. 'What *is* the matter with you?' he ground out. 'How could you go on at her like that, when the poor thing is dripping wet and chilled to the bone. Besides, I've told you before, this is *my* house – my *home*!'

'But you don't even know who she is,' the old woman said stubbornly. 'You know nothing about her.'

'I know she's in some kind of trouble.'

'Huh! You've been swayed by a pretty face. Otherwise, why would you take in a complete stranger?'

'I took *you* in, or have you forgotten that?'

The old woman looked uncomfortable. 'That's different. I'm family.'

Paul shook his head. 'Not so different. You hadn't acknowledged me since I was ten years of age, then suddenly there you were, standing on my doorstep, your suitcases waiting in a cab. You practically begged me to take you in.'

'That's a wicked thing to say!' Sitting bolt upright in the chair she challenged him, 'My circumstances were different. I'd only recently lost my husband. I found it painful, living in the same house we'd lived in for all those years.'

Wagging a finger he reminded her, 'I recall different. I recall you telling me you hadn't loved him in years . . . that he was a miserable old mean-spirited bugger who made your life a misery.'

Agatha's face reddened with the flush of guilt. 'That's got nothing to do with it. Besides, I've got money – plenty of it, but *that* brazen hussy's turned up with nowt but the clothes on her back. What's more, you've even given her the front room, when you knew all along I wanted that room.'

'Aw, come off it, Aggie. You know very well that room is my best earner. Year after year it's booked solid, right through from

March to November. Besides, you heard what Mary said. She won't be staying long. Probably only until she gets work and a place of her own to rent.'

'Hmh! "Mary", is it? You've been taken in by a pretty face, that's what. I bet you she'll be here longer than you think – especially when she finds out what a soft touch you are – as if she hasn't already found out. And as for me not getting in touch with you over the years, it was only because you never stayed in one place for more than five minutes at a time.'

But Paul wasn't about to let her off the hook so easily. 'Even so, I didn't know you from Adam when you turned up here,' he reminded her. 'Yet I took you at your word and agreed for you to stay – for a week or two, that's what you said, but it's been more like two years, and you're still here.'

'Are you telling me to go?' Her bottom lip began to tremble in that childish, familiar way he had come to recognise when she couldn't get what she wanted. 'I'll go if you want me out. I won't stay where I'm not wanted.'

'Of course I'm not telling you to go!' Coming over to her, he chided warmly, 'You know how fond I am of you. All I'm saying is, don't be so hard on this woman. She looks to me like she could do with a friend.' Stooping, he reached out and cupping her face in his hands, he asked quietly, 'Will you promise to be nice to her?'

Wiping away a tear, she nodded reluctantly. 'All right. I promise.'

'Wonderful!' He thanked her. 'I knew you had a heart, hidden away beneath all them nasty suspicions.'

Later, while Paul went to his room to check the incoming bookings, Emily brought Mary's wet clothes down and put them in the copper to soak. 'The lass is out on her feet,' she informed Agatha. 'I lit a fire and warmed the bed, and told her to get into it. She can talk with Paul to her heart's content tomorrow. I saw him going into the office and he said I'd done the right thing.'

'I don't like it, Emily.' The old woman had lied to Paul. 'He asked me to be nice to her, and I said I would – but I'm damned if I will. Never! I don't care for the woman . . . don't trust her neither.'

'That's a bit hard. Why don't you give the poor thing a chance?' Emily paused to rub her hands by the fireside; like all the big old houses along the front, every room carried its own chill in winter, and the bedrooms were no exception. 'Let's talk about it tomorrow, eh? I'm worn out. I promised to take her up a hot drink and after that, I'm off to me own bed.'

'You listen to me!' Drawing her aside, Agatha lowered her voice. 'Watch her! Don't get too close to that one. She's a bad 'un, I can tell.'

'How d'you mean?'

'I mean, she's after him – after my nephew's hard-earned money. She's looking for an easy man and a cosy life with it, but I'll tell you this!' Leaning nearer, she confided in a harsh voice, 'She'll not get her claws into him, I'll see to that. By! I'll soon have the bugger on her way, you see if I don't!' Just then they heard Paul coming down the stairs. 'Not a word to him, mind!' she warned.

When Paul walked through the door, Emily fled to the kitchen, while Agatha greeted him with a smile. 'Emily says she's gone straight to bed, poor thing. I expect she'll feel better when she's had a nice cup o' cocoa and a good night's sleep, eh?'

Secretly, Agatha was thinking to herself that if she'd had a dose of arsenic handy, she'd have put it in this Mary's cocoa and hope she *never* damn well woke up!

Chapter Five

What have you got to say for yourself, my boy?' Thickset, with a scraping of brown hair and spectacles that danced on the end of his nose, Clive Ennington, manager of Galloways Children's Home, was not a patient man. 'Well? I'm waiting.'

'Nothing.' Jack's sullen mood had not mellowed during his stay at the home; if anything, over this past week, it had got steadily worse.

'"Nothing" WHAT?' The man's ice-blue eyes almost popped out of his head.

'Nothing . . . sir.'

Mr Ennington began pacing the floor. 'There was fighting in the dining hall.' Spinning angrily on his heel, he demanded, 'Well? Am I right?'

'Yes . . . *sir*.' The boy's insolent emphasis of the last word sent the older man into a rage. Red-faced and fit to burst he gave Jack a shove. 'Hands out – NOW!'

When, defiantly, Jack held out only one hand, he was taken by the shoulders and shaken so hard his teeth rattled in his head. '*Both* hands, if . . . you . . . *please*!' Ennington uttered every word as though he might choke on it.

Reluctantly, Jack held out both his hands, palms upwards,

fingers together. He had done it often enough this past week to know how.

'I didn't start it, sir.' Looking the man in the eye, Jack kept his head high and his shoulders straight. 'They were making fun of me.' A dark shadow flitted over his uplifted eyes. 'I don't like being laughed at.'

Throwing back his head, the man sniggered at Jack's childish pride. 'So! You don't like being laughed at, eh?' Composing himself, he stared down at the youngster. 'Well now, I hope you like the feel of leather against your skin, because you're about to receive the lesson of your life.' Flexing his muscles, he then took up the cat o' nine tails and flicked it in the air to loosen the flailing leather strips. With a look of pleasure on his face he raised it high in the air and with one swift movement, brought it licking down towards Jack's outstretched palms . . . first one, then the other . . . four lashes on each hand.

He waited for the boy to cry out, and when he did not, it had the most startling effect on Mr Ennington; intermittently flicking the cat-o'-nine-tails as he went, he began hurrying in a strange kind of hop, back and forth across the room. 'Did you see?' he asked hoarsely. Peering sideways at her, he addressed the woman known as Alice Compton, whose duties included overseeing any punishment a child might receive. 'Did you notice how he took his beating?' When he shook his head angrily, the wisp of hair he had combed to one side so as to disguise his creeping baldness fell across his eyes.

'I don't understand what you mean,' she answered respectfully, Alice was the one who had found Jack and his sister on the steps of the town hall a week ago today. In that short time she had come to love both children – even Jack, who could be disruptive and difficult to handle. Unfortunately, and much to his discredit, that was more often than not. But then, after the way he and his sister had been abandoned, who could blame him?

'Really?' Her boss stopped in his tracks, his eyes boring through hers. 'What I mean is, he took it like a *man*!' Again, that curious sideways look. 'Don't you think so, Mrs Compton?'

Alice looked over at the boy, small and straight, and filling the room with his presence; she gave a discreet smile. 'Yes, sir, I think you're right,' she said. 'He *did* take it like a man – yes, indeed.'

Her reply only appeared to irritate him. 'The boy is too arrogant by half,' he gritted out, and suddenly he was across the room and laying into Jack again; this time with the flat of his hand. 'Arrogant child! If you will insist on fighting, then I must insist on you being punished.' For good measure and to drive his message home, he swiped Jack so hard across the head that the blow sent him reeling to the wall.

Realising how he meant to follow it up with another assault, Alice Compton was across the room in two strides. Placing one protective arm round Jack's shoulders, she put out her other hand to ward off the fist that was already closed and poised to strike. 'The boy was telling the truth,' she declared boldly. '*He* didn't start the fight. It was Gerry Reynolds.'

'Nonsense, woman! Reynolds is a trusty lad. In the two years he's been here – why, he's earned everyone's respect!'

'Not *mine*, sir, nor the younger children's, especially the girls. In fact, the fight started on account of Jack's little sister. Reynolds was threatening her well-being, that's what Nelly from the kitchen told me, an' I've never known her tell a lie in all the years we've worked together. Some of us have seen for ourselves what a bully that young fella me lad is. In fact, as you yourself must know, I have reported his behaviour on more than one occasion.'

Squaring her shoulders she looked him in the eye with confidence. 'I expect it's all down on record, sir. I mean, I handed in a written complaint about his manner an' all.'

At once the man's mood changed. He seemed suddenly wary; a look of fear darkening his features.

'Are you saying I run a corrupt establishment?' Narrowing his eyes at her, he advised softly, 'Be very careful how you answer.'

Alice, too, was wary. She knew full well how he had ruined many lives in the past, and that he could ruin hers, too, if he felt the need. 'Of course not, sir. Only Jack here . . . well, he's innocent of the charge.'

With troubled eyes, she looked down at the young boy. There was a long, meandering weal running from eye to ear, and his nose was bleeding badly. But he had no pity for himself. Instead, with shoulders braced and tears of humiliation flowing down his face, he prepared himself for the next cruel blow.

'It's all right, lad.' Alice's admiration for Jack was tenfold as, with a tremble of disgust in her voice she addressed the man in respectful but accusing tone. 'If you don't mind me saying, sir, I think you should talk to Gerry Reynolds. For some reason, he has it in for this young lad. Since the day he and his sister arrived, Jack has been hounded by that scoundrel.'

'Hmh!' Her plain words had a marked effect, because the man seemed to back off with unusual humility. 'Your comments are duly noted, Mrs Compton. Now please get this urchin out of my sight!'

Encouraged by her success, Alice requested, 'After I deliver the boy to his dormitory, could I have a minute of your time, sir?'

Swelling with indignation, Ennington retorted, 'Good God, woman! I'll have you know my time is too precious to waste on trivial matters to do with kitchens and dormitories, and whatever else it is you women take care of. Talk to the bursar. Whatever it is, I'm sure he can deal with it.'

But Alice persisted. 'It isn't trivial, sir, and it isn't to do with my duties. It's a personal matter, you understand.'

'Oh, very well,' he said brusquely.

Bristling with curiosity he wandered to the long casement window, where he stood legs astride, his mind working like a beaver in a trap. With a sickly grin he turned to look her in the eye. 'I do hope you aren't about to offer your notice, but if that's how you feel, then we can talk about it, of course.'

Alice was taken aback. 'Oh no, sir! It's nothing like that.'

Before she could explain further, she was rudely interrupted. 'Away with you now, woman. I have things to attend to. Come back when you've duly delivered the boy, and we'll discuss it then. Five minutes! That's about as much time as I can spare.' With a wave of his hand he effectively dismissed her. And being needful of her place here, she quickly departed.

Alice hoped her errand would prove fruitful, especially as it seemed Mr Ennington had ignored her complaints – and one of them officially written out too. For a manager to ignore such a thing, he was either neglecting his duties, or there was something fishy going on, though she couldn't for the life of her think what it might be.

On the way back, Jack asked nervously, 'Can I say goodnight to my sister?' With his father gone, and his mother before him, Nancy was everything to him now.

'I don't see why not.' Changing direction, she led him towards the redbrick building where the younger children were housed. 'Mind you, it's already seven o'clock,' she warned him kindly. 'Likely as not they'll be off to their beds by now.'

'I need to know she's all right.' Jack had been deeply upset by the other boy's threats on Nancy.

Knowing his thoughts, Alice reassured him. 'Don't listen to Reynolds,' she urged. 'He can't harm your sister. She's watched carefully – all the little ones are, and besides, he's just a big-mouth who likes causing trouble. Deep down, that boy is nothing but a coward.'

'Still an' all, I want to see her.'

'All right, love, but only for a minute, or you'll get me shot.' She wondered if a favour might be repaid with a favour. 'Jack?' There were still a few unsolved riddles.

Jack looked up, but said nothing. He had learned to say only as much as was necessary.

Alice, though, never gave up. 'I wish you would confide in me.'

Still, he remained silent.

'Why won't you tell me about your parents? Who are you, Jack . . . and is that *really* your name?'

Still there was no response.

'I can't understand it.' Alice was now thinking aloud. 'We made all the usual enquiries . . . I even went out and about asking people if they knew anything, but it's as though you two never existed.'

Taking him gently by the shoulders, she drew him to a halt. 'Listen to me, pet.' She smiled at him, her affection evident in her eyes. 'I found you and Nancy, and I've come to love you both . . . I never was fortunate enough to have children you see, and I was hoping . . .' She paused, realising it was not wise to reveal her plans, not yet anyway. 'Never mind that for now, eh?'

She had another question. 'Where did you live before, Jack? Was it out in the country . . . isolated so you hardly ever met anyone? Maybe you didn't have any friends – is that it? Is that why no one came forward when we made all them enquiries? And who wrote the letter we found in your sister's pocket, asking that we take care of you, because you had no one else?'

When Jack deliberately looked beyond her to the redbrick building where Nancy was kept, she grew anxious. 'I'm trying to help you, Jack. Who was it that left you at the town hall?'

Jack's tongue was stilled as ever, and Alice knew she would get nothing out of him. 'All right.' She gave an almighty sigh. 'I'll not ask again, but if you feel the need to talk to somebody . . .

well, I'm a good listener.' She dropped her voice to a whisper. 'Besides, I know how to keep secrets.'

When he seemed not to be listening, she shook her head despondently. 'Come on then, son. Let's go and say goodnight to your little sister.'

Thankful that she had stopped asking questions, Jack quickened his steps. He liked Alice – he had liked her from the very start. But she was authority, and he couldn't bring himself to trust her.

Just as Alice had warned, the younger children were being put to bed. Nancy apparently was still awake, having only that minute been taken in. 'Oh, bugger me, Alice. I'll be hung, drawn and quartered if they know I've let you through.' Edith Charles the nursery nurse was a small, round woman with big brown eyes and droopy ears that stuck out from beneath her hairnet. Ever since being summoned before the housekeeper, on account of two bedsheets going missing, she had developed an unnatural fear of her superiors.

When Alice explained the nature of her errand, she dithered and fidgeted. 'Ee, I daresn't! It's more than me job's worth.'

Alice used her wiles. 'Aw, come on, Edie. Didn't I risk *my* job, when I stood up for you in front of the housekeeper? "Edith might be a bit slow," I said, "but she's no thief, ma'am". That's what I said, and it got you off, didn't it?'

Edith recalled the incident only too clearly. 'Oh yes, it got me off all right,' she chuckled, 'only now, everybody thinks I'm a bit wrong in the 'ead. Honestly, Alice, you didn't do me no favours when you said I were a bit *slow*.'

Alice winked naughtily. 'It worked though. As for what everybody thinks, tek no notice. They're only jealous because they know you've more brains up top than any one of them.'

Edith's big eyes grew even bigger. 'Oh Alice, d'yer really mean that?'

Alice shook her head. 'No, but there's nothing to stop *you* from believing it, is there?'

When she burst out laughing, Edith had to laugh with her. 'You mischievous bugger, you got me going there for a minute.' Creased with laughter, she slapped Alice so hard on the back, it knocked her sideways.

Jack grinned. He thought they were both as mad as hatters, but he couldn't help but like them. However, right now he needed to see his sister. 'Can we go now?' he asked anxiously.

'Sorry, lad.' Alice had not forgotten. Turning to Edith she asked, 'You heard young Jack here. Can we go through now?'

'Go on then.' Alice was her friend and good friends were hard to come by. 'Being as you got me out o' trouble, I dare say I can turn the other way for now. I mean, it weren't my fault if you an' the boy went and sneaked by me when I weren't looking.' She glanced at Jack and gave a cheery smile. 'By! You're an 'andsome little fella an' no mistake.' She laughed out loud, when Jack blushed bright pink. 'Aw, look at him, bless his little heart.'

Her laughter faded when Jack, impatient, assumed one of his more hostile stares; head bent and eyes peering up, he gave her a fright. 'Bloody hell, gal, I bet 'e's got a right shocking temper!' Instinctively backing off, she saw another side to Jack – one that she didn't much care for. 'I reckon you've got yer 'ands full there, Alice, an' no mistake.'

'You could say that.' Alice knew all about Jack's temper, for hadn't she herself been on the receiving end of it more than once. 'You're right, Edith. Jack can be a really bad boy when he puts his mind to it.' She gave him a crafty wink and he knew what she was at.

Suddenly, Edith was like a cat on hot bricks. 'Go on, be off with yer, but don't wake the bairns, and for Gawd's sake, don't stay longer than two minutes. The buggers'll be round to check on me any time now.' Agitated, she glanced at the door. 'Hurry up, gal, get going.' She gave Alice a gentle shove. 'Two minutes, mind.'

The pair hurried down the corridor and across the galleried landing. When they came to the nursery, they paused a moment by the door. Jack's searching gaze raked the room, until at last he spotted Nancy's fair head. 'She's over there, look!' As he went to run on ahead, Alice reminded him, 'Go softly now.'

Beneath their feet the wooden floorboards creaked and groaned, heralding their arrival. Glancing about, Alice saw how the tiny babies were already fast asleep in their cots; ugly wooden affairs cobbled together by the older children at the home, they resembled crates rather than cots. 'Poor little beggars.' Alice's kindly heart felt heavy every time she walked these dormitories.

There were no home comforts in a place like this; no curtains at the long grimy windows, no pretty rugs on the floor and no delicate hand-knitted covers to keep the bairns warm. Instead they were swathed in coarse grey blankets and the bonnets on their heads were ill-fitting and itchy, with thin ribbons that knotted under the chin and made red marks that took all day to fade. It had even been known for bairns to be strangled by the thin ties while they slept. Because nits and lice ran rampant through the children's heads, it was a rule that they wore sleeping bonnets, and whatever the cost, rules must be kept.

As Alice followed Jack down the room, her troubled eyes roved every inch of that desolate place, and her heart grew heavier. In every dormitory there lingered a certain musty smell – the accumulation of years of neglect, but here in the bairns' building there was another kind of smell. It was like a curious presence in the air, a sense of awful loneliness; a feeling that touched you deep inside.

She raised her eyes upwards, to the heavy wooden beam that spanned the entire width of the room. *God loves us all* it proclaimed in large, gilt-edged lettering; two outstretched hands embracing all below.

Alice smiled cynically. 'He must love some more than others,' she muttered, and immediately felt ashamed.

Thankfully, most of these bairns would be placed in loving homes. Others were not so fortunate. In the older children's dormitories, there were orphans who had been here for many years. Some even stayed until they were old enough to be turned out to find their own way forward. Many of them returned, pleading to be taken in, but of course they never were. It was a cruel world.

'Are you all right, Nancy?' Jack's love for his sister shone out in the warm, soft smile with which he bathed her pretty face. 'You mustn't be afraid, I'm only across the yard.'

'When are we going home?' Her pretty blue eyes shone with tears and her bottom lip trembled. 'I want my daddy. And I want Mary.'

At once, Jack took her hand in his and, whispering in her ear, he reassured her. 'Don't worry. We'll be all right, you and me. Just do as you're told and try not to get upset, and nobody will hurt you.'

'I didn't tell them anything, Jack,' she whispered in return.

He put his arm round her and held her for a time, and when she appeared to be asleep, he held her a moment longer, just to be sure.

From a discreet distance, Alice looked on. What she saw only intensified her determination. She saw how Jack was savagely dedicated to his sister, and how even in sleep, the girl held on to him, and she thought she had never seen anything so beautiful. It was obvious that these two had been through bad times together, for only that kind of experience could create such a bond.

Stepping forward, she leaned down and breathed, 'It's time we went.'

Jack's troubled brown eyes looked up to Alice, but the woman had no words of comfort. What could she say that would make things right?

'Time to go, lad,' she repeated.

Laying Nancy tenderly against the pillow, Jack covered her over with the blanket. As they walked away he didn't speak; only time and again he glanced back at his sister. 'I *hate* him!' His features distorted with disgust. '*I hate them all!*'

'Who do you hate, Jack?' Alice could only hope this might be the breakthrough she had been hoping for.

He bowed his head. 'Nobody.'

Having betrayed his true emotions for the first time since coming here, he did not utter another word until they arrived at the main building. 'Thank you,' he said, and in a rare moment of gratitude, he actually touched her hand.

'Why won't you let me help you?' Alice persisted. 'What happened to your mammy, Jack? Why were you abandoned like that?'

But he only shook his head and kept his gaze down.

Another moment, and Alice had taken him right to the door of the dormitory. 'Goodnight, son,' she said gently. 'Sleep well.'

A nod of his head, and he was gone, into that soulless room, where other boys of his own age and older dreamed of things beyond their means – of a home and love and family . . . precious things which some of them would never experience.

Alice waited for him to go inside. She heard the door click shut, and still she made no move. Instead she waited, her instincts keeping her there. A short time passed, and she wasn't surprised when she heard the soft sound of laughter coming from inside the room. Wasting no time she flung open the door and her suspicions were confirmed.

Standing tall and defiant, Jack was in the centre of the room. Just as she had feared, he was already surrounded by three larger boys; the ringleader being none other than Gerry Reynolds.

In a run she went down the room. 'What the devil's going on here?' she shouted.

Seeing her anger and fearing punishment, the other two boys scattered. Leaping into their bunks they drew the covers over their faces, only their eyes peering over the top to see what would happen next.

Reynolds got in first. It were 'im!' he accused. 'He jabbed me in the stomach as he went by.' Some four years older than Jack, he was a large, red-faced boy, and so skilled in the art of lying that he actually believed his own lies. 'I were fast asleep in me cot, when this divil 'ere woke me up. Aye, an' 'e woke the other two up an' all.'

Alice questioned him. 'Tell me, Reynolds, why would he do that?'

''Cause 'e were looking for trouble, like always.'

As a matter of course, she had to question Jack. 'Is that right, Jack?'

Raising his eyes to the other boy, Jack looked at him for what seemed an age, his gaze darkening, and his fists closing by his side.

'Jack, answer me!' Alice knew the truth. She just needed him to speak out. 'Is that the way it was?'

The older boy held Jack's probing gaze, while behind Alice's back, he mouthed three words. 'Don't forget *Nancy*.'

Jack wasn't afraid for himself, though he worried that this boy might have a way of getting to Nancy, and he knew he meant to hurt her if he could.

He gave Alice her answer, but it was not the one she wanted. 'He's right. It happened just like he said.'

Alice's heart sank to her boots. 'Oh, Jack!' She bent her head to speak softly to him. 'He can't do you any harm. Nor can he hurt your sister. Believe me.'

Experience had taught Jack not to place his trust in anyone. 'It was like he told you, Mrs Compton. I punched him in the stomach as I passed his cot.'

Reynolds was overjoyed. 'Ain't that what I said?' Eyeing Alice with contempt, he then turned his attention to Jack. 'No hard feelings, matey,' he bragged. 'An' I won't report you if *she* don't.' Deep down he was afraid of Jack; afraid of that black hateful look in his eyes. But he would never admit it; especially in front of the gobshites in this place!

Alice was no fool. 'Into your beds, the both of you.' She was angry. Why wouldn't Jack trust her? Why did he let that bully get the better of him? But then she had seen the look in Jack's burning brown eyes, and her instincts warned her that Reynolds had it to come. All the same, she couldn't help but worry about Jack . . . so filled with loathing and bitterness, and too ready to lash out at the world. But there was no doubt in her mind that he had good reason to feel the way he did.

After seeing them into bed, she warned the entire dormitory: 'Any more of your tomfoolery, and you'll have Mr Ennington to reckon with. So think on!' And they knew she meant business.

Losing no time, Alice made her way over to the main office, where she hoped the manager was still free to speak with her. More than ever, she needed to do what had been on her mind this past week and more.

In fact, she had to wait outside his office for some time before he was free. 'He's got a gentleman in there with him.' Iris Dayley was the housekeeper; a rough-looking woman of middle years, with iron-grey hair tied into the nape of her leathery neck, and a deep scowl etched permanently into her forehead. 'What business have you with him?' She was nothing if not nosy.

'If you don't mind, it's personal, Mrs Dayley.'

'Hmh! Well, don't hang about here for too long.'

'Thank you, ma'am.' Alice didn't mind the woman, not really.

After all, despite the courtesy tide of 'Mrs' she was a spinster without family of any kind, with a large workforce to look after, and a job that kept her on her toes from morning till night. So, in Alice's books, she had a right to be grumpy.

With the housekeeper gone, Alice thought she might beg a cup of tea from Cook; she had a thirst on her to drink the sea dry, and her tongue seemed stuck to the roof of her mouth.

Before she left she took the liberty of listening in at the office door; the muffled voices told her that whatever business they were discussing would take a long time yet. 'Time to grab a cuppa,' she murmured, and made her way quickly down to the kitchen.

Cook already knew about the visitor. I saw him go in when I took Mrs Dayley's tea up,' she confided. Her round jolly face had grown bright pink in the heat from the oven. 'He looks a real gentleman, he does.' Giggling, she put one hand on her hip and the other up to pat her hair and, to the delight of her scullerymaid, she flounced about the room like a mandarin. 'Matter o' fact, I reckon he's just my sort.'

Groaning, she fell heavily into the armchair. 'Phew! I must be getting past it,' she cried breathlessly. 'There was a time when I could have danced and skipped all day.' Summoning the scullery-maid to fetch her a 'glass o' lemonade, with a drop o' gin to colour it' she went on to explain, 'From the cut of his clothes, I reckon he must be worth a bob or two.'

Intrigued, Alice helped herself to a cup of tea. 'Have you any idea what he's come about?'

Cook was indignant. 'No – and I don't *want* to know, thank you very much. So long as the buggers leave me alone in my kitchen, that's all I ask.'

Alice took her cup of tea and sat at the table, where Cook had settled herself into the stand-chair. 'How's them new childer doing?' she asked, meanwhile sipping her gin and growing redder in the face by the minute. 'I heard that nasty piece of work

Reynolds had his eye on the lad – what's his name now? John . . . Jake, is it?'

'Jack!' Alice smiled. Cook never did have a good memory for names. 'Nancy's craving for her daddy,' she revealed sadly, 'and as for the lad . . . well, he's having a bad time of it with that Reynolds lout.'

'Have you reported it?'

'No.'

'Why not?'

'I happen to think it might just sort itself out.'

'In what way?' Finishing the last of her gin, Cook beckoned the scullerymaid to fetch her another, which the scraggy girl did regretfully, because she knew once Cook had gone over the top, they'd *all* suffer.

Preparing to leave, Alice answered her question. 'Young Jack has hidden depths. I think he'll retaliate if he's pushed too far, and then that little toad Reynolds had better watch out.'

'Mmm.' Cook reflected on Alice's words, 'I've heard it said that Jack is a bad boy.'

Alice brushed her comment aside. 'Only when he feels threatened.'

'Still an' all. Once a boy comes bad, he'll *allus* be bad.' With that she fell off the chair and had to be helped back on. It took both Alice and the scullerymaid to heave Cook into an upright position.

'I must be off now.' Alice glanced at the clock over the range. 'I don't want to miss my appointment with Mr Ennington.'

Cook's slurred voice followed her. 'You'd best watch that bad boy Jack,' she said. 'Like as not he'll get you in trouble when yer back's turned, you see if I'm not right!'

Alice couldn't make out what she was shouting, because she was already running like the wind, on her way to see the only man who could help her.

As it turned out, her errand was futile. 'Am I right in thinking you intend leaving this particular establishment?' Ennington turned and demanded, after she had knocked at the office door and been admitted.

'No, sir, I am not.' It irked her to think he seemed bent on forcing that particular issue.

Disappointed, he banged the desk with his fist. 'Get on with it then, woman. I haven't got all night. What's so important it can't wait?'

Alice took a deep breath and then blurted it out: 'I want to be considered for fostering the children known as Nancy and Jack.' There, it was said, and she felt the better for it.

'What?' Open-mouthed, he stared at her. 'Are you telling me you want to foster children? *You!*' His voice boomed out, his face incredulous as he continued to stare at her. Then came the laughter – great roaring bursts of hilarity that shook the room and made her tremble in her shoes. Finally, when his bulbous eyes had almost popped right out of his head and the dribble ran down his chin like that of a newborn, he rounded the desk and leaning into her face, he asked softly, 'Really, Mrs Compton, have you completely lost your mind?'

Indignant, Alice defended herself. 'Excuse me, sir, but I'm no different from anybody else who comes here to take away the children; some of them, I have to say, I would not let loose with a dog, never mind a child. I have a husband and a nice home, and I have no other children.' She straightened her little body and looked him in the eye. 'I would have thought I were a very suitable candidate, at least as suitable as the others.'

'Then you would be wrong, for two very good reasons.' He had not realised how fiery she could be, and it worried him, 'Firstly, my dear Mrs Compton, you are an employee of this establishment, and as such are not privileged to foster from this house.'

Alice was taken aback. 'I was never told that, sir. And, as you know, I was a clerk in the town hall for many years before I asked to work with the children.'

'What does it matter if you were never told, Mrs Compton?' He smiled charmingly. 'You are being told now, are you not?'

'Please, Mr Ennington, I really want to look after those two bairns. They've been through so much, they deserve the chance of a better life. They'd be happy enough with me, sir. They know me. And they need a regular home-life.' She choked back the emotion, 'Please, sir. Can't you make an exception in my case?'

Smiling slyly, he walked away to seat himself behind his desk. 'I'm afraid not,' he told her with great satisfaction. 'It is a rule of this house, and a rule is a rule, as well you know, Mrs Compton.' With an impatient wave of his hand he dismissed her. 'Leave now. I have work to do.'

Alice knew there was no use arguing the point, and so she quietly turned about and went towards the door, but before she left she reminded him curiously, 'You said there were *two* very good reasons why I would not be able to foster the children.' Her eyes lit up. 'Have their parents turned up? Oh, Mr Ennington, sir . . . will they be going home at last?' If that was the case, she would gladly reconcile herself to the fact that she could not have them after all.

Drumming his fingers on the desk, he seemed to be turning something over in his mind, before remarking, 'You appear to have become fond of these two.'

'I have, sir! Oh yes, I have.'

Hesitating, he wondered if it was wise to reveal his plans. She was a thorn in his side, but she worked hard and had adapted well from her position as a town hall clerk. He wanted her out, but as yet had found no way of being rid of her. Unlike the others, she was no simpleton. However, even she had not found out his secret – that for years now, he had been selling the most desirable children to the highest bidder.

He felt clever. Untouchable. Nobody ever questioned him, and his bank balance was exceedingly healthy. So, it followed that he did not want his little business to break loose, which it well could if she found out what he was up to.

On the other hand, if he could convince her that the children were going to a good home – somewhere they would be loved – she might be pleased for them. The decision made, he stood up and went over to her and quietly closed the door, so they would not be overheard. 'The second reason that you would not be able to foster the children is because I have already found homes for them.'

When he saw that she was about to speak, he anticipated her question. 'No, Mrs Compton, it isn't their parents, I'm afraid. But it's something equally satisfying, I think. So, after tomorrow, the children will be taken good care of, and you can rest easy.'

Alice was torn apart. 'Can I know where they're going?'

Smiling, he wagged a finger and tutted loudly. 'Now, now, my dear, you know better than that. With you having worked in the town hall, you will be well aware of the conditions. The children, and their whereabouts must be protected. After all, it is possible that the home they knew before was a cruel place so, the fewer people who know where they are, the better. For their own sakes, you understand.'

Alice nodded. 'I understand, sir.' Hadn't she herself helped to enforce those same rules over the years.

'I can only assure you that the candidates were well vetted, as always. They are respectable people, who will provide stability and love – the very features you yourself mentioned.' He clapped his hands. 'My word, Mrs Compton, why so gloomy? I would have thought you might be pleased for the children?'

Alice brushed away a tear. 'I am, sir. I *am*!'

'Good. Then may I ask you not to breathe a word of this, until I myself have informed the children personally?' Again he smiled that charming smile. 'After all, my dear, however crusty and unapproachable I may seem from time to time. I really do have their best interests at heart.'

His cunning words made Alice feel churlish for not being instantly delighted at the good news, 'Thank you, Mr Ennington,' she said. 'I'm glad you told me.'

They bade each other goodnight, and while he returned to his desk, Alice gathered her belongings together. Five minutes later the night shift arrived and Alice took her leave.

On the way out she passed Edith, who looked fit to drop. 'By! It's been a hard day, gal. I won't be sorry to get home. But then it'll be cooking and clearing up, before I can even get my tired arse on a chair for the night.' She looked at Alice with envy. 'My old man ain't like yours,' she groaned. 'It don't matter if I'm on earlies or lates, or if I'm on me bloody knees, I still have to make a meal when I get in.'

Alice had to admit that she, too, felt incredibly weary. 'I must admit, I'm looking forward to putting my feet up,' she said. 'And you're right, Edith, I *am* luckier than most. If I know my Anthony, he'll have a stew on the simmer and the kettle boiling fit to bust.'

Edith had another, more personal question. 'And is there still no sign of . . .' she cast a significant gaze down towards Alice's midriff. 'You know what I mean, gal.'

Alice knew what she meant all right, because didn't they talk about it often enough? 'No.' She gave a wry little smile. 'I'm still not with child. I'm beginning to think it's not meant to be.'

'Aw, you never know, gal. I reckon it'll happen when yer least expect it. The thing is, not to give up hope.' Rolling her eyes to the skies, she said, 'As for *me*, I wouldn't want a kid if it came gift-wrapped. I see too much o' the little divils all day long. The last thing I want is to be going home to another.' Now when she sighed, there was real disappointment in her voice. 'Besides, I've already got one – a big lazy bugger who wants waiting on day *and* night . . . if yer know what I mean.'

Alice had a question for her; one which had often come to mind over the years when they had worked together, but being as it was a delicate matter she had not asked before. Now though, she felt it was the right time to satisfy her curiosity. 'I'm surprised you haven't already fallen for a child?'

Edith hesitated with her answer, but then in a lowered voice she admitted, 'I have, gal . . . three times.' She took a deep sigh. 'I got rid though. I went to see that woman along Albert Street. By! She bloody nearly killed me the last time, an' all. Silly cow!'

The revelation that Edith had done away with three unborns, sent Alice into a deep, thoughtful silence.

'I wish I hadn't told you now.' Edith was downhearted. 'I know how you feel about having yer own childer, and how long you've been trying to become a mammy.' Closing her fingers round Alice's arm, she drew her to a halt. 'I'm sorry, gal. Yer must hate me now.'

Alice didn't want her thinking like that. 'No, of course I don't,' she told her friend. 'We all want different things and it's not for me or anyone else to judge what you've done.' On impulse, she embraced the other woman, telling her, 'I could never hate you. Besides, I know you must have had your reasons for doing what you did.'

Edith explained them to her. 'I'm not the motherly sort – not like you, Alice. Oh, I know I work with 'em, but that's all it is . . . just work. I don't feel for the childer like you do. I can go home and happily shut it all out of my mind. Like I say, it's just work to me.'

She began walking on, and Alice went with her. 'Me poor mam had fourteen,' Edith revealed. 'We were a real burden to her. Me dad were a bully an' he didn't give a tinker's cuss for none of us, not the kids, and not our mam, except for the fun o' getting her with child. But it weren't no fun for 'er, I can tell yer. She had no life outside of us kids. She never had a decent frock to wear, and it was the divil's own job to keep us all fed and clothed.'

When she paused, Alice urged her on; if this had been weighing on Edith's mind for all these years, it must be time for it to come out in the open. 'Go on, love. Please. I want to know.'

Edith shrugged her shoulders. That's really all there is to tell . . .' She choked on the words. 'Except to say our mam lost the struggle when she were giving birth to her fifteenth. It were terrible, gal. She were at home in the back bedroom. Us kids could hear it all . . . everything.'

Now, when emotion threatened to overwhelm her, she took a moment to compose herself. 'They took our mam away, and soon after that, Dad were killed in an accident at work. There were them as said he'd done away with himself, but we'll never know. The authorities moved in and all us fourteen kids were scattered like seeds from one end o' the country to another. We never saw each other again.'

Seeing the expression of horror on Alice's face, Edith smiled sadly. 'We all know how the authorities don't care about keeping brothers and sisters together.' She fell quiet for a moment, before saying softly, 'I often wonder about 'em, gal. You know, where they are . . . what happened to 'em.' She shrugged her shoulders. 'I don't suppose I'll ever know.'

When they reached the boulevard, they went their separate ways; Edith to a number four horse-tram, destination Kempston, and Alice to the one which would carry her home to Prebend Street.

'Alice?' Having walked with her to the tram stop, Edith had something else to say.

Alice was already climbing up the steps to the upper deck, but she turned when Edith called her name.

'Thank you.'

'What for?'

Now, when Edith smiled, Alice could not help but notice how contented she seemed. 'For listening,' she called out. 'It helped more than you can ever know.'

Alice nodded. There was no need for words. Her warm, kindly expression said it all, and Edith went away feeling more of a woman than she had felt in a very long time.

Setting herself into the wooden-slatted seat, Alice kicked off her shoes. Her feet burned with weariness, and her eyes were so heavy she would have fallen asleep there and then. But she didn't. She couldn't.

It was only a ten-minute journey to Prebend Street, with three stops on the way. As always at this time of night, there were few passengers. The conductor looked as tired as Alice felt. 'Roll on summer,' he said as he clicked her ticket off the machine round his waist. 'I can't abide with cold days and driving rain.' And what else could Alice do but agree wholeheartedly?

It seemed she had no sooner got on than she was climbing off. 'Goodnight, m'dear.' With his girlish smile and fine long fingers, the conductor seemed a very feminine kind of fellow, she thought, but a nice, friendly enough soul.

Waving him a cheery goodbye, she went at a quickened pace down Prebend Street. As always, the street wrapped itself round her and welcomed her home. Born and bred in this common little street, Alice had never wanted to live anywhere else.

In winter, Prebend Street was quiet, with fewer children and rare sightings of the women who in summer would stand on their doorsteps to pass the time of day. During those same long, warm months of summer, the street came alive. The children would be out skipping or playing hopscotch, or running about, screeching with laughter. The men would gather in little groups, leaning on the wall and smoking their pipes contentedly as they chatted.

In winter, however, the street was ominously quiet, though almost every window was lit from within and occasionally the sight of a family gathered round the table for dinner, or the cheery fire in the hearth, reminded Alice that, winter or summer, this was her life. The only thing missing was a child of her own.

There was no light on in her own front parlour. Alice smiled to herself. I expect Anthony's in the kitchen, up to his elbows in pots and pans, she thought.

She was right. As she came into the parlour, her husband rushed from the kitchen to greet her. 'Hello, sweetheart. Tired, are you?' Stocky of build with grey eyes and a dimpled smile he took off her coat and sat her down. 'I got home from work earlier today,' he told her. 'They sent two bargeloads of the wrong stock down to the warehouse and the boss refused to offload it. It'll be morning afore they can bring the right order.'

After a few minutes' rest, Alice followed him into the kitchen. 'Let me help,' she said, although she knew how he loved to cook. 'I can't just sit and be waited on.'

'You might as well, because there's nothing to do here,' he answered. 'I told you – I got finished early. I've got the taters all mashed up, with lots of butter the way you like it, and the cabbage is done to a treat. The meat pie you baked last night is warmed through, and all it needs now is for the table to be set.' He turned to grin at her. 'There y'are, that's a job I wouldn't mind giving away.' He laughed out loud. 'I've never done it right yet – or so you tell me.'

Alice suspected he missed his old line of work. 'Stop a minute, love, please.'

'What's wrong?'

'Look, I know you hate working at the warehouse, and I also know that there's nothing in the world you love more than cooking. Look at you now!' She gestured at the tempting array of vegetables and the careful, decorative manner in which he was arranging them in the dishes. 'It's what you do best.'

'I know.' At least he couldn't lie about that. 'Only because I'm hopeless at anything else.' He laughed. 'What's all this about anyway?'

'I want you to go back to your old job. Tell the manager at the Bedford Arms that you made a mistake in handing in your notice. I reckon they'd welcome you back with open arms, especially as the new chef is said to be useless.'

'Who told you that?'

'Edith.'

'Look, sweetheart, Edith is a nice person and I like her, but *I* happen to know that the new chef is doing very well, thank you!' Placing his two hands on her shoulders, he held his wife tight. 'Even if he *were* rubbish, as your friend seems to think, and even if they went down on their bended knees for me to go back, I wouldn't. So, don't waste your breath and don't fret over it. Look, sweetheart, I'm all right as I am. I bring home good money, and it's regular work. Besides, there's talk of me getting promotion. What do you think of that, eh?'

Alice wasn't fooled. 'It's the money, isn't it?'

'What d'you mean?'

'You know very well what I mean. They don't pay a chef half as much as they pay at the warehouse. You think you're obliged to bring home a bigger pay packet, don't you?' She pleaded with him. 'We managed all right before, didn't we?'

'Yes, but we weren't too bothered about starting a family then. One day next month . . . next year, you could be carrying our child, Alice. I wouldn't be much of a man if I couldn't provide for the pair of you. There would no longer be your wage coming in, and there'd be another mouth to feed. Trust me, sweetheart, I know what I'm doing.' When he realised she was about to protest he kissed her soundly on the mouth. 'I won't hear any more about it. We both want a family and that family has to have the best I can provide. So, you might as well enjoy your meal, and forget about me going back to the kitchens. The only place I'll be going to from now on is where they pay the biggest pennies.'

'If you say so.' Alice knew him well enough not to press the point.

During their meal he talked excitedly about his plans for the future, and afterwards they discussed Alice's upset at the two youngsters being sent away. 'I know it's best for them,' she conceded, 'but I was just getting to know them.'

Across the table he held her hand. 'You really took to them two kids, didn't you?'

Alice nodded. 'Oh Anthony, you should see the devotion between them. It's so touching.'

He gave a knowing smile. 'You asked to foster them, didn't you? Come on – don't deny it.'

Alice blushed. 'What makes you say that?'

'You could say it's because I know you too well.'

'Would you have minded?'

'Mebbe.'

'Why?'

'Well, for a start I'm not sure I could handle the lad – Jack, the bad one.'

'He isn't really bad.'

Anthony wagged a finger. 'From what you've told me this past week and more, he's a buggeroota. Even halfway that bad is too much for me. If it was my own kid, I hope I might know how to deal with it, I don't know as I'd like to learn on some other man's offspring.'

'So, you would have said no?'

Again he took hold of her hand and squeezed it hard. 'Not if you wanted it real bad, sweetheart. I could have managed to put up with it, if only for your sake.'

Alice took another bite of her meat pie before shoving it aside.

'Well, it doesn't matter now anyway,' she told him sadly. 'Mr Ennington said they were already placed in good homes, so that's an end to it.'

Partly relieved and partly disappointed for his wife's sake, Anthony gave her a playful shove. 'You'd best eat up, Mrs Compton, or you'll get no pudding, and that would be a real shame; especially as I've baked a huge jam turnover, and made thick, creamy custard to go with it.'

Alice was won over. She ate her pie, and afterwards tucked into the best jam pudding and custard she had ever tasted. They finished the meal with a drop of homemade elderberry wine got from the corner shop, and when the washing-up was done, they sat side by side on the sofa; Alice with her legs curled up under her, and Anthony with his arm wound round her shoulders.

He guessed what she was thinking, and needed to reassure her, 'The kids will be all right, you'll see,' he promised. 'Besides, God willing, we'll soon have one or two of our own.' He drew her to him. 'We've never tried it on the rug in front of the fire,' he suggested mischievously.

She laughed softly, looking up at him with adoring eyes. 'Want to try it now?' she invited.

'You little harlot!'

'Shut the curtains then. We don't want the neighbours peering through the windows at us.'

He laughed. 'Well, not unless we charge them anyway.'

While she got undressed, he shut the curtains and turned down the oil-lamps, and right there, shrouded in the rosy glow from the fire, they made love.

Time alone would tell if they had made a baby.

Later when they lay in bed in the dark, steeped in thought and reflecting on the day, Anthony felt contented enough. Alice on the other hand, was beset with thoughts of Nancy and Jack. 'What kind of parents would desert their children like that?' she asked her husband.

'God only knows.' He had no answers, except to say, 'Don't dwell on it, sweetheart. Tell yourself they're among the more fortunate ones. At least they haven't been kept in that hell-hole for as long as some of the poor divils.' He snuggled up to her. 'They'll be away on the morrow,' he murmured, 'to a good home, and a better future than most. Think on that, and be glad for them.'

Alice kissed him goodnight. 'You're right,' she said. 'And I'm being selfish.'

With that she drifted into a restless sleep, fraught with dreams and images.

And at the centre of it all were Nancy and Jack.

Chapter Six

Events had moved quickly and, unbeknown to Alice, arrangements were already underway to place the girl, Nancy, with her new foster-parents. If Clive Ennington had his way, it would be a swift and secret exchange, but already there were slight complications. None however, that he could not deal with.

On this particular evening, as on many others before, Clive was preparing to leave for a long-awaited and exciting night with a Bedford floozie when, to his frustration, an urgent letter was delivered to his office. Curious as to who should be sending him messages so late in the evening, he read the note with interest.

As he scanned the message, he cursed and moaned, and when it was read from beginning to end he threw it back at the unfortunate young man who had brought it. 'Clear off!' he snarled. 'You've delivered the blessed note, now sling yer hook, damn you!'

In trembling voice, the young man asked, 'Excuse me, sir. Will there be an answer?'

'GET OUT!'

Being more concerned about his well-being than any answer there might be, the young man took to his heels, leaving the note on the floor where it had landed.

Shouting abuse which could be heard from one end of the

home to the other, Ennington snatched up the note and read it aloud, hoping he might have misunderstood it in the first place. To his increasing dismay, not a word had changed since he read it the first time:

My dear Mr Ennington,

I know this will prove to be a dreadful inconvenience to you, and for that I can only apologise.

The truth is, I have been summoned to London for the duration of the next week. Consequently, our arrangement will need to be finalised sooner than anticipated. I am to leave for London on the first available train on the morrow, and as we had arranged for me to collect the child at 8 a.m. you must understand it will now need to be much earlier.

In view of the reason for me wanting to take the child, it is imperative that the deal is done and settled before I depart for London. Therefore, I intend to arrive at Galloways, some time between 4 and 5 a.m.

I know this is extremely early, but as I have to make my way there and back, and in between get the child settled before I leave for London, I regret there is no other alternative.

I have everything ready, just as we agreed.

Yours truly,

Edward Cornwall

'Damn and bugger it!' All important, he strutted along the halls and walkways, until he discovered Matron in her office. 'I need you to prepare a child for travelling,' he informed her curtly. 'She faces a long journey, so perhaps you should feed her a good half hour before she goes. After all, we don't want the brat spewing up all over the gentleman's fine carriage.'

Matron was horrified. 'Do you mean right now?'

'No, of course I don't mean right now!' He asserted his authority. 'And I will thank you not to question me in such a way.'

Matron composed herself. 'Of course, sir.'

Her composure melted when he divulged the exact time the child was to be collected. 'The gentleman is expected to arrive between the hours of four and five a.m.' While he spoke his fists clenched and unclenched, as he thought of the pleasures he was having to cut short on account of this certain gentleman. 'From what I understand, some urgent business in London has forced him to change his plans. It is not for us to question. It is for us to make ourselves available.'

'I'm sorry, sir, the children are all fast asleep at that time of the morning.' The Matron was a large, plain creature, with hands the size of shovels and a neck the width of a navvy's top arm, yet she had a soft voice and manner to go with it. 'If we wake one, we might wake them all,' she argued.

Then you'll just have to get them all off to sleep again!' He was a past master at sarcasm. 'If, of course, you feel you can't cope, you only have to say so.'

'I can deal with it, sir.' She had long suspected underhand business going on here. Apart from that, she had no personal liking for Clive Ennington, whom she considered to be a pompous, evil man; however, for all that, she still valued her job far too much to report him to the authorities.

'I wish I'd been told before now,' she protested. 'I might have been able to separate the child from the others and save us a lot of aggravation. But this is the first I've heard of it,' She faced him boldly. 'I wasn't informed of any gentleman visitor, especially one who means to arrive at such a late hour.'

'Well, I'm informing you *now*,' He felt the intensity of her dislike and it put him on guard. 'Have the girl ready at three thirty, and be sure to find something decent for her to wear. This man is no ordinary visitor. He's wealthy and influential, and you can be assured, he won't want to take a ragamuffin away with him.' His eyes flashed a warning. 'Do you understand?'

'I understand, sir.' She understood only too well.

'Good! Now be off with you, and don't be tempted to gossip. The gentleman does not want his private transactions broadcast far and wide.' He paused, a smile on his face that made her skin crawl. 'I believe you are a very sensible woman, Matron, and of course, there are times when sensible people need to turn a blind eye.'

The smile froze on his face. 'I expect *you* to do the same. That is, if you want to remain in work. And I don't mean just here in this establishment. I mean *anywhere*!' The smile faded. 'I trust I'm making myself clear?'

'Perfectly clear, sir.' She hated herself for kow-towing to a man such as this.

'Excellent.' He turned and walked away, delivering an order as he went. 'Send a tray to my office at once. Tea and cakes – oh, and a pork pie. I have a curious appetite on me.'

'Which child is it, sir?'

'What?' Spinning round, he focused his beady eyes on her. 'What was that you said?'

'Which girl am I to get ready, sir?'

'Really!' Ennington drew himself up to his full, formidable height. 'I appear to be surrounded by dimwits!' He had a cruel way of humiliating a person. The girl is called Nora . . . Nelly – oh for God's sake, Matron, you know damned well who I mean!'

'Nancy? Is that who you mean, sir?'

'There you are. You knew all along!' He spat out her name as if it were poison. 'Nancy! Of course that's the one. Have her washed and dressed and make sure she looks the part.'

At the door he turned again. 'On second thoughts, I won't

have time for a tray.' He glanced at the clock above her desk – a flimsy affair when contrasted with her bulk. Ten o'clock already. Mmm.' After a moment's thought, his avaricious eyes lit up. 'Look, Matron, I have an errand in town. I'll be back in good time. Meanwhile, keep an eye on things.'

'Yes, sir.' She rolled her eyes to the ceiling. Wasn't she *always* the one to keep an eye on things, whether he was here or whether he was not?

'Good woman.' A condescending chuckle, then the rush of his coat as he hurried away. And now, a mighty slam of the door to announce his departure.

'Good riddance – and don't bother coming back!' The wishful thinking was issued in a fearful whisper.

A few minutes later, Matron was passing on the instructions to the night nurse in charge of the infant unit. 'What the devil's he playing at, getting the poor child out of a warm bed, to whisk her off like a thief in the night?' With features akin to that of a bird, the nurse was a tiny little thing in comparison to her superior. Even the clothes she wore hung on her like sacks on a washline. Yet she was a strong-minded person, with a way of speaking the obvious. 'I reckon that bugger's up to no good!' She kept her voice soft so as not to wake the children asleep around them. 'I reckon he *sells* the poor little divils to the highest bidder.'

Horrified, Matron cautioned her, 'Mind your tongue, Mavis,' she hissed. 'I've no doubt what you're saying is true – we all know it goes on.'

'Ennington's a bloody rogue, he is! He sells the ones as come in last and gets 'em out afore the authorities even know the poor little sods were ever here.'

'I won't tell you again, Mavis! It's not good to speak it out loud.' She glanced about, apprehensive in case anyone else might have heard.

'Huh! Are you telling me he might be listening round the corner? Well, excuse me, Matron, but if he asks for my opinion, he'll get it – and to hell with the consequences.'

'You don't mean that.' The Matron was well aware of the little woman's background. 'Anyway, he's not here. He's got an urgent errand in town.'

At this, the little woman laughed out loud. 'Hmh! More like urgent *woman* business. A pound to a penny, he's gone to see his bit on the side.'

'We don't know that.' Concerned that the little woman might get herself into hot water, Matron began to wish she had said only what was necessary.

'We *do* know it, Matron. We know he's wed, and we know he treats his wife like the dirt under his feet, 'cause my cousin delivers the papers there. By! He hears 'em fighting and arguing and Mr Ennington going at his poor wife like a madman. Besides, you remember how Cook saw him in town one evening, arm-in-arm with his painted floozie. He's a randy old bugger, an' I hope he gets his comeuppance.'

Matron bade her to be quiet. 'I know all that,' she confessed, 'and I know why he stays here overnight sometimes, when that tart of his comes creeping in thinking we don't know what's going on.' She put her finger to her lips to stop whatever Mavis was about to add. 'But, like I said, it's not wise to talk about it. Walls have ears, Mavis.'

'And who's supposed to get the child ready, tell me that?' Mavis was wearied by all the work. 'What with Anna off to see her sick mother, and me up to my neck in washing the dirty linen, who's to do it, eh?'

Try as she might, Matron could not silence the little woman. 'And what if the others all wake up?' Mavis ranted on. 'Who's gonna get them all back to sleep, 'cause *I* can't! I'm all right at washing and ironing, and changing dirty bottoms, but when it comes to keeping them in a good mood, I'm hopeless. Matter o' fact, the mere sight of me sends 'em off into the screaming abdabs.' Exhausted by her own rampage, she sat down suddenly. The only one as can quiet 'em when they start is Alice Compton, an' she ain't here, is she?' She shook her head. 'Sorry, Matron . . . *you'll* just have to do it.'

Matron smiled knowingly. 'No, I won't.'

Mavis was up in arms. 'Oh, please!' Her face was a picture. 'I can't quiet the little devils, *I just can't.*'

'You won't have to,' the big woman revealed. 'I intend sending for Alice. She's been got out of her bed before when there's a need of her, and I'm sure we can count on her coming to the rescue now.'

Mavis breathed a sigh of relief. 'By! There's nobody can quiet them childer like Alice . . . got a natural touch she has an' no mistake. What's more, she's made friends with the two new ones when nobody else could.' She cocked a wary eye at the other woman. 'Lord only knows what she'll say when she knows they're about to be separated.'

Matron was well aware of it. 'That's why I want her here. I've a feeling there might be trouble.'

A thought occurred to the night nurse 'There ain't no trams running at that time o' the night. Who's gonna fetch her?'

Matron had it all planned. 'I'll send Joe, the caretaker. He'll have her here in the pony and trap in no time.'

Mavis's face crinkled into a naughty smile. 'I bet her fella won't like it. They might even be in the middle o' trying for that bairn they desperately want.'

Matron chastised her. 'From what Alice tells me of him, I'm sure Mr Compton will understand.'

So it was decided, and while Matron went away to organise old Joe, Mavis set about her washing and ironing. She then did her rounds, and before she knew it, the time had ticked over to half past two. 'Time for a brew,' she decided, and toddled off to the kitchen.

She lost no time in putting the kettle on to make herself a cup of tea. I've earned it,' she told herself, and for good measure she sliced herself a piece of fruitcake from the very tray which might have gone to Mr Ennington, had he stayed.

Mavis took a bite out of it. 'What the old sod don't know, won't hurt him!' Chuckling aloud, she took another bite. Then she had a swig of cooking sherry to whet her appetite, and another to warm the cockles of her heart. Then she fell dozing into the chair. She had hardly tucked her legs under her before she was snoring like a good 'un.

When suddenly the kitchen door was flung open she leapt off her chair, clutching at her chest. 'Oh my Gawd, Joe . . . you gave me such a fright!'

A jolly sort with a head of wild red hair and a moustache that covered half his face, Joe laughed out loud. 'Well, I never! You should see the colour o' your face, Mavis. I only came to ask if you'd keep me supper warm, as I'm to go and fetch Alice from her bed.' He chuckled again. 'By! I've never seen a woman scared o' *me* afore. It's a whole new experience, I can tell you.'

Mavis saw nothing to laugh at. 'You cheeky sod! I'll give you a "new experience" if you don't bugger off. As for your supper, you can bloody well sing for it, frightening me like that. Sneaking up on a poor helpless woman – you ought to be ashamed.' With that she grabbed the dishcloth and aimed it at him, shaking with laughter when it landed with a squashy smack all over his face. 'First bloody wash you've had in years, I shouldn't wonder,' she screeched, and when she reached for the saucepan, he was out the door like a scalded cat.

'The woman's mad as a hatter,' he muttered as he hurried along the corridors. 'I wouldn't mind, but I only went in to ask her about me supper.' All the same, he couldn't help but chuckle.

'To think the sight of *me* can send a woman wild.' He stuck out his chest and congratulated himself. 'Seems I ain't lost me touch after all.'

Reminding himself that he was to have Alice here by three thirty, he quickened his step and, thanks to Mavis's reaction to his appearance, his steps seemed curiously lighter and more jaunty than ever before.

Alice Compton had not slept well, so when Joe gingerly called through the letter-box, she was out of bed and down the stairs quick as a flash. It wasn't the first time she'd been called from her bed.

'Who's that at the door?' Missing the warmth of her body beside him, Anthony raised his head from the pillow. 'Alice? What's wrong, love?' With the sleep still on him, he clambered out of bed, pulled on his trousers and followed her.

In the parlour he found Joe explaining the reason for his presence. 'I'm sorry, Alice,' the caretaker apologised. 'There's some sort of crisis at the home, and they reckon you're the only one to deal with it, you being so good with the childer an' all.'

Before Alice could question him further, Anthony's voice intervened. 'What sort of crisis is this, then?'

Joe swung round guiltily. 'Oh, Mr Compton, I'm sorry to have woke the pair of you, only I were sent urgent like.'

Having grabbed his shirt on the run, Anthony quickly put it on; these old houses had walls like paper and the night air brought in the damp. 'It had better be a real crisis,' he said crossly. A kind and thoughtful man he might be, but in that first half hour of waking, he was never in the best of tempers. 'Getting us out of bed this time of a morning.'

Alice answered, 'Go back to bed, sweetheart. There's no need for you to be up. I can deal with it.'

Her husband knew well enough how capable she was, but the

sleep hung over his senses like a blanket. 'I'm awake now,' he grumbled, 'so I might as well make us all a cuppa.'

Joe glanced nervously at the mantelpiece clock; it was already quarter to three. 'I reckon we've just about got time,' he said graciously. 'Thank you – yes, I'd love a cup of tea.' He grinned at Alice. 'Mavis is in one of her funny moods. She wouldn't even promise to warm me supper till I got back.'

Alice grinned back at him. He and Mavis were always having one row or another, but it soon blew over and they were the best of friends again. Right now though, she had more important matters on her mind. 'This crisis, Joe. What's it all about?'

Joe told her as much as he himself knew. 'Matron says it's to do with one of the childer . . . she's being sent away. The gentleman in question is coming to fetch her at four o'clock, that's as much as I were told.'

Alice's heart turned over. 'This child – her name wouldn't be Nancy, would it?'

Joe searched his mind, then shook his head. 'Can't recollect it,' he answered thoughtfully. 'I don't reckon 'er name were ever mentioned.'

Alice needed to get to the home as quick as she could. If it was Nancy, and Jack knew nothing of it, there'd be hell to pay. 'Look, Joe, you sit yourself down and have your tea while I get ready.'

Running upstairs she threw off her nightgown and pouring a measure of cold water into the bowl she dipped the carbolic into it before rubbing the soap between the palms of her hands; she then lathered it over her face, and rinsed it off. That done, she dressed quickly in a brown, ankle-length skirt, together with a blue jumper and matching cardigan; both knitted by her own quick hands. A swift brush of her hair and she was ready.

Within five minutes she and Joe were on their way.

'Mind how you go now.' Shivering on the doorstep, Anthony

waved them off. 'I don't suppose you know what time you'll be back?'

Alice shook her head. 'Go back to bed,' she told him fondly. 'There's no point waiting up.'

He nodded, waved again and by the time they had turned the corner, he was gone.

It was an eerie ride. Every house they passed was in total darkness. Some of the street lamps were off. The ones that were lit emitted a familiar rushing noise, as the gas wormed its way up to the flame. The ensuing light danced and flickered, penetrating the darkness and lingering there, in small shrouded haloes that caught the shadows and shifted them about.

And through it all, the pair of them sat in silence, half asleep, deep in thought, moving through the night to the tune of the horse's hooves dancing against the cobbles.

Alice was so deep in thought that when Joe spoke, she was visibly startled. 'Sorry, I was miles away,' she confessed. 'I didn't hear what you said.'

When cold, Joe's nose tended to drip through his moustache; as a rule he would wipe it away with the cuff of his sleeve, but as his two hands were presently guiding the horse's reins, he sniffed and coughed and addressed her through stiffened lips. 'I were just saying, it's bloody freezing! If there's one thing I can't stand, it's the cold. Seems to go right through me old bones, so it does.'

Alice could see he was uncomfortable. 'Here, lad,' She removed the blanket which he had thoughtfully placed over her legs before setting off, 'You have this blanket. I don't feel the cold as much as you.'

But Joe would hear none of it. 'No, gal, you keep it. We've not far to go now, an' anyway . . .' he chuckled, 'if I can put up with Mavis's acid tongue, I'm damned sure I can put up with a bit o' cold round me arse.'

When Alice laughed out loud, he laughed with her. 'Eh, look, I'm really sorry to have got you out of a warm bed, only Matron seemed really put out.' He lowered his voice. 'If yer ask me, I reckon she were expecting some sort o' trouble – the sort it seems only *you* can tend to.' He glanced at her admiringly, 'It's a known fact, you have a special way with the childer . . . especially them two new ones.'

'And are you sure she never said which child was being collected?' Alice had an instinct that it could well be Nancy.

'No, she never said, honest.' Tweaking the reins, he turned into Midland Road. 'Why? And what if it is this Nancy? Could she mek trouble?'

'I hope not, Joe, but her brother might.'

The caretaker nodded knowingly. 'I reckon Mavis has mentioned them two – Nancy and Jack, ain't it? Weren't they abandoned in the town hall – and weren't it you as found 'em?'

'I didn't find them exactly. A man brought them there and just left them. He went away, and never came back. I thought he was their father, but what sort of man could abandon his children to strangers?'

'No man alive,' Joe answered solemnly. 'Unless he had some powerful trouble on his back.'

Alice had a mental image of the man. 'I only saw him for a minute or two. He was in his early forties, I'd say, and really good-looking. Come to think of it, he did seem troubled somehow – you could see it in his eyes. I hurried away to get them all a hot drink, but now I wish I'd stayed; he might have confided in me and not disappeared like he did. He was a quiet man, very gentle with the children. I've often wondered about him. Where did he go? Why didn't he come back?' And that same niggling doubt. 'Maybe they weren't his children after all.'

Philosophical as ever, Joe nodded and grunted, and sniffed the drips in from the end of his nose. 'I don't suppose we'll ever know.'

'You could be right. We won't learn anything from the children, that's for sure. They won't say one word about him. Nor will they give any information as to who they are, or where they come from. We put adverts out all over the place, but nobody ever came forward.'

'What about school?' Joe enquired. 'From what Mavis said, the lad must be old enough to have been at school?'

'That is *if* he went to school.' Alice smiled sadly. 'Oh, you know what it's like, Joe. Some kids will hide for days rather than go to school. All the same, we tried every school in the vicinity and none of them could help.'

'That tells me two things.' Joe prided himself on his instinct. 'Like you say, either the little sod played truant and never went at all – in which case the truant officer isn't worth the wages he's paid, or he *did* go to school, but not in this area.'

'That was Clive Ennington's thinking, too.'

'Well, it's a strange to-do an' no mistake.'

Alice had no answers. 'We tried everything,' she recalled. 'I even trudged the streets, to see if anybody might know anything, but it's as if the children never existed.'

'Happen they never *did* exist – not round here anyroad.'

Joe was echoing the very same thought that had gone through her mind time and again. 'That's what I thought,' she remarked. 'If they had only just moved into the area, it's not surprising nobody knows them.' She gave a deep, lonely sigh. 'It's a mystery, but one thing shines through, and that's Jack's devotion to his little sister.'

'And is that why you're so concerned it might be his sister who's being taken away, *and* at such an odd hour of the morning?'

'Nancy *was* due to leave the home,' Alice confided. 'Apparently a wealthy gentleman has taken to her. But nothing was said about her being spirited away like this.'

'Happen it ain't her. Happen it's some other little girl.' He turned the horses in through the archway. 'You'll soon know one way or the other,' he declared, ''cause we're here now, thank gawd!'

Clambering down from his seat, he rounded the trap in order to help Alice disembark, though she didn't need much help. 'Right, I'll say goodnight – or good morning as the case may be,' he chuckled into his beard. 'I'm off to me supper and bed, gal, an' once I'm in the Land o' Nod it'll take an army and its cannons to wake me.' He peered at her out of one eye. 'I expect you'll be staying now – at least till the trams start running?'

Alice smiled. 'I'll be fine, Joe, thanks. You get off to your bed. I won't be needing you any more today.'

He gave her a cheeky wink 'You're a good gal!'

Matron was very relieved to see her. 'I would never have got you out of bed if I didn't think it necessary,' she assured her.

Alice brushed aside the older woman's concern. 'I wasn't sleeping well anyway,' she said, 'so don't feel too badly.'

Matron bade her to sit down. When Alice was comfortably seated, Matron settled herself in the neighbouring chair. 'When I heard the pony and trap, I took the liberty of ordering us a jug of cocoa. Did you want something to eat? A biscuit – a sandwich, maybe?'

Alice graciously declined. 'Joe said something about a crisis?'

'I hope it won't come to *that*, but I must admit I am a little concerned. You know, do you not, that little Nancy is due to leave?'

Alice nodded. 'Mr Ennington informed me.'

'And did you know she was going to a wealthy family?'

'He said as much, yes. But that's all he said.'

Just then, Mavis arrived with the tray, and an apology. 'I would 'ave brought some fruitcake,' she said sheepishly, 'only some greedy devil's already wolfed the lot.' The truth showed itself in her bright pink face.

Smiling to herself, Alice looked away. Matron, however, managed to seem her usual self. 'It's all right, Mavis,' she answered. 'The cocoa will do. Thank you.'

Much relieved, Mavis withdrew.

When the door was closed, Matron poured out the cocoa. 'If anyone's been at the fruitcake,' she chuckled, 'you can be sure it was Mavis herself.'

Alice grinned. 'She's always had a sweet tooth.'

'No harm in that, even if it does deprive us all of a slice of best fruitcake.' Smiling, Matron handed Alice her tea. 'Now then, it seems the gentleman due to arrive within the hour is a very wealthy, influential man. He has some kind of business in London, which appears to keep him away from home for days on end. And even when he's home, he's away early in the morning, until late at night.'

'It doesn't seem a very stable life for Nancy to be going into,' Alice fretted. 'Money isn't everything. It doesn't compensate for the lack of parental love or family security.'

'No, and at any other time I would agree, but this is different. You see, Alice, there is a very special reason why Nancy is wanted in this particular home.'

Alice's suspicions were confirmed. 'So it *is* Nancy who's being taken away at this ungodly hour?' Placing her cup of cocoa on the small table at her side, she leaned forward in her chair, her face solemn as she asked, 'What's the hurry to take her away? Why can't she be taken in daylight . . . and what about Jack? Does he know she's going? Will he be allowed to say his good-byes, or will he just wake and find she's gone for good?' That would be so unbelievably cruel.

'Please, Alice, just hear me out,' Matron interrupted. 'Any other time I would be just as angry as you are. In fact, I was up in arms when told what time I was to get the child ready. However, less than ten minutes ago, Mr Ennington explained the situation in full. I believe if you had heard what he said, you might then understand the need for urgency.'

She had seen how riled Alice was, and waited now for her to calm down. 'Right. Well, according to Mr Ennington, there are . . . or *were* . . . three children in the family. Unfortunately, the youngest girl was drowned some weeks ago, and the mother has never recovered.'

Alice was genuinely sorry. 'That's terrible!'

'The mother is distraught, as you can imagine. Being the busy man he is, her husband could not spare the time to be with her as he would have liked, so at great expense he brought in a nurse, but the nurse was not made welcome. The mother understandably did not want treating like an invalid. All she wanted was her child back, but of course that was not possible.'

Suddenly Alice began to see it all. 'So Nancy is to be the replacement for the lost child, is that it?' Altogether it was not a happy situation, she thought.

'In a word, yes. But is that so bad?'

'It won't be bad if the mother can love Nancy for her own sake. But it will be a bad thing if Nancy is to be rejected, in the same way the nurse was rejected. It would be too cruel if that dear little girl was to be sacrificed to a mother's grief.'

'No, Alice. You've got it wrong. It won't be like that! The love is still there, just waiting for the right person to fill that poor woman's heart. I believe Nancy is the right person. This is an opportunity for her to find a place where she'll be cherished and loved, as never before. She's a very fortunate little girl. You must see that?' Taking a deep breath, Matron got out of her chair and stood over Alice, her manner accusing as she demanded harshly, 'Tell me this then: would you rather she was left in this place? Never to have the same opportunity as that poor child who was lost? It's Nancy's best chance at happiness and, as you so rightly said, her chance to have family security and a mother's love. Think, Alice! Would you deny Nancy that?'

'No, no! Of course not.' Again, Alice felt a pang of guilt. 'All I want is for her to be loved and happy.' Not quite true. What she *really* wanted was for Nancy and Jack to come home with her. But it wasn't to be.

'So will you help me, Alice?' Matron continued.

'In what way?'

'As I've already explained, Nancy will be going to a good home, where she will want for nothing. Jack, on the other hand, is to remain here until he, too, is placed. I'm led to believe from Mr Ennington that he's already been approached by someone who might want the boy. A family man – a farmer. Though nothing is settled, so it's best not to mention it and raise his hopes.'

Alice realised now why she had been brought here. 'You want me to tell Jack about his sister leaving?'

Matron nodded. 'You're the best person for the job,' she admitted. 'What's more, Nancy will need reassuring, when she knows Jack won't be going with her.'

Alice was horrified. 'You mean you haven't told her?'

Matron's sheepish expression answered her question. 'I need your help, Alice. I need you to talk with the children. Will you do that – please?'

The young woman gave a wry little smile. 'I don't see that I've got any kind of a choice.'

Matron was visibly relieved. 'You can make it so much easier for the children.' Leaning towards her, she lowered her voice. 'Don't think I'm not aware of how close you've grown to those two. I know what a good mother you'd make, love, and if it were up to me, you could take them home right now.'

When Alice looked up, the sadness was written in her eyes. 'You're right. Nancy is going to a good home – a better home than I could ever offer her. Jack, too. I'll talk to them both, if you really think it will help.' Wiping her face with the palms of her hands, she stood up. 'Where's Nancy now?'

'Mavis is dressing her as we speak.'

Alice hesitated only for a moment but it was then that the older woman placed her hand on Alice's shoulder and said in a tender voice, 'Do your best, love. Make it easy for them both.'

With that thought uppermost in her mind, Alice hurried to the kitchen, where she found Mavis and the child. Seated at the table, woman and child were tucking into a slice of cold apple pie. 'Ooh, Alice! Come in, gal, come in.' Surreptitiously wiping away the juices which had dribbled down her chin, Mavis beckoned Alice into the room. 'We were just having a late-night snack, weren't we, child?' Mavis never learned the children's names. Instead she referred to them all as 'child'.

'It's all right.' Alice sat beside the little girl, whose face had lit up at the sight of her. 'Finish your pie,' she told the other woman. 'Don't feel guilty on my account.' She knew what it was like to feel guilty.

Chuckling and chattering, Mavis polished off her pie, as did Nancy. 'Right, I'll leave the pair of youse,' Mavis said when she'd finished, and made herself scarce by leaving the room altogether.

Alice took the little girl on to her lap for a cuddle. 'You look nice.' She saw how someone had gone to a great deal of trouble to make sure Nancy looked her best. 'That's a lovely dress, pet.'

The child looked up with shining blue eyes. 'It's a present,' she said in her baby-soft voice. 'A present from Mrs Mavis.' She fingered the bow in her hair. 'This, too – look.' Her spontaneous smile was like sunshine on a cloudy day.

'Have they told you where you're going, sweetheart?' It was hard for Alice to choke back the emotion.

'I'm going to have a new mummy.'

'Now isn't that wonderful!'

'Where's Jack?' The smile began to slip.

Alice knew she would have to play this very carefully. 'I expect he's in bed.'

'He's coming, too, isn't he?' Her voice trembled.

Alice held her tight. 'I don't think so, sweetheart. I think there's another nice lady who wants to have Jack as her little boy. That would be good for him, don't you think?'

The blue eyes grew moist and the bottom lip crumpled. 'I don't know.'

'Nancy?'

Close to tears, the child looked up.

'I think you should be very brave, for Jack's sake. Don't you?'

There was a long silence, during which the girl never took her eyes off Alice. Presently, in a soft voice she announced, Jack said I'm *very* brave.'

'He's right, too. You *are* brave.'

'I won't cry.'

'There's a good girl.'

'Will you tell him?'

Unable to speak, for the hard knot of emotion that straddled her throat, Alice merely nodded. A small hand crept into hers and suddenly Alice was holding Nancy so tight she could feel the child's tiny heartbeat against her own.

This was how Matron found them, holding each other, and Alice, looking over the child's shoulder, the tears bright and sore in her eyes. It was so unfair that she must be the one to persuade the girl into leaving quietly. Knowing how much Alice cared for the girl, and how much the girl had come to trust her, it was all Matron could do not to show her own feelings. 'Best go now,' she told Alice gruffly. 'The gentleman is here.'

'Come on, sweetheart.' Alice eased the child away. 'You go with Matron. I'll be along shortly.'

'I want you to come with me!'

'I promise I'll be there to see you leave with your new daddy, but first there's something I have to do.'

Nancy's face broke into a smile. 'Are you fetching Jack?'

'We'll see.' Alice handed her over to Matron. 'Give me ten minutes,' she asked the older woman. 'Don't let her go without me being there.'

Matron promised. 'Besides, I doubt if she'll leave peaceably without you being there. Be quick though. Mr Ennington is in a powerful hurry.'

As Matron went away with the child kept close to her, Alice hurried down the corridor. She had to see Jack. She had to let him know what was happening. She had no real idea how he might react to the news, but she would do her damnedest to persuade him it was for the best.

As she rounded the corner she glanced back and there was Nancy, being run down the passage, her little legs going twice the speed of Matron's. Straining against Matron's hold on her, she had twisted her neck round so as to see which way Alice was going. 'It's all right, sweetheart,' Alice whispered. 'It'll be all right.'

But she didn't know that. She could only hope, and pray that everything would turn out right.

Having talked to the woman on duty, Alice went softly into the dormitory, where she found Jack fast asleep. She shook him gently, whispering, Jack, it's Alice. I have something to tell you. Wake up. *Jack, wake up*.'

Stretching and groaning, the boy peered up at her through small, sleepy eyes.

'We need to talk.' Rolling back the covers, Alice urged, 'I have to tell you something.' Taking hold of his hand, she helped him out of bed. 'I'm sorry for waking you,' she breathed.

Rubbing his eyes, Jack walked alongside her as she led him out of the dormitory and into the open area beyond. 'What's wrong?' He was instinctively suspicious. 'Why did you wake me up?'

Alice didn't answer until they were in the duty office; she had already asked if she could use the room for a minute or two, and that was all the time she had, to let Jack know what was happening. 'You had an idea that Nancy was being found a good home, didn't you, Jack?'

'Yes, but I told them we wanted to be together.'

'I know that, but sometimes it just isn't possible.'

Leaping out of the chair he eyed her like a cat might eye a mouse. 'They're taking her away, aren't they?' he demanded. 'They've found somebody to have Nancy . . . but they don't want *me*!'

Alice was half-relieved that he had guessed the reason for her errand. 'I'm sorry, love.' Reaching out, she touched him affectionately on the shoulder, but he cringed away, his eyes blazing and his voice shaking with temper.

'I won't let them take her away, I *won't*!' Pressing himself against the wall he stared at her with a kind of hatred. 'I promised her I would never leave her . . . and I won't!'

Alice remained at a distance. 'Even if it means you'll be doing her a great harm?'

'What are you talking about?'

'Nancy has been given a wonderful opportunity to be raised as a lady. She'll be well educated, and want for nothing. If you spoil her chances now, she may never get another offer like that.'

'She won't go without me, anyway!'

'Oh, Jack.' Alice was torn two ways. Even now, she didn't know for certain that Nancy would be loved in the way she had just described to Jack. On the other hand, this family had suffered a terrible loss, and Nancy could be just the ray of sunshine they needed to help them get over it. Moreover, she was such an adorable child, they couldn't help but love her. 'Listen to me, lad.'

'Where is she?' Now, when Jack ran to the door she went to him; holding the door fast shut, she spoke softly, believing every word with all her heart. 'I'll tell you something now, that I've never told a living soul. I love you and Nancy as if you were my very own. If it was possible for me to take you home and keep you for myself, I would move heaven and earth to do so. But it isn't possible, so I'm prepared to do my best for both of you, in any way I can.'

Suddenly he was pleading with her, clutching her lapels and crying openly. 'You can have us,' he said. 'Tell them you want to have us. It'll be all right, you'll see.'

Alice shook her head, tears in her own eyes. 'I can't, Jack. It's not allowed.' She held him away, so as to look into his troubled eyes. 'The gentleman who wants to take Nancy home to his family is very wealthy. He can make sure that she has everything any girl would ever want. She'll have her own bedroom, and a nurse to take care of her. And when she's ready for learning, she'll have someone to come and teach her – another language, how to play the piano, how to be a lady. Think of it, Jack. Would you take all that away from her?'

For a long moment he looked at her, and ever so slowly his face began to crumple, until now he was sobbing helplessly. 'I wanted us to stay together. She needs me.'

Alice took him into her arms. 'I know.' She stroked his hair and kissed his forehead, and whispered, 'Sometimes, things don't work out the way we want them to.' And who knew that better than Alice Compton herself?

With a shivering sigh he drew away. 'Are they taking her now?'

Alice nodded.

'Can I see her?'

She held out her hand. 'We'll have to be quick.'

He went with her, and all the way to the outer hall, he spoke not one single word.

When they opened the door, the scene that greeted them was cordial and easy; Clive Ennington was talking to Matron, while only a few steps away Nancy was asking a gentleman questions. Tall and elegant with greying whiskers and a kindly face, he was stooping to hear what she had to say. Suddenly he burst out laughing, and Nancy did the same.

Alice was as surprised as Jack to see how comfortable Nancy was with the gentleman. 'They've taken to each other straight off,' she murmured.

While Jack and Alice watched from a discreet distance, the gentleman reached into the pocket of his long-coat and drawing out a China doll with blonde hair and huge blue eyes, he gave it to Nancy. 'She looks just like you,' he said with a smile.

Thrilled with her present, Nancy flung her arms round his neck and hugged him hard. 'She's lovely! Thank you – oh, thank you!'

Jack was visibly moved. 'She's forgotten me already,' he whispered.

'Don't think like that,' Alice urged softly. 'She's just a bairn . . . they're easily distracted.'

Taking hold of his hand, she would have gone forward with him, so that he could talk with Nancy and be assured. But in a swift movement that caught her unawares, he broke away and ran back in the direction of the dormitories. Knowing how distraught he was, Alice fled after him.

The only two to see what had happened were Matron and Clive Ennington. 'Get the girl into the carriage!' he told Matron in a harsh whisper. 'Then go after the boy. I want no trouble!'

As quickly as her great bulk would allow, Matron swept the

girl into her arms and rushed her out to the waiting carriage, while behind her, a considerable wad of money changed hands between the two men.

'Thank you for organising things so quickly,' Edward Cornwell acknowledged, to which Ennington replied with a smarmy grin. 'You can rely on me to keep my word,' he lied with conviction.

The transaction over, they shook hands and parted.

By the time Alice caught up with Jack, he was already halfway along the corridor. With his face turned away and his nose pressed against the window he didn't hear her soft footsteps as she approached with caution.

When she quietly called his name, he turned with a look of surprise, but made no attempt to flee; instead he continued to gaze out of the window at the waiting carriage. 'She'll be gone in a minute,' he said brokenly.

Knowing there was little she could say that would comfort him, Alice put her arm round his shoulder, and looked out of the window with him. Outside, the gentleman was just climbing into the carriage with Nancy, who could be seen peering out of the back window, as though searching for someone.

'I don't want her to go.' Jack was telling himself that he must accept what was happening, if only for Nancy's sake. But it was hard; even harder than when his mammy deserted them, and even when Mary left, and then his daddy. 'I won't have anybody now.' His voice trailed away.

'You're wrong, Jack.' Alice knew how hard it must be for him. 'You'll soon be part of a family again.'

'Will she be all right?' Jack's mind was on Nancy.

'I think so, Jack,' she answered. 'I *hope* so.'

'When she gets to know them properly – living in their fine house and doing all the things you said – she'll forget me. She'll forget what I look like, and all the things we talked about.

She'll forget *everything*!' The small boy turned to look at her; his stricken eyes and forlorn expression shaking her to the core.

'Listen to me, my lad.' Taking him by the shoulders, she gave him a gentle shake. 'Your sister will never forget you. You'll *always* be her hero.'

'I'll never see her again, will I?' His voice was dead.

'I can't answer that, Jack, but I dare say there'll come a day when she'll want to find you.'

'I don't want to wait till then. I want to go and see her *now*. I want to see where she lives and what these new people are like. It's my place to look after her.'

'My! That's such a heavy burden for a boy. But I'll tell you what, Jack. You've done a fine job, but now the burden has been lifted from your young shoulders. You can live your own life now, with the family who want you for their son. Nancy has gone to good people, and so will you. The man who enquired after you is a farmer. Think of it, Jack! *A farm*! Animals . . . sheep and cows and maybe even a horse for you to ride. There might even be a lake for you to fish in, and a spinney where you can play and climb to your heart's content. Oh, Jack! It'll be a boy's paradise, with wide open fields, and all manner of things to do.'

'When will I be going?' There was no excitement in his voice, but anywhere must be better than being here at Galloways.

'Tomorrow maybe, or the next day – but it will be soon, so I've been told.'

'I want to see Nancy first. I need to know where she is.'

Alice knew it was an impossible request, but she didn't want to dash his hopes altogether, so she answered as discreetly as the truth would allow. 'When all the excitement has died down, I imagine Nancy will be asking after you. As to whether you can visit her, we'll have to wait and see, won't we?'

Jack wasn't listening, because now the carriage was pulling away and he was waving like mad. Nancy didn't see him. And for a long time he stood there, the palms of his hands spread across the window pane. 'She didn't wave,' he murmured. '*Nancy didn't wave*.'

'She probably did, only you couldn't see her. Remember, Jack, she's only small. I expect she's been told to sit very still, so as to be safe. Besides, it's difficult for her to see out of the back window when the carriage is being driven off.'

He didn't answer. All he could think of was the fact that his sister didn't wave goodbye. 'I told you, didn't I?' He gave a sorry little smile. 'She doesn't want me any more.'

'Please don't think that.' Alice's heart was breaking for him.

Jack didn't look at her; he didn't speak. Instead he hung his head and sobbed, quietly at first but then the sobs seemed to consume his whole body. With his arms folded across the window pane and his head bent over them, he made a pitiful sight.

'Come here, sweetheart.' Alice eased him away from the window, but instead of falling into her arms, he began screaming at her: '*You sent her away! I hate you! I hate you!*' When she tried to hold him, he was like a mad thing, hitting out with clenched fists, and kicking at her with his boots. 'LEAVE ME ALONE!'

There was a tussle and suddenly he broke away, fleeing down the corridor, towards the front door.

Alice went after him. 'No, Jack. It won't do any good. JACK!'

With an echoing thud, Jack ran straight into the formidable figure of Clive Ennington, who grabbed him sharply by the ear. 'What the devil's going on here?' His eagle eye caught sight of Alice approaching at a run. '*Explain!*' Swinging the boy to one side he kept a tight hold on him, while waiting for Alice to offer an explanation.

Thinking quickly, she did her best to defend Jack. 'It was my fault,' she said. 'I promised he could say goodbye to his sister, but the carriage had gone before I realised. Naturally the boy is upset.'

'You had no damned right to promise any such thing!'

'It was little enough to promise,' Alice retorted. 'It seemed cruel not to let them say goodbye to each other.'

Peering at Alice through angry eyes, he warned her softly, 'If you want to remain in my employ, Mrs Compton, you will have to remember that any such decision is for *me* to make . . . not you.' Taking in a deep breath through his enormous nostrils, he satisfied himself that she was not about to question his authority then, with a sense of glee he turned to Jack, who all the while had struggled and fought against being held captive.

'As for *you*!' Digging his nails into Jack's earlobe he swung him a full circle, until the two of them were looking eye to eye; with the big man staring down threateningly, and the boy staring back up with defiance in every bone of his body. 'It seems to me you need the arrogance knocked out of you, for good and all.' Stooping nearer, he covered the boy's face in spittle as he went on excitedly, 'You really are a bad boy, Jack! We'll have to put that right, won't we, eh? I mean, it would be wrong of us to send you to the good farmer, until we're absolutely certain you won't cause him any trouble.'

Jack's answer was to sink his sharp teeth into those huge, podgy fingers. '*You sent her away!*' he screamed. Ignoring Ennington's howls, he bit him again. 'She didn't want to leave me, but *you* sent her away. *You're the bad one, not me! I hate you!*'

Even though Jack had bitten him through almost to the bone, the man held on to him before, filled with an uncontrollable rage, he said something that hurt Jack far more than Jack had hurt him. 'Of course we sent her away,' he whispered out of earshot of Alice. 'Because she *asked* to be sent away.' His eyes opened wide at Jack's look of disbelief. 'Oh yes, that's right. What's more, she never wanted to say goodbye to you, *your dear sister*.' He hung on to the last three words, emphasising them, and revelling in Jack's distress. 'I gave her the opportunity, and she said no.' His face close to Jack's, he grinned like a maniac. 'So you see, Jack, she wanted rid of you. She told me she never wanted to see you again.'

With every cruel word, Jack seemed to shrink before his eyes. When the man straightened himself, Jack's face was a study in hatred; the eyes like dark slits in his head and his teeth bared like that of a crazed dog. Lashing out with all his strength, he cried out bitterly, '*You're a liar, mister!*'

Enjoying himself immensely, Ennington smacked him hard across the head, effectively silencing the boy while he smiled down on him. 'I'm no liar,' he said sweetly. 'What I told you was the truth. I'm afraid you'll just have to live with it.'

At that moment, old Joe came in on the scene, asking if he could lock up. 'Ah, the very man!' To Joe's astonishment, Clive Ennington pounced on him. 'Now then, Joseph, you must tell this boy how I asked his sister if she wanted to see her brother before she left, and how she told me that she never wanted to see him again. Tell him, Joe! He believes I'm a liar, and we can't have that now, can we?' His veiled threat was obvious to all but the boy.

'Now then, boy.' Ennington addressed Jack with a sly grin. 'This man was here when I spoke with your sister, and he'll tell you what happened. He'll confirm that I'm speaking the truth.' Taking the old caretaker by the arm, he led him to where Jack was eagerly waiting, hoping Joe would deny it all.

Sensing straight off that Ennington was up to no good, Joe hesitated. 'I'm not sure I know wha—' He winced when the other man spitefully squeezed his arm, though only Alice noticed it.

'Tell him, man!' Ennington growled. 'Tell him how she wanted nothing more to do with him.'

Swallowing hard, Joe glanced at Alice, who was shaking her head discreetly.

'What's the matter?' Ennington grinned jovially. 'Cat got your tongue? All I'm asking is that you confirm that I am telling the truth.' The smile never left his face but, like Alice, Joe knew that behind the smile lay a monster of a man, with an unenviable talent for making people's lives a misery – especially if they did not conform with his wishes.

To his shame, Joe's courage crumbled. 'He's telling the truth, son,' he told Jack reluctantly. 'Mr Ennington asked your sister if she wanted to see you before she left, and she said no.'

'Thank you, Joe,' the manager said briskly. 'Now get off and lock up, but be sure to be back by eight.'

'Yes, Mr Ennington.' He tipped his cap and was quickly gone, leaving behind him one elated man, and one devastated little boy.

Where Jack had refused to believe Clive Ennington, he trusted the old man. Though he found it hard to believe that Nancy would turn against him like that, it must be true, for hadn't Joe said so?

While he silently cried, his young heart aching, he was told, 'Now then, you *bad* boy, we can't let you go unpunished. And if you cause any more trouble, we'll have to punish you all over again – and yet *again* if needs be.' Ennington took a long, shivering breath that seemed to shake the very windows. 'If the badness is still in you after that, then we shall have to keep you here for as long as it takes. If that happens, we will send a more deserving boy to the good farmer.'

Thrusting the boy towards Alice, he instructed sourly, 'He's to be locked up, and kept without food for two days and nights. After that bring him to me, and we'll see if he's learned his lesson.'

Alice nodded, albeit reluctantly. She then took charge of Jack, who went to her meekly. He was quiet and still, not at all like that lively, desperate boy who had run down the corridor wanting to kiss his sister goodbye. Instead he was shocked to the core, because the idea that Nancy could reject him was a terrible thing.

Holding him close, Alice faced Clive Ennington without fear. 'I'm sorry, sir, but was it really necessary for you to tell him such a terrible thing?'

Satisfied that he had broken the boy's spirit, Clive Ennington even afforded her a smile. 'I told him what he needed to hear. I told him the truth,' he lied. 'Now perhaps he'll stop whining.' Wagging a finger he warned Jack once more. 'Remember what I said, boy? Buckle under, or face the consequences.'

In all her life Alice had never loathed anyone, but she loathed now, and it was like a bitter taste on her tongue. 'Come on, Jack.' She led him away, 'Best do as Mr Ennington says.'

Much later, after she had delivered Jack to his punishment, Alice went looking for old Joe. After a lengthy search, she found him enjoying his pipe in the boiler room. 'For pity's sake, Joe, what in God's name possessed you to lie like that?' she demanded hotly. 'Can you even *imagine* what you've done to that boy?'

'I'm sorry, gal.' Joe was ashamed of what he'd been made to do. 'But I'm just an old man with a few years of work left in me. I don't want throwing out on me ear at my time o' life. I need a pay packet to keep the roof over me head and food on me plate. Surely you can understand that?'

Alice saw his remorse and her attitude softened. I've tried to tell Jack it was all Mr Ennington's doing, that it was all a pack of lies from beginning to end, but he won't listen to me. He really believes that Nancy went away with no love in her heart for him. He'll never think of his sister in the same way again.'

'Aw, he's young. He'll get over it, gal.'

Alice was dumbfounded. 'How can you say that? He's had so much heartache in his young life. Nancy was everything to him.'

'Look, gal. I know what I'm saying. Me and you, we've got used to our lot, and it ain't much, I must admit. But young Jack is only just starting out. He's got a life to come, all new and shiny. He's a bright boy, and I dare say there'll come a day when the whole world will lie at his feet.'

He puffed on his pipe and blew the used air into the atmosphere. 'Mark my words,' he remarked thoughtfully. 'He'll soon forget what happened here. Kids are like that. Besides, he would never have seen his sister again anyroad! So what was the harm?'

Unconvinced, Alice left him to his conscience.

That night, when she lay in her bed, she began thinking on what he'd said. It was true. Jack *was* a bright boy. 'I hope Joe's right,' she told Anthony in confidence. 'I hope there *will* come a day when Jack finds the world at his feet.'

And her husband, being the practical man he was, said we all had to make our own way in life. 'Time will tell,' he murmured before he rolled over to sleep. 'Time will tell.'

After his two days and two nights of punishment, though thanks to Alice he had not gone hungry, Jack was released into the custody of a farmer by the name of Justin Lyndhurst. Justin was a big, gruff fellow with a laugh that would wreck a ship, but he was kind and funny, and Jack took to him straight off.

'I hope you're a good boy,' he told Jack as they went away in a carriage to the station. 'I hope you know how to work hard, and look after them as look after you. You see, I've no son of my own,' he revealed, 'and mebbe there'll come a day when I can leave it all to you.'

Jack didn't appreciate the full meaning of Justin's words, but he laughed at his jokes, and enjoyed the excitement of the journey to his new home.

And, because he couldn't bear the pain of knowing what Nancy had done to him, he thrust her from his mind.

It was the only way.

Chapter Seven

The man called Geordie had been watching at the window for over an hour. 'Where is he? What devilish mischief has he got up to now?' he said out loud. Though it was bitter cold outside, the sweat pulsated through his skin, forming small, shiny droplets which systematically broke open to trickle down his face and neck.

'He's a damned lunatic!' Wiping the sweat from his brow with the sleeve of his shirt, he thumped the sill with clenched fists. 'What in God's name was I thinking of, to get mixed up with a bloody madman like that?' he moaned.

Hearing a noise down in the street, he glanced back through the window. It was just a dog, mooching about in the middens. A large black animal with an appetite to match, it foraged about the dustbins one after the other until, growing frustrated, it turned one of them on its side, spilling filth and rubbish in every direction. 'You mangy cur!' he yelled. 'Gerrout of it!'

Flinging open the window, he threw a piece of firewood which caught the dog on its rear. With a yelp of pain and not a backward glance, the creature took off down the alley with its tail between its legs. 'And don't come back,' he bawled, 'or it'll be more than a piece o' wood next time!'

Turning from the window in a rare temper, the man eventually calmed down and even began chuckling. 'By! I've lost count o' the times me and Marlon 'ave been chased off with our tails between our legs!' Memories of foiled burglaries and women trouble set him off laughing. A moment later the laughter had died away and a scowl darkened his features. 'It ain't like that *now*, though. It's all threats an' fights, and mixing wi' ruffians who should be swinging from the end of a rope!'

Anxious and afraid, he started pacing the floor. The thought of what his companion might be up to at that very minute sent him into a panic. His steps quickened to such a frantic pace, that he was almost running back and forth across the room. 'I'm getting too old for this business,' he told the walls. 'He's taking us into places I've no liking for. There are some bad buggers out there and now he's mingling with 'em, he's getting as bad as they are – but can you tell him that? Can you buggery! By, that young whippersnapper will be the death o' me yet!'

The sweat trickled down his neck and soaked into his shirt. He couldn't stomach the thought of going back to prison. *Where the devil was Marlon?*

Going to the fireplace, he took a cigarette from his pocket and placed it in his lips; tearing a strip from a nearby newspaper, he rolled it into a spill and dipped it into the fire. When it was lit he touched the end of the cigarette with the flaming paper, and drew in a great breath. Once the cigarette was glowing, he threw the paper hastily into the fire, still for a minute, lost in thought. Grim thoughts that haunted him . . . memories of a certain fight, and a family man who was mangled under the hooves and wheels of a carriage and pair. 'A bad thing,' he murmured, shaking his head. 'A terrible, bad thing!'

He remembered Robert's face and torn body as if it was yesterday . . . skin and bone ripped apart by the hooves, until it was almost unrecognisable. Shivering, he shut his eyes, unable to think of it any more.

After a while, he went to the window again. There was still no sign of his mate. He grew agitated. 'I can't wait here,' he said. 'For all I know, he could be gone all bleedin' night. He might even be in jail – that wouldn't surprise me.' He glanced round the room – at the tiny drop-leaf table and the two worm-eaten chairs got from some back-street junk shop. The dresser that held the bowl and jug was an upturned crate snatched from the market while still full of oranges. There were no curtains; they weren't really necessary as the windows were thick with grime and smoke and, as he'd had pointed out when Marlon commented on his lack of privacy some time ago, the rear windows overlooked a little-used alleyway.

The place stank unpleasantly of stale smoke and beer, and of a drainage system that had long ago given up the ghost. 'I'll not wait.' His mind was made up. All this hanging around was driving him mad.

Searching about for a pencil and paper, he found a note under Marlon's pillow. The younger man sometimes slept in the spare room when he was on the run or lying low for some reason. 'What's this, eh?' Deciphering the childish, badly spelt scrawl, he read: *At last I've manujed to get in on the gamling. I'm feelin lukky tonite, so the buggurs had best wach out.*

Geordie gave a huge weary sigh. 'How he gets through the day, Gawd only knows.'

Taking pencil and paper, he went downstairs and seated himself at the table. It's my turn to leave *him* a note, he thought sourly – tell him I've had enough. I want out! I should have known better than to pair up with a maniac like him. Damn and bugger it. He's more trouble than he's worth.

Despite this, he still felt a degree of loyalty to the young thug, so he threw the pencil down and took to pacing again; groaning and cursing as he strode up and down the room. Puffing furiously on his cigarette, he began to cough. Smoke filled his eyes and brought tears, but he didn't remove the cigarette; instead he puffed all the harder. 'Jesus! I'm a bag o' bloody nerves,' he cursed, 'an' all 'cause o' that daft bugger!'

Returning to the window he looked out. When he could see not a soul in sight, he went and sat by the fire and cursed his mate up hill and down dale, then he got to his feet and took off again, striding across the room like a caged animal.

'He shoulda been here long since. What's keeping him?' He laughed – a dry, cynical kind of laugh. 'He'll be in the pub, drunk as a bleedin' lord, opening his big mouth and telling folks what we've been up to – and never mind that it could put us both away for a bloody long time!'

Startled by the sound of men's voices yelling and screaming, he snatched the cigarette from his mouth and threw it on the fire. Running to the window he looked out. From what he could see in the light from the street lamp, four men were in the alley outside. Two of them seemed to be holding another back, while the big fellow in the group kicked and punched him.

When the victim began pleading with his assailant to show mercy and let him go, Geordie recognised his mate's voice. 'God Almighty . . . it's *him*!'

Rushing out of the room, he ran down the passageway and out of the door. By the time, he got to the alley, it was all over; the three men were gone, and young Marlon was lying face down in the gutter, bathed in his own blood and seemingly lifeless. 'Oh Christ, look what they've done to you.' Geordie was sickened – and something else. In his mind's eye it was *Robert* he saw lying there, not Marlon. A surge of anger rose in him. 'I told you they were a bad lot, but you wouldn't listen, would you? You never do!' Dragging him up by the arms, he helped to steady him on his feet. 'Come on, let's get you inside.' Step by painful step, he took the younger man up the stairs and into his room, where he laid him down on the bed.

Opening his bruised eyes, Marlon gave a crooked smile. 'They followed me.' He took a minute to wipe the blood from his mouth. 'Another minute and I'd have been home and dry.' Judging by his slurred voice, he'd been drinking.

'You're a mess.' With a sense of horror, Geordie observed his wounds; the nose that was bent at such an angle it must be broken, and the eyes swollen like oranges and swimming in blood. His mouth was split asunder and one ear was torn at the tip. Jesus, mate, what did you do to deserve this?'

One obscene eye winked. 'I played 'em at their own game, and won all their money, only they didn't like the idea,' he winced, 'of me keeping it.' He tried to sit up but fell back again. 'Leave me be. I'm all right.'

'You're a daft bugger, that's what you are!' After two years of working the streets with him, Geordie had come to expect anything. 'One o' these days they'll fetch you home in a bag.'

'Piss off, go on!' Angered, the younger man lashed out with his feet. 'I don't need you.'

'I'd say you need me more than you realise,' Geordie snapped. 'But I'm at the end of my tether so if I were you, I wouldn't get too bleedin' cocky.' Physically pushing the young man back into the pillow, he warned, 'If you want to walk out of here right now, I will gladly let you. But if you want my help, you'll do as you're told.'

The look on Geordie's face told the wounded man he meant every word he said. 'All right, but stop going on at me,' he said sullenly. 'I've taken a bad beating, and all you can do is complain, like some bloody fishwife. Just shut your mouth, that's all I want.'

'I'll shut my mouth when I'm good and ready and not before,' Geordie told him smartly. 'Now just you lay still. There's some warm water in the kettle. I'll clean you up the best I can. But if you ask me, it's a doctor you need.'

The young man began to panic. 'No doctor!' Swinging his arms about he almost fell off the bed. 'I don't want no bloody quack nosing about!'

Geordie shrugged his shoulders; at this moment in time it didn't matter to him whether the hot-headed Marlon lived or died. 'Whatever you say.' He went downstairs to the kitchen where he collected the bowl and towel; the kettle stood in the hearth. He poured a small measure of water into the bowl and tested it; the water was still warm. 'That's about right.'

Returning with the items, he found his friend sitting up, smoking a cigarette, as arrogant as ever, 'I thought I told you – I'm all right,' he said sulkily.

'Sit still and do as you're told for once!' Stripping off the younger man's shirt, he washed the blood from his neck and chest, dried him and found a clean old shirt for him to wear. It was cold in the tiny bedroom. That done, he dabbed gently at his face with the wet flannel, after which he checked the nose. 'It don't seem broke, but it's taken a real bashing. You'll not breathe easy through that for a day or two, I'll be bound.'

Marlon was in no mood to be lectured. His wounds stung and a poisonous hangover was setting in. 'Why don't you just bugger off, like I said?' he mumbled. 'I don't need you preaching at me like some country vicar. Just clear off out o' my sight.'

'When I'm done with you, yes, I'll go, *and I won't be coming back.*' Geordie had practised his speech so often these past few weeks; it was meant to be a long and apologetic parting, and now, here he was in the heat of anger, blurting it out in one breath.

Marlon was visibly shaken. 'What d'yer mean you won't be coming back?'

Standing over him, his eyes fixed on the other's anxious face, Geordie explained in cold hard words. 'I've had enough. When we started out it was just petty thieving to earn a few bob, that's what we said. We did the warehouses and the odd house and sometimes we picked the pockets of the well-off.' When Marlon opened his mouth to protest, the older man put up a hand to stop him. 'Hear me out. I only want to say this once.'

Taking a deep breath he went on, 'At first it was a bit of a lark. We had enough to fill our back pockets and do as we pleased, but it's all changed, and I don't like it.'

'It *had* to change!' Marlon burst out. 'Can't you understand that, mate? It were never enough – a few wallets here, a silver cameo or a crate o' booze there. What good's that, eh? These days I'm after the big stuff.'

'Shut it! I asked you to hear me out.'

When Marlon slumped back against the pillow, Geordie told him of his fears. 'It did *not* have to change. We were doing all right. Then suddenly it weren't just thieving. It got heavy – smacking somebody over the head so we could take his wallet, or pinning some frightened woman to the wall, while the other one of us ransacked the house. And as if that wasn't bad enough, you started mixing with sewer-rats – moving into the kind of crime that I want no part of. You've got reckless, my friend. You're not satisfied to take their money, you want to half kill 'em at the same time.'

'Sometimes they ask for it—'

'I told you to shut it!' Savagely cupping Marlon's battered face in his two hands, Geordie stared at him with a kind of loathing, his voice trembling as he spoke. 'What about the bloke we robbed the other week . . . was *he* "asking for it"?'

'Get yer 'ands off me.' With his face contorted out of shape and his voice strangled by the big man's hands pulling him up by the chin, Marlon was scared witless. 'Anyway, it were *his* fault.'

'No.' Geordie shook his head. 'He were just an ordinary bloke. A family man. He even talked to you like you were decent – human even. And what did he get for his consideration? You followed him in the dark, then you set on him like a crazed animal.'

The young man gave a nervous laugh. 'We got his wallet though, didn't we? Oh, an' he were carrying a pretty penny, too.'

'Mebbe. But you didn't have to shove him under the wheels of that carriage. Christ Almighty, the horses' hooves chewed him up like meat through a mincer. The last thing I ever wanted was for you to kill somebody. If that's how you mean to play it, you're on your own. When they put that rope round your neck, I don't intend to be dancing on air next to you!' With a groan he thrust him aside. 'You're beginning to sicken me, d'you know that?'

'We didn't kill him.' Brimming with arrogance, Marlon had a sly little grin on his face. 'The bloke ain't dead, if that's what you think.'

'What d'you mean?' Grabbing him by the collar, Geordie hauled him up, his voice thick with anger. 'You saw what that carriage did to him.' Confused, he let him go. 'You're a bleedin' liar!'

Convinced he now had the upper hand, Marlon persisted. 'I'm tellin' yer the truth, mate. Y'see, I'm beddin' a certain woman – married, she is, to one o' them sewer-rats you mentioned.' He actually laughed out loud, even though it hurt him to do so. 'By! If ever he found out I were stealing his missus as well as his money, there's no tellin' *what* he'd do. But then he's a bit short in the brain department. It's only a matter o' time afore I take his business away altogether.'

'Get on with it!'

'Well now, his missus, Sally, she happens to work behind the desk at the Infirmary, and she's already told me that the same bloke as were brought in from the street that night is in a terrible way, but he ain't dead. Not yet he ain't.' He chuckled. 'So you see, we ain't murdered nobody.'

Geordie took the information in with astonishment. It was

good news and gave him some measure of relief from the terrible guilt he'd felt ever since that night. 'How does this Sally know it's the same bloke we robbed – the same one that *you* sent under the wheels o' that carriage?' he demanded. 'How can she know that, eh?'

'Because she's got a loose mouth an' likes to gab.' He snorted with disgust. 'Even when we're at it, she can't stop talking – yap, yap, yap the whole time. But she's worth it, I can tell you that.' He gave a rude wink. 'Loose-mouthed or not, she knows how to mek a man happy.'

Against all his instincts, Geordie believed his story. 'Well, I for one am glad he's alive. Happen I can sleep in me bed of a night now.'

'What!' The other looked at him in amazement. 'You mean to say you've been losing sleep about some bloody stranger? Huh! I'm damned sure *I* couldn't give a bugger whether he's alive or not, although to tell the truth, I'm sorry we didn't do a better job on 'im. Mebbe I ought to creep in that ward one night an' finish him off, eh?' With a self-satisfied smile he laid carefully back against the pillow. 'At least now we'll not be had up for murder.'

Having heard enough, Geordie grabbed up his coat. 'You mean *you* won't be had up for murder. It was you that pushed him under the carriage. Not me.'

The younger man chuckled sleepily. 'Aw now, come on, Geordie. You know full well, you'd never have let me take all the blame. You know what a coward I am. I don't know as I'd like to be dangling from the end of a rope all by meself.'

'You're a callous bugger, I know that,' Geordie said now. For a long time, he had seen the violence festering in his partner, and what he heard now only reinforced his misgivings. 'You were right in what you said afore,' he disclosed quietly. 'You don't need me, so I'll be on my way, and like I said – I won't be coming back. You can keep whatever goodies we've got stashed away. I want none of it.'

With that he took his leave, but not before he had issued some hard, parting words. 'You've got badness in you, Marlon. You're a dangerous man to be around.'

As he closed the door, the younger man's voice followed him. 'Piss off then! I'm well shot of yer. But I'll never be far away, mind, and if I find out you've opened yer mouth too bleedin' wide, I'll have to get some o' me newfound friends to shut it. Drop me in it, matey, an' I'll 'ave yer shakin' in yer boots afore yer know it. *D'yer hear me, old man?*'

At the foot of the stairs, Geordie paused. 'I hear you,' he muttered, 'but you'll never see the day when I'm shaking in me boots because of *you*.'

Outside, he took a deep invigorating breath of cold night air. 'I'm rid of you, thank God,' he said gratefully. 'I'm only sorry I didn't do this months back.'

As he let himself out of the squalid little dwelling for the last time, Geordie racked his brain. 'Now then, what was that woman's name . . . Shirley? Sally?' Jubilant, he clicked his fingers. 'That's it! *Sally*.'

Realising what he must do, he pulled up his coat collar against the cold and spoke out loud. 'Sally, my dear, I'm about to pay you a visit.' With this in mind, he quickened his steps in the direction of the boulevard.

A few minutes later he was heading for the Infirmary. Determined but apprehensive, he settled into deep thought as he paced the darkened streets. Deciding to go to the Infirmary was the easy part. He now needed to work out in his mind what he should do, once he got there.

Aware of his heart beating rapidly with anticipation, Geordie walked in through the Infirmary entrance; he paused for a moment to look about. There were only a few people in the waiting area at this early hour; a lad with his arm in a sling, a man holding a bloodstained wad to his eye, and an old couple comforting each other in a corner. Other than that, it was fairly quiet.

Glancing across to the desk he took discreet stock of the two women there. Painfully thin, with sallow features and long fair hair, the younger one seemed to be under instruction, listening hard to what her older colleague was saying, while her gaze remained fixed on the ledger in front of them. The older woman was attractive in a rough sort of way; with her thick black hair and wide-awake dark eyes, she carried an air of self-confidence, together with the knowledge that she was undeniably attractive to men.

That must be Sally. Geordie smiled to himself. She was all of ten years older than that daft sod, Marlon. Yet he could see why the young man might be attracted to her, even though he was risking life and limb in playing such a dangerous game.

Just then she caught sight of him. 'Excuse me, sir, are you waiting for somebody?'

Stepping forward, Geordie smiled politely at her. 'I've come to see an old friend. He's the man who was recently mangled under the wheels of a carriage . . . left for dead, they said, but now I've heard as he's still alive. So, did I hear right?'

'Well yes, but I'm sorry to say he's still in a bad way.'

'I'd like to see him.'

'You can't. Visiting hours were over some time ago. You'll have to come back tomorrow and even then, the doctor might not let him see anyone.'

'I need to see him *now*.'

'Are you deaf?' Forgetting her place, she thumped the desk, glaring at him with obvious irritation. 'I've already said you *cannot* see him tonight, and if I know Dr Morrison, not tomorrow neither.'

'Dear, dear!' Using his last card, Geordie shook his head. 'And Marlon promised you'd be understanding. He said you would let me see my old friend for certain.'

'*Marlon?*' The woman's face bled white. 'And who might that be?'

'Oh now, I can't believe this.' Knowing he'd already won, he feigned shock 'I was told you and he were on . . .' Glancing at the younger woman, he lowered his voice to an intimate level '. . . *very good* terms.' His implication, together with a knowing wink, had the desired effect.

Catching her breath, the woman called Sally was momentarily lost for words. 'I've no idea what you're talking about!' Eyeing him suspiciously, she appeared to grow another inch when she bristled from the neck up.

Delighted by her reaction, Geordie knew she must be Sally, and that he had managed to put the fear of God in her. 'It's Sally, ain't it?'

Glancing at her younger companion, Sally said, 'Victoria, go and check the linen, will you? I've an idea the laundry sent the wrong order.'

Victoria shook her head. 'Oh no, they didn't. It's the right order, 'cause I checked it when I came into work.'

'Well, go and check it again!' Sally ordered her, flustered.

Sensing there was some kind of funny business going on here, the younger woman was not about to argue. Instead she took up pencil and paper and hurried off.

Addressing Geordie in a harsh whisper, Sally protested, 'I think you've got the wrong woman. I don't know anyone called Marlon!'

Geordie explained his visit in a low voice. 'I can understand you not wanting to admit you know him, 'cause he's a rough 'un, is our Marlon. But you *do* know him, and very well, too, if I might say so. *Bedmates* – that's what he told me.' He gave her a knowing wink. 'I wouldn't mind betting your old man doesn't know you've got a sweetheart. Tut tut. I reckon there'd be hell to pay if he ever found out. I'm given to understand he's got a terrible temper.'

Taking a minute to steady her nerves, the woman realised she was in a dangerous situation. 'Can I be sure you'll not say anything of what you know . . . not to *anybody*?'

He nodded. 'I'm a man of my word.'

'All right. But you realise my job's in jeopardy if it becomes known that I let you in to see this patient?'

'Like I said, I'm a man of my word.'

'Five minutes then, and I'm to accompany you the whole time.'

'Sounds all right to me, Sally.'

Bristling again at the nerve of him, she said nothing. Instead she called Victoria back and left her browsing the ledger for mistakes. 'I'll not be gone long,' she informed her briskly.

To Geordie she urged, 'This way,' and he followed silently, grateful that he had found a way.

Hurrying through the passages and corridors she led him via the longest, but lesser used route, until at last they arrived at the ward. 'Take those heavy boots off,' she ordered at the door. 'I don't want you waking everybody.'

Sneaking past the nurse's office, Geordie was relieved to see that she was knee-deep in paperwork and totally oblivious to what was going on around her. 'She'll not see us if we're quiet enough.' Sally pointed to a side ward. 'He's in there. And be quick about it.' She glanced furtively down the corridor. 'I'll wait out here and keep watch.'

Geordie had a question. 'What name does he go by?'

Surprised, she asked, 'I thought you said he was a friend of yours?'

'So he is.' Geordie had to think fast. 'Trouble is, he changes his name that often, I don't know what to call him.'

Still suspicious, she regarded him a moment. 'Call him Robert,' she revealed. 'Robert Sullivan – that was the name we found on his person.'

Nervous and unsure as to what he might find, Geordie proceeded on soft footsteps.

The sick man's room was small and dimly lit, the light from the lamp throwing a garish glow over the bed and the man inside it. And there was a smell, that certain nauseating smell that lives in every hospital, a thick, dry smell that covers the tongue and invades the skin. The air was rancid with it, so much so that Geordie could hardly breathe. For a minute he almost turned tail and ran, but he couldn't do that, not now he'd discovered that the poor man still lived.

With his heart in his mouth, he sneaked forward. 'Hello.' His voice was small and trembling. 'I'm Geordie. 'I've come to . . .' Suddenly he saw, and was sickened to his soul. Trussed up like a chicken ready for the oven, Robert was a maze of bandages; his legs were hoisted some twelve inches above the bed, and his arms, encased in plaster, were stretched out and secured to his sides by means of a wide, leather belt. Only the tips of his fingers showed; once-long, fine fingers were now held stiff and straight, by means of long wooden stints.

'My God!' Geordie's horrified gaze was drawn to Robert's face and head. The face was swathed in bandages, with only slits for the eyes to peer through; though from the look of him, Robert had not seen anything with those eyes for a long time. The top of his head was completely bald and curiously dented in places, and swollen out of all proportion in others.

'Oh, my God!' Geordie moaned over and over, 'My God, look what he did to you!' In his mind's eye he saw Robert as he had been that night, tall and good-looking despite the strain evident on his face, a vibrant fellow, talking of his children and looking forward to taking them away.

'May God forgive us.' And then he was sobbing like a bairn, the tears rolling down his face and tasting like salt in his mouth. Seeing this fine man in such a terrible state was not what he'd expected, and it was too much for him to bear.

Reaching out with big coarse hands, he laid them tenderly on Robert's confined fingers. 'I came to say how sorry I am,' he whispered brokenly. 'I never meant for this to happen. I couldn't stop him, y'see. Oh, but don't think I'm laying all the blame on him, 'cause I'm not. Oh no! I'm as much to blame as he is, 'cause I should have stopped him long since.'

When there was no response – and he didn't expect one – he bowed his head and gently squeezed Robert's fingers. 'I'll come and see you again if they let me,' he confided. 'I need to make amends, you see.' His voice still shook and he couldn't speak for a minute, then he confessed, 'Since that night, I haven't been able to sleep. I lie awake thinking about you, then I fall asleep and all I can see is you falling under the wheels o' that carriage, and the horses . . . oh, dear God, how they dragged you down.'

The tears fell fast, blinding him, and for a minute he had to look away.

Just then the door opened and Sally appeared. 'It's time we went.' Just as suddenly as she had opened the door she closed it with the warning, 'There's somebody coming! Wait there for a minute.'

Geordie returned his attention to Robert. 'I've got to go now,' he told him, 'but I'll be back, you can count on it!' He wiped his eyes and sniffled back the tears, and straightening his shoulders he drew away. 'I'll pray for you, matey – you *an'* yer family. I promise. It's the best I can do.'

As he turned to leave he thought he heard a sound – a ruffle of linen or a groan. Whatever it was, it made him go back. 'Robert?' There was nothing, so he leaned forward and tried again. 'Robert, what is it?'

He sensed a flicker of response, but for the life of him he couldn't see it. *Then he saw!* Through the slits in the bandage he saw the tiniest glimmer in Robert's open eyes. *They were looking straight at him!*

Startled, Geordie instinctively recoiled. 'Christ Almighty!' Ashamed, he bent forward again, peering through the bandages into those dark, stricken eyes. 'What is it? What are you trying to tell me?' In that garish light, he detected a definite flicker of awareness. 'Is it the nurse you want? I'll fetch her, don't you worry.' When he straightened to leave, he was shocked to find Roberts fingertips move and touch him on the hand, keeping him there.

'What is it then?' Intrigued and excited, Geordie held on to him. 'You *don't* want me to fetch a nurse, so . . . is it summat else you want?'

Never having been in a situation like this before, he was unsure as to what he should do. 'Was it summat I said?' He thought about what his parting words had been. 'You want me to pray for you? Yes, of course, I will. I've already promised to do so.'

The dark eyes continued to implore him. 'No? What, then?' He was growing frantic. 'What did I say . . . was it something about your family?'

The eyes softened. Deep down inside, in his heart and soul where the damage was limited, Robert knew he could trust this man. He closed his eyes then opened them again, hoping the man would understand.

'My God!' Geordie knew he had struck the right chord. 'It *is* your family, ain't it?'

Robert felt his heart well up with relief. He couldn't reply, not even with a nod, but he had to let this man know about his children. *Somehow, he had to let him know!* The need, and the emotion was too overwhelming.

'Jaysus!' Geordie saw the tears well up in Robert's eyes and he was so moved he could hardly speak. Gulping hard he recalled, 'You and your wife were split, if I remember?'

Robert closed his eyes and opened them again.

'But the children? You were taking them away somewhere?'

The fingers flickered and the tears spilled out. It was the first time since the accident that Robert had managed to communicate with anyone. And it was unbelievably wonderful.

Geordie wasn't sure what he was meant to do. 'You don't need your wife, but you're worried about your children, is that it?'

This strange but beautiful conversation continued for some minutes, before Geordie had tweaked out the necessary information. 'All right, matey. I'm not sure how, but one way or another, no matter how long it takes, I'll find your children and bring them to you.'

For the next agonising minutes, through the means of opening his eyes when Geordie said the right letters, Robert was able to convey the letters of the alphabet that spelt out his children's names.

'Nancy,' Geordie concluded excitedly, 'and Jack. Those are the children's names, have I got that right?'

Robert confirmed this with a flicker of his eyelids. But that was his last response, because now, exhausted and spent, he lapsed into a deep, dangerous sleep.

Filled with a sense of wonder, Geordie lingered awhile, his gaze fixed on those tiny slits that were now closed and seemingly lifeless. He, too, was exhausted by the effort between himself and Robert, and at the end of it all, he felt greatly humbled by the other man's immense courage.

The door opened and startled him, 'Now!' Sally had made sure the coast was clear. 'We've got to go *now*!'

He nodded, but before he left he had to look again on that face that was not a face, and he felt saddened to the point of tears. 'Rest easy now, son,' he whispered in the sleeping man's ears. 'I'll do what I can.'

Once they were safely back at the front desk, Geordie asked Sally if they knew anything about Robert's children.

She told him they had no knowledge of any family at all. 'We found his name inside one of his boots, though why a grown man should label the inside of his boots is beyond me.'

Geordie knew the reason for that. 'I used to do the same,' he confessed, 'as did many others. You see, if you work in a place where you need to change your boots in order to do your job, you want to be sure somebody else doesn't lay claim to what's yours.'

'But why would you need to change your boots?'

'Regulations.' He cocked a thumb in the direction they'd just come from. 'Our friend back there was a freight-loader on the trains, so I believe, but at some time before that he must have worked in an iron foundry, maybe, where there's allus a danger o' summat landing on your feet and breaking your toes clean off. Things are beginning to change, you see? At one time the boss didn't give a bugger whether you did your work in bare feet so long as it got done. Now though, there are regulations, like I said, and some o' the more decent employers are starting to provide proper boots to them as can't afford 'em.'

Sally nodded. 'That's good. Some factories can be bad places. I know of at least two men who have lost their toes, and another who lost his life.'

'Aye well, like I said, there are regulations being brought in and employers don't want to be fined half their year's profit. Mind you, there are still them as haven't yet got the message.'

'Get on with your work!' Seeing her younger colleague Victoria straining to hear their conversation, Sally began to grow worried. 'Look, you'd best go,' she told Geordie. 'You never saw that poor man back there. And I never knew anybody called Marlon. So remember to keep your mouth shut.'

She wasn't too bad.

Geordie grinned. 'Like I told you already, I'm a man o' me word. Oh, an' there's something you should tell the doctor.' He cast a glance towards the corridor. 'Robert *can* communicate with you, if you only take the time. It's all in the eyes. Look in the eyes and you'll see what's in the mind. Tell the doctor that.'

When he was gone, Sally recalled his last remark and sighed. 'Hmh! Thank God he's gone. And if he thinks I'm going to start telling Dr Morrison any such thing, he must reckon I'm as mad as *he* is!'

Back outside Geordie looked up at the stars and picked over what he had learned. 'I'll do my best,' he murmured, 'but it'll take time. I know that much. There are two young 'uns to find called Nancy and Jack.' He glanced up to the heavens. 'Well, Lord, I've been a bad man in me time, but I'm looking to You now, 'cause I reckon I'm gonna need some help. Nancy and Jack,' he said thoughtfully to himself. 'It's not much to go on – not much at all.'

In his mind's eye he saw Robert's twisted form and stricken eyes, and he knew that however long it took, he would not give up, until he had found the whereabouts of them two childer.

Part Two

JUNE 1895

STRANGERS

Chapter Eight

It was the most glorious June day. At midday the sun was high and the skies were a magnificent blue. On a day such as today, when the impossible heat soaked a man's back and drained his strength, all work stopped at noon, and restarted some two hours later; at least it did on Weatherfield Farm in the hamlet a few miles west of Burnley, where Justin Lyndhurst had taken Jack to be his fostered son.

Justin had followed that same procedure every summer for nigh on thirty years, and today was no different. 'I've never known it so hot,' he complained to his wife, Viola, 'an' I've a crippling thirst on me. I tell you what, lass, I'd not say no to a mug o' your best tea an' a bacon buttie or two.'

'Aw, you're allus hungry!' she retorted. 'Still, it's time I were away indoors and out of this sun.' Viola Lyndhurst hated the sun and the heat. In fact, she hated the cold and the rain, the snow and the wind, and more than anything, she hated the work that living on a farm entailed. To tell the truth she craved the life of a lady, with nothing to do but laze about and spend money as if it had gone out of fashion.

Seven years ago, after the TB took her first husband and left her a widow with a one-year-old child, she had wed Justin in desperation, on the offchance he might 'pop his clogs' sooner rather than later; especially as he was nearer to sixty years old than she was nearer to forty. So far, however, she had been bitterly disappointed, even though these past two years he had suffered the odd, lingering symptoms of ill-health.

All the same, he showed no real sign of imminent demise – so much so that the idea of lacing his food with rat-poison seemed more attractive as the years wore away.

And now there was a new threat to what should be all hers one day. That damned lad to whom Justin had taken such a shine, Jack, was like a thorn in her side! She could think of nothing more wonderful than being rid of them both at one and the same time. If only some accident or another would occur and leave her and her daughter sitting pretty!

'Cat got your tongue, has it?' Unaware of her hostile thoughts towards himself and the lad, Justin gave his wife a playful nudge.

'What?' Red-faced and weathered, Viola was a big, rough sort of woman. Never in her miserable life had she ever felt the need to wear anything pretty, or paint her face, or curl her lank brown hair. Her hands were almost as thick and strong as her husband's, and unlike Justin who was lately beginning to delegate the harder tasks about the farm, she had the strength and stamina of an ox.

'Are you all right, wife?' Justin didn't like it when she lapsed into deep thought.

'Well, o' course I'm all right!' she snapped. 'Why on earth shouldn't I be?'

'You just seemed so far away, that's all.'

'Aye, but I'm *not*, am I? I'm out here in the blazing sun, been working my poor fingers to the bone, getting old before my time.' She gave an almighty sigh. 'Oh well, happen things will improve one o' these days . . .' When you're under the turf and I've got my hands on what you've left behind! she thought greedily. 'So, it's bacon butties and a mug o' tea, is it?'

'Thank you, m'dear. I'll be along in a minute.'

She could hardly hide her sense of loathing. 'Waiting for the lad, are you?' It was as well her husband didn't know how much she hated that little bugger. 'You dote on him far too much if you ask me!' she couldn't resist saying.

'Just look at him though. Look at the way he puts his back into the chopping and piling o' that wood, an' he's only just eight year old.'

'Aye, but he's no more willing than any other poor lad you might have taken out of the orphanage and given a home to.'

'Mebbe not, but I've been watching him. He's a natural farmer, I can tell.' Pride and affection ebbed through his voice.

'If you say so, husband.'

From the barn door, the two of them watched Jack as he went about his work. 'He's got the makings of a real man, don't you think, Vi?'

There was a measure of pride in Justin Lyndhurst as he spoke about the lad. When he first brought Jack to Weatherfield Farm, he couldn't be certain how things would turn out, but now, as he watched him deal with the work in hand, he was convinced he had made the right decision. What was more, he had told Jack the very same time and again, and having someone who believed in him seemed to have helped the lad settle more quickly into his new home.

'You lay too much praise on that lad,' she muttered. 'You'll have him getting above himself.' Viola had no liking for Jack, whatever he might do, or however hard he might work. In fact, she had no liking for children of any kind, except for her own daughter by her first husband. The same age as Jack, Lizzy, it seemed, was destined to be a plain-looking, unexciting girl, and for that reason alone, she was her mother's pride and joy.

Viola Lyndhurst believed with ferocious passion that the day would never come when there was a man on this earth good enough for her offspring.

'You do *like* the lad, don't you?' Justin's anxious voice invaded her thoughts. 'I mean, you know how much I've tekken to him. I'd be real disappointed if I thought you couldn't tek to him the same way.'

'Well, o' course I like him.' She lied so easily. 'And I'm glad you've got him here to give you a hand. I've already told you – it's good to have a man in the making about the place.'

All along, Viola had been careful not to let on how she felt towards Jack; indeed she made it appear that she had the same admiration and affection for the lad as did her gullible husband. But when Justin was away or out of sight, she treated Jack like some vagabond off the streets, or a slave to run and fetch, to labour and sweat, until he ached in every bone in his young body.

As for Jack, he never complained or revealed the truth to the man who had put his trust in him, but he had come to hate this woman, with a bitterness that he could almost taste.

'As I said, he seems to be a natural farmer,' Justin rambled on. 'What do *you* think, wife?'

'Oh, he's doing very well, yes.' Having to admit it though, was like cutting off her right arm.

The old man gave her a curious look. 'Are you *sure* you like the lad?'

She turned with a smile. 'I've just said so, haven't I?'

He was relieved. 'Yes, but are you sure you're not just trying to please me?' It was so important to him that she should feel the same way towards Jack as he did. 'Only the last time we had a lad working here you seemed to tek agin him.'

'I never did! He just didn't pull his weight, that's all. *You* know that as well as I do. Besides, it were you as sent him away, not me.' She narrowed her eyes. 'Or have you forgotten that?'

'No. And you're right. That Clem were a lazy little sod. He didn't belong on a farm, not in a million years. I made a mistake with that one.'

'But not this one?'

The last intruder she had successfully got rid of, but she knew this time it would be that much harder because, as the old farmer said, Jack was a hardworking lad, who kept himself to himself.

Up to now, she hadn't managed to turn her husband against him. But there was still time. And she had a good many cards up her sleeve yet.

When the tea and bacon butties were on the table, Justin went in for his wash. Towelling himself dry at the sink, he called: 'Fetch the lad in, will you, wife? He must be famished.'

Reluctantly she went out to where Jack was working in the yard. 'He wants you inside,' she snapped. 'If it were up to me, you'd not set foot inside my house, not today nor any other day!'

'I know that, missus.' Jack did not look at her. Instead he carried on chopping the wood, desperate not to let her know how she always managed to get to him. 'I can eat in the shed,' he told her. 'I don't mind.'

'Aye, an' that's where you belong . . . in the shed with the other rats and rubbish!'

With the axe in his hand, Jack stopped his work and turned to face her. 'Why do you hate me so much?' His dark eyes burned with resentment.

For a moment she was desperately afraid; she looked in his eyes and saw that the hatred she felt for him was akin to the hatred he felt for her. She saw, too, the axe in his hand – and the next instant, her fear turned to rage. In a minute she had pounced on him and wrenched the tool from his grasp. 'I don't hate you!' she growled. 'I loathe the very ground you stand on. Oh, but you think you've got it made here, don't you, eh? You think you've got him wrapped so tight round your little finger that he'll leave his heart and soul to you when he's gone – but he won't! You can worm your way into *his* affections, you calculating little swine, but not mine!'

'You've got it all wrong, missus.' The last thing on Jack's mind was to take anything from the man who had shown him such kindness. 'All I want to do is work and help him. I just want to show him how grateful I am.'

'*Liar!*' Lashing out with the axe handle she caused him to fall backwards, into the woodpile. 'I promise you this, you little bastard. The second after he's gone, you'll be gone, too – out the door and back to the gutter where you belong, and bloody good shuts to you, that's what I say!'

Scrambling to his feet, Jack gave as good as he got, though it only served to antagonise her further. 'How many times do I have to tell you, missus? I don't want *anything*!' he shouted. 'I think a lot of Mr Lyndhurst.'

'Oh, I'm sure you do, 'cause you're expecting the silly old sod to leave you well-off, but you remember what I said: if he goes, you go, too, and if I can find a way to be rid of you afore that, you can depend I'll have you up that road so fast your feet won't touch the ground.'

'If Mr Lyndhurst wasn't here, I wouldn't stay anyway.'

'Wise boy. I think you're very wise as well, not to have told him about our little conversations. But then again, it all fits in with your devious plan, doesn't it? If he thought I was set agin you, he'd be even more protective than he is now, and that would never do, would it, eh?'

'You're *mad*! Why won't you listen?' Driven to tears of anger, his voice shook with emotion. 'I don't have any devious plan. It's *you* that's devious. Mr Lyndhurst is a special man; he deserves better than you. My dad left me like I were a bag o' nothing. Then my sister left me just the same. But not Mr Lyndhurst! *He* took me from that stinking place in Bedford and gave me work and a home. He's the only friend I've got, and I'll always do what I can to repay him. After that, I'll be gone from here, don't you worry.'

'Vi? Jack? What's keeping the two of youse?' Justin called from the house. 'Them tea and butties are gerrin' cold!'

When neither Jack nor the woman answered, so intent were they on outstaring each other, Justin came out in person, addressing the lad as he approached. 'Come on now. It's time you had a rest.'

'I were just on my way, sir.' Brushing himself down, Jack stretched his back and wiped the sweat from his face. 'Mrs Lyndhurst told me I was wanted.' He gave her a shrivelling glance. 'I was just finishing off, but I'm ready now.'

The entire meal was an ordeal for Jack. Sitting there at the same table as the woman who hated him made him feel uncomfortable; it also filled him with bitterness that she had the ability to unnerve him every time she looked at him, or found him on his own, working in the field. There were even times when she made it her business to seek him out in order to belittle and humiliate him, especially in front of Lizzy, and that was extremely painful to him.

There was an unforgiving, lingering anger in him at what his daddy and mummy and even Mary had done; they couldn't have loved him and Nancy or they would never have gone away and left them like that. In spite of that, he still loved and needed them all, but for what they had done to himself and Nancy, he could never forgive them.

It was Nancy who had broken his heart though. Yet he didn't feel rage towards her. He felt only sadness and regret. Even now, if she called him he would rush to her side. But she wouldn't call him. After the way she had gone, without even waving goodbye, he believed she had cut him out of her life for ever. The truth was, if it hadn't been for Mr Lyndhurst and his stepdaughter Lizzy, he would have run away before now. But he had found precious friends in these two, and feeling heart-sore and vulnerable, he was not ready to throw that away.

So, he ate his sandwiches and he answered any questions that were put to him, and when the woman smiled at him, he smiled back, because he knew the man was watching.

'That's it, then,' Viola remarked, in a kindly voice that made him cringe. 'We'd best get back to work – eh, son?'

For a minute the reply clogged his throat. It was only when Mr Lyndhurst intervened that he was made to look up. 'Summat wrong is there, lad?' Justin Lyndhurst stared from one to the other. 'Look there, wife,' he told Viola. 'Our Jack hasn't eaten enough to fill a mouse's shoe!'

Viola glanced at Jack's plate and was suitably horrified. 'Oh my, but you'll never last the day if you don't eat.' Scrambling out of her chair, she took the boy's plate. 'You don't like the sandwiches, I can see that. So, you hang on here an' I'll get you summat else. Happen you'd like a barmcake filled with fresh-cured ham, eh?' Leaning close to Jack, her smile was wicked. 'We don't want you going hungry, do we? Young lad like you, doing a man's work with axes and such. Mr Lyndhurst is right. You need to keep up your strength, or who knows *what* might happen to you.'

Feeling threatened, Jack clambered up from the table. 'I'm all right, thank you.' His answer was directed to the man. 'I were more thirsty than hungry.'

As always, Justin was understanding. 'It's the sun . . . fierce it is at this time o' year.' Addressing his wife, he asked her to, 'Fill a bottle with cold tea, m'dear. It's the best thing for a raging thirst. Oh, an' wrap him a barmcake up. Like as not he'll find a minute or two to eat it as we go over the fields.' He gave a hearty chuckle, 'Matter o' fact, wrap one up for me an' all.' He turned to Jack. 'A man's work is hungry work, ain't that right?'

The old man's laugh was infectious, and the broad smile on his homely features made Jack feel good inside. 'Yes, sir, it is.'

Justin got out of his chair and gave a long, noisy stretch. 'Tell you the truth, I'd rather be tekking an hour's nap, only there's so much to be done, I'd only lie there feeling guilty.'

The idea of her husband under her feet galvanised Viola into reminding him sharply, 'You'll be better off out there, or like you say, you'll only whittle and worry.' The highlight of her day was when he set off down the hoggin-path and out of her sight.

Winking at Jack, he nodded. 'She's right. Weary or not, there's no time to lie about. I've said I'll open the lake to the fishermen and so I will. Besides, I'll not be earning afore they start fishing, an' they can't fish if there's no road to it.' Rubbing his hands, he gave another wink. 'A shillin' a day from each fisherman is not to be sniffed at. Like as not, once word gets about it'll fetch more money in than all the cows and heifers I've sold in a year.'

Taking his hat from the door-peg, he plunged it over his head, where it settled into its regular spot over his ears, like one of his wife's upside-down puddings.

As he prepared himself for leaving, he chatted on. 'I don't want the fishermen trudging through my pastures, mekking a permanent path wherever they think fit.' The old chap was proud of the manner in which he kept his pastures. When one of the locals remarked some time back 'it's more like parkland than grazing' he was like a dog with two tails.

Now he gave a long, shivering yawn. 'I must be gerrin' old.' Another minute while he waited for his wife to finish making their barmcakes, and he was chattering away. 'You see, Jack, I shall have to mek a new path from the old entrance at the other side o' them woods. It's not been used in many a year, so we'll have us work cut out, I can tell yer.'

Jack was intrigued. 'I didn't even know there was another gate into your land.'

'Oh, aye. It's not been used since . . .' Looking puzzled, he scratched his head thoughtfully. 'Well, it were that far back I can't remember. I know this much though, if we tek the path from that old entrance and run it right the way through the woods, it should be easy enough to follow it down to the lake. That way, you see, the fishermen will be in and out, without bothering the cows, and I'll not even know they're there.'

He gave a crafty wink. 'Until I goes to collect the money on a Friday, that is.' He cocked his head and congratulated himself. 'It's a good plan, though I say so meself!'

Jack had to agree. 'It *sounds* good.'

'Aye, it sounds good to me an' all, lad. So, let's be off then. If we're about to earn us money we shall do it with a good heart and learn not to grumble. Oh, an' when we've done with the woods, there's the lake to dredge. Mind you, we'll not be doing it on our own, 'cause I've arranged for the help o' three good men from Harwood. It's a big job, dredging a lake.' He groaned from his boots. 'By! I feel weary just *thinking* about it.'

'*I* can cut a way through the woods, if you need to have a nap.' Jack welcomed any opportunity to show what he was made of. 'You've already taught me how to use the axe, an' I know how to keep a look-out for grass snakes. Oh please, sir . . . I know I can do it!' His face was flushed with excitement.

Justin looked at the boy, and his heart warmed to bursting. 'By! Yer mek me that proud, lad,' he said brokenly. 'I've no doubt you've got the heart and the guts to do it, but you see, son, you ain't quite big enough nor strong enough to do it on your own. Oh, but I'm sure the day ain't far away when you'll be slicing your way through that wood and dredging the lake like you were born to it. But not yet, eh?'

He cast an appreciative glance at Viola, who was inwardly seething at the deep affection growing between these two. 'The wife is right,' he said throatily. 'We don't want nowt bad happening to you, do we, eh?'

He put a strong arm round Jack's young shoulders. Just for today, you'll have to let an old man help you, eh?'

All of a sudden, he chuckled. If I get in the way, you can tell me to bugger off home. Mind you, I'm not saying as I'll tek any notice . . . seeing as I'm the boss round 'ere.' He cast a wary glance at his unsmiling wife. 'But you can tell me to bugger off all the same, an' I promise I'll not tek offence.'

A short time later, they were walking off down the hoggin-path with their snacks tied up in muslin and hanging from their belts. Viola watched them go. 'Why don't the pair of youse fall in the bloody lake an' drown?' she grumbled. 'You'd not be missed, neither of you.'

She moaned and swore and cursed them until they had entered the woods and were gone from her sight. Then she marched into the scullery and took her temper out on the washing-up, swearing like an old trooper when she threw a plate into the enamel bowl, and got soapy suds blown back in her face. 'That damned boy – thinks he's got one over on me, does he?' She dabbed at her face with the dish-cloth. 'Well, he can think again, 'cause I'm not done with him yet, not by a long chalk I'm not.'

With a spring to his step and the axe thrown over his shoulder, Jack walked beside the man and felt a great sense of pride. 'I love the woods,' he confided. 'Sometimes when I've finished my work, I like sitting quiet and listening to all the animals round me. Once I saw a deer, and oh, it was so beautiful.' He looked up at Justin and his eyes were alight with wonder. 'It came real close – nearly close enough for me to touch. I could see all the colours in its coat.'

Justin smiled down on him. 'Have you never seen a deer afore, then?'

Jack shook his head, and when a sadness seemed to envelop him, the old man left him be.

For the next half hour they walked leisurely, meandering in and out of the Jersey cows and their young as they negotiated the pastureland. Now they were coming up the headland that went straight on to the woods, and still, Jack walked with his head bowed and a silence over him that Justin was reluctant to break.

As they strode on, and Jack kept his silence, Justin asked quietly, 'D'yer mind if I make a suggestion, lad?'

'No, sir.' Jack considered him to be the wisest person in all the world.

The old farmer slowed his step, and in a kindly voice, he told Jack, 'Whenever I'm worried about summat, I find it's good to tell somebody.'

Jack looked up, and it broke the old man's heart to see his dark eyes so troubled. 'I'm not worried, sir,' Jack answered. 'I were just thinking, that's all.'

Justin kept on walking. 'Thinking about yer dad, was yer?'

Taken aback, Jack took a minute to reply, and when he did there was bitterness in his voice. 'Why should I think about *him*? He didn't care anything about *me*! Nor my little sister!' There was such anger in him, and pain, and a sense of bewilderment that wouldn't go away.

'So, yer don't think it would help if yer was to talk about him? Y'see, lad, you've never told me about what happened . . . not that it's any o' my business, but it might help to put things right in yer own mind.'

'I don't want to talk about it.'

'Fair enough. I'll not ask again, but remember, I'm here if you ever feel the need to get it all off yer chest.'

'Thank you, sir.' But he never wanted to mention his dad's name again, or his mother's, nor what they had done to him and Nancy. As for Mary, he knew well that the blame lay with him, but that was something he could scarcely bear to recall.

'Right you are.' Justin had something else to say, though.

'Look, if it's all right with you, there's summat I want yer to do.'

Jack's mood lightened. 'Course I will!'

'Now that we know each other a little better, happen yer could stop calling me "sir". It meks me feel like some country gent, instead of an old farmer.'

'Oh, si—' He stopped himself. 'Are you sure?'

Justin tousled the boy's hair. 'O' course I'm sure, else I never would have suggested it in the first place.'

'Thank you.' Head up and shoulders straight he spoke the name as if it belonged to him. '*Justin!*'

The old man laughed out loud. 'That's better!'

A thought occurred to Jack and it almost spoilt the moment. 'What will Mrs Lyndhurst say when she finds out?'

'Oh, she'll not bother, an' if she does, I shall explain that it were my idea and I'll not hear no argument over it. All right?' He wagged a finger. 'Though you'd best not go thinking you can call the wife by her first name, oh dear me no. She's a traditional kinda woman is my Viola.'

'I won't.' The very idea of calling that woman by her name went against his every instinct.

Justin nodded. 'That's all right then.'

Again, they walked on in silence for a time, before Justin again spoke. 'Can I ask yer summat, lad?'

Curious, Jack looked up again, enjoying a sense of comradeship as he spoke the man's name for the second time. 'Course you can, Justin!' It felt incredibly good.

Drawing the boy to a halt, Justin placed his hands one on each of Jack's shoulders, a look of apprehension on his face as he went on quietly, 'I know I can never replace what you had, and I know some of it must be painful, but I've never had a son, d'yer see? Never had a child of me own, though Lizzy is a lovely little thing an' I love her with all me heart.'

His soft whimsical smile told the truth of that. 'But a man

has need of a son. One day you'll understand that.' He paused, stroking Jack's thick mop of hair while trying to find the right words. 'What I'm saying is, I went to that orphanage to see if I could help a child – a *boy* – yes, that's what I had in mind. For my sake, and so that Lizzy would have somebody to look up to.'

Again he paused, finding it difficult to tell Jack what was in his heart. He didn't want the boy to think he was taking over his life, nor that he was trying to replace the father he so obviously loved, in spite of him being abandoned.

Taking a deep breath he spoke softly, six wonderful words that struck Jack to the heart. *'I want you for my son.'* His old smile wrapped itself round Jack like a warm fire on a cold night. 'I'll admit, I weren't sure at first.' He laughed. 'A right little horror you were, angry and rebellious, doing yer best to mek life difficult for me. I don't mind admitting there was a moment there, when I had half a mind to send you back!'

He paused, his face crinkled with emotion. 'Then I saw how you were hurting inside, and I knew the anger must go away some time or another. Oh, I know it ain't gone altogether even yet, but yer ain't the bad boy you were, an' I'm glad o' that.'

He shook Jack gently by the shoulders. 'I've seen the love yer have for the countryside, an' I've seen the goodness inside yer, an' oh, I'm that proud of yer!'

Feeling the tears welling inside, the old man choked them back. 'If ever I'd've been blessed with a son o' me own, I'd've wanted one just like you.' Taking another deep breath and sniffling back the threatening tears, he smiled down on Jack with a fatherly love. 'So! What d'yer say then, Jack lad . . . will you be me son?'

Deeply moved, Jack's gaze fell to the ground. He had loved his own father, and Mary, too, and even his mother, who had never told him she loved him, and they had all turned their backs on him, just like they'd turned their backs on Nancy. Now, here was this wonderful man whom he had come to love, asking him to be his son, and it was unbelievable.

Thinking he had offended Jack, the old man apologised. 'I'm sorry, lad, I should have kno—'

His words were cut short when suddenly Jack began sobbing; wild, uncontrollable sobs that racked his young body. Unable to speak, the boy simply threw his arms round the old man's waist and held on with a fierceness that shook Justin to his roots.

He knew then, that the fear was still in the child, and now that he had taken this sorry young lad as his own, he would have a long, hard job to do over the coming years. But it would be a job he would carry out with all the love in him, because this unhappy boy was very special. For all the brashness and defiance that rose now and then, Jack had the makings of a fine man. He had seen that in him from the start, and he saw it now.

After a while, he drew the boy away. 'It's time we went, son,' he urged gently. 'There's work to be done.'

In silence, they walked away, the old man and the boy; deep in thought, each marked by the emotion of what had happened.

Now, in a moment Jack would never forget, the old man draped an arm round his shoulders; he didn't look down at the boy, nor did he speak, but the tender, loving action spoke volumes.

Something wonderful had come into their lonely lives. Chance and circumstance had brought them together, and now, with time on their side, they could build and grow together. Even so, the bond they had forged on this day would last for the rest of their lives.

Over an hour later, hot and sweated, they were almost through to the other side of the woods. Having worked like they had never worked before, they painstakingly forced a way into the light. Justin led the way, slashing at the overhanging boughs and dismantling the many tangled bushes which over the years had taken too strong a foothold.

Behind him, Jack cleared away the smaller branches and twigs; creating a wide, open pathway by carefully shovelling back the low undergrowth that had grown across the earth like a suffocating blanket.

Inch by inch they broke through; the searing heat and the heavy going making their work that much harder, but neither of them stopped or complained as they cut a way through.

When at last they came into the open air, Justin took a breath like it was his last. 'By! I never realised it were as bad as that.' Falling to the ground, he bent forward, catching his breath and wiping the sweat from his face. 'I should have tackled it years ago,' he remarked wearily. 'I should have kept that path open, but I never needed it, d'yer see? I've allus gone to the lake by way o' the pastures.'

Jack, too, was exhausted. Throwing down his axe, he dropped flat to the ground, arms wide and eyes open to the skies, the sweat dripping from his face and melting into the ground, until he seemed almost a part of the earth itself.

They stayed like that for a while; catching their breath and cooling in the gentle breeze that came up from the lake.

Jack was the first to sit up, his eyes wide with amazement as he glanced about him. 'Oh, Justin! Look at the lake . . . it's so beautiful!' In the sun the lake surface shimmered and danced, catching the light and throwing it back until it seemed alive. On either side, the long green fields stretched away; cows grazed and hares sat upright, ears sharp, bright, beady eyes glancing in all directions. From above, the sun sent out its golden rays, warming the earth and lighting the world, and in all this magnificence there wasn't a sound; save for the birds in the trees, singing their pretty song.

Stirred by the wonder in Jack's face, Justin sat up to look.

'Aye, lad,' he murmured, 'it's beautiful right enough.' He went on to tell Jack how, 'Me own daddy worked this land and his daddy afore him . . . aye, an' *his* grandaddy, too!'

He glanced at Jack and his love for the boy was evident. 'Now that I've got a son of me own, I can rest easy,' he confessed. 'It would have broken my old heart to see all this beauty gone out of the family after so many years.'

He pointed to the lake. 'Y'see there?'

When Jack nodded, he went on, 'I've fished that lake all me life, man and boy.' Smiling nostalgically, he shook his head and taking in a deep invigorating breath, he blew it out on the crest of a contented sigh. 'By! There's nowt like sitting quiet, with only the animals and the fish to keep yer company.' His eyes grew wide, and his voice dropped to a reverent whisper. 'It's that quiet, I swear you can hear the fish turning circles under the water. An' if yer listen hard enough, you can even hear yer own heart beating. It's magic, son. *Pure magic!*'

Jack was mesmerised. 'We lived in the country,' he heard himself say. With mixed feelings, he recalled how it was. 'It were quiet there an' all, just like it is here – a bit lonely, too. We didn't know many people. Sometimes we didn't see anybody for days on end; it were like we lived in another world.'

Stretching out his arms to encompass the woods and surrounding landscape, he filled his eyes and heart with what he saw, but it was the lake that caught his imagination. 'We didn't have a lake,' he said regretfully. 'It was pretty where we lived, but it wasn't beautiful, not like this.' His voice fell to a broken whisper, his mind reliving the past. 'It wasn't so quiet, neither. Dad and Mary got to arguing just like he and Mum did, then she went away.'

He dropped his head and stared at the ground. 'I was bad, you see, Justin. It was *my* fault Mary went away.' A sob rose in his throat as he thought about all the repercussions of his behaviour.

The moment was too painful, too private, and he could say no more.

'D'yer know, son, that's the first time you've told me owt about yer life, about how it were *afore*.' Justin could see how wretched Jack was feeling, and needed to reassure him. 'I'm glad yer told me. But you've no need to tell me anythin' at all, if yer don't want to.'

Annoyed with himself for confiding these secrets, Jack looked away; the hurtful memories already creeping up to haunt him. And though he tried hard to suppress it, the rise of anger inside him was too powerful. 'Can we go now, please?' he asked.

Seeing the way it was, the old man made a move. 'Aye, we'd best get on. There's still the lake to be seen to.'

As he strode on, Jack followed. 'There's a shed along here,' Justin informed him. 'We need to collect a heap o' tools and such, afore we can get started. The men should be along shortly and they'll expect us to be ready.' Pausing for a minute he asked, 'Can yer swim?'

'I sometimes used to swim in the brook.' Though it was never as often as he would have liked.

Justin nodded appreciatively. That was another snippet of information Jack had let slip. At last, the boy was beginning to open his heart, and that was good. But slowly, slowly. There was no rush.

A short time later they had two barrow-loads of tools set out along the lake's edge; shovels, planks, ropes and other necessary implements including huge nets with which to scoop up the fish. These were to be kept in the big tank already in place alongside the lake. 'There yer go, son. That's us ready now.' Proud but weary, the two of them sat down, awaiting the arrival of the men from the village.

Deciding it was as good a time as any to enjoy their snack,

Justin urged the boy to open his muslin wrap. 'Let's see what goodies we've got, shall we?'

As it turned out there was nothing extra, only the barmcakes and a bottle of cold tea, with a stiff, stark-white napkin to wipe their hands on. 'I were sort of hoping there might be a chunk o' cake,' Justin revealed, licking his lips. 'She's a damned good cook is my Vi, when the mood teks 'er.'

While they ate their barmcakes and drank their cold tea, Justin explained how they might go about dredging and restocking the lake. 'It's not that big a job,' he remarked. 'If we were attempting to completely empty the lake it would be a different thing altogether, but we're not. All I want is to cut back all the debris that's choking an' dirtying the water, and to skim the surface where it's beginning to thicken.'

'When do the new fish come?' Jack had heard how the cart would be fetching tanks of new fish for the lake.

'Not yet, son. I've no intention o' putting more fish into the lake, until I'm satisfied that it's free and clean enough to keep 'em healthy. By! Them fish 'ave cost me a mint o' money, an' I don't mean to lose 'em, I can tell yer that!' He went on, 'Y'see, lad, if the water is badly choked, the oxygen is fast used up, an' if that happens, not only does the whole thing start to look unpleasant, but the fish begin to suffer, and we don't want that now, do we, eh?'

'What sort of fish are they?' Jack knew little about that kind of thing, but he was keen to learn.

'Carp, mostly. The lake used to have a good supply o' carp once upon a time, but I've no idea what's alive down there nowadays. All the same, when they come with the new fish, it'll send new life into that there lake . . . plenty to keep the fishermen happy, eh?' The thought of earning money for nothing made him chuckle. 'I reckon they'll be happy as can be, once they get to pulling them carp out one after the other.'

While they were still chatting, the men from the village arrived, and with them a big machine, which Justin referred to as a 'Navvy'. 'It'll have the banks clean as a whistle in no time at all,' he explained to Jack. 'It's got a long arm, d'yer see?' Pointing to the steel girder that stretched some twenty feet into the air, he went on, 'See that bucket on the end? It'll be dropped into the water and sent as far down as it can reach. We'll have the muck and rubbish out, an' loaded on to that there wagon as quick as a wink.' Pointing to the high-sided wagon that had drawn up behind the 'Navvy', he called out to the driver, 'Hiya, Malcolm. How yer doing, mate?'

'Never better, and you?' With legs no longer than Jack's, dressed in green breeches and a starched apron, and wearing a little pointed cap, the fellow didn't look strong enough to drive such a big wagon drawn by such big carthorses. Sucking his pipe and grinning from ear to ear, he looked more like a happy goblin.

'Oh, I'm the same as allus,' Justin replied. 'Too much work an' never enough hours in the day.' Addressing Jack he told him to stay clear of the big machinery. 'Keep outta the way, son. Watch an' learn, 'cause there'll come a day when it might be *you* out there organising the business. All right?'

'All right . . . Justin.' Saying the old man's name always gave him a burst of pleasure, which showed in the broad smile on his face.

'Aye, that's it, son.' His smile was as bright as Jack's. 'Now think on. You stay well back. When I've need of yer, I'll give yer a shout.' With that he went away to organise the men. There were four in all – five including Justin – and, according to him, that was more than enough to get the job done in good time.

Watching the men at work was a fascinating experience for Jack. He saw them position the big machine and the bucket being dropped into the water; a few minutes later, it brought up an overflowing load of filth and greenery, with tree roots and other smelly stuff he didn't recognise, and didn't want to.

Twice over, the wagon was filled to brimming and twice it went away, the excess water draining from its rear as it moved off down the track towards the midden.

The whole procedure was repeated another four times before the shout went up. 'By God! Look at that!' Suddenly all was brought to a halt. Justin came to tell Jack. 'There's a monster of a pike lurking deep down in the mud. Stay where yer are, son.'

'Why?'

''Cause them pikes are a nasty piece o' work, that's why. For all we know, there could be more. Even one on its own would have yer for breakfast if yer got too close. So, you sit yersel' down and enjoy the sunshine. We're likely to be a while yet.'

Jack did as he was told, and from his vantage point he watched as they drew out the huge pike . . . some eight feet long, dark and slithery as Satan himself, it was. Then another, smaller but fierce-looking all the same.

When the pike were safely despatched to the grass verge, far enough away so they couldn't slide back into the waters, Jack could hear the men laughing excitedly. 'Make a tasty meal tonight, eh?' they shouted. It seemed a shame to Jack that such magnificent monsters were to be cut up and eaten.

A moment later, Justin came to reassure Jack, remarking with a sense of awe, 'By! I don't mind tellin' yer, son – them pike are the biggest I've ever seen, and I've seen some in me time!' He added how they must have got to that size from eating all the carp that once swam free in the lake. Taking off his cap he wiped his brow with it. 'We shall have to be sure there are no more o' the devils lurkin' down there, afore we dare put the fish back or release that new batch o' carp.' With that in mind he returned to the men.

It was some time later when Justin came back to ask Jack if

he might do him a favour. 'I'm likely to be working here till dark,' he said, 'and I promised the wife I'd meet Lizzy from the schoolhouse. Will yer do that for me, son? Will yer go and wait down the lane and keep a watch out for the lass? Tek her straight home, an' tell Vi I'll be some considerable time yet.'

Always eager to do his best for the old man, and having already taken a liking to Lizzy, Jack agreed without hesitation.

'An' are yer able to find yer way back through the woods?' Aware that Jack was still new to much of the area, Justin was understandably anxious, 'You'll not get lost, will yer, son?'

'If I go back the same way we came, I'll not get lost, no.'

'Go on then. An' tell the lass why I weren't able to meet her, will yer?'

Jack promised he would and set off at a run. 'Hey!' Calling after him, Justin warned, 'Best to go steady once yer get to them woods, or you'll likely lose yerself. You'll not be the first – not by a long chalk.'

He watched Jack as long as he could. 'What's the lad turning out like?' Curious, his pal Malc had come up behind Justin, interested to know about Jack and the progress he was making.

'Oh, he's a fine lad,' Justin answered proudly. 'I couldn't 'ave got better if he'd been me own flesh and blood.'

Malcolm gave a hard, dry laugh. 'Huh! It don't allus work that way, Justin me old mate, 'cause I've got a son that's all my own, and he's bloody useless! Bone-idle an' good for nowt! If he walked away from me tomorrow and never came back, I'd thank my lucky stars.'

Justin knew the youth's unenviable reputation, and his heart went out to this man. 'Sadly, we don't allus get what we'd like in this life,' he replied thoughtfully. 'No matter how hard we might wish it.'

As they walked back to the lake's edge, the two old friends talked more about Malc's wayward son, and what he heard made

Justin thankful that he'd been blessed with a lad like young Jack.

'Deserted by his family, you say?' Malc was intrigued.

'That's as much as the 'ficials could tell me, aye.'

'Still, I'm glad you're content with this one.' The story of how Justin had long yearned for a son was well known hereabouts. The last boy he'd taken on, Clem, was a disaster from start to finish.

'I don't understand it though.' Like many others, Malcolm couldn't help but wonder about Jack's past. 'Where's his mammy? And how could a father turn his back on a son like that?'

Justin shook his head. 'From the few snippets I've managed to pick up, I've an idea the lad's parents must have split up. I reckon the mother went away . . . then there's somebody called Mary, but that's all I know. As for the father, I'm like you, matey. I can't for the life of me understand how he would want to be rid of young Jack.'

Unaware of the interest he'd aroused, Jack wended his way through the woods until he came out at the very spot where he and Justin had started, some long hours before.

It took only a few minutes from there, to run all the way into the village, and another few minutes to locate the lane, and the schoolhouse at the end. A converted stone-built cottage it had once belonged to the gentry hereabouts, as did all the houses within a four-mile radius.

The last remaining member of that family was a reclusive old spinster who had lived out her entire life in this village. In her will, she left instructions that the main house was to be sold and the monies used to renovate each and every tenanted property that was rented from her family. The deeds to each property were thereafter to be freely given to the tenants in residence.

Her own spacious cottage was left to the village, with the instructions that all remaining monies from the estate were to be used in converting it into a schoolhouse for the children of that same village. When the good lady was laid to rest, a plaque was erected in her memory, and not a child passed through that school without learning of its history and the generosity of its benefactor.

Jack had only minutes to spare before the school doors were opened and the children let loose into the care of their respective parents, who as always were waiting by the gate.

Lizzy was one of the last to emerge. Jack saw her straight off; a small-built figure with long, light-brown hair and quiet blue eyes, she made a welcome sight.

On seeing Jack, she ran to him. Jack! Where's Daddy?' Looking beyond him to the lane, she seemed concerned.

'Don't worry.' Jack quickly explained. 'He had to stay at the lake as there's a lot of work still to be done, draining it. They found pike and they have to be sure there are no more, before they put the fish back in.' His chest almost burst with pride. 'He sent *me* to take you home.' A slight blush ran over his face. 'If that's all right with you?'

'Oh Jack, you *know* it is.' Her somewhat plain but pleasant features grew pink under his searching dark eyes.

'Come on then,' he urged. 'We'd best not hang about, or I'll have your mother after me.'

Lizzy was disappointed. 'Daddy promised to take me along by the canal. Will *you* take me, Jack? Will you?'

'If you like.' How could he refuse?

The canal was not on the straight route home, but it was only a matter of turning right instead of left. Afterwards they could find the road home, in no time at all.

Together they went into the village and down the main street to the bottom field; then across the stile, and over the little bridge, and in minutes they had clambered down the sloping embankment and were sitting side by side on a fallen tree-trunk, waiting for the barges to appear below them.

Lizzy saw it first. 'Look, Jack. There's one!' The barge moved along, pulled by a massive horse, loaded down with cargo and painted colourfully from stem to stern. The man on the tiller waved at them and they waved back, and Jack thought it was all too wonderful.

From their vantage point, only an arm's reach from the water, the two of them sat laughing and chatting as if they had known each other for ever. 'There aren't any ants inside here, are there?' Lizzy had a fear of small things that might bite.

He laughed. 'No, and if there were, I'd soon chase them away.' From that first day when Justin introduced him to the girl, he had felt a powerful sense of protectiveness towards Lizzy.

They watched the barge chug by, and then came another, and they watched that go out of sight, but even when it was gone, neither of them made any move to leave. Jack?' Lizzy kept her gaze on the canal.

'Yes?'

'My mother *does* like you really.'

Surprised by her remark, Jack didn't know what to say, so he thought it best to say nothing.

'She can be nice when she wants to.' Lizzy so much wanted him to feel at home. 'You'll see I'm right, when you get to know her better.'

Jack gave her a warm, shy smile. 'If you say so.' Except *he* knew different, but if it pleased Lizzy to think her mother was a better person than she really was, then who was he to disappoint her?

'What was *your* mummy like, Jack?'

Startled by her frankness, Jack took a moment to answer. 'She was moody, I suppose.'

'Was she pretty?'

In his mind's eye Jack saw his mother as plain as day. Mathilde Sullivan was a small, bright creature, with masses of fair hair and blue eyes like Nancy. But her eyes were hard and cruel, while Nancy's were soft and pretty.

Gently nudging him, Lizzy asked again, 'Your mother . . . was she pretty?'

'She had nice hair, and she wore nice clothes.' He imagined 'pretty' to be loving and warm, and his mother was neither of those things.

'She *sounds* pretty.'

'She left us.' His back stiffened and his mouth was suddenly set in a hard line. 'She didn't want us any more.'

For a moment, Lizzy wished she hadn't asked, but once again her curiosity got the better of her. 'Was it your mother who left you at the town hall in Bedford?'

Jack felt the anger rising again. 'We'd best make for home, Lizzy. We don't want to get into trouble.' He wanted to tell her everything, but he was afraid she might not like him any more if he did.

Still, he made no move and neither did she. Instead she said in a sorry voice, 'I shouldn't have asked you those questions.'

Her apology softened him. 'It's all right.'

'Does it still hurt . . . what happened?'

'I don't want to talk about it,' he answered kindly.

'Nobody can understand.'

'If you like, you can talk to *me*, Jack. I'll try to understand.'

Now, as she slid her hand into his, he knew he had a friend and suddenly it seemed the most natural thing in the world for her to know how it had been for him and Nancy. All the same it took another minute or two before he could bring himself to mention it. 'Mam and Dad were always arguing,' he muttered. 'Once, she left and then she came back again, and they argued even worse, so she went away and told us she would *never* come back again!'

'And did she?'

A shake of his head gave the answer. And oh, the memory of it all was like a knife in his chest. 'Soon after that, Dad met Mary, and we moved to Hilltops. It was all right, but . . .' He shrugged. 'I didn't . . .' He paused, recovering his emotions. 'I was . . .'

'What?'

He gulped, shame and regret marbling his voice as he went on quietly, '*I was bad to her*. I wanted her to go away. I thought, if she stayed long enough the rows might start and then she'd go and we'd have no mother again. I wanted our proper mam back, and I blamed Mary. I wanted to hate her. I was bad to her.'

His voice fell to a whisper. 'Then she told Dad how I was making her life a misery and wouldn't give her a chance. She said I was driving them apart, and it was true, but I didn't care . . . not then.' Now he did, but it was too late. 'Dad didn't believe her, so she went away for a whole week. It was awful. Dad was so unhappy. Sometimes he'd lock himself in his room and sometimes he would just go out and not come back until it was dark. Me and Nancy, we used . . .' He had to stop; he couldn't speak for the hard lump that straddled his throat.

Lizzy squeezed his hand. 'Go on, Jack. Daddy says it's good to tell somebody how you feel inside. Tell *me*, Jack. It'll be our secret, I promise.'

'Me and Nancy used to sit in the dark and wait for him, and it seemed like for ever and ever before he came home . . . and he'd be so drunk.' He choked on the words. 'It wasn't his fault, and it wasn't Mary's fault. It was *mine*!'

'Did Mary come back again?'

'Yes. But she said that, if ever I was bad to her again, she would go away and this time she would *stay* away, and that I could explain to Dad whose fault it was.' Jack shook his head slowly from side to side. 'I just wanted Mam and Dad to be together again. I thought if Mary went away for good, we'd all be a real family again!'

Lizzy understood. 'You were unkind to Mary again, weren't you?'

Jack nodded affirmatively.

'So, she went away, didn't she?'

Again, Jack nodded. 'It was terrible! The very next day, after she'd gone, our dad took us to the town hall and left us there. I don't reckon as how he was in his right mind somehow. He really liked Mary, but he knew she wasn't coming back.'

'You said something about Nancy. Who's she?'

Jack was shocked that she didn't know. He thought Justin might have told her; although in a way he was glad he hadn't, because if Lizzy didn't know, then neither did her mother, and that was how it should be. 'Nancy was my sister, but she's not any more.' Tears trembled bright in his dark eyes. 'She didn't want me either. She went away to a rich man's house and she didn't even wave goodbye.' Suddenly he was stamping his fist on the tree, so hard that it drew blood. 'My mam and dad didn't want me, and neither did *she*!' His voice shook with emotion. 'That's because I'm *bad*! That's why! Bad Boy Jack, that's what they called me, and it's true. Mary was a good person . . . my dad loved her, and I sent her away.' Soft, plump tears ran down his face. 'I didn't mean for it to happen like that.'

Lizzy slid her arm round him. 'Don't be unhappy,' she pleaded. 'Your sister and your daddy, and Mary as well – they'll all come back one day, I *know* they will.' She had a sudden fear. 'Oh, but if they do, you won't leave us, will you, Jack? I wouldn't want you to go away.' Her troubled eyes searched his face for reassurance.

But before Jack could answer, he and Lizzy were suddenly and cruelly wrenched apart. '*What the divil d'you think you're doing!*'

Viola Lyndhurst came at them like a crazy thing, her face red with rage and her arms flailing the air. 'You!' Pointing at Jack she went straight for him. 'Get away from her!' With both arms outstretched she gave him an almighty shove that sent him helplessly hurtling towards the water's edge. He tried hard to stop himself going into the water, but the momentum was too great.

The last thing he heard before he splashed into the canal and sank down to the depths, was Lizzy's frantic voice, screaming his name.

The shock of the water closing over his head, and the speed with which he hit the water, temporarily disorientated him, and he was choking. But before he could upright himself and make for the air, Lizzy was beside him. A competent swimmer, she was helping him, her sweet plain face written with horror at what her mother had done.

When the two of them scrambled to the water's edge and clung to the bank, Viola could be seen hopping about, screaming and shouting like a crazy woman. In minutes, two men from a nearby barge had dragged both children out of the water and deposited them on the canal path.

'See what you've done!' Shaking a fist at Jack, Viola took hold of the shivering girl and pressed her close. 'I knew you were trouble the minute I set eyes on you,' she raved. 'Wait till her daddy gets home. He'll take the whip to you . . . *and* he'll show you the door, if *I've* got owt to do with it!'

Breaking from her iron-like embrace, Lizzy pleaded Jack's innocence. 'We were only waiting for the barges. Daddy told Jack to fetch me from school. Don't blame Jack, it wasn't his fault. *Please*, Mam.'

Amazed and infuriated by the girl's plea, the woman took hold of her by the shoulders and shook her like a dog might shake itself when it's been for a swim. 'You'll do as you're told,' she said gruffly, 'and be led by *me*, young lady! You're far too precious to be in the company of rabble!'

When Lizzy began protesting, she was grabbed forcibly by

her soaking-wet collar and marched away almost at a run, with the woman all the while grumbling and shouting, and making Lizzy feel even more miserable than she already did.

They hadn't gone far when a local man drove by with his horse and cart. When he saw what was happening, he drew to a halt, and promptly offered the pair a lift back to the village.

At first, Viola refused. 'I'm not getting in *that*!' The cart was half-loaded with sacks of coal. 'Besides, it'll teach this young madam a lesson to walk all the way home, wet and uncomfortable,' she snapped. 'It might make her think twice before she throws herself into deep water, to help some worthless good-for-nothing!'

'I'd think again if I were you.' The man's argument quickly convinced her. 'You'll want to get the lass home and in a hot tub as fast as you can,' he warned. 'Hot day or not, she'll catch pneumonia in them wet things.'

In a minute, Lizzy was being bundled on to the cart, with her mother beside her, still arguing and complaining, and wagging a finger at her daughter as she blasted Jack up hill and down dale. 'The boy's a bad lot, not fit to be with ordinary decent human beings!'

Oblivious to her ranting, Lizzy's sorry face was turned to the solitary figure standing dripping on the embankment. Jack caught her glance and smiled, and continued to gaze after her as she was driven away.

Lizzy's gaze remained fixed on Jack, silently pleading with him to follow them. But she knew he wouldn't. He was too proud. And maybe even a little afraid.

When he could see her no longer, Jack gratefully accepted the offer of being taken on board the barge, where he was stripped, given a blanket to wrap round him and a hot drink to drive out the shivers, until his clothes had dried out. 'We saw what happened,' the young bargee told Jack. 'She must be some sort o' bloody witch to throw you in the cut like that!'

But Jack would not be drawn into making a comment. He drank his tea and when his clothes were dried he thanked the boat people for their kindness, and made his sorry way back to Weatherfield Farm, where he went straight to Justin's barn and hid up in the hayloft.

Some time later, Jack was woken by a man's angry voice, then the slam of a door followed by an ominous silence. Someone was rowing, and his mind flew back to his dad and mam, and the way it had been with them. Instinctively he crouched down into the hay, silent as a mouse.

A moment later, the barn door opened and Justin was silhouetted there. Looking about, he called out his name. 'Jack? Jack, lad, are you in there?'

Needing a friend, Jack nervously stood up; Justin heard the rustle of hay, and held the lamp high. 'Thank God!' He was visibly relieved to see Jack safe and sound. 'Come down 'ere, son,' he urged kindly. 'Don't be afraid.'

When Jack came down, albeit hesitantly, the old man clutched him to his chest. 'Oh, Jack! Whatever d'yer think of us?' Holding the boy at arm's length, he said, 'I were told what happened. I went to the canal an' I looked all over, an' when I couldn't find yer – oh son, I were that frantic. Then I stopped to think, and I wondered if yer might have come 'ere . . . into the barn.'

His voice broke. 'I should have realised, son – 'cause where else would yer go, eh? This is yer home! It'll *allus* be yer home.'

'I'm sorry, Justin.' Jack's heart was like a lead weight inside him. 'I thought you'd be angry with me.'

'I *am* bloody angry!' When the old man stood up to his considerable height, as he did now, he made a formidable sight. 'But not with *you*, son, oh no!' His voice shaking with heightened emotion, he demanded, 'What in God's name were she thinking of, to leave yer there, on yer own – frightened, too, I shouldn't wonder. And by the sound of it, half-drowned in that damned canal!'

'I wasn't frightened.' Now it was Jack's turn to be angry. 'And I wasn't half-drowned neither. I already told you, I used to swim in the brook.'

'Mebbe so. But the brook and the canal are two very different things. That there canal is dangerously deceptive. I've known grown men drown in that same spot where you and Lizzy went in.'

Jack's first thought had been for Lizzy. 'Is Lizzy all right? She came in after me, to try to rescue me. Her mam was so angry, I thought she might hit her.'

Placing a hand on Jack's shoulder, the old man led him out of the barn. 'There's nobody gonna get hit,' he said quietly, 'but there will be some straight talking. Oh, aye! There's a few things need to be ironed out round here, and this is the time to do it.' With that he marched Jack up the path and into the house.

Seated by the fire with Lizzy close by, Viola was catching up on her mending. When she heard the door open she looked round, infuriated when she saw who it was. 'Get him out!' Scrambling out of her armchair, she snatched Lizzy to her. '*Get him out of here!*' She pointed a trembling finger, a look of defiance on her face as she stared at Jack. 'I'll not have that creature in my house,' she cried. 'I don't want to see that boy anywhere near my daughter, not ever again!'

Lizzy's voice sailed across the room. 'NO! It wasn't Jack's fault. If you hadn't pushed him so hard he would never have tumbled into the water. *It wasn't his fault!*' She burst into noisy tears.

'Shut up, child,' Viola said sternly. 'You don't know what you're saying.'

Quietly, with great dignity, Justin loosed Jack from his hold and walking across to face his wife, he told her in a cold, firm voice, 'Don't make Lizzy a liar,' he warned. 'As it happens, I've heard the same story from the bargee who took Jack in after you left him there. Apparently you came up behind Lizzy and Jack and went for Jack like a crazy thing . . . hollering and shouting, an' calling him all kinds of terrible names. Not content with that, you then gave him an almighty shove that sent him hurtling into the canal, and when Lizzy went to help him, instead of thanking her for being the brave little thing she is, you gave her a real bad time.'

'She had no right going into that canal after him. Oh, I know she swims like a fish, and it weren't so much that I thought she were in any danger. It were *him*!' The big woman shuddered with the force of her loathing. Pointing at Jack, she addressed Justin in lowered tones. 'You've picked another bad 'un, husband. Why don't yer admit it? Get rid of him. I don't want him here.'

Justin simply smiled. In firm tones he advised her, 'You, me, Lizzy and Jack . . . we're a family now. This lad is my son – *our* son, Vi – every bit as much as Lizzy is our daughter. He's as welcome in this house as any one of us, an' don't you ever forget that.'

Turning to Lizzy he said gently, 'Is that all right with you, lass?'

'Yes. Oh yes, Daddy!' Running to him she threw her arms round his neck. 'I *never* want Jack to go away. Never.'

Putting Lizzy to the floor he turned to Jack. 'Go an' get yerself ready for dinner.' He sniffed the air. 'By the smell of it, I do believe it's meat pie and fresh greens – am I right, m'dear?' Smiling at his wife, he waited for an answer, his eyes fixed on her the whole time, and his determination concerning Jack plainly written on his face.

'Yes,' Churlish in her manner, she retorted, 'Only it wouldn't be so stewed over if you'd have let me serve it up before you went out in the dark, looking for . . .' It was on the tip of her tongue to call Jack some unsavoury name, only she thought better of it. There would be other ways, other means, to be rid of that little swine.

Time was on her side. She consoled herself with the thought that Justin would not always be here to defend him.

So, Jack went away upstairs to wash and change, and when he came down, the dinner was all laid out. 'Sit down, son.' Justin pulled out the chair next to Lizzy. He himself sat opposite, beside his sour-faced wife.

The meal was delicious, as usual; but then, as Justin had claimed time and again, Viola was an exemplary cook.

Throughout the meal, they talked of Justin's plans for his new business. 'I reckon to mek a lot o' money,' he told his wife. 'I've been thinking about the whole thing, an' I've a mind to start up a fish farm into the bargain. I've heard tell it's a fast-growing business. But first we'll get the fishing thing off the ground.' His grin was wider than a Cheshire cat's, as he looked from one to the other. 'I don't mind tellin' yer, I've had so many enquiries, I reckon I'll be swept off me feet in no time.'

Viola was always thrilled when there was money to be made. 'You think it'll be a big success then, do you?'

'Oh aye, I'm sure of it. If all goes well, we could have more money than we've ever had afore.'

The big woman's eyes lit up. 'So, could we get this cottage done up, d'you think?' She could spend money faster than he could earn it.

'I don't see why not. Aye, an' young Lizzy here can have that new piano I've allus promised her. After all, according to you an' the teacher, she's doing very well in her practices on the old one.'

While the adults talked, the two children spoke of other things. 'What was the barge like?' Lizzy wanted to know. And he told her about the little stove and all the brass things that shone like gold – jugs and water carriers and such – and the girl's pretty eyes brightened like sun in the afternoon.

As the youngsters chatted excitedly, Viola listened to Justin outlining the future, but her eyes were on Jack the whole time, her wicked mind brooding.

Jack saw this and was wary.

He knew that he had made a terrible bad enemy in this woman.

If he wanted to stay here with Lizzy and Justin, he must learn not to turn his back on her. Not even for a minute.

Chapter Nine

Edward Cornwell owned the finest house in Woburn. He had a collection of art that was his pride and joy, a staff of six and a wife, Rosemary, who wanted for nothing. However, Rosemary, though still attractive and attentive in her own way, was not enough to satisfy his carnal needs any more.

His son, David, aged nine, was a credit to him; his daughter, Pauline, aged twelve and a promising pianist, was totally spoilt and extremely demanding; if there was anything she wanted, she whined and showed off until she got it.

Edward also had a mistress some twenty years his junior. And an expensive apartment in Bagley Road, where Noreen was kept in style, ready to meet his every need.

Today was no exception. 'I can't stay long,' he warned her now. 'I have to be back at the house by teatime.'

Having made herself look beautiful, with a shining new hairdo and expensive lingerie, she had looked forward to having him to herself for at least a few hours. 'Dammit, Edward! You know how I hate it when you have to rush away.' Noreen Drew was long and slim, with black eyes and rich, dark hair. Her tapered fingers dripped with the rings he'd given her for the favours she bestowed on him, and the apartment was bedecked with the best that money could buy.

While Edward had no love for her, she had none for him. Their relationship was simply a business transaction, with each getting what they wanted in return. However, when Edward went away from his frequent short visits, completely satisfied, Noreen was left frustrated in a number of ways.

In Edward she had found a benefactor who, though demanding of her time and energy, made sure she was well provided for; yet from the very beginning, his mistress had had a secret agenda. She intended persuading him to leave his wife and marry her. As yet there was no sign of it happening, but Noreen was a determined woman, not easily defeated.

Now, as always, there was little time for talk. Already, Edward was stripping off, and when he stood there in all his naked, aging glory, she slipped off her garments one by one, slowly, tantalisingly, watching his member grow and expand with its need of her. 'Come here, you little bitch!' he growled, and opening his arms he took her to him. In a minute they were rolling on the bed, she with her legs wrapped round his nakedness, and he with his hands on her buttocks, clawing at her skin, desperate to be inside her, where he would stay, prolonging the moment, tormenting himself with delight for as long as he could.

Afterwards, she sponged him down with warm milk and licked it away with her tongue, while he lay there luxuriating in her attentions. 'You know you drive me crazy, don't you?' he murmured in a harsh, broken whisper. 'Sometimes I think you must be a witch!'

'I'm not happy with you, Teddy,' she said petulantly. 'You're leaving me again. You *never* stay longer than an hour. We make love, then you go, and I'm all on my own. We never get to talk! It's not fair. What's so important that you need to rush back this afternoon? Why can't you stay . . . at least for another hour or so?' When she could get to work on him – make him want to always be with *her*.

Recognising that she was about to become moody, he chastised her. 'You knew what the arrangement would be – that my work and family would always come first' While he began to dress, he smiled a warning. 'Are you telling me you've had enough of our little arrangement? Because if you have, we can end it all here and now. There are plenty of women who would give me what I want, in return for a place like this.'

'You're a hard-hearted bastard!' she purred. 'Do you really mean you could let me go as easily as that?'

'If I had to, yes.' He could not afford for her to think she had him at her beck and call, though in truth he would find it hard to replace a woman of her kind. All the same, he must not let her see his weakness. 'One woman is as good as another, I know that from experience.'

'I don't believe you.' Opening up her robe, she drew him down and straddled him, suggestively thrusting herself forward, while licking at his mouth with the tip of her tongue. 'Nobody could give you what *I* give you.'

He began to melt. 'You *are* a witch!'

'Will you stay then?'

Angry now, he pushed her off. 'I've told you . . . I *can't*.'

She realised she would have to be careful not to frighten him off altogether. 'I'm sorry,' she said sweetly. 'It's just that I miss you, Teddy darling, I really do wish you could stay a bit longer now and then.'

Pacified, he fastened his trouser buttons and pulled on his jacket. 'So do I,' he admitted. 'But I can't, and you have to understand that.'

'So, why do you have to rush away this afternoon?'

'It's the youngest girl's birthday. She's *four* already.' Rolling his eyes to the ceiling he admitted wearily, 'I can't believe how time has flown, since I brought that child back to Paisley Hall, just over a year ago.'

'What!' His mistress was both amazed and irritated. 'D'you mean to say you're rushing away because you've got a *birthday* party to go to – and it's not even your own child?'

Unaffected, he kissed her goodbye. 'That's exactly right, but I'm afraid there are times when I must be seen to be playing the dutiful father. As I've already been away on business for three days, and my wife knows that I'm due time off, I have no more excuses.'

Before she could open her mouth to protest, he was out the door and gone, and he didn't even wave to her when she ran to the window. He simply climbed into the waiting horse-cab and kept his gaze forward. 'Bugger off then, you miserable devil!' Feeling cheated and infuriated, she smacked the window hard with her clenched fist. 'I don't give a sod whether you come back or not!'

When the vehicle was out of sight and her temper had cooled, she gave a sneaky little smile. 'Birthday party or no birthday party, there'll be a time in the not too distant future, when I'll make it so you can't bear to leave me. If I have my way, Edward Cornwell, you'll soon turn your back on that precious family of yours.'

She glanced round the light, spacious room, impeccably furnished with the best that money could buy. But it wasn't enough. 'I want more than this,' she murmured. 'I need a husband, and a house. I need roots and security . . . everything you've given *her*!'

Going to the cabinet, she poured herself a glass of wine, sipped it thoughtfully and savoured it to the last drop. 'I want to be the next Mrs Edward Cornwell. I demand respect – money, position and status. I've worked hard enough, been at your beck and call long enough, so I reckon I'm entitled!' She licked her tongue round the rim of the glass. 'You'd best keep looking over your shoulder, *Mrs* Cornwell. It's only a matter of time before I step into your very expensive shoes.'

* * *

At Paisley Hall, Rosemary Cornwell had only one thing on her mind at the minute, and that was a birthday party. She wanted everything to be perfect, and to this end she hurried down to the kitchen, where she found Cook already decorating the birthday cake. A huge triple-layered thing of beauty, it was decorated with pink and yellow icing, and right in the centre stood the delicate china figure of a little dancing girl in green dress and shoes.

'Is everything going all right, Mrs Bellamy?' Addressing the rotund figure of the cook, she crossed the room where, seeing the cake in all its glory, she clapped her hands like an excited child. 'It's beautiful!' she cried. 'In all the years you've been with us, you have never once let me down.'

Having checked the cake, she then perused the other delights that Cook had lined up ready on the side: crimson jellies in the shape of rabbits and teddy bears, pink blancmanges, tiny fairy cakes sprinkled with hundreds and thousands, and little sugar dollies, dainty meat sandwiches and rounded pastries, and plates of cheese and miscellaneous goodies to finish. And beside all that, a row of glasses, with four jugs containing elderflower cordial and homemade lemonade.

'My, my, you've excelled yourself,' she told Cook. 'It all looks splendid. The children will be thrilled.'

Cook blushed with pleasure. 'I do me best, ma'am,' she replied. And nobody there doubted it for one minute, least of all Meg, who was Cook's little helper.

When the mistress had gone, Meg came to see how Cook was doing; she watched her write the name on the cake, and make all the squirly marks round the edges. There was a question she was dying to ask, but knowing how Cook did not like being pestered, she was afraid to open her mouth.

Cook sensed the little woman's dilemma. 'Out with it then!' she demanded impatiently. 'What's on yer mind?'

Meg bit her lip, then she looked again at the cake, and in a small squeaky voice, she remarked curiously, 'You've put *Sara-Jane* on the cake.'

'Indeed I have, and why not?'

'Because she's called *Nancy*, not Sara-Jane.'

'Is that right?' When she was frustrated, Cook had a habit of blowing loudly through her nose, which is what she did now. 'And have you taken leave of your senses?'

'Oh, no! She told me herself – her name is Nancy. It's *allus* been Nancy. She doesn't want to be called Sara-Jane, and neither would I.'

Replacing her icing tool into the bowl, Cook took the wretched woman aside. 'Now you listen to me, Meg,' she warned quietly. 'The instruction is that we call the child "Sara-Jane", and that is what we must do. Never mind what the child tells you herself. It's the master and mistress who pay our wages, and we do what we're told. Do you understand me?'

Big-eyed and wondrous, Meg had to say it, albeit in a fearful whisper. 'But Sara-Jane is . . . She was . . .' Try as she might, she could not bring herself to say it.

'*Killed!*' Cook said it for her. 'The poor child was drownded and not even her sister could save her. Is that what you're trying to say, you foolish creature! And do you think *I* don't know that? Of course I do, but it seems to me that this little girl was brought here to ease the mistress's pain, and if she wants to call her by her own daughter's name, who are we to say different. Besides, where's the harm?'

'It just don't seem right somehow, that's all.'

'Ah, well, right or wrong, it's none of our business.' She held the other woman with her gaze. '*Is it?*'

When Meg didn't answer, she was roughly shaken. 'I said, it's none of our business . . . is it?'

'No.' Meg shook her head obediently. 'It's none of our business.'

* * *

Unaware of the conversation taking place downstairs in the kitchen, Rosemary continued on her rounds. She checked the room where the party was to be held and counted the twelve little presents all lined up and prettily wrapped in paper; eight for the girls and four for the boys, each one finished with a flourish on top.

The room was lavishly decked out with multicoloured paper chains; and a big magic lantern awaited the visitors' attention. Even now, the tables were being set with pink plates for the girls and blue plates for the boys. At the far end of the room, a space had been cleared for the clown, who would arrive later to entertain the children. 'Wonderful!' Sweeping across to speak with one of the servants, Rosemary congratulated her on the appearance of the room. 'The children will love it!' she cooed.

Next stop was upstairs to see how the birthday girl was getting on. In fact, it was only half an hour to the party, so she should be dressed and ready to meet the other children.

In her room, Nancy was being pampered; her hair had been shampooed with camomile and brushed to a shine, and now she was being dressed in a smart velvet dress, cream in colour with brown collar and belt. The ankle-strap shoes were also brown, and matched the bow in her hair.

'Oh, my!' Rosemary appeared just as the maid was tying the belt around her waist. 'You look like a princess.' Rushing across the room she hugged the girl. 'I'm so proud of you, my pet. Your father will be, too.'

The little girl hugged her back. 'Will he be here for my party?'

Rosemary laughed. 'He promised us, didn't he?'

The child nodded.

'Then he'll be here.'

As it happened, Edward was opening the front door even as they spoke. He did not seek his wife out, nor did he enquire about the children's whereabouts. Instead he went straight to his office, where he engrossed himself in papers of business.

After a time he heard the children arriving, noisy little things, squealing and laughing, until his concentration was gone. 'Dammit!' Realising he could do nothing more just now, he piled the papers together and set them aside for later.

As he was about to open the door, Rosemary pushed it from the other side. 'Oh there you are, Edward!' She let him peck her on the cheek. 'The children are all here. Pauline and David are downstairs with Sara-Jane, and we're about to bring in the birthday cake.' With that she hurried away, back to their young guests.

Her own two children, David and Pauline, were hanging around, waiting for Nancy to appear. 'She's not even come downstairs yet!' Pauline had been a surly child for most of her twelve years. 'If she doesn't come down soon, I'll cut the cake without her.'

'Don't be such a bully.' David warned her off. 'She's shy, that's all. She's not used to big, noisy parties like you are.' Some three years younger than his sister, he was the exact opposite in nature; kind and considerate, he had taken the tiny girl under his wing right from the start, though this attention to the new member of the family only served to antagonise his sister.

'I'm sorry.' Nancy came up behind them, her face smudged with tears. 'I didn't mean to be late.'

Rosemary took her into her arms. 'It's all right, poppet,' she said. 'I know you didn't want a big party last birthday, and I could understand that. But this time we talked about it, and you said you'd be all right.'

Still nervous and unsure, Nancy wiped away her tears. 'I want my party. Honest I do.'

'*Liar!*' Pauline gave her a push in the back. 'You don't want it, because you can't have that other ragamuffin here – the one you cry about in your sleep. What's his name? Jack. Who is he anyway?'

'Pauline! That's enough!' Rosemary was furious. 'Another word from you, and I shall send you straight to your room. I will not have you spoiling Sara-Jane's first real party,' Turning to Nancy, she asked tenderly, 'This boy whose name you keep saying in your sleep. Was he at the children's home? Was he your friend?'

Nancy's eyes glittered with tears. 'I don't know.' All she could remember was his name, and his face. She had never forgotten his kind face. 'I don't know *who* he is.'

'Well, never mind, my dear, it doesn't matter now. It might have been a nasty little boy who frightened you, or just someone you happened to see there. Besides, you were only a tiny infant when your daddy brought you away from that dreadful place. There were so many of you there, it's no wonder you can't recall any one particular child. And maybe it's as well, because that's all in the past now. You have a new life here with us, your family. You're *our* baby now, and nothing will ever harm you again, I promise.'

With the noise and the laughter and everyone making such a fuss, Nancy soon put her worries aside and joined in the fun. But at the back of her mind, she could see Jack's face, and her heart was saddened. Somehow or another, she knew he had been kind to her. *She hoped with all her heart, they would meet again.*

Later, when the children sat down to tea and the cake was brought in, she was taken by Rosemary to blow out the candles. 'Take a big breath,' the woman told her lovingly, 'and just blow.'

Amazed by the size of the cake, Nancy took a deep breath and prepared to blow, but then she saw the name there and the breath was let out in a gasp. 'It's not my cake!'

Rosemary was beside herself. 'What do you mean, child? Of course it's your cake.'

Nancy was adamant. 'No! Look, it says somebody else's name. My name begins with a "N".' A bright child, she had come on in leaps and bounds with her alphabet, for the nursery at Paisley House was full of the most wonderful books and toys.

Rosemary smiled. 'Oh, I see. It says *Sara-Jane*,' she confirmed, 'but it isn't someone else's name, my love. It's *your* name now.'

Backing away, Nancy shook her head. 'Not my cake . . . not mine.' Taking to her heels she ran across the room towards the door. All the other children stared, wondering what the matter was.

Going after her, Rosemary told the servants to let the children begin their party feast. She wanted to talk this through with her little girl, away from prying eyes, 'You know you were telling me how you couldn't remember who that boy was – the one whose name you call out sometimes in your sleep?' she began.

In tears now, Nancy nodded.

'Well, that was another life, you see. I've already told you that now, you have a new life, a new family. So we needed to give you a new name. After all, how did we know that Nancy was even your name at all? It might have been one they picked out of a hat at the children's home. How were we to tell? We called you Nancy in the beginning, and that was all right, because you were used to it. But it was never meant to be for ever. I always wanted something else for you.'

She held the child close, telling her in a whisper, 'I want you to take the name Sara-Jane as your very own. It's a gift from me to you. You see, I had a little girl before, and she was lost to me in a terrible accident. I was very, very sad until your daddy brought you to me, and after that I could see that here was another little angel to replace the one I'd lost.'

At this, Nancy stopped crying. 'I didn't know you had another little girl,' she said. 'I thought there was only Pauline and David.'

'Oh, but she was so much like you.' Cupping Nancy's face in the palms of her hands she entreated her, 'You've given me so much happiness since you came here. If you would only take the name of Sara-Jane, I would be the happiest woman in the world. Will you do that for me? Will you show me how much you love me? Will you?'

Too young to understand the implications, Nancy thought on what her 'mother' had said. All she knew was that this woman had loved her and treated her kindly, and now, she wanted to repay that kindness if she could. Taking on a new name was not much to ask. 'It *is* a lovely name,' she said shyly.

'So, will you be my Sara-Jane?' As she looked on Nancy, the face of her own dear, lost child swam before her, and it was almost more than poor Rosemary could bear.

There was a long, poignant moment before Nancy nodded. 'All right.'

Rosemary embraced her. 'Thank you,' she whispered. Holding Nancy at arm's length, she said casually, 'Very soon, we shall have to arrange for the priest to baptise you.'

'What does that mean?'

'It means that you really *will* be Sara-Jane.' She stroked the girl's fair hair. 'I don't think you will ever know how much you mean to me.'

Deeply touched by Rosemary's affection for her, Nancy hugged her. 'I love you, Mummy,' she whispered, and for a long, precious moment, Rosemary would not let her go.

The rest of the party was a tremendous success. The children ate every scrap of food and had the time of their lives, and the clown was a hit with everyone; at the back of the room, even the servants were curled up with laughter.

When it was time to be collected by their nursemaids and be taken home, the children were given their presents. Nancy got a huge china doll, which was almost as big as herself. When

Rosemary went to carry it upstairs for her she insisted on taking it herself, though it took her twice as long, and once she almost went headlong down the stairs with it, but Rosemary was there and, much to Pauline's disappointment, caught her safely.

Later, Nancy told one of the servants that it was the first real dolly she'd had in her life. The news was carried down to the kitchen, where they all said what a delightful little unspoiled creature she was. Cook went further. 'She's too good and innocent to live in this house,' she said darkly. It might have been better if she'd gone to some ordinary place.'

'Whatever d'yer mean?' Meg asked, nosy as ever. '*I* wouldn't mind landing up in a house like this . . . all that money and everything. That kid has even got her own governess to come in every morning.'

'Money is all very well,' Mrs Bellamy said heavily, 'but it's not everything. I don't mind telling you, I'm worried for that poor little mite.'

'Why?'

Cook lapsed into silence for a time, before giving an answer that appeared to satisfy Meg's curiosity. 'I reckon Pauline has it in for her, that's why.'

'Oh, I already know *that*. You should have seen that one's face when the child were given that great big doll. By! If looks could kill! But then the mistress has the measure of her eldest daughter. She'll soon put her in her place, like she did this morning, when Miss Pauline were having a go at the girl.'

Cook nodded. 'I suppose you're right.' However, she had been here a long time; long enough to be disturbed by this latest chain of events. There were things playing on her mind that would not let her be.

Terrible things, that she would never dare tell another living soul.

* * *

The following morning at breakfast, Nancy arrived carrying her doll, which she sat beside her at the table.

'That's a bit stupid, isn't it, fetching that ugly creature down to breakfast.' Pauline never missed an opportunity to torment the younger girl. 'You wait until Mother comes down. She'll soon have it away from you.'

David chided Pauline, while assuring Nancy that their mother would do no such thing. He then sat on the other side of her and they chatted happily about the party, with Pauline looking on jealously, hating them both.

A few moments later, when Rosemary came down, she told Nancy it was all right for her to have the doll with her at breakfast. 'But only for today, sweetheart,' she said. 'It's best if you keep her in your bedroom from now on.' She glanced worriedly at Pauline, for her eldest daughter was glaring at Nancy, her hatred visible for all to see.

Choosing to ignore Pauline's resentment, Rosemary made an announcement. 'Nancy had another birthday present,' she told the others, 'one of which I hope you will both approve.' Looking from her son to the two girls, she went on, 'Your sister has a new name. From today, she will be known as Sara-Jane Cornwell.'

Her news was received quietly, although David made the point, 'Wouldn't Nancy prefer her own name?' He had seen how she'd reacted about the name on the birthday cake, and it worried him.

'Nonsense! Sara-Jane and I have already discussed it, and we both agree that the name suits her. It . . . *belongs* to her.'

Pauline smirked to herself. She hadn't realised it until now, but her mother was playing right into her hands. 'You're right, Mama,' she remarked approvingly. 'The name *does* belong to her,' And she for one was delighted.

After breakfast, Rosemary took Sara-Jane by the hand. 'Come

into the study, my dear. Your father needs a word.'

Clutching her dolly, Nancy obediently followed Rosemary into the study, where she lingered a moment at the door. 'Come in, my dear.' Edward Cornwell was torn two ways as far as this child was concerned. He had always nurtured certain dark suspicions, even though he dared not voice them to anyone, although he did ask now, 'How did Pauline take the news that her sister is to be known as Sara-Jane?'

'She was fine about it.' Rosemary was surprised that he should concern himself about that. 'In fact, both Pauline and David seemed delighted, although at first, David needed some reassurance.' She smiled proudly. 'He appears to have taken on the role of protector to this little one.'

'Really?' Edward wasn't sure he liked that. Now, as he looked down on the girl, for a fleeting moment his heart almost overruled his head, but then, in a crisp voice, he informed her, 'My wife and children seem to have taken to you, so I now intend seeking permission from the authorities for us to adopt you legally. Do you have any thoughts on that?'

Seeking guidance from Rosemary and seeing how she was nodding in agreement, Sara-Jane answered, 'Yes, sir.'

'Oh?' He had already noticed what an intelligent girl she was, despite her very young age. The assessment from her governess had confirmed his findings, and now the girl herself was questioning his intentions. 'And what thoughts might they be?'

'What does it mean?'

'It means we will be your legal parents. Are you happy with that?'

For a minute, the face of Jack crept into her mind. There were others, too – a man, and maybe a woman. In that unsure moment she needed them here. She had felt safe with them. 'I don't know, sir.'

'I see.' Impatient, he bowed his head to his work. 'Take her away, my dear,' he instructed his wife. 'We'll discuss this later. Right now, I have a million and one things to do.'

Later that afternoon, Pauline waylaid Nancy in the hallway. 'So, you're stealing my sister's name, are you?' she whispered. 'Well, they say you only get what you deserve. *She* was a nuisance, just like you. I never liked her, not from the day she was born.' Her smile was wicked. 'But it's all right now, because she's not here any more. But *you* are, and now you've even got her name.'

Crouching down to look Nancy in the eye, she warned, 'You'd better watch out, brat . . . *or you might end up the same as her*.' When she saw David approach, she stood up and backed off hastily. 'Don't say a word to anyone, or you'll be sorry!' she hissed, and ran off down the hallway.

David asked what his sister had been saying. 'She wasn't being nasty to you again, was she?'

Nancy shook her head. 'I don't think so,' she answered. In fact, she wasn't exactly sure *what* to think.

Later that evening, when she was lying in her bed, she thought about what Pauline had said, and when it began to worry her, she climbed out of bed and going across the room to where her dolly was seated in a rocking chair, she knelt at its feet and looking up with worried eyes, began to talk to it. 'I don't like Pauline,' she whispered. 'She made me frightened.'

The doll stared back with its big black eyes, silent and unknowing. Convinced it could hear her, Nancy went on in hushed tones, 'She's not nice, is she?' Continuing to look up at the doll, she seemed to be waiting for an answer.

When there was none, she collected the doll into her arms and struggling to the bed, she propped it against one pillow. Then, climbing in, she sat beside it, holding its hand. Leaning over, she put her mouth close to the doll's ear, and in hushed tones, she opened her heart. 'She's not my friend, and she says naughty things sometimes.' Her face lit up in a smile. 'But I like my new mummy . . . she's nice.' Again, a scowl. 'But I'm not sure about my new daddy.'

A tear trembled in her eyes. 'What happened to my *old* daddy? Pauline said I used to have one, but he was bad, because he gave me away.' With her two fists she wiped away the tears. 'If he did that, I don't want him back!' Then she smiled, a sweet, innocent smile that came from the heart. 'I like David though. He's nice. He takes care of me.'

She felt safe with David. 'He's like . . .' Her mind became confused whenever she thought of Jack; it became confused now, and lately it was becoming hard for her to remember him. 'He's like *Jack* – but I don't know who he is. Where is he, Dolly? Where's Jack gone?'

She shook her head, as if to clear the fog in her mind. 'I told Mummy about him, but she said he's gone away and he'll never come back, so I have to forget about him.' She shrugged. 'I expect I'll have to, then, because I can't see his face any more.' And that was a very sad thing.

She shivered. 'I wish Pauline would go away,' she whispered. 'You do, too, don't you?' She peeped at the door, as if afraid someone might come in. 'Pauline *frightens* us.'

Suddenly she was sobbing – soft, racking sobs that strangled her throat and chest. After a while, with her two arms wrapped tight round the big china doll, she fell asleep.

Outside on the landing, Pauline moved away from the door.

She had heard enough to put a smile on her face.

Chapter Ten

'An' how are you today, matey?' This was Geordie's umpteenth visit to the Infirmary in Bedford, where Robert was still recovering from the vicious attack on him over a year ago. 'Are they treating you well?'

Robert nodded. 'Doing . . . all right.' With his mouth stitched on one side, and his neck held in traction, it was agonisingly difficult for him to talk. His life seemed to be one round of pain and helplessness, but he was always cheered when Geordie came to visit. This genuine, homely man was a precious lifeline to the outside world, and the only hope he had of finding Nancy and Jack. But he was more than that, because now he had become a devoted friend and confidant.

Arranging his gift of fruit in the bowl at Robert's bedside, Geordie gave him a snippet of news. 'It ain't much,' he warned, 'but it seems that soon after your children were taken to the orphanage, they were shipped out to two different foster homes. That's as much as I can find out for now, and even *that* took some doing, I can tell you.'

He gave a hint as to how he got the information. 'A smile and a friendly word can sometimes do wonders, but finding out what goes on at Galloways is like getting blood from a stone. They all seem to be frightened o' losing their jobs.' Or something else, he thought wryly, though he didn't make that comment to Robert, because the poor bloke had suffered enough and, God help him, was *still* suffering.

He gave a mischievous grin. 'I've not given up though,' he promised. 'Now that I've managed to make friends with one of the women who works there, I shall keep on trying.'

He could see by the look in Robert's eyes that he needed to know more, so he volunteered a description of the female in question. 'Her name is Iris Dayley.' He spoke softly, out of earshot of anyone else in the big ward. 'She's the housekeeper there.' Rolling his eyes he groaned like a man in pain. 'By God, but she's ugly! As bootfaced and miserable a woman I don't believe I've ever come across – not unless you count my wife when I lived with her. *She* could turn the milk sour on a winter's day!'

Then, realising how Robert was only interested in one thing, he continued in a more sober tone, 'She's awful tight-lipped as regards the goings-on at that place, so I'm gonna have to play it softly, softly for a while. But I'll find out more, you can depend on it.' He beamed at the sick man. 'She'll not be able to resist my charm, will she, eh? I mean, a man of *my* good looks? What? Tough nut she might be, but I'll soon have her eating out o' my hand.'

Robert began to wonder if something underhand was going on in the Galloways Home, or if it really *was* like Geordie said – that folks were afraid of losing their jobs if they were caught tittle-tattling. Either way, after what he'd been told, he was more afraid than ever. 'Speak to . . . her!' Straining up from the bed he steadied himself with one hand while with the other, he took hold of Geordie's lapel, his eyes wide and anxious; his breathing erratic. 'Tell her . . . I want . . . them . . . *back*!'

Exhausted, he fell on to the pillow, eyes closed and his

breathing laboured – so much so that Geordie had to call the nurse.

After checking that the patient was all right, and that his brief lapse was probably due to over-exertion, she warned Geordie, 'He needs to be kept quiet, otherwise I'll have to ask you to leave,' She knew how dedicated he was to Robert, but the patient was her main priority. 'Remember, he's not out of the woods yet,' she imparted in lowered tones.

Geordie was beside himself. 'Look, matey, just keep yourself calm, eh? All I want to do is help, I never said you wouldn't get them back. I've already promised you that I'll move heaven and earth, and I will. But it'll take time.'

Regaining his strength, Robert murmured a response. 'I . . . nobody else.'

Geordie understood that, and said so. 'Tracing them is harder than I imagined,' he admitted. 'And now that I've got a job and become a respectable man, I haven't got the spare time that I had before.' He laid a hand on Robert's. 'But you have to trust me,' he said softly. 'I won't let you down.'

'I . . . know.'

When Robert looked at him now, his eyes brighter, and his breathing a bit easier, Geordie was made to realise how much pain this man had endured, and once more he was filled with guilt. 'Look, I'd best go,' he said awkwardly. 'You get some rest, eh?'

Robert did not protest. Suddenly desperately tired, he thanked the Good Lord for this unusual friendship. Slowly, with great difficulty, he reached out and sliding his fingers over Geordie's hand, he gave a half-smile. It was enough.

Choked with emotion, Geordie sat quiet for a time. But before he left he needed to know something. 'D'you want me to go to the authorities?' he asked. 'Happen they can get the information a lot quicker than I can.'

Frantic, Robert put up his hand in a warning gesture. 'Too dangerous.'

Geordie nodded. 'Fair enough. I should have known you wouldn't go for that, being as I've asked it before an' you've said no every time. I reckon I understand why you're not partial to the authorities getting involved. They'd say as how you weren't capable of having them kiddies back. That's it, ain't it? That's what worries you.'

Slowly nodding, Robert fought to answer. '*You* . . . find them.'

For a long time, Robert had found it hard to accept him; especially as it was Geordie and his mate who had put him here in the Infirmary. But for now, the big man was his only hope.

Geordie sensed what he was thinking. At the back of his mind, he always suspected that one day, Robert would be strong enough to confront him about that shocking night when he had been deliberately thrown under the carriage. Where would their friendship be then, eh? He wouldn't blame Robert if he tore the head off his shoulders; his mate's, too, for what they'd done.

Even so, he hoped there might be a measure of understanding. He hoped that after all the visits he'd made and everything he was trying to do to make amends, Robert might find it in his heart to forgive him.

Reaching his gaze across the ward, Robert watched as Geordie made his way to the door. There was a faint smile, then when the door closed behind the other man, Robert shut his eyes and drifted into a troubled sleep, calling out and crying until the nurse came to administer a sedative. 'Poor, tortured thing,' she said to Matron as she returned to the desk. 'Do you think he'll pull through?'

'Who knows?' came the reply. 'If you ask me, with the terrible injuries he had when he was brought in, he's done wonders to get *this* far!' She glanced across at Robert. 'Something, or *someone*, must be driving him to get well. It's a strange friendship those two have, don't you think, Sister?' She gestured to the door where Geordie had left. 'I would never have thought they had anything in common.'

The nurse nodded. '*I* thought that, too,' she confessed, 'but there seems to be a special bond between them. I overheard the older man talking to him – something about how he would not rest until he'd made amends for what he'd done.'

'Well, I don't know what it is he's done, and I'm not sure it's any of our business, but I know this much.' Matron glanced at Robert and her heart went out to him. 'I honestly think our visitor would gladly walk over hot coals to help that fine man there.'

That night, Geordie visited the same pub he'd frequented every Friday night, on the off-chance he might catch sight of Iris Dayley or anyone else who worked at the nearby Galloways Children's Home. So far he hadn't had much luck, but he had to keep on trying. Somebody must know something about Robert's children, and in his experience, everybody had a price. It was only a matter of time before he got to the bottom of it.

Strolling in with the confidence of a man who had made himself known hereabouts, he ordered a drink from the landlord. 'A jar of ale, and one for my friend here.' He greeted the man leaning on the bar beside him – a long, lean fellow with a ruddy complexion, probably got from too much beer and bad food. 'Hello again.'

Grunting a reply, the man gave a sideways glance. 'Don't give up, do you?'

'Not as a rule, no.'

The other man gave a sly little grin. 'Still asking questions, eh? Still hoping you'll get some answers?'

'That's right.'

'Hmh!' He looked Geordie up and down, much like a cat

might regard a mouse. 'Waiting for the spinster, are you?'

'What spinster?' The one and only time he'd spoken with the woman in question, Geordie thought he'd been most discreet.

The thin man gave a cocky grin. 'Don't play games with me. She goes by the name of Iris Dayley. Her as works at the orphanage, as if you didn't know. Her as comes in here every Friday night with her jug, to be filled with ale. She's the same spinster as you talked to last week.' He pointed to a corner where two gentlemen sat chatting. 'You sat in that corner where the toffs are now, thinking you couldn't be seen,' He grinned. 'I've got a keen eye, and I don't miss nothing.'

Geordie was impressed. 'I can see that.'

'You're wasting your time with that one. You'll not get anything out of her.'

'Oh? And why's that?'

''Cause she's like the rest of them as works there – tight-lipped about what goes on. As I told you some time back, I collect the rubbish every week so I know what I'm talking about. Iris Dayley is no different than any of them women who work over that place. She thinks more about her job than she does of a few measly shillings. When the shillings are all spent, what then, eh?'

Geordie wondered if the man was fishing. 'Look here, what I'm told never goes any further, so who's to find out, eh?'

'Makes no difference. She'll not talk tonight, any more than she would last week. If there's no work, there's no money. If there's no money, she can't pay the bills, and how long will it be before she's out on the streets? Gossiping about what happens over there is more than she dare risk, it's as plain as that. She can't afford to lose her job, mate, however grim and unpleasant it might be. It's all she's got, an' she won't risk losing it, not for anything, she won't.'

When the landlord returned with their ale, Geordie put the

money across the counter and thanked him. He waited a minute or so, before the landlord moved away to serve another customer, then he turned again to the thin man. 'What about you?'

'What about me?'

'What do *you* know?' He winked. 'It's worth a half-crown if you've summat to tell me?'

The man slurped at his ale, wiped the froth from his chin and placed the jar on to the counter. 'I won't deny I could do with the half-crown,' he admitted, 'but I've nothing to tell you. Sorry, but thanks for the ale anyway.' He raised his glass to Geordie's. 'Here's wishing you get what you want.'

'Hmh! I'm not likely to, am I? Not when everybody clams up every time I open my mouth.'

'Aye, but it's a delicate business. What goes on in that establishment has always been a bit dodgy, if you ask me.'

'Explain.'

Closing one eye, the thin man peered at Geordie through the other. 'First, I asked you a question, and you didn't give no answer, so I'll ask it again. Why exactly are you so interested in them two brats? Is there summat you're not telling? Is there a price on their heads, or what?' He took another long, slow drink. 'Even if there is, you'll be hard pressed to find out what goes on behind closed doors. Them as are in charge are nothing but rogues, and them as work there are obliged to walk about with their eyes shut. If they so much as sneeze outta place, they're in more trouble than you or I can ever imagine.'

Leaning closer he confided, 'It's even been known for folks to go missing after they've been asking questions – *if* you know what I mean?'

Geordie was left in no doubt as to what he meant. 'If it's that bad, why hasn't somebody brought in the authorities?'

The man laughed. 'Are you simple or what? I've just told you: them as run the place *are* the authorities, or as good as!'

On learning the truth of that place and the people in charge, Geordie began to wonder if he had a cat-in-hell's chance of finding Robert's children. He asked the other man outright about the missing children.

'I know nothing about these brats you're talking of,' came the reply.

'All right, I believe you. But you've heard things. So, talk to me. Tell me what you know.'

'No. I've said too much already.'

Geordie slapped half a crown on the table. 'Happen that'll help loosen your tongue.'

Snapping up the money, the thin man took another gulp of his drink. Slamming the empty jar on the counter, he told Geordie in a frightened whisper, 'It seems the devils cover their tracks only too well. According to what I've heard, they're clever enough to place a number of children in the right homes, just to satisfy any authority that might want to take a look at the ledgers.' Sniffing away a dewdrop, he squeezed his nose with the tips of his finger and thumb. 'The few childer who get taken to genuine homes are the lucky buggers. It's the others you should feel sorry for.'

'What do you mean?' Geordie didn't like the sound of that.

Sidling up to him, the thin man rubbed his fingers together under Geordie's nose. 'Talk ain't cheap.'

Slipping him another half-crown, Geordie complained, 'That leaves me nearly broke.' But he reminded himself it was all in a good cause and, as it turned out, the information he got was eye-opening.

'Like I say, there's been talk,' the man confided in a soft, intimate voice. 'Whispers, idle gossip about childer being left there and never being seen or heard of again. Some say the poor little sods are sold off to the highest bidder, though the Lord only knows where they might end up! Then there's the youngest and prettiest who get rented out – if you understand my meaning? Some of the poor little sods go mad and are locked away for ever.'

'Good God above!' He had suspected there must be something going on in that dreadful place, but until now he had had no idea of the scale of it.

Not yet finished, the man spoke so quietly Geordie had to strain to hear. 'Two year ago, one of the women who live in was woken by a terrible screaming and shouting. When she ran downstairs to see what was going on, she was bundled back into her room and told to keep her mouth shut, if she knew what was good for her. But before they dragged her away, she caught sight of a little girl – one she'd never seen before. The girl was being manhandled, crying for her mammy . . .'

Sickened to his stomach, Geordie asked nervously, 'What happened? Did the woman go to the police?'

'Apparently, she toyed with the idea, 'cause she mentioned it to her husband, who told her to keep her nose out of it, or she'd end up in more trouble than they could handle.' He went on in hushed tones, 'When she got up in the morning there was no sign of the girl. So she put it out of her mind, just like her husband told her to. Then, two days later, that same girl were found floating in the River Ouse.' He gave a cynical little laugh. 'Word went out from official circles that the girl was a bad 'un – out of control, they said. They claimed she'd escaped and run off. Them as run the place were out all night searching for her, so they'd have you believe! Next thing, poor little bugger turns up drowned, and they're all wide-eyed and sorry, I don't think!'

Geordie was shocked. 'Happen she *did* run away?'

The thin man stared him in the eye and smiled; in a voice as telling as the smile, he said quietly, 'If you think that, you're more gullible than I reckoned.' With that, he bade him good night and quickly departed, glancing warily about him as he went.

Behind him, Geordie was so shocked with what he'd heard, he began to think there must be a way of bringing the guilty to justice. First though, he had to finish the job he'd started. He was heart and soul committed to finding Robert's two young 'uns, or he'd never rest easy again.

No sooner had the man left, than Iris Dayley came in. Her usual habit was to walk up to the counter and hand her jug to the landlord for him to fill with his best ale. This she did tonight, the same as always, blatantly ignoring the disapproving stares from the men seated about. It was not the done thing for a woman to set foot in a pub. This was *their* little empire, and they bitterly resented her presence there.

The landlord had no such qualms. Money was money as far as he was concerned, no matter where it came from. 'Evening, missus.' He gave her one of his best smiles. 'Want your regular, do you?'

The smile faded when she accused, 'That's right, you old bugger, and I don't want short-changing neither, not like last week.'

'Hey!' Affronted, he demanded, 'What d'you mean by that?'

'What I *mean*, Mr Landlord, is that last week I paid for a full pint, and you only filled the jug three-quarters. So this week, I'll have a full pint if you please, and I'll pay for three-quarters of it. That way we'll be even, won't we?'

The landlord was so taken aback by the brass neck of her, that he roared with laughter, as did all those within earshot. 'I'll tell you what, missus,' he chuckled, 'being as you caught me out fair and square, I'll fill your pretty jug to the brim, and not charge you a farthing. What d'you say to that?'

Giggling like a schoolgirl, she told him what a gentleman he was, 'You certainly know how to treat a lady,' she said coyly.

While she waited for her jug to be filled, Geordie kept a keen eye on her. 'Could we have a little talk, you and me?' he asked, moving up beside her.

'Oh, it's you!' Recognising him as the man who had come after her the week before, she told him in no uncertain manner, 'Kindly go away. I've nothing to say to you.'

'Look, I won't be a nuisance, only I'd like a minute of your time.' He bent to her ear. 'It's worth a bob or two.'

She began to waver. 'Oh well, I expect I can spare a minute. I've a good quarter of an hour before I have to leave.'

He gestured to a corner table. 'We can talk in here if you like, or I'll walk you home and we can talk on the way?'

'All right.' Having cast a quick glance round the room, she was wary of the two toffs, deep in conversation not too far away. 'There's too many folk in 'ere,' she said, 'and I've no more to say this week than I had last week. Still, if you've a mind to hand out shillings for the pleasure of my company, you're more than welcome to walk with me for a while.'

When her jug was returned full to the brim, she took a clean muslin cloth out of her wicker basket and placed it tenderly over the top of the jug. She then secured the muslin with string, and placed the entire thing into her basket, making sure to pack it upright with even more muslin. After that, she placed a folded newspaper over the top. 'Can't let folks be peering into my basket, can I now?' she told Geordie and, much amused, he readily agreed.

For the landlord she had a final parting word or two. 'In future, kindly do not address me as "missus". I am not wed, and never likely to be, but don't feel sorry for my predicament, because I'll have you know it's from choice. I could have wed any man I wanted.' Raising her face to look him clear in the eye, she held his gaze for one long, daring, heart-stopping moment before, head in the air, and carrying her basket with pride, she marched across the room and out of the door, leaving a pub full of chuckling men in her wake.

Outside, puffing and panting, Geordie went after her as she hurried away at a cracking pace. 'Hang on!' Crooking his hand round her elbow, he begged, 'Slow down, woman! Are you trying to finish me off or what?'

She paused, but only to look into her basket and make sure her ale was intact. 'You men are all the same,' she told him loftily. 'Only after a woman for what you can get!'

'What?' Open-mouthed, he stared at her – at the plain, almost ugly features, the scraggy hair, and the unwholesome figure that no man, however desperate, would want his arms around, 'I'm not after your body,' he said sincerely, trying not to chuckle. 'It's information I want.'

She took a pace back. '*What* information?'

He walked beside her as she took off again. 'The two children I told you about.' Digging into his trouser pocket he fumbled for a shilling. When it was got he took hold of her hand and dropped the coin into her palm. 'I have to find them.'

Coming to a halt, she opened her palm and peered down, a little smile enveloping her features when she saw the shilling there. 'You won't.'

'Why not?' All kinds of terrible things ran through his mind. 'Has something happened to them, is that what you mean?'

Squeezing the shilling tight in her hand she went on at a quickened pace, 'Leave me alone. I've nothing more to say.'

Persistent, Geordie ran after her. 'Their names are Nancy and Jack Sullivan – they're brother and sister. They were left at the town hall over a year ago now and taken to Galloways. For God's sake, woman! Where are they? Why won't you help me?'

Now she was almost running. 'I told you to go away. I don't know anything. I've never heard the names and even if I had, I wouldn't tell *you*.'

Still he persisted. 'Their daddy needs to know they're safe. He's been in an accident, that's why he couldn't fetch them away. I've promised him I'll find them. Where are they? Look, I'll pay for whatever you can tell me. I've no more money now, but I'll get it. If you've any heart at all, *please* just tell me where they are!'

When she suddenly stopped, his heart rose with hope, but then it fell like a stone when she threw the shilling back in his face. 'Keep your damned money! It'll only bring me trouble. Besides, I've told you, I know nothing!' She wagged a finger at him, her face contorted with anger. 'You'd best stay away from me, or I'll tell the police how you keep following me, frightening me for no good reason. I mean it! I'll have you locked up without a second thought.'

Like a scalded cat she ran off, with no thought for herself or her ale. Scrambling on board a passing tram, she went straight through to the compartment where Geordie could see her, clearly agitated, leaning back in the seat, eyes closed and her face sweating, either from hurrying or from fear.

Now, as the tram moved away, he saw her take the jar of ale out of her basket. She carefully checked it before putting it to her lips, when she took a long gulp. She then replaced the jug, covered it over and for one split, unexpected moment, turned to stare at him out of the window.

In that minute, Geordie was taken aback by the sheer, naked fear he saw on her face. Ashamed at having harassed her, he moved away.

As he walked on, hands in his pockets and downhearted yet again, he began to mutter about the man who had given him only enough information to worry him, and this poor woman, who appeared frightened out of her wits.

'There's something real bad about that place,' he muttered. 'Folks seem too frightened to open their mouths. Time and again 'I've come up against a brick wall.'

Pausing, he looked ahead, as if talking to somebody, but with Robert in mind. 'I'll keep trying, matey,' he murmured, 'but it seems to me, the more I talk to folks, the more I find to worry about.'

He shook his head forlornly. 'The truth is, Robert, however hard I try or whichever way I go, I'm beginning to think . . . *you may never get your children back*.'

Chapter Eleven

'Come on now, lad, let's be 'aving yer.' Justin's voice woke Jack out of a deep sleep, 'Old Maisie's started with her foal and I need all hands on deck. Move yerself and be quick about it. I'll be down at the big barn.'

By the time Jack got out of bed, Justin was out of the room and away. In a rush, Jack pulled on his trousers and jumper and shoes, ran downstairs and, grabbing a coat from the back-door hook, went out into the settling snow, across the yard and into the big barn, where Justin was already at work.

'Good lad.' The old man smiled from ear to ear when he saw Jack. 'Come an' hold her neck while I see what's going on down there.'

Jack did as he was told, and straight away he could see that the old horse was in trouble; sweating profusely, she was clearly agitated and in pain. 'It's all right,' Jack soft-talked her. 'Don't worry. You'll have your baby soon enough. We won't let anything bad happen to you.'

Seeming to understand, the mare stood still, while Justin did a quick examination. When it was done, he swilled his hands and arms in a bucket of hot water mixed with soda. Drying them on an old towel brought across for the occasion, he told Jack sombrely, 'I'm no vet, but I reckon it's a breech birth. She can't do it on her own. If we don't get help, we could easily lose her.'

Upset by the news, Jack stroked the animal's head. 'What's a breech birth?'

Throwing the towel aside, Justin explained, 'The foal is coming out feet first instead o' head first. It's the wrong way up for delivery, I've seen it happen afore. If it don't turn itself round, they're both done for, an' I don't mind telling you . . . it ain't a nice way for this lovely old girl to go.' Patting Maisie on her neck, he told her, 'You just hang on, sunshine. We'll do everything we can to 'elp yer.'

'Do you want me to fetch the vet?' Jack read the signs. 'I know where he lives. I can run across the fields and be there in no time.'

'Aye, lad.' Justin knew he could count on the boy. 'As quick as yer can. But mind yer go back to the house first. Put your long boots on, an' wrap up warm. It's no weather for a dog out there.' In fact, it had been snowing for most of the night, though it was only now beginning to settle.

Jack was back at the house in minutes, and in even less time he changed his shoes for long boots, his jacket for a good, thick coat and finally, he pulled a woolly hat on, right down to his ears. That done, he left the cottage at a run, climbed the stile at the bottom of the orchard and took off through the fields and over the bridge that straddled the brook. It was not an easy journey, wrapped up the way he was. In fact, by the time he'd crossed the top field and come out into the village square, he had taken off his hat and was beginning to limp with the weight of his boots, now made heavy with snow.

The vet was woken by Jack's heavy-fisted hammering. Flinging open the upstairs window, he looked a comical sight with his sleeping cap on. 'Good God, man! Are you trying to wake the dead or what?'

Jack cupped his mouth and shouted again. 'You've to come

to Weatherfield Farm, quick! Maisie's in trouble!'

That was all the vet needed to know. 'Stay right where you are, Jack. We'll go back together.'

Within five minutes he was at the door, togged up in big boots and topcoat, with his bag of tricks in his hand. 'Take hold of that, boy.' Thrusting the bag into Jack's grasp, he went off in the direction of his yard; a moment later emerging with his horse and trap. 'C'mon, now. Let's be off.'

Greatly relieved, Jack scrambled up and they were soon on their way.

When they arrived at Weatherfield Farm, Jack was surprised to see Lizzy there in the big barn. While Justin prepared for the vet, bringing fresh buckets of hot water and such, his daughter kept the mare calm and still.

'I heard you go out,' she explained to Jack. 'I knew there must be trouble with Maisie, so I came down.'

'Aye, an' to tell the truth I don't know how I'd have managed without her,' Justin admitted proudly. 'For a lass of only eight year old she's got a sensible head on 'er shoulders. By! I swear I couldn't have kept old Maisie calmer, if I'd stayed with her meself.'

The vet was quickly ready; one glance at the old man and he was as worried for him as he was for the mare. 'Sit yourself down,' he told Justin. 'I don't need you for the minute.' Turning to Jack he added, 'You and I can manage on our own for now. Your daddy looks done in.'

Justin wouldn't hear of it. 'Hey! I'm not ready for no knackers yard yet!' he retorted. 'I've had this old mare for night on twenty years an' I'll not desert her now.' With that he stood by Maisie's head, and sliding his arm round Lizzy, he told her, 'You've done a grand job.' He winked across the barn to where Jack was watching every move the vet made. 'You, too, son. I do believe you're a farmer after me own heart.'

Such praise made Jack's heart swell with pride. 'That's what I want to be,' he answered. 'A farmer.'

With one arm all the way into the mare's insides, and at the same time listening to the conversation, the vet looked up at Justin's words, but his address was to Jack. 'To make a good farmer you'll need to be a stubborn old bugger – like you, eh, Justin?' He chuckled at his own joke. 'That's one thing he'll definitely learn from you – because you're the stubbornest old bugger I've ever come across!'

'Is that so?' Justin asked politely. 'I reckon you'll be going thirsty the next time you're looking to me for a bottle of home-made elderberry wine!'

The banter between these two long-time friends set the children giggling.

The laughter stopped when the vet withdrew his arm and gave them his conclusion. 'It's a breech all right,' he told Justin. 'She's not able to do it herself.' Washing his hands in the bucket, he promised, 'It'll be a long night. Perhaps you'd like to send these two back to their beds?'

With cries of protest coming from both quarters, Justin shook his head. 'They're neither of 'em squeamish,' he replied. 'They're med o' good, strong stuff, the pair on 'em.' He winked at each in turn. 'They can stay till they faint, an' no longer!'

The vet made his own conditions. 'If the lad can fetch clean hot water as I work, and the lass calms the mare, and *you* sit back and watch the proceedings until I ask for your help, it's fine by me.'

So, Jack ran back and forth while Lizzy stayed and talked soothingly to Maisie. The vet got to work, and Justin was made to sit by on a bale of hay, taking it easy after his frantic dashing about.

Just as the vet promised, it was a long, worrying night. Easing the foal out bit by bit, without tearing or damaging the mare, was not an easy task. Occasionally, he had to rest, and so did she. At one stage they thought Maisie might give up, but Lizzy and Jack soft-talked her, and she seemed to gather a momentum of strength and determination.

In the early hours of the morning, the foal was delivered; after one final pull, he slithered out and plopped on to the straw like a bag of coal down a shute. 'By!' Justin was astonished. 'That's as big a bugger as I've ever seen!'

Never having witnessed a foal being born before, Jack looked on with eyes of wonder. 'It's beautiful!' His voice trembled with wonder. 'Can I touch it?'

'Not yet.' The vet was a careful man. 'Let his mammy wash him first, then she won't mind too much.'

When the licking and washing was done, the foal struggled to its feet and several times it wobbled over and then tried again.

With tears in her eyes, Lizzy fell to her knees beside the newborn. Reaching out with tender hands, she stroked the foal's wet, shiny nose. 'Look, Jack.' Taking his hand, she placed it on the foal's face. 'Feel how silky he is.'

For the next few minutes, while the men and mare watched, Jack and Lizzy talked with the foal, making themselves known to it, and finding great joy and pleasure in the way it seemed to take to them. 'Can we keep this one?' the little girl asked, looking up at her stepfather with anxious eyes.

Justin coughed and spluttered and stood firm with hands in his pockets and a look of regret on his homely features. 'I don't think so, lass,' he replied. 'That's a fine foal – mek a splendid stallion, will that.' He turned to the vet with a discreet wink of the eye. 'You remember old Henry Armitage has allus wanted a stallion out of our Maisie?'

The vet played along. 'How could I forget, being as he rants on about it every time I pay him a visit. He's always said what a fine mare your Maisie is, and how a foal out of her would make him a happy man. And if it was a foal of this calibre, he'll think his Christmases have all come at once.'

'So, you reckon he'll pay a fine price for this one, do you?'

With as mischievous a nature as his good friend Justin, the vet said thoughtfully, 'No doubt in my mind at all. In fact, I've never seen a foal with such good bones as this one. Yes, I'm sure he'd pay you a whole mint of money to take it away.'

Just when the children were beginning to despair, Justin's weathered features spread with a smile, and they knew his little game. 'We *can* keep it!' Jack whooped for joy.

Lizzy ran to her daddy and, throwing herself round his neck, she cried with relief. 'Thank you,' she said, and he held her tight.

'He's yours,' Justin assured her. 'Yours and Jack's.' Putting her to the ground, he asked, 'What name should he go by, d'yer think?'

Jack knew. 'Samson!' he said, without a shadow of doubt.

Everyone turned to look at him, with Justin being the first to speak. 'By! You're right, lad. Samson . . . aye, it suits him, so it does.'

They all agreed. 'Strong and handsome,' the vet said. 'There's no other name that'll suit him better.'

Lizzy asked the mare, who was at that moment taking a motherly interest in her new offspring, 'What do *you* think? Would you like your foal to be called Samson?'

She stroked the mare's nose and, raising her head, the old mare nuzzled her face. 'She likes it!' Lizzy laughed. 'She's saying thank you.'

So it was settled. For the first time in his life, Jack was part-owner of a stallion in the making.

In that special, joyous moment he had only one secret wish – that his sister Nancy could be here to share it with him.

But he had Lizzy. And he was glad of that.

* * *

It was seven o'clock in the morning when they finally emerged from the barn. The skies were just beginning to lighten with the start of a new day, and under their feet the layer of snow had melted into the earth, like sugar over rice pudding. 'It'll all be gone soon,' Justin declared. 'Good job an' all. Happen if the weather picks up, we can get on with urgent work outside.' If there was one thing the old farmer hated, it was wintertime, although he would be the first to admit there was a special magic about snow on the ground, and the sparkle of an early morning frost.

They watched the vet drive off in his trap and, with one last peep at mother and foal, they closed the barn door and slid the bolt to. Before he set off across the yard, Justin stretched his back and rubbed his neck and told them how weary he felt. 'It's been a long night,' he said. 'You two get back off to bed for a couple of hours. By! You've done me proud today, the pair of youse.'

He slid one arm round Jack and the other round Lizzy, as they made their way back to the house. 'Wait till I tell your mam what a magnificent creature we've brought into the world.' With that in mind he quickened his steps. 'Our Vi'll be interested to know what we've been up to all this time.'

He was wrong. His wife was neither interested nor impressed. Having only a moment before come down from her bed, with her hair in curling rags and her early morning face on, she grunted and grumbled and set about making breakfast with a grudging heart.

'Horses is horses,' she said. 'They all look the same to me. "Magnificent" indeed! I'd rather have a dog to carry my basket from the shops.'

Justin checked her on that. 'We had a dog once, and if I remember rightly, he used to fetch and carry, but you were allus moaning about how he got under yer feet. When he popped his clogs, you never shed a tear.'

'Hmh! While you, you old softie, cried like a baby.' She had never let him forget how she was the strong one, but only because she had never liked the mangy dog. 'Anyway, stop going on, or you'll have to cook your own breakfast. I've got a shocking headache. You know I can't abide much chatter when I've got one of my heads. You can see how it is, and yet you still go on and on, about a blessed horse giving birth. Don't you think as a mother, I know enough about that already? I'm not well, can't you see that?'

Knowing her from old, Justin chuckled. 'I can see you've got a mood on,' he said. 'All right then, I've only to ask you one more thing then I'll shut up like the dutiful husband I am.' Winking at the children he asked her, 'What d'yer think to the name we've give it? *Samson*. There now, don't yer reckon that's a grand name for a grand foal?'

'Samson!' Having broken two eggs into the pan, she wiped her hands on the towel, and spun round, her accusing eyes going straight to Jack. 'That *your* idea, was it?'

Lizzy leapt to his defence. 'It's a lovely name, Mam,' she protested, 'I reckon Jack did well to think of it.'

'Oh, do you now?' She'd had a mind to deride the name just as she derided everything else Jack had a hand in, but she stopped herself. She mustn't be seen to dislike the brat, not in front of Lizzy, and certainly not in front of Justin. So, to maintain her reputation as a good mother and wife, she had to pretend; by now she was so used to deceiving Justin, it came easy as breathing. 'I suppose it's all right,' she commented with a smile in Jack's direction. 'An' if my little Lizzy likes it so much, how can I not like it as well, eh?' The false smile enveloped one and all. 'Yes, it sounds a good enough name.' Silently hating Jack for the upset he'd brought to this house, she got back to her cooking.

'Aye, you're right. It's a *grand* name.' Justin was pleased at her approval. 'The vet said as how it were the only name that suited.'

Viola had said more than enough on the matter, so she kept quiet and made her plans, and finished cooking the breakfast; thinking how, the sooner Justin was fed, the sooner he would be out of the door and messing about with his animals and machinery. With any luck, Jack would be by his side.

Made hungry by their night's work, the three ate their breakfast and to Viola's annoyance, continued chatting about the mare and foal, saying what a wonderful thing it had been, to see the newborn animal come into the world.

After a time they fell silent, while they polished off their first meal of the day.

Whatever faults Viola had, she could certainly put a wholesome meal on the table, be it breakfast or dinner, or just a plate of sandwiches outside in the garden on a summer's day. She herself had never been seen to eat before eleven in the morning, when she might take time off to nibble at a freshly baked scone, or a teacake with honey.

This morning, Lizzy had toast and homemade jam, Jack had bacon and egg, while Justin as usual had two eggs, two fat sausages, a rasher of bacon and a generous helping of fried potatoes from last night's leftover dinner. Just what the doctor ordered!' he declared, patting his stomach.

Seeing how he shovelled the food away, Lizzy and Jack exchanged amused glances. They each loved him as much as the other. And how could they not, when he was such a fine, homely sort of a man, with a wagon-load of love to share between them?

Viola had only a cup of tea. As always, she could not manage food first thing in the morning, just as she could never manage a smile nor a good word for anybody.

'Right then.' Bringing up a hearty burp and apologising for it in good humour, Justin took his empty plate back to the sink, where he announced, 'I'll mek meself scarce now. I've a thing or two to tend outside.'

'What things?' Jack was worried about being left there with Viola.

'Let's see . . .' Justin stroked his chin while he mentally went through all the unfinished tasks that had waited since last autumn, together with the more recent ones that couldn't wait another day. 'Well now, there's the spoke on the wagon needs fixing – it'll have to be done afore I can fetch the chopping wood from the spinney. After that, I need to replace that broken panel in the shed, and there's a slat outta the barn door that needs replacing. We can't have the mare and foal open to the winter cold, can we now, eh?'

'Huh!' From the table, Viola waved her teaspoon at him. 'You've spent that much time in that blessed barn these past weeks, I don't know why yer don't move in there!'

'That's not a bad idea.' Justin greeted her remark with a smile. 'This place is like the Antarctic when the wind blows from the east, but I don't reckon I've ever known either of them barns to be cold.'

Viola had to have the last word. 'Happen we should *all* move in there.' The crafty look she gave Jack told him he would not be invited.

Whistling a merry tune, Justin made his way to the back door where he donned his long-coat and boots.

'Don't whistle in the house,' his wife chided. 'I've told you before, it's bad luck.' He could whistle in the barn to his heart's content, she thought wickedly. If the roof caved in on him, it wouldn't matter one iota.

'That's an old wives' tale, so it is.'

'I mean it, husband. Don't do it.'

'Aw, well, I'd best be off then,' he said. 'The young 'uns are going back to bed for an hour or two. Why don't you do the same?' He winked aside to the children. 'Happen you'll get outta bed the right side next time, eh?'

'Cheeky devil!' Pouring herself another cup of tea, she stood by the stove, yawning. 'I might just do that for half an hour or so, if you don't mind?' In truth, she didn't give tuppence whether he minded or not.

Like the good man he was, Justin had no inkling of the way she felt towards him. Stepping forward, he planted a kiss on her forehead. 'You go on, m'dear,' he urged. 'Get yersel' back to bed.' He wagged a finger at the children. 'You two do the same, mind. It'll tek me about an hour to fix the wagon wheel and fetch the wood from the spinney. I'll mek enough noise to wake yer all, when I get back.' A moment later he was through the door and out.

'Are *you* going back to bed, Jack?' Tired to her bones, Lizzy had started yawning.

'Don't know.' Whenever Justin was out of sight he felt threatened.

Viola put away the breakfast things, talking as she went. 'It doesn't matter what Jack wants to do,' she told Lizzy. 'Yer father said you were to get off to bed, and that's what you'd best do.'

Coming near the child to take her plate, she gave her a hug. 'We don't want you losing your beauty sleep, do we?' Over Lizzy's shoulder she gave Jack a burning glance. The hatred she sent was like a physical presence in the air.

Lizzy was concerned about Jack. 'Aren't you tired?' she asked.

'A bit.' If he went to bed now, he knew he would find it hard to sleep.

With her daughter's help. Viola finished clearing away. 'Right. All done – let's get off to our beds. Your father will wake us when he gets back.' Opening the door she gestured towards the stairs. 'Come on then, young lady.'

Lizzy glanced at Jack as she went. 'I'll see you later, eh?'

Jack nodded. 'All right.'

When they were gone, Jack sat for a time, elbows on the table and his head bowed low. Whenever he was downhearted, he thought of how it had been, with Nancy and his father, and Mary, and a well of guilty sadness and regret began to rise in him. Then he thought of Lizzy, and of Justin, and his heart was uplifted.

Suddenly the door opened and there was Viola.

'You'd best get to your bed,' she said, closing the door as she came in. 'I don't want you down here on your own. You might make off with my china or summat. After all, I don't know you from Adam when it comes right down to it.'

'I'm no thief!'

'Oh? And how am I supposed to know that, eh?' She was close enough now for him to see the whites of her eyes. 'Happen you've stolen before! Happen you were put in that home because you were a bad 'un. Who can tell *what* you've been up to! See? It's no wonder I don't dare trust you.'

'I've never stolen anything.'

'Liar!' In a swift, unexpected move she had him by the throat. 'I'll tell you what you *won't* steal, and that's my daughter and this land. If that man out there was to pop his clogs tomorrow, I'd sell this place faster than you could turn about. Horses, cows, barns and all . . . gone! You, too. By! It would do my heart good to see you turned out on to the streets, because it's where your sort belong. On the streets . . . begging for a living. Lazy, idle thing that you are!'

Squeezing his throat so hard she could hear him choking only made her all the more cruel. 'You're on borrowed time, my lad! So don't get your feet too far under my table, 'cause I mean to be rid of you, first chance I get. I don't want you here, and I don't want you near my daughter. Because of *him*,' she glanced towards the window, 'I'm made to see you and my precious baby walking the fields, talking and laughing together.' She leaned closer, until he could feel the warmth of her breath. 'I've got my eye on you, don't worry.'

With a flourish she threw him aside. 'Just you think on what I've told you, and if one dark night you want to run off, I for one would not be sorry.'

With that, she went to the sink and made herself a hot drink as calm and quiet as you like, as if nothing had happened, while behind her she could hear Jack choking.

A moment later she was gone, and Jack was left rubbing his throat and gasping for breath. He had never felt hate as he felt it then; so strong he was shaking with suppressed violence.

Suddenly he was up and out of his chair and putting on his boots and coat. As quietly as he could, he opened the back door and tiptoed through it, closing it just as gently.

But not so gently that Lizzy didn't hear.

Getting out of bed, she went to the window and looked out, and there he was, a fast, strong figure running at speed across the yard and down towards the barn. 'He's going after daddy.' She began to panic. For a split second she had a mind to follow him; she even went to the chair where her clothes hung. Then she thought better of it and returned to the window. 'Mind how you go, Jack,' she whispered. 'I'll see you later, eh?'

Climbing back into bed, she closed her eyes and the last thing she saw in her mind before drifting into sleep, was Jack's laughing face; which she had come to know and love so well.

As Jack neared the barn, he saw the wagon just turning the corner of the lane. With a burst of energy he was away, criss-crossing the field and leaping the brook, to find the shortcut. As the old man was about to enter the main track, Jack was almost on him. 'Wait for me!' he shouted. Out of the shrubbery he leapt on to the wagon, hanging on at the back while Justin brought the conveyance to a halt.

'What the devil d'yer think you're doing?' the old chap spluttered. Helping Jack aboard, he scolded him like a father should. 'I thought I told you to get some sleep afore I got back?'

Jack said he was sorry to have disobeyed him, but, 'I'm not all that tired, and anyway, I wanted to come with you.'

Justin stared at him. In the morning light he thought Jack had been crying. 'Are yer all right, son?'

Feigning a bright smile, Jack answered, 'Course I am . . . now that I'm with you.' He was even more determined now, that however hard that woman tried to be rid of him, and however difficult she made his life here, he would not leave; not without Lizzy and this wonderful man.

'Here yer are then, son.' Handing Jack the reins, the old man leaned back in his rickety seat and yawned. 'You drive, while I sit here an' rest.'

Jack didn't need asking twice, though he was a mite nervous. 'I've only driven it twice before and that was just round the yard.'

'Aye, well, yer did all right, or I'd not be asking yer to take the reins now, would I?'

Encouraged by Justin's faith in him, Jack asked hopefully, 'So can I drive it all the way there and back?'

When he got no reply, he turned and what he saw brought a smile to his face. 'Well, I never!'

The old man had gone right off to sleep.

Another minute, and he was snoring loud enough to frighten the fearless.

Jack loved the spinney. In the early mornings it shone with dew and in late evening the stars lit the darkest corners. This morning, with the scatterings of snow on every tree-top, it was magical.

'Nowhere in the world like it, and it must never be spoiled.'

Justin woke, just as Jack drew the ensemble to a halt. 'For every tree I chop down, I plant another. That way the wood never dies.' His face wreathed with pleasure, he climbed down and stood a while, hands in pockets, his gaze roving the trees and undergrowth, soaking up every small detail. 'I played here as a lad,' he confided for the umpteenth time. 'I courted the girls here as a young man, and when my father passed on, I was made custodian.' His chest almost burst with pride. 'I've never cheated on these woods, never once!'

Coming to where Jack stood, he put an arm round his shoulder. 'Promise me you'll do the same, and I'll be a happy man to me grave.'

Jack looked up. 'What do you want me to promise?'

'That you'll always look after these woods, same as I have all these years. If anybody comes along offering you large amounts of money for 'em – as they will, 'cause they've already approached me many a time – I want you to promise me that you'll send 'em on their way.'

'Why would anybody offer money for a wood?'

'For the timber, lad. By! There's a fortune to be made out of it.'

'You mean they'd cut all the trees down?'

'Aye, every one. That's exactly what the buggers would do, if only they could get their hands on it! What's more, they'd neither think nor care to replant as they went. So the woods would die, and we don't want that now, do we, eh?' Taking Jack by the shoulders, he turned him round to face him. 'You still ain't made me that promise.'

Jack was unsure. 'But . . . how can I promise? They don't belong to me. They belong to *you*. And Lizzy.' Somehow the idea of Viola Lyndhurst wanting the woods never even entered his head.

'Lizzy will be looked after in other ways. Besides, the lass wouldn't know how to deal with all this, an' it wouldn't be fair placing such a burden on her shoulders. She'll likely be wed one day an' it could easily be to somebody who has no love for nature, or this kind of beauty. I might as well tell you now, son. When I'm no longer here, these woods will be yours. It'll be up to *you* to mek sure nobody harms 'em.'

Jack felt honoured. 'Do you really think *I'm* up to it?'

'Aye, lad. I've never doubted it.' With a gentle nudge he persisted, 'So, will yer mek me that promise, so we can get on with us work?'

Jack nodded. 'I promise,' he answered. 'I'll never let anybody harm them.' Frightened by the way Justin was talking, he made a condition. 'You'll need to stay with me though, so you can show me how to look after them.'

At that, Justin laughed out loud; he recognised the fear behind Jack's thinking, and respected it, 'You're a fella after me own heart, so yer are,' he said. 'To put yer mind at rest, I can tell yer I'm not planning to go anywhere just yet. Not for a very long time, God willing.'

His fear dispersed, Jack showed his relief in a boyish laugh. 'We'll be the guardians of the woods, won't we?'

'Aye, son, that we will.'

Side by side, content in each other's company, and armed with sapling trees, ropes and shovels, they set about their work.

First the old trees were brought down branch by branch, with Justin astonishing Jack by scaling the trees like an acrobat. 'I've been doing it so often it's like second nature to me,' the old chap explained. 'When you're a bit older and wiser, I'll show you how to do it.'

Jack learned a lot merely by watching. And when the two old trees were down, he was given a shovel. The two of them dug out the hole and filled it with bark mulch, and tenderly as can be, they set the saplings in place of the old ones.

'There!' With his back aching and his heart filled with wonder, Justin stretched himself to full height. 'See that, my son? Them saplings will grow tall and strong, much like yersel',' he promised. 'By the time you're a young man, you'll see their branches blossom and spread. They'll be part of the woods, an' you'll be part o' them.'

Jack was mesmerised; in the place where the saplings had been planted, the ghostly daylight found its way in and lit the spot with a softness that was almost reverent. Beside them lay the old trees, gnarled and spent, fit now only for firewood. 'It's so beautiful in here,' Jack told the old man, 'I won't let you down, I promise.'

Justin had no doubts whatsoever. 'I know you won't,' he said. 'I saw what kinda man you would be, the day I first set eyes on yer.' Emotion shook his voice. 'I followed my instincts and took you home, and I've never regretted it, not for one minute.'

Suddenly and much to Jack's astonishment, the old man was crying; soft, crippling sobs that bent his body and bowed his head.

'Don't cry. Please, don't cry.' Jack hung on to him, the tears rolling down his own face as he felt the emotion ripple through this giant of a man. Was it something he had done? Had he let him down in some way or another? Jack blamed himself. It had to be his fault, or why would Justin cry like that? To Jack's tormented mind, it was like a punishment for every bad thing he had ever done.

Soon enough, the minute was spent and the tears all gone. Shame-faced, Justin apologised.

'Sorry, lad,' he murmured. 'I know I've done this to you before. Only, you see, I've lived a long time and never had a son. Now I've got you, and now I know there'll come a day when I can safely hand Weatherfield Farm over to your capable hands, I can rest easy inside meself . . . if yer know what I mean?

Sometimes I can't believe my luck – that God has given me a wonderful son like you, when it was almost too late.'

Seeing this lovely man cry like a baby had been a sobering experience for Jack. In that very special, unforgettable moment, he had grown from boy to man. 'I'm glad,' he answered softly. 'And I'm proud that you think so much of me.'

As they went away to fetch the saws and bags in which to put the chopped wood, Justin had another question, 'Will yer mek me another promise, son?'

'What's that?'

Justin's mischievous old face lifted in an elfin grin, 'Don't dare tell anybody that I cried like a babby.'

Jack didn't hesitate. 'Course I won't.' There was one other thing though. 'So long as . . .'

Justin stopped in his tracks. 'So long as what?'

'So long as you let me drive the wagon back home.' He so much wanted Lizzy to see him arrive with the reins in his hands.

For a minute Justin was open-mouthed, then he began roaring with laughter. 'Why, yer little sod! Yer really had me worried there for a minute.'

The sound of their laughter rang through the woods.

Man and boy. Father and son.

Their unique relationship, strengthened tenfold.

Chapter Twelve

'It's good news, Mrs Marshall!' Putting down his pen, the doctor smiled up at Mary. 'At a calculated guess and going on the information you've given me, 'I'd say you were three months' pregnant, give or take a day or two.'

It was not the news Mary needed to hear. She wanted children, of course she did. But not now. Not like this. It was the wrong place; the wrong time. *The wrong man.*

'Thank you, Doctor.' Hiding her innermost feelings, she took his expert advice and made another appointment at the outer desk. 'August the fourth,' the receptionist said. 'In three weeks' time?'

'Yes, that's fine, thank you.' Mary left as quickly as she had arrived, but with a heavier heart and a multitude of doubts over the future.

Emerging from the drabness of the doctor's consulting rooms into a glorious summer's day, Mary thought it a shame to feel so sad on such a day as this, especially when there was a new life growing inside her.

Confirmation of her worst fears had left her feeling thirsty, so she made straight for the café on the promenade. 'Tea, please,' she told the girl, 'And one of those scones.' The pyramid of delicious-looking scones was covered by a large glass dome.

'That one under there.' She pointed to one at the bottom, one that helped to support all the others, but the girl didn't seem to mind.

'People always want the one underneath,' she said cheerfully. 'Even if I changed them all over, they'd still want one from the bottom.'

'Sorry.' Mary felt guilty, but that was the one she fancied.

The girl glanced down at Mary's open jacket. 'It's always the same,' she observed, 'in your condition.'

'What do you mean?'

'I mean being with child. It always makes you crave something or another. With you, I expect it's the scones.'

'How did you know I was with child?'

'I can always tell. It's the look in the eyes, or the glow in the face, I'm not sure.' She giggled. 'It could be the scones, though – you know, wanting the one that's underneath.'

Mary was both surprised and dismayed. 'I thought I wasn't showing yet.'

Sliding the scone out, the young woman dropped it on a plate with a pat of butter and a knife. She put this on a tray with a pot of tea, a small jug of milk, cup, saucer, strainer and spoon. 'You'll find sugar on the table,' she said.

'Thank you.' Taking out her purse Mary waited for the girl to add up the total, which she did in a laborious, comical manner, talking to herself all the while.

'That'll be sixpence halfpenny please.' She took the money, a sixpence and a threepenny bit, and gave the change of tuppence halfpenny, and when Mary was walking to her table, she turned to her colleague who was preparing sandwiches close by. 'I'll tell you summat,' she said. Mary could hear every word she said, although this was not intentional.

Curious, her colleague looked up. 'Oh, an' what's that?'

'That lady there . . .'

Licking the butter from her fingers, the other girl glanced at Mary. 'What about her?'

'She's with child.'

'So?'

'So! It's not her husband's, I'll bet you anything you like.'

'What on earth makes you say that?' The other girl snorted.

The first one shrugged. 'I just know it, that's all,' she said sagely.

'Hmh! Like you knew that man fancied me last week, 'cause he kept looking at me, eh? It weren't just *him* looking though, was it? And you never even told me. Oh no! You'd rather let me walk about mekking a fool o' meself!'

'Hey! Don't blame me for that. How was I to know you'd got your skirt tucked in your drawers? Next time, take more care when you go to the lavvy.'

'Yes, and I might be able to, if you didn't look at the clock every time I need to go. What kinda boss are you anyway? Five minutes for a wee and eight minutes for the other. How's a girl supposed to tidy herself up in a rush like that, eh?' Getting angrier by the minute, she dug her superior in the ribs. 'It would serve you right if I walked out here and now!'

'Huh! Go on then. See if I care.'

Taking her at her word and throwing down her butter knife, the girl reached under the counter to collect her jacket. 'I'll get better treated at the mill, and earn more money, too!'

Aware that she couldn't manage without her, the manageress barred her way. 'Don't be so hasty. How about if I offer you an extra tanner a week?'

'Not enough.'

'How much then?'

'A shilling?'

'Tenpence.'

'And a full ten minutes when I go to the lavvy?'

'That's daft! Eight'

'Nine. Or I'm off!'

'Oh, shut up. Get back to your work.'

'And?'

'Tenpence a week more and nine minutes for the lavvy. Satisfied?'

'For now.'

Mary had witnessed the whole exchange and it made her grin. She wished she had a friend like that – someone she could argue with, then make up with. Someone to whom she could pour out her heart. It was a sad state of affairs, to have no friend at all.

It was when she took a second bite of her scone that she thought of Emily. *There* was a friend, of sorts. She was kind and helpful, and since Mary had first arrived at Paul's guest-house, she had taken her under her wing. 'Emily!' Even saying the name gave poor Mary a measure of comfort. I'll go and see if she can advise me, she thought.

Taking the doctor's appointment card out of her bag, she looked at it. *Mrs Marshall*, it said. Feeling ashamed, she put it away. It was the first time she had lied like that. Unmarried and pregnant. How could she have allowed it to happen?

For a moment she stared out of the window, at all the people walking by. She wondered what their problems were. Everybody had them, but hers seemed to weigh especially heavy. She must talk to Emily. With that thought in mind she drank her tea, but left her scone half-finished.

'Bye then.' The girl watched her leave. 'I'm telling you,' she said as Mary moved on up the street, 'it's *not* her husband's baby.'

'I don't care if it's the *pawnbroker's* baby! We've another customer, look. So stop your chatting and get on with it.'

'Don't tell *me* what to do!'

'Why not? You're always telling *me* what to do.'

The argument went on, long after Mary was out of sight.

Emily lived in one of the terraced houses alongside the market-place. Having been there before when she had carried heavy shopping home for the dear lady, Mary was familiar with the house, and so she had no trouble finding it.

Fronted by a white door which was flanked either side by flower pots with pink geraniums now in full bloom, it was a pretty little place; small enough to keep tidy, yet big enough for one.

Mary walked up the path and after hesitating a moment, she knocked on the door.

From inside she could hear someone padding along the passage, then the door opened and Emily stood there, happy to see her. 'Mary, lass. Come in.' Stepping aside she invited her again: 'Come on in.'

Mary followed her along the narrow passage and into the parlour, a tiny room with well-polished furniture – sparse but accommodating. At the window were bright-flowered curtains and in front of the hearth a colourful peg-rug, made by the woman's own hand. In the hearth stood a jug of flowers from the back garden, and the windows were flung open to let the sun shine in. All in all, it was a pleasant little room, with that certain homely atmosphere which Emily carried with her wherever she went.

'What brings you here?' she asked now. 'It's not Aunt Agatha, is it?' Her eyes widened with concern. 'She's not been taken ill, has she? I saw how peaky she looked this morning, after she tackled Paul about his new ideas on expansion. I told her – "it's none of your business," I said, "but you will insist on getting yourself all worked up about something and nothing". But will she listen? Will she heck as like!'

'No, it's not Agatha. She's the same as usual – or she was when I went out earlier on.' Mary didn't feel happy about worrying the woman, but she had to talk to somebody or go out of her mind. 'It's *me*,' she said quietly. 'I need to talk.'

Misreading the signs, Emily thought she had seen this coming. 'Look now, you sit yerself down.' She glanced towards the window. 'Or, if you like, we can go and sit in the garden.'

'Yes, I'd like that.' Mary loved to be outside when the sun was shining.

'Good!' A smile enveloped Emily's kindly features. 'I were working out there just now, weeding and such. It's so pretty at this time of year.'

Mary nodded. 'I know what you mean. Paul has made a real feature of the garden at the hotel. The guests love it. And so do I – when I get the time, that is.'

'Aye, you do work hard, and I don't envy you that.' She rubbed her hands together. 'Right then, I'll get the refreshments. You sit in the garden, lass. I'll not be long. Then we can talk to our hearts' content.'

Emily was right; her garden *was* pretty. Mary sat at the white, wrought-iron table, under an old floral parasol. The table was set out on a square of slabs, and from there the path ran centrally through the long, spacious garden. On either side there were flowers and shrubs of every colour and shape imaginable; tall slender lupins in dazzling shades, a deep crimson hydrangea, and various other shrubs and flowers which Mary didn't even recognise. And all of it lovingly tended.

'You keep your garden really nice,' she remarked as Emily arrived with cold drinks from the pantry and homemade biscuits.

'It's my pride and joy,' the woman declared. 'But we're not here to talk about my garden.' Drawing up a chair she poured a glass of sarsaparilla for Mary and another for herself. 'Now then, love.' She offered the plate of biscuits, but it was graciously refused.

'I had a scone in that café near the doctor's surgery,' Mary told her.

'Doctor's? Are you ill, lass?'

Mary shook her head. 'Not ill, no.'

'So what's troubling you?' Slapping a hand over her mouth, Emily stared at Mary with wide open eyes. 'It's that bugger Agatha, isn't it? I knew she'd get to you sooner or later, the old besom! But look, you mustn't worry too much about her. She's just a cantankerous old devil who doesn't know when to mind her own business!'

Mary took a sip of the sarsaparilla. 'It's nothing to do with Agatha,' she confided. She hardly knew how to begin.

'So, what *is* it to do with?' Emily was trying to be helpful.

'It's to do with me and Paul.'

Emily began to understand, yet dared not voice her suspicion in case she was wrong. Instead she gently urged, 'Whatever you tell me will go no further, I hope you know that?'

Prolonging the moment, Mary took another sip of her drink, after which, in one outflowing breath, she told her the truth. 'I'm having his child.'

'Oh my dear!' The older woman was visibly shocked. A child out of wedlock was a serious matter – though seeing Mary's anxiety, she was determined to hide her own feelings on the matter. 'Does Paul know?'

Mary shook her head. 'I only had it confirmed myself today.'

'You *are* going to tell him, aren't you?'

'I haven't decided what to do yet.'

'But you *must* let him know!' Emily believed in openness and honesty. Anything else brought nothing but trouble. 'It is his child, isn't it?'

'Oh Emily, who else's would it be?' She was surprised that

the other woman should even ask such a question.

'Of course. It was a stupid question, forgive me.' She didn't even know why she had said it. 'But if it's *his* child, why would you not tell him?' she persisted.

Mary had asked herself that same question over and over again, and still she wasn't sure in her own mind. 'It's difficult to explain,' she answered. 'I don't know if I *want* him to find out. I don't know what kind of answers I could give him.'

'You do love him, don't you?'

'I love him, yes, but not in the way he thinks.' She took a moment to voice her innermost thoughts. 'I made a mistake. I should never have let him believe I felt the same way as him.'

Having grown fond of Mary, Emily so much wanted to help. 'Summat's troubling you. Happen you should get it off your chest, lass. You know you can trust me.'

Mary knew that was the truth, and so she followed her instincts and told the other woman everything, from start to finish. She told her the reason why she had come to Lytham St Annes. 'It could have been anywhere,' she said sombrely. 'It didn't matter to me, not then. I was desperate. I needed to get away.'

'Away from what – from whom?'

'From Robert, the only man I've ever truly loved.' There, she'd said it. And the pain of her loss was for a moment excruciating.

'So why did you leave him?' Like Agatha, Emily had always wondered what kind of circumstance had brought Mary to seek accommodation at the hotel, without money or baggage. 'Was he bad to you – is that it?'

'Oh, no.' Mary's thoughts took her back to Robert, a good, kind man; a man whom she had let down badly. 'We could have been so happy,' she murmured sadly.

'But I don't understand, lass. If he was a good man and you loved him, what made you leave?'

'His son, that's who made me leave.' She went on to tell Emily about Robert, and Jack, and little Nancy, and how she was driven out by the boy, who was determined to be rid of her any way he could. 'He hated me too much.' She remembered how it was, but seeing it all from a distance now, she wondered if she could have been kinder to him, talked with him more, but then she *had* tried so hard and yet nothing had changed. If anything, the situation had only got worse.

'He wouldn't let me get close to him. You see, his mother had left them all – for greener pastures, Robert said. The boy seemed to blame me, even though she'd been gone for some time before I came along.'

'But he was just a child. Why did you let him drive you away?'

'For Robert's sake and little Nancy's, I stayed as long as I could bear it.' The memories flooded back. 'It got so bad I knew it was only a matter of time before he turned his father against me, and I loved Robert too much to let that happen.' She began to shiver; even with the warmth of the sun on her arms, she felt the cold rush of regret. 'He was wicked, Emily . . . *wicked*!'

'In what way?'

'In every way imaginable. He told tales – terrible lies about me smacking him, when I never once laid a hand on him. I wouldn't do that. At first Robert didn't believe him, but then he began hurting himself. He even threw himself down the cellar steps once, and lay there screaming until we came running. He told Robert I'd pushed him. From that minute on, I could see the doubt in Robert's eyes. He *said* he didn't believe the boy, but somehow he changed, enough for me to think he might have an inkling of suspicion that Jack was telling the truth.'

'And did you tackle this Jack about it?'

'He didn't seem to realise what he was doing. There were times when he began to believe that *I* was the villain, and not him. He and Nancy had piggy-banks. Robert would put tuppence a week into each one. After a time, there was a tidy little sum for each of them, but the boy played a terrible trick on me. He emptied his pig into my purse, then caused a stir, saying somebody had taken his money. I had my suspicions, and found the money in my purse, which I returned straightaway.'

Mary hated recalling these disturbing memories. She shuddered.

'I told Robert I'd had nothing to do with it, and the matter blew over. But there was a shadow over our relationship. Every time he looked at me, I could feel his doubt.'

Emily was shocked. 'It sounds to me like the boy was deranged.'

'Yes, I think he was. Deranged with grief because his mother had left him and his sister. They were such babies, Emily. It was a sad situation. I tried so hard to make up for the loss of their real mother, but the boy resented me from the start. Bit by bit, he came between me and Robert. He was a clever child, ingenious, Robert never knew the half of it – like the time Jack watched me put the washing out on the line, then the minute my back was turned he pulled the lot down and dragged it through the mud.'

'He really tried you to the limit, didn't he?'

'There were so many little, irritating things, too. Many a time I'd put something away, and it would be gone when I went for it the next time. He did aggravating things to get under my skin. After a time it was all too unnerving. As much as I loved Robert, I began to wonder if I loved him enough to put up with it all. Years of endurance lay ahead of me. I tried talking to him, telling him how the boy was ill, that he needed help, I said if it went on, I'd have to leave, but he begged me to stay.'

'Did he speak to the boy?'

'Yes, and for a time things would improve, but then they started up again. Flowers I'd only just set in the garden were pulled up out of the ground to die; rubbish from the midden was poured all over the steps. It was awful. I didn't blame Jack; I blamed his mother. By all accounts she was a selfish, greedy woman who wanted more out of life than Robert could give her. But it was the children who suffered.'

'What about the girl?'

Mary smiled. 'Nancy was a sweet, quiet little thing, confused by it all and probably hurting just as much as Jack.'

'How was the boy towards his sister?'

Mary could never forget that wonderful relationship. 'Absolutely devoted! He loved her so much – idolised her, and she looked up to him – wouldn't go anywhere without him. He was so protective and loving towards her. I think deep down he was trying to make up to her for having lost her mummy.'

'So there was some good in the boy then?'

'I'm sure there was a lot of good, Emily. Like I say, I don't blame Jack. He was hitting out the only way he knew how. He was a victim, just like me.'

When the memories became too much, Mary's deeper emotions escaped in the soft, bitter tears that whispered down her face. 'In the end I was no better than his mother . . . The last straw came when he told Robert he'd seen me with a man in the barn, kissing. I told Robert he was lying, but there was an almighty row.'

Discreetly wiping away the tears, she went on, 'In the end, I think I persuaded him that Jack was trying to make trouble between us, but it was too late. Something had changed between us for ever. After that, I knew I had no option but to leave.'

Emily's heart went out to her. 'You still love him, don't you?'

'I always will,' she confessed. 'That's why I feel so guilty about Paul. I could never love him, not in the way I love Robert. But I let him sweep me along, because I do have feelings for him. Still, I should have told him the truth, and I didn't. Now, I'm carrying his child, and I don't know what to do. The last thing I want is to hurt him.'

Emily churned the matter over in her mind. 'It seems to me you have three choices; *don't* tell Paul you're carrying his child. Go back to Robert, tell him the truth and hope he still loves you enough to take on another man's child. Or, go off on your own and try to make a life for yourself – although it won't be easy, I can tell you. There are no easy ways for a woman with a child on her own.'

'And the third option?'

'Forget about Robert if you can. Let Paul believe you love him – you've already said you have feelings for him, and I for one know what a lovely couple you make. Build a life with him and your child, and one day – who knows? You might find you *do* love him enough after all.'

'But wouldn't taking that option be unfair on Paul?'

'I don't think so. I can see you care enough to make him happy. And once the baby comes, I believe you'll be content enough with your life.' She wanted Mary to do the right thing, but she also wanted her to be happy. 'Remember, love, you can't change what happened in the past, and too often it's the past that writes the future. Happen your future is here in Lytham at Bluebell House, with Paul and the baby.'

She clambered out of the chair. 'So there it is, lass. As I see it, there's only you as can decide, and while you're doing that, I'll make us a brew.' That said, she was away into the scullery, leaving Mary to think on it.

That same evening, Paul took Mary out to dinner; the fish restaurant was a regular haunt of theirs. Overlooking the sea, with a wide terrace and soft-lit lamps, it was a romantic place, where they could hide away from Agatha's prying eyes and be by themselves. Mary had been greatly relieved when Paul said he was taking her out; here in this quiet, intimate place, it would be so much easier to tell him what he had to know.

The meal was always a gastronomic delight; the baked fish was fresh as the morning and the vegetables melted in the mouth. As always, they both enjoyed what was put in front of them, especially the apple pie and custard, which was one of Mary's favourites.

When the meal was over, they talked of this and that, and Paul told her how much he loved her.

'I have to tell you something,' Mary started, but he closed her lips with the tip of his finger.

'Not yet,' he said, smiling into her eyes. 'I just want to look at you for a while.'

Bathed in the lamplight's glow, Mary was flattered when he commented on how beautiful she looked. 'Radiant!' was what he said. He kissed her on the mouth, not caring who saw them.

With a flourish, he beckoned the waiter and ordered a bottle of best wine. 'I've got a surprise for you,' he revealed. 'I've been itching to tell you all day, but Aunt Agatha seemed to be everywhere, and I so much want you to know before anyone else.'

Mary was intrigued; she was also very nervous, because after seeing Emily that morning she had been agonising over what to do for the best. Now, having decided, she needed to tell Paul as soon as possible, before she changed her mind. And now here *he* was, with news of his own, and she would have to wait that much longer before confiding in him.

When the wine came, he chinked glasses with hers, and gave her the news. 'I've bought the Old Palace Hotel.' The smile on his face was wonderful to see.

Mary was thrilled for him, and said so with a kiss.

'I can't believe I got it! There must have been at least six people interested, and *I* got it!'

Mary congratulated him. 'I didn't even know you were after it.'

'Ah! That's because I wanted it to be a surprise if I got it, and if I didn't it wouldn't be a disappointment, because you would never know.'

She laughed. 'I had an idea you were up to something, but that place is derelict, isn't it?'

'At the minute, yes. But it stands on at least two acres of ground, *and* it overlooks the promenade.' His excitement was infectious. 'Don't you see, Mary? The potential is enormous.'

'I thought the builders told you it would take a small fortune to renovate?'

'Well, yes, they did. But it's all right. I've got it all worked out. We can go through that later. The main thing is, it's ours now . . . yours and mine. Our first venture together.' He took both her hands into his, his loving gaze enveloping her. 'I got it for you, my darling.'

Mary was cautious. 'I hope you didn't,' she said. 'I hope you bought it because it was a good investment?'

'That as well, of course. It *is* a good investment, or I would never have gone into it. But it was you who gave me the confidence to go for it. If I didn't have you behind me, I would never have dared take such a huge gamble.' Lifting her hand to his mouth he kissed it lightly, his gaze never leaving her face. 'I don't think you realise how you've changed my life. You make me want to climb mountains, swim rivers, build empires!' He laughed out loud. 'Oh, Mary Honeywell, I do love you so!'

Filling her glass again, she raised it to him. 'Here's to your success,' she said, and meant it from the bottom of her heart. Paul deserved it. He worked from morning till night and asked for little in return. This was his dream, and she was glad for him.

After they drank to that, he put down his glass and reminded her, 'Sorry, my love, I got so carried away, I almost forgot you had something to tell me?'

In that moment, with Paul waiting for her to speak, Mary realised there was only one option open to her. How could she leave him now, when he had taken such a huge gamble on her account? 'It's nothing,' she said. 'It can wait.'

Paul insisted. 'No, you must tell me or I'll be for ever wondering what it was you had to say.' He leaned forward across the table. 'It's not so terrible, is it?'

Mary smiled, '*I* don't think it's terrible.'

'So, tell me.'

Nervously watching for his reaction she told him, 'I went to the doctor this morning, and he confirmed what I'd suspected all along. I'm three months' pregnant.'

At the news he fell back in his chair, open-mouthed, eyes like saucers. 'Oh, my God,' he whispered. 'Oh, my God! I'm about to become a daddy, is that what you're saying?' Mary nodded and he was on his feet, shouting for the waiter. 'Champagne!' he cried. 'Champagne for everyone! I'm about to become a father!'

Much to Mary's embarrassment and delight, everyone there called out their congratulations. Paul laughed and cried and took her in his arms, and told her how she had made his life perfect; in a voice inaudible to the others, he told her, 'We'll get wed as soon as it can be arranged. Tomorrow, next week – it can't be soon enough for me. Oh, Mary! What news! What wonderful, wonderful news!'

Mary went along with his madness; she saw the tears of joy in his eyes and all her misgivings went out of the window.

Later, as they walked home arm-in-arm, Paul seemed disturbed by her quiet mood. 'What's wrong, my love?'

Calmer now, Mary looked up at him. 'What could be wrong?' Not knowing how to answer, she turned the question back to him.

Drawing her to a halt, he held her by the shoulders, his anxious gaze raking her face. 'You're not sorry – about the child, I mean?'

'Never!' Already she was impatient to hold her baby in her arms.

'And you *do* want to marry me, don't you?'

Mary wished she was brave enough to tell him he was getting the raw end of the deal; that she could never love him as she ought to, because she was still in love with another man. But now, seeing him so happy and filled with plans for their life together, she felt it would be too cruel to dash all his hopes.

Besides, how could she bring herself to go back to Robert and ask him to take on another man's child? It was too much! And, as Emily had said, a woman on her own with a child in tow would find it hard to make ends meet – although that had never really been an option, because Paul would never let her take the baby, and who could blame him? He was the child's father. He had a right to raise it and love it, and map out its future. And it was *her* child, too. She had a duty as a mother.

After all, she had seen from first hand what it had done to young Jack, when his mother deserted him.

Paul's desperate voice shook her out of her reverie. 'Mary? What's wrong?'

Turning to him she painted on her brightest smile. 'Nothing's wrong,' she answered tenderly. 'And why would I not want to marry you, eh?' Reaching up, she slid her arms round his neck. 'Besides, how can I let you down now?' she asked mischievously. 'After you've gone and bought me a hotel?'

He laughed at that, then he kissed her hard on the mouth and, sliding his arm about her, walked her home to tell Aunt Agatha the news. 'I hope she doesn't get it into her silly head that she can be Maid of Honour!' he joked.

Mary loved his sense of humour. It was one of the things that had attracted her to him in the first place. 'Oh, I think they'd make a lovely pair at the wedding . . . dressed in silk and lace, with pretty bows in their hair. Red and yellow flowers, I think, and cream satin shoes.'

'Whatever are you talking about?'

'Agatha and Emily, of course. I'd like them as bridesmaids, if that's all right with you. I think they'd look wonderful.' It was hard for her to keep a straight face.

'Er, I don't think so,' he laughed. And opening the door, bundled her inside.

The following morning, after Emily had arrived and was about to get breakfast, they thought it a good time while they were all together, to announce all three items of news.

Firstly, Paul told them he had bought the Old Palace Hotel. This was greeted with a cry of horror from his aunt. 'You fool! It's dead money. Any decent businessman wouldn't touch it with a barge pole!'

Undaunted, Paul told her there was nothing for her to concern herself about, that he had only informed her out of courtesy anyway, and that it was his money and not hers that he was gambling with. At that, the old lady sat back in her chair, bottom lip hanging to the ground, and her eyes fixed in a downwards, sulky stare.

The second piece of news was greeted with shocked silence from Agatha, and sincere congratulations from Emily. 'I hoped as you'd end up getting wed,' she said with a sly little wink at Mary. 'I'm thrilled to bits for the pair of youse.'

At the third piece of news, Agatha almost had a fainting fit. '*Pregnant!*' Scrambling out of her chair she stared at Mary with disgust. 'You should be ashamed of yourself! Unmarried and with child . . . how could you?'

Paul intervened. 'If you don't mind me saying, I think *I'm* partly to blame there, Aunt Agatha. I can't ever recall a time when a woman got with child all by herself.'

Infuriated, Agatha shook her fist at them both. 'You'll rue the day . . . you see if I'm not right!' With that she marched off to her room, muttering and cursing, and bringing a rueful smile to the others.

'She'll get used to it,' Emily promised. 'I'll talk to her when she's calmer.'

From the top of the stairs came Agatha's voice, raised to the roof. 'You'll do no such thing! In fact, you can get yourself off home, because I've no need of you any more. The pair of them bring shame on the house of Marshall, and here's you, congratulating them. It's a damned disgrace, that's what it is! Go on. Be off with you. You're sacked!'

Emily merely sighed and smiled. She was long used to the old woman's tantrums. 'Like I say, I'll wait till she's calmer, then I'll have a quiet word.'

'You do that,' Paul agreed sombrely. 'And while you're at it, tell her she'll have to accept things the way they are, or she'll have to look for other accommodation. I've put up with her moods and taken them all in my stride for long enough. But this is different. I won't let her come between us – not now, not ever.'

Taking Mary in his arms, he gazed down on her with the look of a man deeply in love. 'The truth is, I've never been happier than I am right now.'

Five weeks later, Mary and Paul were married in the little church not far from the hotel he had recently acquired. It was a delightful place, with beautiful stained-glass windows depicting the steps of the crucifix, and over the altar a cross the size of Jesus, arms outstretched as if giving His blessing.

Over the past few months, Mary had spent many an hour in this church, talking to God, asking His advice, praying for guidance. And now it seemed she had her answers, because here she was, marrying Paul, and bearing his child. And still the doubts weighed heavy on her heart.

Throughout the service, Paul could not take his eyes off her. Dressed in a cream linen two-piece with fitted jacket and long skirt to the ankles, a simple short veil over her eyes, and carrying red roses, she made a stunning sight. 'You look lovely,' he told her time and again, and she smiled back, wondering how she had got herself into such a tight corner, and knowing that today was the day when she really had to say goodbye to any chance of reuniting with Robert.

She told herself there was nothing she could do about it now. It was all too late. All she could hope for was a good life with Paul and their child. In her heart she knew it would not be the joyous, contented life she might have chosen for herself and Robert, though the love for him would always be there. However much she might want to, for Paul's sake, she could never change that. Her love for Robert would remain as strong as ever, she had no doubts about that.

That was the secret she must keep from Paul. A secret she could never share.

It was a good service. There were numerous people there – guests from the hotel, a neighbour or so, and of course Emily, who smiled on Mary the whole way through the service. Mostly though, they were business friends of Paul's, with their wives and sweethearts, all done up in their Sunday best, with pretty hats and frills, happily chattering among themselves as they gathered for the photographer and were told to 'watch the birdie!'.

Bullied by Emily, Agatha had reluctantly allowed herself to be marched to the church; grumpy and sour as ever, issuing hostile glares at Mary as she walked down the aisle towards the door. 'They're wed now,' Emily told the old lady. 'So you might as well get used to it.'

'I'll *never* get used to it,' the old woman hissed. 'I'm only here because I don't want her to get the better of me.'

'If you can't get used to the idea of Paul and Mary being wed, then you'd best do what he says and look for another place to live.'

'Don't be silly. He didn't mean that. It was said in the heat of the moment, that's all.'

Emily gave her a meaningful nudge. 'Ah, but you can't be sure, can you?'

Emily was right. Ever since that terrible night, Agatha had wondered whether she'd pushed her nephew too far. She realised she had gone about it all wrong. She had to keep in good relations with Paul and set about getting rid of his wife at the first opportunity. 'I honestly don't believe Paul would turn me out,' she replied in a whisper, 'but I'm not giving him the chance. Besides, I would be failing in my duty if I left him to the grasping wiles of that one.' Raising a thumb she gestured to where Mary and Paul were leaving the church arm-in-arm. 'She's after his money, that's why she cornered him into getting her with child. But she's not so clever that she'll not make a slip at some time or another, I've got my eye on her. She'll not get away with anything where *I'm* concerned!'

Emily took it all with a pinch of salt. 'Put your best smile on,' she suggested. 'You can't be throwing confetti with a face like thunder.'

Once outside, Agatha did her best to smile as she pretended to throw the handful of rice given her by Emily.

All of the guests laughed and cheered and wished the happy couple well as they showered them with paper-confetti and brown rice; though, standing some distance away, the old caretaker groaned as he realised it was himself and his little helpers who would have to scrape it off the ground afterwards.

At the follow-up celebration in a nearby inn, Paul got waylaid by some of his colleagues from the catering trade. While they discussed his latest acquisition in the hotel stakes, Mary took the opportunity to go out into the garden, where she sat by the pond, lost in thought, praying that she had done the right thing, yet already suffering regrets.

'Ah, sure you'll be fine together, you and Paul and the baby.' Having come up softly, Emily sat herself down beside her, 'Give yourself time to adjust, love. I have a feeling it'll all come right in the end.'

'I hope so,' Mary said in a low voice. She herself was not so sure. 'Because if it doesn't, I will have made the biggest mistake of my life.'

That night, in the hotel suite they'd booked for a week, Mary lay in Paul's arms as his wife for the first time. But as it was not the first time they had made love, it wasn't a new experience, nor was it for Mary an exciting experience. They had only ever made love once before, and that was after Paul had found Mary sad and alone in the kitchen, when she'd woken in the early hours and couldn't sleep.

That was a gentle lovemaking, a kind of comfort-giving. From that togetherness the child was conceived, and Mary was caught in the trap.

On this their wedding night, it was a different kind of lovemaking, because now they were man and wife. Paul had a right; Mary had a duty.

As he tenderly laid her beneath him, she succumbed because it was the right thing to do, but her heart and soul were not in it.

'Are you happy?' he whispered, and she told him yes, she was. She felt his flesh against hers, and she felt his kiss on her mouth, but it did not move her, nor did it excite. After a while, when he had roved his hands over every precious inch of her body, he drew open her legs and entered her with a cry of anguish and, just for one brief moment, her own senses were stirred, but only because she was a woman, hungry for love.

Now, as he thrust into her time and again, she closed her eyes and thought of Robert.

Almost without her realising, the tears crept up on her. When they trickled down her face to wet the pillow, Paul didn't notice. Head high and arms outstretched, he rolled away, gasping, satisfied.

Until the next time.

Chapter Thirteen

After several years of being only half a man, Robert could hardly believe what the doctor was telling him. 'We're very pleased with you, and because you've done so well, we've decided it's time to get you out of that wheelchair and on to your own two feet. We've devised a programme to get you started and I've no doubt, given your background,' raising his eyebrows he gave a wry little smile, 'and sheer stubbornness, that you'll be walking unaided before too long.'

The wonderful news took Robert's breath away. Having been brought here for what he believed to be a routine check-up, he had expected to be looked over, given his week's exercise programme and sent back to the rehabilitation unit of the Infirmary, where he had been a resident for some many months now.

Instead he had just been given the best news of his life. 'Oh my God!' Catching his breath in a sob, he fell forward, his outspread hands over his face to hide the emotion. 'You can't imagine what this means to me,' he muttered. 'How can I ever thank you?' Looking up now, his green eyes moist with unshed tears, he asked, 'When do we start?'

The doctor ventured a stern warning. 'I know how impatient you are, and I know how hard you've pushed yourself, but I don't want you spoiling it now, at this late stage.'

Dr Morrison had been in medicine for more years than he cared to remember; he had seen all kinds of accident and emergency cases, and many was the time he despaired at the frailty of mankind, but Robert Sullivan was a different story altogether.

Robert was anxious. 'How long will it be before I'm walking, doc? I have things to do . . . a family to find.' His words tumbled one over the other in his haste.

The doctor understood. 'I know about your family, Robert,' he had been told in confidence of Robert's search for his children, 'and I want you to gather them round you almost as much as you do yourself – but I *must* stress the need for caution.'

He paused, hoping his warning had sunk in. 'Let me tell you something,' he went on. 'As God is my judge, I don't know how you've managed to get this far. From a twisted, shattered thing with no expectation of life longer than a day or two, you've emerged strong and wilful. All right, it's taken a damned long time, but in *all* of that time, you've never wavered once in tackling what you knew had to be done, in order for you to get well again.'

Getting out of his chair he walked over to Robert and, sitting on the edge of the desk before his wheelchair, he shook his head in disbelief. 'In all my experience, I've never seen a man suffer so much pain and injury, and come out of it the way you have. It's taken *years* of hard work on our part, and pure grit and determination on your part, to get you where you are now. Just look at the way it was . . . the coma, then the fits – and after that not knowing where to start because there was so much to be done, and you still in a dangerously weak state. I tell you, man, we nearly had to give up on you.'

Robert remembered. 'But you didn't, did you?' he said emotionally.

'No, but it could have all gone wrong. We performed God only knows how many operations – fractured skull, arms and legs broken, with hardly an inch of clean bone anywhere. Almost every organ in your body bruised and near shredded. Your brain so shaken the fits nearly took you from us on their own! Good God, man. You've been rebuilt from top to bottom. Is there anything we haven't repaired, replaced or simply thrown away?'

Robert was amazed. 'You've never told me all that before.'

'That's because you were never ready for it. But now, well . . . you've done wonders. In short, Robert, you are an amazing man, for whom my staff and myself have nothing but admiration. Please don't risk all that good work now, by being too impatient.'

'Don't worry, Doctor. I haven't got this far to throw it all away,' Robert promised. 'But I still need to know . . . when do I start? How long will it take?'

Returning to his desk, Dr Morrison also returned to his formal manner. 'It will start when I give the go-ahead,' he replied. 'As for how long it will take, I have no idea. Weeks, months . . . a year. It's not an easy thing, Robert. First we have to get the muscles in your legs strong enough to carry you. Then there are other things to be considered – co-ordination, for instance, that will take time and patience. The heart will need to work harder than it has already. Then the depression will set in; there will be days when you feel as if you're going backwards rather than forwards, and there'll be other days when you want to scream with frustration. But, in the end, one way or another, however long it takes, you *will* walk out of the hospital on your own two feet. Then, God willing, we'll be rid of you at long last, and you'll be on your own.' He made the last remark with a grin on his whiskered face.

It was the last statement that shook Robert to his roots. 'On your own'. It was a frightening prospect when for years now, he had lived in institutions. All this time he'd had no life of his own. But that would all change soon, because he was ready now. Ready and raring to go.

* * *

That evening, he waited excitedly for Geordie's regular visit, so he could tell him the news.

'Waiting for someone, are you?' The nurse was new on the ward.

'I'm waiting for Geordie,' Robert replied. 'He's my friend.' The very best, he thought proudly.

The evening meal was served and though he was hungry, Robert could not eat. His stomach was churning with excitement, and all he could do was watch the clock, hoping Geordie might be early tonight.

The minute hand seemed to fly round, then an hour had passed and still Geordie hadn't arrived. 'He'd best be here soon,' the nurse told him, 'or he'll miss visiting time.'

Robert watched the door, then the clock, and again the door, his eyes constantly shifting from one to the other, with no thought other than if he left it much later, Geordie would not be allowed in, and his precious news would have to wait until tomorrow.

Because he had more pressing things on his mind at that minute, Geordie himself had lost all sense of time. 'I'll take the money *now,* dammit!' he cursed.

'Don't yer think it might be more sensible if we waited, at least until the cops stop looking for whoever robbed that poor man?' Marlon's remark was laced with sarcasm.

'I said *I'll take my share now*! I have need of it. I've lost my job as well you know, or I would never have got tangled up with you again. In fact, after this, you needn't count on me. I'll get meself another job. I'm not finished yet, not by a long chalk. I'm not like you, y'see. I don't mind working for a living.'

Geordie turned to the other young man who had done the robbery with them, but since then had said very little. Right now he was standing in the shadows, listening, but not taking part.

Geordie wanted him to know what danger he could be in. 'If I were you, I'd get out of it while you can,' he advised. 'Stealing wages from a carrier, and other bad stuff . . . it's a mug's game. As for this fella here,' he pointed to Marlon, his old-time partner, 'he's about as bad as you can get.'

The young man gave a low, wicked laugh. 'Is that right?'

'Did he tell you he almost killed a man by pushing him under the wheels of a horse and carriage? The poor bastard was pulled halfway along the street by the horses' hooves – torn to shreds like a piece of meat between a pack o' dogs. It's only by God's hand that he survived. As it is, he's already spent years in hospital and lost his family into the bargain.'

'What's that to me?' The young man came out of the shadows – a bright-haired ruffian by the name of Gerry Reynolds, one-time orphan at Galloways Children's Home, bully, and now a crook, up to all manner of mischief. 'You can't tell *me* anything about bad stuff, matey! So your bloke spent years in hospital, did he? He should try spending time in an institution like I had to. I spent half my life in an orphanage, and I know all about bad stuff. So don't preach to me, you cowardly bugger!'

At this, Geordie leapt at him, but was soon dragged off by Marlon. 'Now then, Geordie, keep yer flamin' hair on. We don't want no trouble. Gerry 'ere is straight outta prison, an' he don't want to go back just yet.' Turning to the other he gave a conniving wink. 'Ain't that right, Gerry my son?'

Gerry was still bristling, aching to get a punch in, but seeing as how he was being given the word, he backed down, though he still had something to say. 'If he wants to go, let him clear off. We can do without him! Me an' Marlon'll do all right,' he told Geordie fiercely. 'In fact, we did a lot better before he invited *you* in with us.'

Loosening himself from Marlon's grip, Geordie gave a second warning. 'I'll say it once more. Think hard before you go along with him, son. This one here is a murderous devil when he sets his mind to it.'

'Is that so?' Arrogant as ever, Gerry Reynolds had never learned to take advice.

'Take my word for it. He might be friendly with you today, but tomorrow he'll have yer heart out soon as look at yer. I've already told yer what he did to that man – and all because his own missus had left him an' he were jealous o' that poor sod's family.'

'Oy, shut it!' Marlon was none too pleased at having his past thrown up in his face, especially in front of this new recruit, who should know only as much as Marlon himself allowed. 'And what about *you*, Geordie boy?' he sneered. 'Turned coward didn't yer, eh? Went running at the first sign o' trouble!'

'I didn't run far enough though, did I?' He began to realise what a fool he'd been, for getting drawn into it all again.

Needing to establish his superiority, Marlon went on, 'Yer might as well know, I would never have let you back in if it hadn't been for the fact that Gerry here needed back-up while I did the job. The laugh is, I could 'ave done the job all by meself if I'd known. The bloke with the money-bag was a pushover. One smack on the head and he went down like a poled ox.'

'Look, I don't want all the details.' Geordie didn't like the look of Marlon's new partner in crime, nor did he like the way things were going. 'Just give me my due,' he held out his hand in anticipation, 'an' I'll be out of yer hair for good an' all.'

Silently fuming, Marlon peeled off a bundle of notes. 'There's your share,' he told Geordie. 'Now clear off, before I have to deal with you altogether.'

Without another word, Geordie was gone, out of the old warehouse and into the alley beyond. He didn't stop to look round, nor did he close the door behind him. All he wanted was to get away from there, and get to the Infirmary in time to see Robert.

As he hurried up the alley, he murmured, 'It's all right, Robert, me old son. I've got the money now to keep us going for a while yet. It won't be long before I get another job an' a place of my own. When you get out o' there, you'll need somewhere to stay, won't yer, eh?' He had come to love Robert like a brother. These days, everything he did was for the sick man.

Back in the warehouse, Marlon was still fuming. 'Bastard! I should never have let him in on the job. I didn't even need him!'

Gerry knew the score and worked it to his own advantage. 'You an' me could've shared that few quid you just gave him,' he pointed out deviously. 'After all, he didn't really earn it, did he?'

Taking his meaning, Marlon went over to the door, where he wrapped his hands round an iron bar, kept here for warning off intruders. 'D'yer know summat, Gerry? I reckon you're right.' He held out the bar. 'In my opinion, Mr Big Mouth needs teaching a lesson.' He tapped the bar against his leg, smiling at the other man with evil intent. 'He's got so bloody pious he could even turn on us and open that big mouth of his to the law. We can't be doing with that, now can we?'

His face set hard and cruel, Gerry Reynolds walked across to where the other man stood. 'Leave it to me,' were his quiet words; though it was not a 'quiet' task he had in mind.

Geordie was halfway up the alley when he heard a sound behind him. There was no time to turn or even cry out, before he was violently knocked to the ground, and even when he was struck hard on the head for a second time, he didn't know what was happening.

Time and again the iron bar came down, and still he didn't understand, until in the last throes of life he looked up through blood-drenched eyes and saw Gerry's leering face. '*You!*' As the light faded from his eyes, he thought of Robert, and the sadness was for him alone.

Bending to rifle through the dead man's pockets, Reynolds emptied them of every scrap – what looked like a letter of sorts, bits of paper and tag-ends of baccy which stuck to his fingers. He threw them all into the gutter. All except the money, which he jubilantly waved in the air, giggling like a madman as he stared down at Geordie's broken form. 'You'll not be needing this, old son!'

Blood-spattered and satisfied, Gerry Reynolds strolled away. 'I reckon I've done you a favour, Geordie boy,' he chuckled to himself, glancing back at the lifeless body sprawled in its own blood. 'At least *you* won't have to spend years of your life in hospital.'

Chapter Fourteen

Panting and groaning, Edward Cornwell pinned his woman to the bed with outstretched arms. 'There are times when I could kill you with my bare hands,' he said passionately, 'and other times when I can't bear to leave you, not even for a minute.'

Growling like a wounded animal, he bent his head to her neck and bit into the soft flesh. 'You make me crazy,' he told her. 'Why is it I could always throw my women off when I tired of them, but not you. God help me, Kitty, I can't seem to get enough of you.'

She laughed in his face. 'That's because I'm better than any woman you've ever had,' she taunted. 'I've put you under my spell, Teddy.'

'Ssh! Don't talk.' With his entire weight bearing down on her, he probed her body with his; licking and kissing and cradling her breasts in the cup of his hands, 'You're so beautiful.'

'More beautiful than the others?' She craved admiration, never happier than when some gullible man was feeding her vanity. She needed to know she was the best, that she would only have to click her long, fine fingers, and he would come running. She didn't love Edward Cornwell. She didn't even desire him. What she wanted was his money, as much of it as she could get before she moved on to pastures new.

He didn't answer straight away. Instead he stripped naked and, with his member so obviously eager for her, he gave a strange, gargled cry before thrusting hard into her, delighting in her cries of ecstasy as she arched towards him, bursting her passion into his, wanting more and more, faster and faster, until they were both dripping with sweat.

For a long time afterwards, they lay side by side, taking great gulps of air, their moist bodies touching, and their arms flung wide. They didn't speak. They never did, after such wild, crippling lovemaking.

Nor did they speak when he got off the bed, went to the bathroom and washed himself down. They remained silent after he came back and began to dress, and still she lay there, wonderfully naked, extraordinarily beautiful, with her shock of fiery red hair and green cat-eyes. Long and slender of limb, she was a picture of womanhood in full bloom.

'Come back here.' Smiling invitingly, Kitty patted the bed beside her.

'I have to go.' Drawing on his trousers, he blew her a kiss. I'll see you later. Don't forget I'm taking you to dinner at the Marchant tonight.'

Her smile deepened. 'Aren't you afraid your wife will see us?'

He shook his head. 'No chance of that, my lovely. It's the evening when she accompanies the girls for their music lesson.'

'Music, eh?' Mimicking him, she gave a refined and cynical laugh. 'Teaching them to be *ladies*, is she? So they can play the piano when the vicar comes to call?'

Unamused by her sarcasm, he stared at her for a moment, his voice hard as nails. 'Something like that, yes.'

'Oh dear. Have I upset you?'

'Not at all.' Putting on his coat, he hooked the umbrella over his arm. 'I'll see you tonight.'

'Aw, come back . . . just for a while.' Her voice was husky, inviting.

He smiled, foolishly flattered by her need of him. 'Put on your loveliest clothes,' he instructed. 'That black outfit suits your colouring wonderfully. And do your hair the way you had it the last time I took you there . . . long and loose, falling about your shoulders.' He gave a curious little chuckle. 'I do so like it when the other men can't take their eyes off you.'

'Is that the way *she* used to dress for you?' Jealousy tinged her voice.

'Who?' As if he didn't know.

'That Noreen – her that was here until a few weeks back. The one you used to lay here, in this very bed. She used to work at the same agency as me, until she got picked up by you.' She half-closed her eyes in a gesture of submission. 'I wanted it to be me. Only you didn't even look my way.'

'I must have been blind then.'

'Was she as good as me?'

'She was . . .' he hesitated. 'Dispensable.'

'But was she as *good*?'

'I've told you before, there's no comparison between the two of you.' He became anxious when she started asking questions about her predecessor. 'She ran out of surprises, and I ran out of patience.'

'They say she was murdered. "Found by the river with her throat cut from ear to ear". That's what *I* heard.'

'Then you heard wrong!' His heart lurched as he thought about the way it had been. 'As far as I know, she went to London intending to start her own business. She talked about it long enough, and with the money she saved, she obviously wanted to give it a try.'

'You paid her too well,' Kitty said sulkily.

'No more than I pay *you*!'

'If you say so.'

'I do say so.' Irritated, he issued a warning. If you insist on talking about things gone and forgotten, I might not find you so attractive.'

Knowing when to shut her mouth, she promised, 'You won't hear another word about her, not from me anyway.'

'You're a sensible woman.' As he went out of the door, he wagged a finger. 'Remember, I'll be here sharp on eight. I won't be pleased if you're not ready and waiting.'

She laughed, a light, girlish laugh that thrilled him. 'Aren't I *always* ready for you?' And to prove her point she opened her legs, for him to see everything. 'I'm ready now,' she murmured, sending all kinds of pleasure rippling through his senses.

'You're shameful!' But it was why he craved her so much. His life was full of decency and restrictive regulations. When he was here with her, he could be as wild and wanton as he pleased.

'Come on,' she purred. 'Come back?' Putting out her tongue she ran it round the edge of her lips invitingly.

For a moment he was sorely tempted, his hardened member positively throbbing in his trousers. 'No!' Shaking his head decisively, he reminded her, 'Eight p.m. Don't forget.'

Within a minute, he was gone; hurrying to round after round of boring meetings and afterwards, a desk of papers a mile high to peruse.

Early that same evening, his wife Rosemary spoke to him several times and each time he appeared not to have heard. 'What's wrong, my dear?' She had noticed his absent-mindedness these past weeks and more. 'Is there something worrying you?'

'Not at all,' he lied. His mind was on the red-haired woman. Day by day, he found it harder to shut Kitty out of his thoughts. 'Why do you say that?'

Rosemary smiled in that lazy dog way she had. 'Oh nothing,

only I've been talking to you for at least five minutes and couldn't seem to catch your attention.'

'Sorry.' Flicking the evening paper on his lap, he opened it to read, then threw it aside. 'I have an important meeting tonight, as I've already told you. I suppose my mind was on that.'

She sighed. 'You work too hard.'

'It's what brings the money home, my dear.' Stretching out his arms to encompass the room with its rich tapestries and silver artefacts, he reminded her, 'If I didn't work every minute God sends, we'd never afford to live in such a grand style.'

Rosemary felt ashamed. 'I'm sorry, dear. I do understand.' Folding away her embroidery she remarked, 'It's a good job I ordered dinner early tonight. At least you won't be going out on an empty stomach, though I would have liked to see you eat more than you did. Pecking at your food like that! It's always the same when you have these late meetings, and they go on so long sometimes. Last week it was two in the morning when you got home.'

Folding the embroidery into her tapestry bag, she clicked the bag shut and set it beside her chair. 'I really don't see why they can't hold these meetings at a more civilised hour.'

'That's because there is never enough time in the day.' Becoming impatient at her constant fussing, he told her sharply, 'The house and children are enough for you to worry about. I don't think there's any need for you to concern yourself with *my* business.'

'In other words, I should mind my place?'

'Exactly, my dear.' He made the point with a half-smile, but his meaning was clear. Like all other men in his position, he did not take kindly to being questioned about his activities.

Rosemary took the hint, and quickly changed the subject. 'I suppose I'd better get the girls ready. Last week we got there at seven thirty-five, which was five minutes late . . . unforgivable!

As it is, Miss Drewer has gone to great trouble to fit these lessons in, out of the goodness of her heart.'

He laughed at that. '*I* tend to think it's because she's being paid handsomely for her trouble!'

At that Rosemary wagged a finger. 'I won't tell her you said that,' she chided. 'Miss Drewer is a very sensitive lady.'

Ignoring her chit-chat, he glanced at the mantelpiece clock. 'I ought to be getting ready myself quite soon. I don't want to be late for such an important meeting.' The thought of seeing his woman again made him positively blush with pleasure.

'It's such an inconvenience though.' Oblivious to his carnal thoughts, Rosemary chattered on. 'Goodness only knows when that wretched man is coming to tune our piano. I don't enjoy dragging the children across town like that.' She eyed him quizzically. 'You *did* remember to talk with him about it, didn't you, dear?'

He offered her a fleeting kiss as she passed him by. 'Would I forget an important thing like that? In fact, I've decided that if he doesn't come soon, I may order another piano, and have that one taken away.'

Rosemary didn't like that idea. 'Oh no, don't do that.' Her gaze went to the grand piano in the corner by the bay window. 'It was your father's, and it's such a beautiful thing.' She reassured him, 'I can wait if I have to. Besides, I expect the man's busy just now.'

'As you say, my dear.' He had known she would protest at the idea of getting rid of that splendid piano, with its family history. He had completely forgotten to contact the tuner.

With time creeping up fast on her, Rosemary excused herself and departed the room. Making straight for the kitchen first, she asked the cook to prepare a flask of fruit juice and maybe a little snack. 'After the children have had their lessons, I might walk them through the park,' she told Mrs Bellamy. 'It's so lovely there at this time of day, we might linger for a late picnic of sorts.'

It being a sunny September evening, the youngsters were presently out in the garden. From where Rosemary stood she could see them clearly. 'They *are* beautiful children, don't you think?'

Cook came to see. 'Yes, ma'am,' she agreed. 'They are.' All but Pauline, she thought. That one grew uglier with the passing years, not only in shape, but nature-wise, too; though her doting mother would never agree.

The one admirable feature about Pauline was her thick strong, dark hair, which hung down her back in folds. Always a big girl, now in her seventeenth year she had filled out all over. She was also strong and clumsy, with a nasty streak, especially towards the girl who had been Nancy, and was now known by everyone as Sara-Jane for reasons that did not bear thinking of.

Time and again, Cook had seen Pauline go for Sara-Jane, and often the younger girl was left in tears at the taunting she received. But she was a brave little thing and took it all in her stride.

It was a rule below stairs, that no one should intervene when the bullying started. 'She must learn to stand up for herself. It's not our business, unless it gets so ugly it has to be stopped,' Cook reminded them. 'Besides, she won't always be small and helpless. There'll come a day when she retaliates, and when that happens I would not like to be in that bully's shoes. Like all cowards, she won't be so clever when the tide turns.'

So far, the bullying had only been verbal, and so there had been no real call for anyone to intervene, but Meg the kitchenmaid's hackles were up whenever she saw what was going on. 'If the mistress could see her going at Nancy like that, she'd punish her, for sure. I, for one, think she should be told.'

'Really? Well, if you have any idea of telling the mistress that her eldest daughter is a bully, you might as well start looking for another job now!' Cook said smartly, also firmly reminding her that the girl's name was *Sara-Jane* and not Nancy. In fact, never a day went by when she did *not* have to remind her at least once. And this when the girl was rising nine years old, even though it still seemed like yesterday when she arrived at Paisley Hall, a frightened toddler.

Cook was startled when Rosemary's voice cut through her thoughts. 'Sara-Jane is making such a pretty little thing, don't you think?'

The older woman could not argue with that. 'Oh yes,' she said, a smile creeping over her ample features. 'She'll break a few hearts when she's grown.' Appraising Nancy as she ran along the small brick wall round the garden edge, Cook saw how long of limb she was becoming, and how her fair hair danced in the breeze. She saw how the sunlight caught those pretty blue eyes, sometimes laughing, sometimes sad, and her old heart was warmed. 'Such a kind, loving little thing,' she added, 'and so knowledgeable for her age.'

Opening the window, Rosemary called them in. 'Time for your lesson, girls,' she said, and almost immediately they began to make their way towards the house.

'Master David is such a fine boy,' Cook observed fondly. 'My! He's grown so tall and handsome, he'll soon be making the girls' hearts all of a flutter, I'll be bound.'

Now just past his fourteenth birthday, David was indeed a handsome young man. With his dark hair and eyes of brown, he had lost that softness of boyhood to the firm, chiselled features of blossoming manhood. Thoughtful and generous of nature, he still retained that protective attitude towards Nancy. If anything, the two of them had grown closer with each passing year. 'He'll not let any harm come to the girl,' Meg claimed, and having watched them together at different times, and seeing how fond they were of each other, Cook wholeheartedly agreed.

Once inside, the girls were instructed to go upstairs and make themselves ready with the help of Meg who, after the governess's abrupt departure for 'domestic' reasons, doubled as scullerymaid and dresser. It was widely known below stairs that it was not her mother's illness that had forced the young woman's hasty departure, but Pauline's nasty, cruel nature, and so far the family had not been able to replace her.

At seven-fifteen, Rosemary and the girls filed into the drawing room to say goodbye to their papa. Dutifully allowing the girls to kiss him – Pauline first because of her jealous disposition – Edward told them curtly, 'Tend your lessons well. I would hate to think my money was being wasted.'

'I shall see to it,' Rosemary promised.

'I already know a little tune,' Sara-Jane said excitedly. 'I can play it for you now if you like?' The smile she gave Edward was magic. 'I'd like to, if you please?'

Pauline soon put a stop to that. 'Stop showing off, you spoiled brat! You know very well the piano's out of tune!'

Edward wagged a chastising finger. 'No need to be spiteful,' he reminded his daughter. Addressing Rosemary he asked, 'Where's the boy?'

'He's on his way. Please don't keep him perusing over the books too long, Edward,' she requested. 'He much prefers to be outside – chopping wood and such.' She smiled. 'If you ask me, he's a born farmer.'

Scrambling out of the chair, Edward faced her down. 'I do *not* want him farming, woman! My son is especially adept at figures. He has a clever head on his shoulders, and a strong instinct for business. When he's old enough and has finished his tutoring, I shall take him under my wing and make him one of the best brokers in the City of London. That's where his future lies – in the City, in finance. Not on some isolated farm in the middle of nowhere!' Ever since the boy was born, Edward had laid down certain plans for his son, and they had grown stronger as David's ability matured.

A little afraid, Rosemary stood her ground on this matter. 'But Edward, you *know* his heart isn't in finance. He hates it every time you take him to the City.'

'Has he told you that?' His chin went up in anger and his eyes bored into hers.

Rosemary lied. 'Well, no, not as such.'

'There you are then.' Edward relaxed. 'It doesn't pay to go making assumptions. Besides, it's for *me* to decide where his future lies. The boy is born for finance and matters of commerce and investment.'

Rosemary nodded. 'As you say.'

Looking towards the door he told her, 'Send him straight in. I'd better have a word with him before I leave.'

'Very well, Edward.' Once again, she had lost an argument with this arrogant, bull-headed man.

'Right then. Off you go.' With a wave of his hand he effectively dismissed them when, one behind the other, they filed out again; though on second thoughts, Edward called his wife back for a discreet word. 'My dear, I think Pauline is beginning to lose her shape. It might be a good idea if she was put on a strict diet? After all, it won't be long now before we need to decide on *her* future.'

He gave an exasperated groan. 'Though I don't know how we shall place her with a good husband if she doesn't trim her figure. Oh, and you really must do something about her awful plainness. Young Nancy is twice as gentle and pretty, and with such impeccable manners.' He chuckled knowingly. 'She's a bit wild and wilful at times, I've noticed, but some men like that in a woman, I'm sure we won't have any trouble marrying *her* off, when the time comes.'

Rosemary drew him up on one particular point. 'Her name is

not Nancy, my dear. You'll remember, her name is now Sara-Jane.'

'Mmm,' He had not liked that arrangement from the start and he liked it even less as time went on, 'I'm not so sure it was a good idea to call her after our lost daughter.'

'I don't agree. The name suits her. Pauline, too, is pleased to have her sister back, if only in name alone.'

After a pause to think, he nodded affirmatively. 'Yes, you may well be right, my dear. I recall how devastated she was at the time, and yes, she does appear to have found solace in the newcomer, although she does get rather bullish with her – just as she did with our own Sara-Jane. I expect it's another trait in her character we should try and discourage.' There was another short pause, and then Edward said reflectively, 'After all, where's the harm in giving the child a new name, when we don't even know for sure what her old one was?'

Rosemary agreed wholeheartedly. 'And what exactly will you have me do about Pauline?' she asked next. 'How can I start to help her?'

'Oh yes. Well, it might be an idea to arrange some lessons on good posture, and to somehow improve her general manners and conduct. In fact, I rather think you might model her on the girl?'

Seeing some element of common sense in his suggestion, Rosemary promised she would give it her consideration.

Outside the door, Pauline and Nancy heard every word. 'Huh! Who in their right mind would want to be modelled on *you*!' The older girl gave Nancy a spiteful push which sent her flying against the wall. 'You're a nobody – Dad said so himself. We don't even know what your real name is.'

'It's Nancy.'

'Not any more, because now you've got the name of a dead girl. Somebody who was ten times prettier than you, but not as clever as me.' She pushed her face close to the younger girl's. 'It doesn't pay to be *too* clever, does it? It doesn't pay to think you're *better* than me.'

'I don't think that.'

'That's very sensible. It's just as well to remember your place.' With the tip of a stiff finger she prodded Nancy painfully in the ribs. 'My father doesn't like you, if that's what you think. He only had you here for Mother's sake. Nobody really wants you. In fact, it might be best if you ran away.' Bending forward to bring her face on a par with Nancy's, she hissed, 'I hate you. I hate you being here, in my house.'

Nancy stared her out. 'I don't *hate you.*' She felt no fear or envy towards this girl, however much she was provoked.

Her direct remark took the other girl by surprise. Backing off, she stared at Nancy with hatred. 'You don't even know what trouble you're in, do you?'

'What do you mean?' A shard of fear stabbed at Nancy's insides.

'I already told you about my sister – the one whose name you stole?'

'I didn't steal it.' It was a sore point with Nancy to be addressed by a name that didn't belong to her.

The older girl laughed in her face. 'I shouldn't worry too much, if I were you. *It doesn't matter anyway, because you won't have it for long*.'

After all the fuss Rosemary had made about her keeping the name, Nancy thought it was a strange thing to say. Still, it would suit her if Pauline managed to change her mother's mind, because she much preferred her own name.

A short time later, Rosemary marshalled them together. She titivated their hair and made sure their shoes were well polished, and when she was satisfied with their presentation, she ushered them out of the front door to the waiting carriage.

As they drove away, David watched from the window.

Catching Nancy's attention he waved to her and she, delighted, waved back. A moment later she was out of sight, and he was the lonelier for it.

Already incensed when eavesdropping on her parents' discreet conversation, Pauline witnessed the warm exchange between these two fast friends, and was filled with rage. A dark, terrible rage that festered and grew as they travelled towards their destination.

As always, Rosemary chatted the whole way – about the beautiful September weather, about the clothes passers-by were wearing, and how it might be 'a good idea if we were all to lose some weight'. She didn't have the nerve to tackle Pauline straight out, so she tried to disguise her motives by including herself and Sara-Jane in the programme. 'With winter coming up, a person always eats far too much. We shall have to be careful this year, won't we?' She smiled at Nancy then Pauline, and though she got a return smile from Nancy, her older daughter merely scowled out of the window and pretended not to hear.

The entire journey took no more than fifteen minutes, but it would have been too far to walk; the music teacher's house was on the other side of Woburn, lying on the edge of the Ridgmont village.

'Here we are then.' The driver helped them down one after the other. 'That'll be just one shilling, if you please.' He took the coin from Rosemary and climbed back into his cab, enquiring as he did so, 'Would you like me to wait, or shall I come back at a given time?'

Rosemary had completely forgotten to tell him. 'Oh yes, thank you. After we've finished our business, we intend walking through the park. If we've finished in time we might even stop for a picnic.'

The cabbie thought that was a fine idea, 'The park is especially pretty at this time o' year,' he agreed. 'Pity of it is, I don't have no time to go there. When me work's done, I'm often too tired to even undo me shoelaces.'

'Yes, I'm sure.' Rosemary gave him one of her 'understanding' smiles. 'I think if you came to the park-gates about quarter to nine or thereabouts, we should be ready for home.'

'Will do.' Tipping his cap in respect, he clicked the horse into motion and went down the street at a leisurely pace.

The music teacher's home was a pretty thatched cottage tucked behind the High Street. It was an ancient place, with low walls covered in climbing flowers, and tiny little windows criss-crossed with leaded light. At either side of the door and all along the slabbed area stood pots of different kinds of plants, all blooming in every possible shade of red, pink, yellow and white, and each with its own wonderful fragrance.

'It's like Fairyland!' Nancy had been here three times already, and each time she loved it more. 'I'd like to live in a pretty house like this.'

Rosemary was horrified. 'Oh, my dear! I don't imagine that will ever happen. When the day comes for you to be married, your father and I have something much grander in mind for you girls.'

Nancy didn't say anything, but was quietly disappointed.

Lifting one gloved and delicate hand, Rosemary knocked on the door. Almost at once it was opened and there stood this comical little woman; short and narrow with a green top on, and wearing little pink slippers on her feet, she befitted that tiny cottage.

Her smile was impish. 'Come in, my dears.' She stepped back and saw them pass one at a time, and she bestowed a special smile on Nancy.

Having spoken quickly with Rosemary and taken the fee for her trouble, the little woman soon had them organised. 'You sit and browse through this music lesson,' she told Nancy, 'while I work with Pauline at the piano.' To Rosemary she suggested, 'I expect you'll be off on your little walk, while I see to the girls?'

Rosemary told her how she would be back within half an hour as usual, and gratefully went away.

Once outside the cottage, which she found very claustrophobic, she walked along the lanes towards the open fields, where she sat on a milestone, watching the children at play in a nearby garden. She had a great deal to think about, and when she was at home, it was not an easy thing to do, what with three children to mind, and a big household to run. In fact, Rosemary had come to value these few quiet moments while the girls went through their piano lessons.

Inside the cottage, to the delight of Pauline who stood by, Nancy was making mistake after mistake. 'No, no!' The little woman gently tapped her knuckles with the ruler. 'Go back and play that again, child, and this time remember what I told you – listen to the metronome. Strike the note in accordance with its every tick.'

Nancy tried again, but found it hard to stretch her fingers to reach the respective keys. 'Look, let me show you.' Asking Nancy to shift along on the stool, the little woman sat down and began to play. The girl was mesmerised by her wonderful ability, and by the length of her fine, beautifully shaped fingers, in comparison to the rest of her short, slightly bent little body. 'Like that, you see?' She shifted back on the stool. 'You play the piano, like *that*!'

Nancy tried again, and this time she managed to play the piece without interruption, though it pained her fingers to stretch them so unnaturally.

The teacher was exhilarated. 'There, that wasn't too bad at all. Though you'll find it much easier when your fingers grow to the keys.'

Pauline had no such difficulty. An experienced pianist now,

she had been taking lessons at school for years. With fingers the length and strength of a man's, she easily commanded the keyboard. There was no denying as she played that she was a very talented pianist. In those few moments while she drew the most magical sound from the piano, her new teacher sat beside her, eyes closed and her little body swaying to the melody.

When the last note died away dramatically, Nancy instinctively clapped. 'Oh Pauline, that was so lovely!'

She stopped clapping when the older girl turned and sneered, 'Like it, did you? You'll *never* learn to play the piano properly.'

'Now now!' the teacher chided. 'That isn't fair. The child is new to all this. It's bound to take time for her to feel comfortable with the keys.' She patted Pauline on the back. 'All the same, my dear, you do have a wonderful instinct for the piano. I have no doubt if you keep up with your practice and concentrate on the mood of what you're playing, you will one day make a very accomplished pianist.'

A moment later, Rosemary was at the door. 'How did they do?' she asked, and was told, 'They did very well indeed. I've given them each a piece to practise, but of course that depends on whether you have your piano in order. You *will* let me know, as soon as you have it ready, won't you?'

'Of course.'

'Good, then I can begin to come to Paisley Hall to give the lessons. If not, I shall see you here again, at the same time next week.'

Once outside and on their way to the park, Pauline complained to her mother about Nancy's poor performance. 'Her playing was rotten,' she moaned. 'I told you it was a waste of money teaching her the piano. She's no good at it.'

Nancy protested, 'It's only because my fingers are too short.'

'It's not your fingers, it's *you*! You haven't got a musical note in your entire body.'

'That's not fair! You've been playing longer than me. I'll catch up when I'm grown more, you'll see.'

Quickly, before the argument worsened, Rosemary came between them. 'Of course you will, Sara-Jane.' Addressing Pauline she told her sternly, 'I won't have you upsetting her when she's trying so hard.' Whereupon the older girl sulked all the way to the park.

Finding a dry corner under a cherry tree, Rosemary settled them all down. 'We can see the lake from here,' she observed. 'We have a little time before we need to make our way to the gate, so when we've eaten we might go down to the water's edge and feed the leftovers to the ducks.'

Opening the picnic hamper, she took out the white napkins which Cook had so beautifully packed; she spread these out and arranging the sandwiches and flask of juice, she told the girls, 'Tuck in,' which they did. Meanwhile, she got out the beakers and poured them each a measure of fruit juice.

Later, when the food was all but gone, and the juice drunk to the last drop, they went down to the ducks and fed them the crusts and scraps. 'It's been a lovely outing.' Rosemary left them to pack away the picnic items while she herself lingered by the lake.

'It's so beautiful here,' she said dreamily. And peaceful, she thought. Sometimes, just now and then, she wished she could move away from the hustle and bustle of her life in the big house and live like that comical little woman, in a pretty cottage with only the flowers and her music for company.

But then, she reminded herself how much she loved the children. And there was Edward. She smiled devotedly. However would he manage without her?

On the way back in the cab, Rosemary went through what they had done, and told them she was really pleased with their progress. She promised that the piano would be tuned properly before too long and, taking their minds off the matter of music, went on to talk about a holiday in France that their father had planned for them over Christmas.

Nancy was thrilled, but Pauline took it all as her right; she had already been abroad several times, so she knew exactly what to expect.

Rosemary continued to chat and they continued to listen, and soon they were in the middle of Woburn town.

While Rosemary explained to her newest daughter how it was in the place they usually stayed, Pauline turned away to look out the window, and got the shock of her life.

In the fading light and onset of evening, she caught a glimpse of her father climbing out of a carriage. Smiling and attentive, he turned back to reach up; taking a hold of her slender, gloved hand, he took great pleasure in helping the woman down from the carriage. She was stunningly beautiful, with loose shoulder-length, flame-coloured hair, around which a cream chiffon scarf was tied at the shoulder; draping to her breast, it was momentarily lifted by the slight warm breeze.

Stiffening with horror, Pauline took in every detail; how tall and slim she was, how she stepped like a gazelle across to Edward, and how her father seemed utterly mesmerised by her beauty and presence.

Having got her close, Edward leaned to kiss her on the mouth, his admiring gaze raking her face while he whispered something in her ear. She laughed girlishly and, as they went arm-in-arm to the foyer of the hotel, she looked up at him, cooing and smiling and cunningly twisting him round her little finger, as only she could.

In a minute they had disappeared into the hotel. Anxious, Pauline glanced at her mother, who was still chatting excitedly. 'Oh, but you'll love it,' she was telling Nancy. 'I can hardly wait for you to see the Alps. They're so wonderful!'

For the remainder of the journey, while the other two talked about France and how it would be, Pauline could not get the picture of her father and that woman out of her mind. With every turn of the carriage-wheel her mood darkened, until she was positively seething with hatred.

The following morning, Rosemary came down with a cold. She spent the best part of the day in bed, being cosseted by the servants and swathed in blankets to keep out the chill.

While the children got on with their studies and homework, the piano tuner arrived and brought the piano back to life. 'There you go,' he told Meg. 'You can tell the mistress it'll play like the harps in heaven now.' And to prove it he ran his fingers along the keyboard, to produce a silvery velvet sound that had Meg almost swooning.

After he'd gone, Pauline was the first to practise her music.

On this particular occasion it was a wild, dramatic piece, played with such passion and feeling that everyone in the house stopped work to listen, awed. 'If I could play like that, I'd never have been a cook, that's for sure,' Mrs Bellamy said.

Meg agreed. 'It's all right for some,' she said miserably. 'It's a pity we ain't *all* born with a silver spoon in our mouths, eh?' In fact, she got so depressed about it, Cook told her to, 'Pull yer socks up, woman, afore you turn the milk sour!'

When the piece was finished, Pauline sat at the piano, deep in thought. Try as she might, she could not get the picture of her father and that woman out of her mind. It had haunted her sleep last night, and kept her virtually silent all day. And now, so bitter was she, that when he came into the drawing room, she made her excuses and took her leave of him.

Nancy waited until Pauline had gone to her room, before she practised her own music piece; a soft and pretty melody, it did not command the same wide-eyed attention as had Pauline's powerful performance.

The following day, Rosemary seemed much worse, but when Edward suggested that he should send for the doctor, she dared him to do so. 'I only have a chill, not pneumonia,' she told him with a brighter smile. 'If I keep warm in bed for a day or two, I'll soon be right as rain.' And when she put it like that, how could he argue?

That evening, Edward came to her room and told her he would have to go out for a while. 'An urgent business matter has come up,' he explained. 'There's an investment deal going through and I'm meeting with the partners. I'm sorry, my dear, but I may not make it back before midnight.' He feigned concern. 'Shall you be all right?'

'Stop fussing,' she said. 'It's only a cold. I'll be fine. Cook is preparing a special broth, said to ward off evil spirits.' When she laughed, he laughed with her. 'Perhaps it will make me sleep soundly.'

She gave a cough that momentarily seemed to take her breath away. They do say sleep is the best medicine of all.'

'Of course.' He was only too pleased to agree. 'Look, my dear, I've had the bed made up in the guest room, so as not to wake you when I come in.'

Rosemary appreciated his consideration. 'That's very thoughtful of you,' she said sleepily. 'I hope to feel a lot better in the morning.'

When the front door closed on Edward, Pauline went into the kitchen, where to Meg's disgust, she helped herself to slices of cold meat, pies and cakes, and a huge hunk of cheese, and stuffed her face until fit to burst. 'Blimey! I've only ever seen someone wolf it down like that once before,' Meg whispered to Cook, 'an' that were the pigs in me dad's field.'

'Ssh!' Mrs Bellamy gave her a warning dig in the ribs. She knew the trouble Pauline Cornwell was capable of. Seeing the real fear in Cook's face, Meg soon got back to her work.

Later that evening, David and Nancy took it into their heads to go and see Rosemary. 'Are you all right, Mama?' David gave her a gentle shake.

Opening her eyes Rosemary was delighted to see them. 'Yes, son, I'm feeling better already,' she said. 'But you two shouldn't be here. I don't want you to get this terrible cold.'

Nancy came closer. 'I miss you.' Since being brought to Paisley Hall, this woman had been so kind and loving, until now she was really very fond of her. 'When will you be coming back down?'

Rosemary stroked the girl's worried face. 'We'll see,' she answered softly. 'Maybe tomorrow.' Addressing David she told him, 'Tell Cook I'm ready for her special broth – oh, and I wouldn't mind a cup of hot cocoa to help me sleep.'

Both children gave her a fleeting kiss on the cheek. 'I'll ask her right away,' David promised, and he did.

In fact, a short time later, as soon as she had eaten every last drop of Cook's delicious broth, Rosemary fell into a deep, restful sleep, first leaving instructions that the children must be in bed no later than nine o'clock. 'But don't tell their father I allowed them to stay up so late.' She asked after Pauline and was told, 'She's in the drawing room, ma'am, reading through the journals, I believe.'

Downstairs, in the drawing room, Pauline had a photograph in her hands, of herself and David with their parents. For a long time she held the face of her father in her quizzical gaze. After a while, the gaze turned to a hard, evil stare. 'You should be punished for what you've done.' The menace in her voice was like a physical presence.

Then she replaced the photograph and picked up the one beside it; a picture of Rosemary with Pauline, David, and the child who had tragically drowned – and who bore a striking resemblance to Nancy. She didn't say anything. Instead she pressed her thumb against the face of her late sister. She held her thumb there for a time, obliterating every feature. Then calmly replacing the photograph, upside down, she walked away.

A few moments later she was out in the garden, not far from where David and Nancy were seated on the grass, contentedly talking. They could not see her, nor she them, but from the kitchen window, Meg and Cook could see them all.

'Just look at that one!' Meg had no liking for Pauline and was not afraid to show it. 'She's like a trapped animal.'

Cook watched for a while; she saw how Pauline was walking up and down, back and forth, clearly agitated. 'Something's worrying her,' she agreed. 'There's trouble brewing.'

'What d'you mean by that?'

Already regretting her words, Cook urged Meg, 'Come away. She mustn't see us watching her.'

As they went about their work, Meg had to ask, '*Is* she mad, d'you think?'

Cook wagged a finger at her. 'We're not paid to think. Just get on with what you're doing and don't concern yourself with summat that's none of our business.'

After that, and because there was something here she did not fully understand, Meg kept her silence and worked hard to take her mind off things. In record time, and much to Cook's surprise, she had finished preparing the dough for tomorrow's bread.

At ten minutes to nine, after supper and a bath, the children were marshalled ready for bed. It wasn't long before Nancy was hard and fast asleep. And, as instructed, David went through his notes on *Matters of Finance* before finally shoving it all under the bed and going off to sleep.

Pauline, however, did not sleep. Nor did she undress for bed. Instead, she waited until the house was silent from top to bottom, before secretly and as softly as she could, going out of her room and along the landing, carrying her shoes as she went.

Outside David's room she put her ear to the door and listened. When she was satisfied he was asleep, she moved on to Nancy's room. Here, she gingerly opened the door and went inside, tiptoeing across the rugs so as not to waken her. For what seemed an age she stood by the girl's bed, staring down on her, smiling softly. 'Sara-Jane.' She whispered it twice, each time her smile deepening. Then as softly as she had come into the room, she went out.

At her mother's room she stood at the door and listened. There was no sound, and looking down at the narrow gap under the door, she could see there was no light on. Satisfied, she quickly went down the stairs and into the hallway, where she took her coat from the cloaks cupboard and slunk out of the house into the night.

As she closed the door behind her she heard the grandfather clock strike eleven.

Once clear of Paisley Hall she began to run, along the drive and out on to the main street. She looked for a cab and soon discovered one parked along the highway; its driver asleep inside, hopefully waiting for fares from late-nighters. 'Hey, you!' Banging on the door, she scared the poor fella half out of his wits. 'I need you to take me to Bagley Road.'

'Jesus!' Scrambling out of his seat, he rubbed his eyes and stared at her, thinking she was too young to be wandering the streets at this late hour. But she was a fare, and fares meant money, and money meant he could pay the rent. 'Bagley Road, eh?' He nodded as she climbed in. 'That'll be threepence, please, miss.' He held out his hand, but was unlucky.

'I'll pay you when you get me there,' she snapped.

In fact it wasn't far. Bagley Road was out towards Heath and Reach, some four miles away. There was a smattering of houses along there, owned mainly by them as had plenty of money to throw about.

'That's where you live, is it?' the driver enquired over the sound of his horse's hooves trotting along the deserted road.

She didn't answer, so he didn't ask again. 'Miserable young bugger!' he sniffed. At first he had thought she was only a child. Now he preferred to believe she was some kind of high-class whore, albeit an unattractive one, out on the prowl. Added to which, he knew for certain that one or two of the houses along Bagley Road were kept for that very purpose.

When she asked to be dropped at the corner of Bagley Road, his suspicions were confirmed. If she didn't want a particular address, it was because she had it in mind to wait for a well-breeched gent to stroll along the road, looking for a night's entertainment.

When the cab was gone, Pauline walked down the street to a certain address; she knew it well as she had been here on other occasions. For a time, she stood outside, looking up. There were no lights on, and no sign of a cabbie waiting to take her father home. 'Not back yet. Good!'

Finding a convenient spot, she hid in the darkness and bided her time. She didn't have long to wait before a carriage drew up not all that far away from where she was standing; so close, in fact, she could hear every word that was said.

'Pull up here, cabbie!' That was her father's voice. Being the devious man he was, he ordered the cab-driver to stay just far enough out of sight so that he was unable to see which house the woman returned to. Nor did he show his face too clearly, for fear the man might some other time recognise him. Instead, as part of his plan, he said goodbye to the woman there and then.

'Will I see you tomorrow?' Kitty was ever greedy, wanting to grab him, and his money.

His answer was a quick fondle of her breasts, a kiss, then she was walking away and he was being driven off. Pauline, for her part, was delighted it all seemed to be going to plan. *But then she knew his routine. She had seen it all before.*

Suddenly, what seemed to be a drunk approached from the other end of the street. Pauline cursed. 'Dammit!' Waiting a minute, she pressed back, into the darkness. She would have to wait, until she and the whore were alone again.

It was almost 2 a.m. Being a sufferer of indigestion, Cook had gone to the kitchen for a glass of water with which to take her medicine, when she heard a noise outside. Terrified that it might be burglars, she quickly put out the lamp and hid, rolling pin in hand, behind the kitchen door.

After a time, she began to wonder if she had been hearing things. But no! From where she stood, she caught a movement outside in the back garden; a small fire was burning, and a moving figure was clearly silhouetted against the flames.

On tiptoe and being careful not to be seen, she went across the room to look out the window. *It was Pauline.*

Furtively cramming what appeared to be clothes on to the small fire she'd built, she kept glancing back at the house, obviously nervous about being seen. Suddenly she gave Cook the worst fright of her life, when she swung round and seemed to stare right into the kitchen window.

Trembling to her very soul, unsure whether she had been seen or not, Cook bowed her head and remained quite still, not moving a single muscle; though for the time it took for Pauline to look away, she ached in every bone of her body.

Quickly now, and still shaking from the shock, Cook left in such a hurry that she forgot her glass of water and medicine as she scuttled back to her quarters.

She daren't think what Pauline was up to. But one thing was certain. She had not been surprised to see the girl's curious goings-on.

Somehow, she had been expecting it.

* * *

The next morning, after a restless night, Cook was making her way into the kitchen when she came face to face with Pauline. There was a heart-stopping moment when they passed each other in the narrow passageway, and it looked like Pauline might say something. Instead, she dropped her gaze to the floor, and walked on.

Greatly relieved, Cook scurried to the kitchen where Meg was already preparing breakfast for the family. 'Where've you been?' Hot and flustered, she was rushing about like something gone mad. 'I thought I were gonna have to fetch the upstairs maid to help me out.'

In spite of her ordeal, Cook had to smile. 'Hmh! You'll not get much change outta that one,' she said, tying on her apron. 'She's been here six months and I don't reckon she's said half a dozen words to anybody. She's a bit like the piano tuner – comes in, does her work, and she's off again.'

'She might not have much to say, but she's good at her work. Them bedrooms are allus spick and span, even underneath the bed, not a speck o' dust.'

But Cook had already stopped listening. Instead, she dropped the eggs on to the griddle and turned the bacon over to crisp, and all the while she couldn't get her mind off last night. There was something very strange about it all. Later, when she could do it without anyone seeing, she would go out and have a look at what Pauline had been up to.

'COOK, CAN YOU HEAR ME?' Meg's upraised voice shot through the air.

'Jesus, Mary and Joseph!' Clasping her heart, Cook swung round angrily. 'Are you trying to finish me off or what?' By this time Meg had come up on her and was so near she got knocked sideways by Mrs Bellamy's bulk.

The unexpected way she'd swung round like that gave Meg a

right turn. 'Boody hell, Cook!' Still shaking, she had to sit down. 'There's no need to go at me like that. I were only trying to make you hear. You seemed to have gone deaf all of a sudden.'

'Get off yer backside and get them tureens over here!' Cook was in no mood to play games this morning and, seeing how she was about to be slapped with the greasy spatula, Meg went at the run.

'Come on, come on! Hurry up or the breakfast will be good and spoiled.' Cook waved the spatula like a weapon. 'We'll have the family down here in a minute, looking for their breakfast. Get a move on, you worthless creature!'

Staggering across with the heavy china tureens, Meg placed them on the table. 'Whatever's wrong with you?' None too pleased, she watched Cook fill the tureens; one with bacon and layered with sausage, the other arranged with beautifully cooked eggs. 'You're like a bear with a sore head.'

'Fetch the trolley.' By now Cook had calmed down. 'Right – take it to the dining room before we both get the sack.' She almost forgot. 'Is the mistress coming down, do you know?'

Meg shook her head. 'She's still full of cold. In fact, I wouldn't be surprised if the doctor doesn't have to come out to her before long. If you ask me, she's got a temperature.'

'I wasn't asking you that!' Cook was too worried for casual chit-chat. 'I asked if she was coming down.'

'Well, o' course she's not. She asked for some more of your broth.' Meg gave a little snigger. 'I reckon she thinks it's magic or summat.'

'Hmh! It's a good job I made enough to last a couple of days.' Impatient, she gave Meg a little shove. 'Go on, woman! By the time you've come back from serving breakfast, it'll be heated and ready. With a bit o' stock stirred in, it'll taste good as new.'

She was as good as her word. By the time Meg returned for a

second pot of tea for Edward, the broth was simmering nicely on the stove.

When the tea was made, Meg ran it into the breakfast room and came back scowling. 'That Pauline gets on my nerves, so she does. Nasty little bugger.'

Cook was sitting at the table, surrounded by boxes of vegetables, her face white as a sheet. 'Summat terrible's happened,' she said hoarsely to the kitchenmaid. 'The greengrocer's just left his order and he's told me a murder was done last night in Bagley Road – some redheaded woman were found butchered on her own doorstep.'

Meg was alarmed when Cook seemed near to fainting. 'I'd best get you a glass o' water,' she said kindly. 'You've had a nasty fright.' As she got the water she chatted in her inimitable way. 'Bad business though, I'm sure. Fancy! Somebody murdered on her own front doorstep. Meks you wonder what the world's coming to, don't it, eh?'

When she turned round with the water, Cook had disappeared, 'Cook, are you all right? Where are you?' Looking this way and that, she called several times, but there was no answer, so she drank the water, herself. 'Gone for a lie-down, I shouldn't wonder,' she said to the empty room. 'Poor old bugger.'

Realising she was on her own, she set about the work Cook had left behind. She dished up a small measure of steaming broth, put it on a tray with a silver spoon and fresh traycloth, and took it up to Rosemary. 'Eat it all up, ma'am,' she said cheekily, bursting with responsibility at Cook's untimely disappearance. 'There's plenty more where that came from.'

She was on the point of telling Rosemary about the murder, when she was asked after the children. 'Oh, they're fine, ma'am. In fact I passed them on the way to the library, where the tutor is all ready and waiting to start their lessons.'

That seemed to settle her mistress's mind, because by the time

Meg had opened the curtains wide and tidied the bed, Rosemary had eaten half the soup.

'I can't manage any more,' she informed Meg, 'but you may tell Cook it was delicious.'

Then she took a nasty wet, sneezing fit and Meg had to fetch two clean hankies. 'I'd best be off then,' she told Rosemary and, not wanting to catch such a filthy cold, she almost ran out of the room.

When the last sneeze had taken its toll, Rosemary called after her, 'You were about to tell me something, weren't you?'

'Was I, ma'am?' Meg had suffered influenza some time back and it had laid her low for a fortnight, so she didn't want to take any risks. Besides, now wasn't the time to burden the mistress with news of a murder. 'Oh, it was nothing, ma'am.' Closing the door behind her, she peered back through the narrowing gap. 'It can wait, I'm sure.'

Rosemary nodded. What a strange little creature Meg was, Rosemary thought to herself. But she was a good sort at heart. Then she took another sneezing fit that rattled along the landing and down the stairs to where Meg was about to enter the kitchen. 'Gawd bless!' she called, then went about her work at the double.

She was itching to tell somebody – *anybody* – about the dreadful news, but Cook had gone to bed, the mistress wasn't up to being frightened out of her wits, and that miserable upstairs-maid wouldn't even give her the time of day. So, having only her own company to hear, she started a long and lengthy conversation with herself. 'Murdered! Flippin' 'eck! Whoever would do such a terrible thing? Ooh! I shall need to be extra careful on my way home of a night-time.' Scaring herself out of her wits, she peeped about with saucer-like eyes. 'Gawd only knows what kind o' madmen are wandering the streets.'

She was still chattering to herself when she brought the last batch of plates to the sink. Then, glancing up, she happened to see Cook hurrying down the path towards the gate. 'Good heavens! First she's brought down by the news of the murder, and now here she is, gadding off to the Lord knows where.' She tutted and sighed and shook her head, and held another conversation regarding Cook and her funny habits, concluding, 'The way she's been acting of late, I reckon she might be growing senile, bless her old heart.'

It was almost a mile to the church, and every step of the way, Cook was constantly glancing behind her, fearing that she might have been followed.

Sneaking into the church like a thief in the night, she went straight to the confessional box and let herself in. At once, the priest's face was pressed close to the screen, his voice soft as velvet as he greeted her in the name of the Lord.

'Bless me, Father, for I have sinned,' Cook whispered fearfully.

He gave his blessing and waited for her confession.

In a breathless whisper, she told him, 'I know something really bad. I should have told someone before,' she went on, 'but it's so terrible, and I'm afraid. I'm not sure what to do, Father. It's making me nervous. I can't sleep of a night. I just don't know what to do for the best. Oh, I'm that frightened.'

'Tell me what it is that makes you so afraid.'

'I can't, Father. I daren't!'

'If you can't tell the Lord what's worrying you, how can He help you?' He paused. 'Can I know your name?'

Cook thought about that for a minute. 'It's Annie,' she muttered. 'But that's all I can say.'

'Trust in me, Annie,' he urged. 'Whatever you confess to me now is heard only by the two of us, and the Lord Himself.'

'You won't tell?'

'No, Annie, I won't tell. I promise you that.'

There followed a moment of silence while she thought it over before, longing to trust him, she leaned as close as she could to the screen. 'I know someone who's committed murder . . . *three times, Father*!'

From the other side of the screen came a harsh intake of breath, then a brief span of silence, while he whispered a prayer. In a voice filled with awe, the priest told her solemnly, 'That's a terrible cross to be bearing. You know what you must do.'

'What, Father? *What* should I do?'

'Go to the police at once.'

Cook leaned back in the chair. She had shared her secret and felt better for it, but the fear was still there. 'Will you pray for me, Father?'

'We'll pray together, then you will find the courage to tell the police what you know.'

'You won't tell, will you, Father? You won't betray me?'

'I can never betray your confidence. It is *you* who must go to the police. But first we'll pray for the Lord to help you.'

He began the prayer, and for a time, Cook prayed softly with him. By the time he had finished, she was gone; having sneaked out as softly as she came in.

As soon as he realised, he ran through the aisles, searching for her. When he couldn't see her anywhere, he hurried outside, catching the last glimpse of her as she rounded the corner. Going in pursuit he hoped he might catch up. But she was already rushing away as if the devil himself was on her heels.

Another frantic minute and she was gone; together with her terrible, frightening secret.

Walking back, he recalled what she had said; '*I know somebody who's committed murder . . . three times, Father!*'

Absent-mindedly, he looked about him, at the well-tended gardens and the lanes beyond, everything neat and normal as always. But there were things the eye could not see, and these were the things that played strong on his mind at that moment.

As he thought of the consequences of today, his heart sank. 'God help us all,' he murmured. 'If only she'd had the courage to do what she knows to be right.' But she hadn't. Instead, she had taken fright and run away.

And there was not a thing he could do about it.

Two nights later, after she'd plucked up the courage to visit a dear, sick friend, Cook imagined someone was following her. Several times she looked back, but there was no one behind her that she could see. Nothing untoward, she told herself, but in the dark of night, the fear would not go away.

Hurrying as fast as she could, she continued her way home, so nervous she was almost running by the time she came to the High Street. 'Lord help me,' she kept saying. 'There's bad things happening.'

Later that same night, a courting couple found her in the centre of Woburn, doubled up in a shop doorway, in a pool of her own blood. She had been viciously attacked, her throat cut from ear to ear.

There appeared to be no apparent motive, for her purse was still secure in her handbag and the ruby ring she always wore was still on her finger.

The police enquiries were long and thorough, but there was nothing for them to go on. The inspector was puzzled as to why a dear old soul, as his wide enquiries had led him to believe Mrs Bellamy was, should be cut down in such a cruel, brutish manner.

'What about the way she near fainted when she heard the news of the whore's murder? The maid said she was positively shaking.' The sergeant had looked at the crime from every angle, until he was beginning to lose faith in himself.

'That means nothing,' the inspector said dismissively. 'I

should imagine every decent person in Woburn, especially at her age, would be made to near-faint at such terrible news.'

'Ah, but then according to this Meg, she took off suddenly. So where was she going? It wasn't to her friend's, because she hadn't seen her for a week, until the night she was killed.'

'That's easily explained. I should think she simply needed to get out in the fresh air after the shock of hearing news like that. As to where she was going, we'll just have to persevere with our enquiries. We may never find out.' He stroked his chin thoughtfully. 'We'll assume that she merely went for a walk, and as we can't find evidence of anything else at this minute, that has to be my thinking.'

The sergeant had a theory, 'The murderer might not even come from these parts,' he suggested. 'What with the two whores, and now a poor old woman, it wouldn't surprise me if we're not dealing with some sort of maniac who's found his way into the area. Perhaps we should think along those lines?'

'Hmh.' The inspector had already considered that theory. 'The fact is, whoever is killing these women must be either stark crazy . . . or pure evil.' He sat for a moment on the edge of his desk, nodding his head as though agreeing with the thoughts in his own head. 'Three women already murdered in a barbaric manner.' He looked across at the sergeant who had begun pacing the floor. 'The truth is, I can't help wondering if it'll end there.'

'What makes you say that?'

'Well, for one thing, there doesn't appear to be a motive – at least not one that we've found so far. At first I thought it might be because these other women were known to be loose women – and you know how some folks take against them. But now, with this older woman – a respectable cook, no less – I don't know *what* to think. You see, if there's no motive, he must be killing for the fun of it. And that means we could see another poor devil cut to ribbons before the day's out.'

The sergeant was made to halt his pacing. 'In that case, we'd best get down to some serious work and catch the bugger! Or it'll be *our* necks on the line next time.'

In the nearby church, the priest was on his knees before the altar. 'What am I to do, Lord?' He raised his face to the crucifix. 'I'm not altogether sure it's the same woman, but she told me her name was Annie, and so was the murdered woman's.'

In his mind he could see Cook running away. 'From the description given in the newspapers and from the woman I saw here, I do believe that the victim and the tortured soul who came to me, were one and the same woman.'

Deeply troubled, he bowed his head in prayer. 'I'm bound by the laws of God and the Church. I cannot betray her confidence,' he murmured. 'But how am I to stand by and keep such a terrible secret?'

Looking up again, there were tears in his eyes. 'I didn't help her, Lord. She came to me for help, and I let her down. Now, for my sins, her burden has become mine. Please, Lord, give me the strength to carry it within me, as I know I must.'

For the first time in his unqualified commitment to the Church, he had doubts he had never experienced before. The thought of that poor woman, terrified by what she knew and afraid to confide even in him, would haunt him for ever.

Chapter Fifteen

On 15 June, 1901, after being moved from one hospital and institution to another, Robert finally left the same hospital he had first been admitted to. It had been a long agonising period of his life, but at last it was almost over.

Having undergone the last of four operations to straighten his right foot, he was making an excellent recovery. 'It will never be absolutely perfect,' Dr Morrison told him, 'but with a bit of luck, you might be the only one who notices.'

He pursed his lips, about to break more, not quite so good news. 'I'm afraid the hip hasn't responded in the same way. You will always walk with the slightest limp, but for a man who's been through the trauma you have, you may think it's little enough to pay for the saving of your life.'

Immensely grateful, Robert thought exactly that. From the bottom of his heart, he thanked this wonderful, talented man who had seen him through the darkest days.

'When will I be able to leave?' he asked. He had things to do. Things that had haunted him for too long.

'A week maybe, two at the most.' Rising from the end of the bed where, much to Matron's annoyance, he always sat when talking to patients, Dr Morrison patted Robert on the back. 'I want you out of here, as fast as you want to leave.' He gave a mischievous grin. 'I need the bed for my next challenge.'

As good as his word, the surgeon discharged his patient two weeks to the day.

Emerging from that hospital into the glorious sunshine was the best day of Robert Sullivan's life. 'I never thought I'd breathe fresh air again,' he murmured, as he gave thanks to that special Somebody up there, Who had brought him through it.

He carried with him a small suitcase, given to him by one of the nurses. It contained two shirts, one spare pair of trousers and some underwear. Other than that, all he owned in the world was the clothes he wore, ten shillings from the hospital charity fund, and two letters in his pocket, given to him by the surgeon as he left. 'They will help get you started,' he explained. 'Take each one to the address on the front. They'll be expecting you. It's all arranged.'

He saw Robert to the office door. 'I don't want you aimlessly wandering the streets after all the time and effort we've both put in to make sure this day would happen.' He stood at the door, watching Robert walk away. Proud and satisfied, he then returned to his work, quietly preparing for the next patient who needed his help.

That morning, Robert had been too excited to eat, so now his stomach grumbled and complained until he had to stop at the local café. 'Tea and toast,' he gave his order to the pretty, half-asleep waitress. 'And lashings of sugar in the tea, if you please.' His ready smile made her blush to her roots, but embarrassing her was not meant on Robert's part; for he was just glad to be alive.

Settling down in the chair, he took the letters out of his pocket. One was addressed to Mr Mortimer Jackson who, according to the surgeon, ran a fleet of carriages. 'I've known him a good many years,' he told Robert, 'and he's always looking for responsible drivers. I've told him you would not let him down if he were to give you a start.'

The second letter was addressed to a Miss Stewart, the landlady of a reputable lodging house on the outskirts of Bedford; she had apparently been a nurse at the hospital in years gone by, and she was also one of the surgeon's grateful patients.

'There you are, sir.' The waitress had obviously tended to her appearance, because now her hair was combed and she had a smattering of colour on her lips; a marked change from the raggedy-hair and plain undressed face which originally greeted him. 'I've put lashings of sugar in your tea as you wanted, and nearly half a pat of butter on your toast. We've got heaps of strawberry jam if you want?'

Robert liked the idea of 'heaps of strawberry jam'. 'Go on then,' he said, with that ready smile which seemed to buckle her knees. 'I don't mind if I do.' So she brought the pot, and shyly smiled down on him as she painted his toast with heaps of jam, accidentally painting his shoe at the same time.

When he'd finished his breakfast and gone to the counter to pay, she blushed and smiled, and blushed again, until Robert didn't know quite what to do. So he gave her a quick kiss on the hand, and she almost fainted. 'Ooh!' That was all she said, and he thought he'd best make tracks before she got any other ideas. After all, he was only just out of hospital.

Once he was through the door and safe, he laughed to himself. 'She needs a better man than me,' he murmured. 'I don't even know if I'm capable any more.'

Suddenly his mind was filled with thoughts of Mary. Her name began in his heart and whispered on his lips. '*Mary.*' His mood became sombre. 'Where are you now, I wonder?'

His children, too, had lived in his heart and mind all these years. He thought of his little family, and his determination was never stronger than it was now. I'll find them,' he vowed softly. 'I'll find them *all*!'

First though, he had to track down the man who had killed his one and only friend, Geordie. He had been shocked to his roots when the news had come to him of Geordie's killing. His instincts told Robert that the same man who had pushed him under the wheels of that carriage was responsible. 'I'm after you, you bastard!' he muttered through gritted teeth. 'You'll pay for what you did . . . to me *and* Geordie. Wherever you are, I'll root you out, and when I do, there'll be no escape.'

It was a strange thing, because he believed himself to be over the trauma of that awful night, but just now, when he went to cross the street, a carriage and four came rushing towards him. Catching his breath he froze on the spot; it took a few minutes and a steely determination to compose himself, before he was able to cross the street.

Unnerved, he began to realise that the outside world was a whole new experience and would take a while for him to get used to. 'Even if I'm offered the work, will I ever be able to drive a horse and carriage?' Until now, the question had not even entered his head.

His first stop was the lodging house.

After a short cab-ride and a wrong turn on foot when he feared he had been put down on the wrong street, Robert finally located the house by the arched bridge on the riverbank. Large and imposing, it was not what he had imagined for a lodging house.

For a long time he stood looking at it. The house breathed character. It was a very old, rambling property with tall windows and stone mullions. There was a meandering flagged path leading to the front door, and long, beautifully kept flower beds on either side. The ancient, giant door was carved with roses around each panel and right in the top centre hung a brass lion-head knocker. It was a most impressive dwelling.

'I don't know that I shall fit in here.' Feeling nervous, Robert edged himself on. 'Come on, Robert m'boy. Dr Morrison wouldn't have sent you here if he didn't think it was right.'

Rolling his eyes to heaven, he shrugged his shoulders and summoned courage. 'Besides, you've got no choice at the minute.'

Somewhat reluctantly, he began his way down the path. When he got to the door he gingerly raised the lion head and bringing it down, clattered it against the plating beneath, alarmed when it made more noise than he'd anticipated.

The door opened almost immediately. 'I saw you coming up the path,' the woman said abruptly. 'For a minute there, I didn't know whether you were coming in or not.'

A tall, gangly woman with large white teeth and piled up mousey-coloured hair, Miss Stewart had that upright, authoritative manner that made a body feel slightly inferior. 'I inherited this house from my father,' she informed Robert as he entered. 'Been in the family for generations.'

Observing her heavily creased face, somewhat scrawny figure, encased in a long dark skirt and severely starched pinnie, Robert didn't know whether she meant the house, or herself.

Yet for all her unlikely appearance she glided across the floor like a swan on a lake. 'Follow me!' She led him gallantly across the hallway, giving a running commentary as she went. 'I was a nurse, you see . . . retired these past twelve years. I never married and never wanted to, so I had no family, apart from my parents. When they passed on, I was left this beautiful house.' She swept through the open hallway with its big windows and many wall-mounted tapestries, and was now moving along the narrow passage towards the living accommodation.

The commentary continued. 'I didn't move into it for a long time, but then I got to feeling lonely and decided to turn this place into a lodging house. Now, of course, it not only gives me a living, but I get to see people come and go.'

As she turned to smile at him, the morning light shone through the stained-glass panel above the door and caught her teeth like paint on a canvas; suddenly they reflected the most dazzling array of colours imaginable. It was a frightening, magical thing to see.

'It's a very interesting house.' Robert thought the house and the woman went together perfectly; both were ancient, both were stalwart and, in a curious way, warmly welcoming.

Gliding past two doors, each closed, she threw out both her arms in an extravagant gesture. 'These are my own private quarters.' Pausing, she looked him in the eye; apart from the raised eyebrows her face was devoid of expression, yet there was a certain element of warning in her voice as she explained quietly, 'No one has ever been invited beyond these doors, and no one ever will. I am a woman who likes my privacy.'

Suddenly, without waiting for a response from Robert, she was off again, turning on her heel and heading back in the direction from which they had just come. Swinging to the left of the hallway, she threw open a door and suddenly it was like the whole world opening out. 'Oh!' Shocked with pleasure, Robert couldn't believe his eyes. 'What a beautiful room!'

'Thank you.' Her face beamed from ear to ear and the teeth were almost blinding in that natural bright light. 'This is the sitting room. I have eight guests staying and there is more than enough room for everyone to be quite comfortable in here. I have newspapers delivered every morning, and keep a good selection of reading material if required.' Turning to face him, she seemed momentarily shy. 'I'm so glad you like it.'

Robert could not deny it was the most amazing room he had ever been in. Flooded with sunshine, the place was huge. At one end, and taking up most of the wall, was a set of three huge windows; one a delightful bay window with a seat all round, and the other two long and wide on either side. The mustard-coloured velvet curtains hung grandly in between, and along the window-seat were a whole collection of pretty, plump cushions to match. 'I made the curtains and cushions myself,' Miss Stewart said proudly. 'A competence in sewing was one of the many things my mother insisted on, from a very early age.'

To the left and right of the room, pictures of landscapes and seascapes hung over the brightly painted walls; there was a long dresser with shelves above it, carrying newspapers and books, and even a vase bursting with summer blossoms. Scattered about in pleasant fashion was an abundance of sofas and three deep armchairs, and every one covered in the prettiest of material. 'All my own work,' she kept saying. 'All my own work,' and Robert was deeply impressed.

Quickly now she completed the tour. The dining room was equally pleasant, with eight small round tables each covered with a white tablecloth and set for dinner. 'The guests have gone off to their various places of employment,' she said. 'Breakfast is finished early, but I'm sure I can rustle up some egg and bacon if you're hungry.' She seemed embarrassed. 'Dr Morrison told me of your history, Mr Sullivan. I do so want to make you comfortable here. I would like you to consider this as your home, for as long as you need.'

Deeply grateful, Robert thanked her and they moved on. She showed him the coats cupboard and the nearby cloakroom with flush lavatory and hand-basin. 'I had all the plumbing put in,' she said. 'As you can see, there's a W.C. here, and two bathrooms upstairs. There are nine bedrooms, each with its own view of the river, and a back access to the street, for frequent comings and goings.'

When he saw the room that would be his, Robert was thrilled. Of medium size, it was cosy and bright, with floral curtains at the window and a hand-basin in the corner. Covered with a patchwork eiderdown, the bed was large and inviting, added to which, along the back wall was a dressing-table with deep drawers and mirror, and beside it a small wardrobe. Everything, in fact, a man might need.

The view of the river was unbelievably wonderful.

From the wide window he could see all the way from the arched bridge, right down to the main street. Six graceful swans mingled not far from where he was, and some way up the river, a canoeist wended his way through the rippling water. Dressed in vest and loose trousers he seemed eminently capable.

All along the bank, myriads of wild flowers were out in bloom; the tended beds which flanked the walkways were a feast to the eyes, and the old willow trees dipped their branches in the water as if taking a drink. 'Magnificent!' he breathed.

'Good!' She flashed her teeth again and rushed from the room; assuming that Robert was right behind her.

Limping slightly, he followed her to the downstairs office, where he was told the boarding-rates. 'One shilling a night without breakfast, and an extra threepence *with* breakfast. Dinner is sixpence extra.' Looking up from her ledger she informed him sombrely, 'I always take seven shillings in advance.'

Thinking how he might not find work quickly, even with his letter of introduction, Robert's heart sank. If he had to pay that much money out now, it would leave him virtually broke.

'But not from you, Mr Sullivan!' She gave him the most understanding of smiles. 'Dr Morrison assured me that you were a dependable sort, with an unusual streak of decency, so on this one occasion I've decided to forgo the advance. I'm sure you will need every penny you've got over the coming weeks.'

With a huge sigh of relief, Robert thanked her. 'You're very kind.' His first impression of her had been that of a woman with a starchy nature; a hard woman of business who would not give an inch. He was glad now, to see he could not have been more wrong.

She handed him three keys – one to his room, and one each for the front and back doors. 'What do you say? Would you like some breakfast?'

'If it's all right with you, I'd much prefer to go out and find work. I have a letter of introduction from the doctor to see a man by the name of Mortimer Jackson. He owns a fleet of carriages, I'm told.'

She stood up. 'You were told right,' she confirmed. 'He is also a man of good reputation. Go and see him by all means. I'm sure you won't be disappointed.'

In the broadest smile yet, she showed her teeth again. 'I have a million things to do,' she explained. 'I run this house on my own, you see. I've had countless helpers and none of them proved suitable. In the end I decided the only person I can rely on is myself. Besides, I find the work very rewarding. I get to keep fit in myself, and make sure everything is done to my liking. And of course, I save on a person's wages, so I win all round.'

Without another word she went from her desk and was gone, along the passage and into her own private quarters, while Robert was left to find his own way back to his room. Which he did without delay.

Once there, he unpacked his things into the wardrobe and washed at the hand-basin. He then combed his hair and tidied himself up, after which, with hope in his heart and a few coins jingling in his trouser pocket, he left the house by way of the back access.

Following the embankment towards the direction of town, he paused to check the address on the letter. Satisfying himself that he had it right in his mind, he set off again, at a smarter pace. Another few steps along the embankment then on to the High Street, where after a good ten-minute walk, he came to the address.

The building was an old warehouse on the very edge of the main street. From the front it looked quite small, but when Robert stepped sideways to look behind the gates, he could see that in fact the building stretched a long way back – almost to the railway lines. There was another, smaller building opposite, and in between a stone-flagged courtyard where, parked there in all their shining glory, were several black carriages, obviously got ready for the day's work.

Returning to the front entrance, Robert noticed the sign above the entrance:

MORTIMER JACKSON
Carriages for all occasions

On entering he went straight to the reception desk. 'Mr Jackson was expecting you,' the young woman there assured him. 'He's asked me to tell you that he'll be out in five minutes. He's just speaking with a client.'

Almost to the minute, two men emerged out of the door to her left. Each one was of middle years and already greying with the pressure of business. One of the gents was a slim man with stooped shoulders and a weary manner; the other was portly, bald and homely-looking. The latter was not a smiler, because not once as he talked to the other man, or even when he wished him good day, did he give even the smallest hint of a smile.

When the slim man was gone and the door had closed behind him, the older gent went to the desk, where he deposited some papers. Having done that, he turned to Robert. 'And you are?' He eyed Robert with interest.

'Robert Sullivan, sir. Dr Morrison sent me.'

'Ah, yes.' He stroked his chin, and looking Robert up and down, seemed to like what he saw. 'I understand you have a letter?'

'Yes, sir. I have it right here.' Reaching into his pocket he handed the letter over with one hand, while holding out the other in greeting. 'It's good of you to see me.' Shaking the other man's hand, he gave a smile but got none in return.

Perusing the letter, Jackson began slowly walking up and down. Robert stood silent, waiting; hoping.

Presently, Mr Jackson turned to address him. 'Mmm. It seems my friend Dr Morrison thinks a lot of you. It says here you've got backbone and courage.'

'I don't know about that, sir,' Robert said modestly. 'The truth is, I couldn't have pulled through without Dr Morrison's help. He shipped me to so many different doctors and specialists, I've forgotten them all, but he promised to send me out of that hospital on my own two feet, and he did it. I shall be forever grateful to him for that.'

The older man observed him boldly. 'It usually takes two,' he remarked bluntly. 'I'm quite sure even Morrison, good man that he is, could never have kept his promise if you hadn't given him every encouragement.'

'Maybe.' Robert had the feeling that Mr Jackson held strong opinions and didn't care much for anyone who questioned them.

'He tells me you've been through a bad time?'

'I have sir, yes, but I'm fit for work now.'

'Mmm.' Walking round Robert he took note of the long, lean figure and the straight back and shoulders. He saw how Robert was leaning heavily on one foot and commented, not without feeling, 'You seem to have a problem with that foot?'

'There's nothing wrong with my foot, sir, except it's not as straight as the other. It would never stop me working.'

'Would it stop you driving?'

'No, sir, I'm sure it would not.'

'Have you a licence to drive a carriage?'

'No, sir.'

'Mmm.' Again he took stock, of Robert's good looks and shock of thick hair. 'Would you *like* to drive a carriage?'

Robert began to relax. 'I would, yes. I'm keen to start work and earn a living. Thanks to Dr Morrison I have a room in a nice house along the embankment. I'm not given to charity, sir. I like to pay my way, so the sooner I start work the better, and driving a carriage sounds to me as good a way to earn a living as any other.'

'I'll have you know, it's a responsible job. Not to be taken lightly!'

'I understand that, sir.'

Of a sudden Mr Jackson was standing in front of him, his eyes looking directly into Robert's, as if searching for the truth. 'Can I ask you something, Sullivan?'

'Yes, sir. Course you can.' Though he didn't much care for the sound of the other man's voice. He prepared himself for the worst.

'Well now, how am I to put it?' He went on kindly, 'I'm told it was a carriage and four that ran you over – that you were dragged under the horses' hooves for some distance, and when they got you to the Infirmary you were just a heartbeat away from losing your life?'

'So I'm led to understand, yes.' It was not a memory he cared to relive but he did so now, and it was a harrowing experience.

'And if that's the case, would it not worry you to drive a carriage and four?'

'Yes, sir, I can't deny it *might* well be unpleasant. But that was a long time since. I have to put it behind me if I can.' He gave a sigh that came from his boots. 'Look, Mr Jackson, sir . . . I believe I would make a good driver, if only you'll give me the chance.'

'Come with me.' Suddenly Jackson was hurrying away, his arm stretched behind him, beckoning Robert with a flick of his finger. 'Hurry up, now! I have a customer arriving in ten minutes.'

Robert found himself being led through the inner office, out of the back door and along to the courtyard where the carriages stood. 'What do you think to this one?' Jackson led him to a particular large carriage. Closed in with hood and apron, it was being shackled to a horse.

'I think it's a grand-looking thing, sir.' Flashes of that night appeared in his mind to shake his confidence.

'Mmm!' With puffed-out chest and the merest hint of a smile on his face, Mr Jackson looked gratified. 'Grand . . . yes, so it is!' He was proud as any man could be. 'One of my newest,' he explained. 'I'm growing that busy, I need to add to my fleet. That's why I'm on the lookout for good drivers.'

Robert had no answer to that. He only hoped he would not lose his nerve when the time came.

'Climb up.'

'Sorry, sir?' Robert had heard but suddenly his knees had gone weak.

The older man scowled. 'I said *climb up*!' Lowering his head he frowned at Robert from beneath long, hairy eyebrows. 'Unless you've lost your nerve?'

Robert's heart took a knock. This was his test. This was the moment when he would find out whether or not he had put the memory of that night behind him.

'Come on, man!'

'Yes, sir.' Taking a deep breath, Robert approached the ensemble with fast-beating heart. When suddenly the horse turned to look at him, he paused, but then moved on again, inching closer, willing his feet to take him all the way.

Both Mr Jackson and his groom Geoff stood by; Mr Jackson with his hands in his pockets and the tiniest doubt in his mind, while the groom stood ready, hand on the reins and talking softly to the horse as Robert approached.

'Show confidence, man!' Mr Jackson's warning rang out. 'A horse can smell fear a mile off. He'll be more frightened than you. Easy now! Easy.'

Swallowing his terror, Robert brought Mary to mind; she had the ability to calm him. He touched the horse on the neck, then he grabbed the side handles of the carriage and hauled himself up, the sweat trickling down his back and standing out like sparkling beads on his temples.

The groom nodded to the boss, and the boss nodded back. 'Well done, Mr Sullivan. Now, take him up the courtyard and back. I know you have little knowledge of how to turn a circle, but I want you to try, and remember – the horse will help, but only if you want him to.'

With Geoff taking him through the motions, Robert went round the courtyard several times before Mr Jackson was satisfied. The groom led Robert back for the verdict.

'Mmm.' Mr Jackson walked up and down, hands in pockets and pursing his lips. 'Mmm . . .' Presently, he looked up at Robert. 'How do you feel?'

Robert felt exhilarated and said so. 'I'll be honest,' he confessed, 'I never thought I'd have the nerve, but yes, I like it, sir. I really do!' He even dared to laugh. 'All in all, sir, I reckon I'd make you a fine driver.'

Mr Jackson looked at the groom. 'What do you think, Geoff? Will he do or will he not?'

Geoff was a happy-looking fellow, with ginger hair to his shoulders and straight, noble features that now broke into a happy grin. 'I think he'll do fine, sir.'

Mr Jackson looked up at Robert, who like the other man was happily smiling, and rapped out: 'I don't like wasted time in working hours. I don't care for chit-chat, and I will not tolerate laziness. If there are no fares to carry, I expect my men to wash the carriages and feed the horses, and when that's done, I expect the courtyard to be so clean you could eat off the ground.'

With hope growing by the minute, Robert nodded appreciatively. 'Yes, sir!'

'I expect the horses to be shining like glass when they go out on the streets, likewise the carriages themselves and the men who sit up in the driving seat. I have a reputation to uphold. Do you take my meaning, Sullivan?'

'Every word, sir.'

'You understand this business is my pride and joy. I have no family, only my precious business. It's taken me thirty years of hard work to build myself up from being a driver in a hired carriage, into the owner of the largest fleet of carriages in Bedfordshire.'

'That's very admirable, sir.' He had taken a liking to this man, but whether the feeling was mutual he couldn't tell.

For a minute the darkest of moods took over Mr Jackson. 'Admirable maybe, but I'm the only one who knows what sweat, blood and tears have gone into making this business what it is!'

Suddenly, for whatever reason, Robert felt he was being cautioned. Glancing at the groom he took the warning, when that man's eyes widened and shut, as if to say, 'Stay quiet!'

'Did you know that we now have motor-driven vehicles threatening our roads?' Jackson boomed suddenly.

'No, sir, I didn't know that.'

'Mmm!' The man thought for a moment. 'Of course, you've been away from it all, I suppose. But yes . . . motor-driven vehicles, would you believe! They seem to be getting a great deal of attention. I dare say there will come a day when these beautiful carriages are replaced by the iron monstrosities!'

'That would be a shame, sir.'

'Maybe, but being the sensible man that I am, and having always kept a close eye on new developments, I have this very morning agreed to go and inspect one of these newfangled things. So, as you can see, I have no intention of letting my business stand still.'

'Yes, I can see that, sir.'

'I'm a fair man and I pay a fair wage, with one week's holiday a year, and an extra day at Christmas.'

'That's very generous, sir.'

Again, and this time only for a fleeting moment, the scowl returned as he stared up at Robert to give the order. 'Get down from there!'

As quickly as he could, Robert scampered down.

When he and Mr Jackson were standing eyeball to eyeball, the older man went on in severe tones, 'If I'm to stay ahead of the competition, I find I must wield a big stick.'

'Yes, sir.'

'Make no mistake, if I should find any man wasting my time, I would not hesitate to show him the door.'

'No, sir.'

'Mmm.'

The silence was unbearable, then just as suddenly it was broken. 'Start Monday, seven a.m. – and don't be late!'

Robert saw the groom smiling and winking, and he couldn't believe that he'd actually got the job! 'Thank you, sir.' Now, as he looked Mr Jackson in the eye, a kind of appreciation passed between them. 'I won't let you down, sir.'

In an unprecedented gesture, Mr Jackson gave Robert a friendly slap on the arm. 'Well done, Sullivan.' With that he marched off, while calling behind him, 'And get some fat on you, for God's sake. I don't want folks thinking I don't pay my men enough to keep body and soul together!'

Behind him, Robert and the redheaded groom were laughing and congratulating each other. 'He's right,' Geoff said. 'You don't look as far through as a hairpin, but at least you've got the job. And don't worry. I'll teach you well. Before you know it, you'll be driving like the best of us.'

Robert was over the moon. 'I'm back,' he said quietly. 'After all this long time, *I'm back*!' It was a good feeling.

* * *

As he made his way into town, Robert whistled and sang and didn't care when folks looked at him as though they thought he was mad as a hatter.

His next stop was the town hall. Once there he stood on the steps, the harrowing memories of that snowy day six long years ago pouring into his heart and soul until he thought he really *would* go mad.

After a while, with determined strides he went up the steps and into the foyer, where he approached the clerk at the desk. 'I need to speak with someone of authority,' he told her. 'Someone to do with the placing of children.'

The girl looked at him curiously for a moment. 'What exactly do you mean, sir?'

'I mean, if a man who was out of his mind with troubles, were to leave his children on this very doorstep, who would be the one to deal with it?'

She wondered about him. He seemed quite normal, if a little unsettled. 'I'll call Mr Thompson, He might be able to answer your questions better than me.' Pointing to the bench she suggested, 'If you could please wait there, I'm sure he won't be long.'

Turning to sit, Robert saw how the bench she meant was the very one where he had abandoned Nancy and Jack. The truth brought a hard, choking lump to his throat. How could he sit there now? He couldn't, not even if his life depended on it.

He became so troubled by it, he couldn't even think straight. His emotions were all over the place. So he paced the floor until the door opened and a man of bent form and strong features came to him. 'Can I help you, sir?'

Robert explained how, some years before, he had left his two children in this place, and since then had been in various hospitals undergoing endless surgery after a terrible accident. 'I left them for a whole day, then when my mind had cleared, I came back to collect them, but I couldn't, d'you see? The town hall was locked up. After that, everything went wrong. But I've come for them now. I've got a place to live, and a respectable job. Look, you must find them. I have to let them know it was never meant for me to leave them.' His voice shook. 'Please! I *have* to find them.'

The man was sympathetic but firm. 'I'm sorry, sir, but if you left them here and never came back, it's a certainty that they would have been placed in a suitable home.' He looked at Robert and thought for a minute, and his eyes lit up. 'I do believe I recall the incident,' he said. 'It was our Mrs Compton who dealt with it, I believe.'

'Where can I find her?'

'Oh, she left this employment a long time ago now.. But she wouldn't be able to tell you anything anyway, I'm afraid. Once the children are placed, it's a matter of looking after *their* interests. After all, if you don't mind me saying, whatever the circumstances, you *did* desert them. Whether or not you had second thoughts won't change that sad fact. I'm afraid you may never find your children now.'

'No! You have to help me!' Taking the man by the lapels Robert almost lost control, but then he released him and apologised. 'Please, I'll do anything to get them back.'

The man was adamant. 'I'm sorry, sir. As far as this establishment is concerned, the matter is closed. It was a long time ago. The children are probably safe and sound and growing up with some fine family. I really can't help you.' With that he excused himself and scurried away, leaving Robert devastated.

'Sir?' The girl at the desk had overheard every word. 'I'm sorry, but you'd best leave now.'

Going to her, Robert asked, 'You heard?'

'I did, yes.'

'I never would have left my children, only I couldn't come back . . . I swear, I would have come back and collected them, but I was hurt bad.'

Seeing him like that, distraught, the tears hovering in his dark eyes, she felt a surge of compassion. 'You could see Alice Compton. He did say she was likely the one to have dealt with it. Maybe she could help?'

Hope surged through him. 'Do you know where I can find her?'

She shook her head. 'She left before I started here, although I've met her once or twice, but I'll try to find out where she lives. If I do, I'll tell her you'd like a word.'

'And will you tell her how unhappy I am? That I love my children more than my own life? I want them back, wherever they are. I want them back. I'm their father. They're *my* children! Tell her I won't cause any trouble. All I want is for her to tell me where I can find them.'

'Yes, sir, I'll tell her all that.'

'Look, I know they were taken to Galloways Children's Home before they were fostered out, but I don't know where they were sent. I mean to make enquiries there. Tell your Mrs Compton that she might find me in the pub by the orphanage. I'll wait there every Friday. I'll watch for her. Describe me to her, so she won't miss me. Tell her to come soon. Will you do that?'

'I'll try. I can't promise, you understand? But I will try.'

More grateful than he could say, Robert nodded. 'Try your very best.'

'I will.'

He thanked her and from there, made his way to the orphanage.

At Galloways, Robert received short shrift. An argument began at the door and as a result, Clive Ennington was brought to deal with the troublemaker. Having been manager at the orphanage for too many years, he had suffered dealings with irate and difficult people before.

'Who the devil do you think you are?' he demanded, grabbing

Robert by the scruff of the neck and hauling him aside. 'Coming in here causing trouble, and for what, eh? Come on now, what do you want here?'

Shaking himself loose without too much bother, Robert answered, his voice trembling without rage, 'I've come for my kids, and I'm not leaving until you, or somebody else, tell me where I can find them.'

'You're nothing but a hobbledehoy! Who are you?' Now, as he stared back at Robert, he thought he saw an incredible likeness to someone . . . a boy maybe? But *which* boy? There had been so many. As his furtive mind sped back over the years, he was shocked to his roots when the lively image of Jack came to mind. 'My God!' Filled with fear he pushed Robert backwards. 'I'll not have my establishment turned upside down by the likes of you. Get out.' He gave him another push, this time more forcibly. 'Go on – get out I say!'

Trying hard to keep his hands from closing round the throat of this nasty piece of work, Robert held his ground. 'I've already told you. I'm not going anywhere until you tell me where I can find my kids . . . a girl by the name of Nancy and a boy named Jack.'

'How am I expected to remember the names of your children?' Inwardly shaking, he knew well enough who they were, but to admit it to this man would be like asking for a beating, and he was not so stupid. 'Good God, man! There are hundreds, possibly thousands of children passing through this establishment over the course of time. I can't be expected to remember every one.'

'Look in your ledger. You do keep records, don't you, of the children you take in and send out? We're talking of some six years ago.'

'The ledgers are official property. After all this time that particular ledger will have been filed away in the main offices.'

'There were troublesome circumstances. I felt I couldn't

handle the situation. I meant to take my life, but someone stopped me. Later that day, after I'd left them, I had a change of heart. I came back but the doors were closed against me, and believe it or not, I wasn't able to come back again until now – through no fault of my own, I swear it before God.'

Unwilling to explain why he had not come back the next day, he insisted, 'Tell me where they are and I'll leave peacable.'

'Huh! You'll leave peacable *now*, or I'll have the authorities here in minutes. They'll remove you quick enough, and you'll not find your children if you're locked up in jail, will you?'

Seeing that this man was not about to help him, and not wanting to end up in another institution where he might be put away for years, Robert wisely backed off. 'You've not heard the last of me,' he warned. 'I mean to get my children back, and get them back I will. And when I do, I reckon there'll be questions to answer.'

Poking the other man in the chest with the tip of his finger, he lowered his voice. 'There's something funny going on here, and I'll get to the bottom of it, you see if I don't.'

With his suspicion confirmed that here indeed was the father of the two children – a girl he had sold for a handsome profit, and a boy who, for the sake of appearances he had sent to a genuinely decent home, Clive Ennington was quietly shaking in his boots.

For the sake of his position, and the very real possibility that it would be *him* going to jail if the truth ever got out, he tried in vain to calm this man, who had obviously passed on his foul temper to that son of his.

'Look here, Mr . . . ?' He didn't even know the family's name.

'Sullivan, father of Nancy and Jack Sullivan, a man who won't be fobbed off. A man who won't rest until he gets his children back.'

'Well, Mr Sullivan, I *can* tell you that your children will have been placed in good homes.' Determined not to spill any useful information, he bluffed and fidgeted. 'Other than that, I am not at liberty to divulge details of any child passing through this institution. That is a matter for the authorities. If you need to trace your children, you must apply to the courts, but I warn you, you're not the only person looking to recover his children after deserting them. Moreover, that in itself is a crime. Why, I've even known a man to be thrown in jail, simply for asking too many questions about the children he abandoned.'

Robert protested angrily. 'I'm no criminal! I came back that same night and they were gone. How is that "deserting" them? I've told you once but I can see I'll have to tell you again: I want them back and I swear, I'll leave no stone unturned, till I do.'

'Then you're a damned fool, sir! The courts don't look kindly on your sort. What makes you think they'll hand over two innocent children to a man who was callous enough to leave them alone with strangers, to a fate nobody could foresee?' Getting carried away with his own false sense of righteousness, Ennington declared arrogantly, 'If you ask me, sir, it was a good job we were on hand to rescue the poor little souls.'

'Oh? And what, I wonder, would the courts think about somebody who commandeers two children, then refuses the father even an address where he can be sure they're being properly treated?'

'As I've already said, I've no doubt but that they were placed in a good home, as we place all our children. Moreover, they're probably very content to have forgotten you. Really, sir, how can you bring yourself to wrench them from a new life, just to appease your own conscience? What kind of a father are you?'

At that moment another voice intervened. 'Best go, sir. You'll not get no change here.' The woman glanced at the manager with a peculiar, hateful expression, which only Robert seemed to notice. 'You don't want the police to come and take you away, but they will if you intend making trouble.'

Clive Ennington beamed across his fat, floppy face. 'Thank you, Edith. I'm sure the young man will take note of your wise words.'

Robert glanced at the woman and when she nodded, with a certain secret message in her eyes, he thought he understood. 'All right,' he told the manager. 'But I'll be back, make no mistake on it.'

'Good man!' Ennington visibly relaxed. 'Now the fuss is over, I shall have to return to my duties.' His smile was sickly. 'Children to see to, and all that.'

With the manager out of sight and hearing, Edith Charles proved to be a friend. 'He means what he says,' she warned Robert. 'He'd have you locked away, soon as look at yer.'

Robert appreciated her warning but, 'I also meant what I said. I will not rest till I find them.'

Glancing first this way then that, and having satisfied herself that no one was about to sneak up on them, Edith confided, 'It's Iris Dayley you want. She's been housekeeper at this place for so long nobody seems to notice her. She comes and goes and doesn't miss a thing. If anybody knows where your kids are, it'll be Iris.'

There was a moment of confusion before Robert recalled something Geordie had told him. He often used to mention the woman Iris Dayley. My God, yes – hadn't he said that she knew things, but wouldn't tell?

'Where can I find her?' Looking about him, he almost expected her to be standing there.

Edith wagged a finger. 'Oh, yer won't find her here. Oh no! She were hounded out, y'see? There were things she spoke up about. She had the courage to go against *him*,' she nodded in the direction the manager had gone, 'an' he warned her, much as he warned you, about the authorities and such. Shame!' She sighed wearily. 'The poor devil were given her notice last week. You see, she were found in the larder, knocking back the booze. It were the very excuse he'd been waiting for, so as he could be rid of her and no questions asked, if you see what I mean? He had her out that door so fast her feet never even touched the ground, poor bugger. She ain't got no family, did you know that?'

Robert knew nothing about her other than what Geordie had told him, and that was very little. From what this woman told him, Iris Dayley had been given a poor deal, but right now, his priority was his own family. 'So, where will I find her?'

'Try the pub across the street. I've heard she frequents it every so often.' Leaning forward, she whispered, 'Some say as she's turned into a drunk . . . can't do without it, or so it seems.'

Robert could afford to be generous, as he'd just been given his first real lead to his children. 'Thank you.' Reaching into his pocket he found a sixpence, which to her surprise he pressed into the palm of her hand.

'Oh, thank you sir. Thank you!' The wages here were so abysmal, that a sixpence was a real godsend.

'These things that somebody told you, about the old housekeeper being a drunk . . .' Robert said thoughtfully.

'What about it?'

'I've always made it a rule never to listen to idle gossip. People and their tongues can be too cruel.'

Looking ashamed, she thanked him again. 'You're right,' she agreed. 'Iris ain't a bad old cow. From now on, I'll not listen to anything nasty said about her.' Glancing about to make certain they were not seen talking together, she looked at him with wide, scared eyes. 'She shoulda kept her mouth shut all the same. No use stirring up trouble if you can't do anything about it, is there?'

And before he could turn towards the door she was off, down the passage at the double, and talking to herself all the way.

Robert was disappointed to find that the pub which Iris apparently frequented was closed until the evening. 'The landlord has had to go north on some personal matter,' a passer-by told him. 'But it'll be open tonight.'

Feeling exhausted after his busy start to the day, Robert didn't go straight back to his lodgings. Instead, as the morning sun grew stronger and he became more optimistic about finding Nancy and Jack, he walked and walked, until his back ached and his feet throbbed; up one street and down the next, not really knowing where he was going and not minding. He took in all the familiar sights and sounds; pausing here and there to look in a shop window, or holding a passing conversation with some lonely person, if they were so inclined.

Finally, in late afternoon he began his way home, but stopped to sit by the river for a while. He watched the swans glide about in their beautiful graceful manner, and marvelled at the canoeists practising their skills, and he felt curiously calmed by it. Except for the matter of his two children, he felt remarkably good. More than that, he delighted in being a free man. After so long being in pain and surrounded by illness, it was like being born all over again.

At three o'clock his stomach took him to the nearby café, where he had two chunky bacon sandwiches and a mug of hot tea. After that, and feeling bone weary, he made his way back to his lodgings, where he went straight to bed and fell into a deep, satisfying sleep.

It was eight thirty when he woke, refreshed and strong of limb. He washed and changed and on the way out he told the landlady that yes, 'I've had a good day, thank you. I've got a job and start Monday, so I'll be able to catch up with what I owe you.'

'Will you be staying for an evening meal?' Miss Stewart prided herself on her cooking.

'Not tonight if you don't mind,' though he was grateful for the reminder. 'I'm hoping to meet up with somebody.'

'Then I won't set a place. But if you intend at any time staying for the evening meal, I'd appreciate it if you'd tell me the night before, so I know how much to cook. As it happens I had put extra on for you tonight, but it's no matter. I expect the others will enjoy more on their plates.' She told him she was glad he'd found work and wished him a good evening. Not being a woman given to chit-chat, she then went away to prepare the food, while Robert made his way back to the pub opposite the orphanage.

Relieved to see that it was now open, he went in, surprised to find it very busy. 'What can I get you?' The landlord was a big fellow, with a jolly nature. While he drew Robert's pint he chatted on, 'New to these parts, are yer?'

Robert wisely didn't give too much away; he knew how landlords passed on gossip. 'Staying with a friend,' he said. 'I suppose it won't be too long before I move on again,' Once he got Jack and Nancy back, he thought, they could pick up their lives together.

'There you go, sir. That'll be fourpence.' The big man shoved the jar of ale across the counter. 'Waiting for a friend, are yer?' he asked lazily.

Now, while the other customers were engaged in conversation, Robert thought it might be a good time to ask. 'D'you by any chance know a woman by the name of Iris Dayley?'

The landlord's eyes opened in astonishment. 'Well, well! Is *that* who you're waiting for? Just now, when I was fetching yer ale, I couldn't help but notice you kept glancing at the door.' His eyebrows went up in amazement. 'Iris Dayley, eh? Well, well.'

'I need to talk with her, that's all,' Robert said coolly.

The big man laughed, albeit kindly. 'She'll not talk with anybody,' he said. 'She's a sour old biddy – been coming to this place for a while now, and she ain't said so much as a how de do in all that time.' He leaned forward, imparting quietly, 'She got kicked out of her last drinking-place.' He was only conveying what he had heard. 'Summat about she threw a jar of ale all over some poor bloke . . . bit of a madwoman, so they say.'

'Really?' Robert wondered if he was doing right approaching her. After all, he didn't want to draw attention to himself, but then again, he had to know where Nancy and Jack had been sent, and according to the woman at the children's home, Iris Dayley was the likeliest one to know the truth of it all.

'Oh, aye.' The landlord explained, 'Apparently this bloke would insist on asking her questions, worrying her every time he clapped eyes on her, if yer know what I mean? The poor bugger waited for her, he did, every Friday, 'cause that's the time she went in for her booze.' He frowned. 'This 'ere fella as wouldn't leave her alone, well, it meks you wonder, don't it? He must have been bloody hard up, 'cause she's wrinkled as a prune an' ugly as the day's long. Huh! You'd have thought he could find summat better to do with hissel', than worrit an ugly old bugger like her.'

He chuckled. 'Like I said though, he must have been desperate.'

Suddenly Robert's mind flew to Geordie, though he'd never mentioned about being swilled over with a jar of ale. Mind you, he told himself, Geordie wouldn't have wanted him to know about such things. All he ever wanted was to bring him good news – though unfortunately there was precious little of that!

'As a matter of fact,' he confessed to the landlord now, 'I've a thing or two to ask the lady myself. You see, I'm looking for an old friend. Somebody said as how this Iris Dayley knows everything about everybody.'

'Oh, that's true right enough, yes. There's not much she don't know, an' not many folks who don't seem to know her by sight. She used to work in that there orphanage, but she caused a lot o' trouble there an' all, or so I'm told.'

Suddenly the door opened. 'Hey! Look what we got 'ere then.' He gave a mischievous grin. 'Yer can ask her to yer heart's content, 'cause this is the very woman. But don't get her pickled and don't get her riled, 'cause I don't want to be mopping up after the pair of youse.'

When Robert turned to look at the woman in question, he was shocked. Bent over with a crooked back, her advance across the room was painfully slow. Her long grey hair flew in wisps about her shoulder and the dirty clothes she wore made her look like a tramp off the streets.

The landlord had a word or two to say before anybody else. 'I thought I told you – I don't like you coming into the bar.' Angered by her boldness, he meant to assert his authority. 'I've asked you time and again, to wait at the door until somebody can fetch the ale to you!'

Shuffling the long narrow jug on to the counter, she removed the sparklingly white cloth from over its mouth; the look she gave him was murderous. 'Fill it!' she ordered gruffly.

The only other option being to throw her out, and somehow he didn't have the heart for that, the landlord grabbed the jug and began to fill it, all the while grumbling at her. 'This is men's territory,' he warned. 'They don't tek kindly to old women and their boozy habits turning 'em off their drink.'

She didn't answer. Instead she threw two coins on to the counter; placed the white cloth over her jug and snatching it covetously to her bosom, began her laborious way back to the door.

'NEXT TIME DO AS YER TOLD AN' WAIT AT THE DOOR!' The landlord's voice followed her. Feeling especially brave and partially pickled, every man then took up the cry. 'Women don't belong in 'ere! Bugger off with yer!'

And bugger off was exactly what she did.

After a discreet interval, Robert followed.

Having reached the top of the narrow street, Iris stopped to take a drink; that was when Robert caught up with her. Spilling her ale in fright, she backed away. 'Who are yer? Look, I've not said anything to anybody. Go away! For God's sake, leave me be! Haven't you done enough? You told me to keep my mouth shut and I have. Honest to God, I have!'

'No, you've got it wrong.' Realising she thought he was one of the people who had scared her, he tried to calm her fears. 'I'm not here to hurt you.' Seeing how frightened she was, Robert's heart went out to her. 'A minute of your time,' he asked. 'I just need to find out what happened to my son Jack, and his sister Nancy. They were taken to the children's home some five or six years ago. I need to know where they went from there.'

Cramming the jug into her basket she began to scurry away. 'Piss off, or I'll scream blue murder.'

Undeterred, Robert ran after her. 'I've got money. I don't want information for nothing.'

'I know nothing, and I say nothing.'

'You *must* know about Nancy and Jack. You were there at Galloways at the time. I was told you'd know where they were sent. Please, they're my own flesh and blood. They could be in danger for all I know. I *have* to find them!'

Suddenly she stopped, consequently bringing him also to an abrupt halt.

'Won't you please help me?' Taking his last few coins out of his pocket, he held them out to her. 'I'll pay . . . anything!'

There was a moment when she quietly observed him, before in a kind of frightened whisper she told him, 'They got rid of me.' She trembled with fear as she spoke. 'There was another man kept asking me questions. I never told him nothing, but they wouldn't believe me.' Raising the cuff of her sleeve she showed a thick angry scar, encircling her wrist like a bracelet. 'See that?' She glanced about fearfully. 'They said as how next time, it would be me *neck*!'

Robert was shocked. 'Who?' When he stepped closer, she stepped back. 'Who did that to you? Was it someone from the orphanage?' He recalled the unwelcome greeting he had got there. 'Is there something untoward going on at that place? For pity's sakes, tell me, woman! What have they done with my children?'

'They've sent 'em away . . . like they send *all* the children away.'

'Where, Iris? *Where* did they send them?' His heart bumped with hope.

Cupping her ear as if deaf, she had a question of her own. 'What did you say they were called?'

'Nancy and Jack. Try to remember . . . you must have seen them, dealt with them. Where were they sent? That's all I need to know. I won't ever bother you again.'

Suddenly, out of the corner of her eye, Iris thought she saw something, hiding in the shadows. She cried out and Robert spun round, but there was no one there. When he looked back again, Iris was gone, melted into the shadows like part of the night.

For almost an hour, Robert ran around the streets, looking in every alley, calling her name and going half crazy when he knew she was gone for good.

Dejected, he made his way back to the lodging house.

Some time later, he lay in his bed, listening to the sounds from the street below; he heard the hallway clock strike midnight, then one hour past, and now two, and he was still wide awake.

It was almost three in the morning when he finally drifted off to sleep, and even then his vivid dreams and nightmares kept him turning and fighting, until out of exhaustion he sank into a deep, dark sleep.

That weekend he took to the streets again, walking miles and asking questions of anyone he thought might know where he could find his children.

When everyone he questioned either deliberately put up

obstacles or genuinely didn't know, or thought he was mad and hurried away, he sank to the very depths of despair.

But he never gave up. In his heart he knew he would find them. He *had* to, because when all was said and done, and more to his never-ending shame, it was *his* fault they were lost. It was he who had wanted to end his life instead of fighting for their sakes. And it was he who had left them to the mercy of strangers.

One thing he did discover, however, and that was the place where they had laid to rest his dear friend Geordie.

Late afternoon on the Saturday, he spent fourpence at the market on a small but pretty bunch of flowers, and another tuppence on an earthenware pot. He then caught the tram to the outskirts of Kempston, where he had been told that Geordie was taken. To the paupers' corner,' they said.

Having alighted from the tram, he then walked the few hundred yards to the church. 'You'll find the paupers' corner over there.' The caretaker was sympathetic. 'I've put crosses on most of them,' he said, 'but there are some who don't deserve either crosses *or* prayer.'

Robert skirted the grounds until at last he discovered the small, neglected plot situated in a corner some distance from the church walls. Here the unholy souls, together with the poor unfortunates with no money nor family, were hidden away out of sight.

Some of the names were almost obliterated, but after persevering, Robert found him. Set beside an old beech tree, the small wooden cross had been partially protected from the weather. Geordie's name was carved there in a large, childish scrawl. There was no surname, nor any dates. All it said was simply the name of *Geordie*.

For a long time Robert stood there, gazing at the name, thinking of that man who had been the cause of his years of suffering, and yet, when he thought life was worthless, that same man had lifted him out of his pain and given him hope.

'I never did find out his other name.' The caretaker had come up behind Robert. 'It were an old woman who told me his name,' he revealed. 'A dirty old thing she was – nervous, frightened of her own shadow, poor devil.'

Robert was astonished. The description was so accurate he thought it *must* be her. 'Was she called Iris?'

The man shook his head. 'She never said,' he answered thoughtfully. 'All I know was, I were putting him into the ground and she tapped me on the shoulder. Gave me a bloody fright, I don't mind telling you!' He shivered as though a cold chill had rippled through him. 'Anyway, she said as how he once told her his name. "Geordie" she said, and then she was gone and, as far as I know, she's never been back.'

That said, he took off his flat cap, scratched his head and put it on again. 'Work calls,' he muttered. 'Best get on.'

Left alone, Robert spoke to his old friend. 'I'm glad they gave you your name,' he said. 'I'll put a proper stone over you when I can.'

Falling to his knees, he pulled out the weeds and surrounding grass-clumps, and once the ground was level and tidy he laid his humble bunch of flowers at the foot of the cross. 'You were a good friend,' he said. 'I don't suppose you'll ever know how much I miss you.'

He murmured a prayer and a promise. 'They'll not get away with what they've done,' he said. 'I'll make them pay, if it's the last thing I do.'

Another moment of reflection and he went softly away.

Chapter Sixteen

On Monday morning Robert presented himself to Mortimer Jackson. 'I'm ready for work,' he and there was a new purpose about him, a kind of quiet depth found from visiting Geordie's grave and from the many different emotions he had experienced in his short time out of hospital.

Mortimer Jackson sensed something about Robert that touched him deeply. He saw the straight shoulders and the look of commitment on his face; he felt the anger and the fight in him, and the hardness of his determination, and he knew that here was a man who had things to do, a purpose to fulfil. It made him inquisitive. But he was not one to search a man out. Instead he felt respect and liking for Robert Sullivan. A man of calibre if ever he saw one.

'Right!' He led him to the courtyard, where a trap was already tacked up and ready with driver. 'You're to spend a couple of days out and about with Stan, and you're to listen carefully to everything he has to say. There'll be no going out on your own until the two of us are absolutely satisfied you can handle yourself.'

He introduced Robert to the man, who was so large there was hardly any room for Robert to climb in beside him. 'Off you go then, and mind you keep your eyes and ears open. Like as not, if he feels you're ready, Stan here will let you take the reins for a while.'

Addressing Stan, he warned, 'If he *does* take the reins, mind you keep him to the back streets, away from the canal. We don't want the lot of you falling into the water and drowning. If you've no more sense it'll be your own faults, but I don't want you losing me one of my best horses and training vehicle.'

As they drew away, the boss winked at Stan, who knew his manner only too well and, unlike Robert, knew he was being deliberately callous.

Excited about his first day at work after so long, Robert savoured every minute; even when after a time Stan let him take the reins and he almost took them into the side of a warehouse. Scattering the men in all directions, before he finally managed to control the horse, he felt the heat of their anger. 'He's a bloody madman!' they yelled. 'Get him off the road afore he kills somebody!'

To his own amazement, Robert did not panic, though when they were safely stationary, the sweat dripping down his face and the fat man clutching the sides of the trap with whitened knuckles, it took a minute for them to recover. 'He's right!' Stan gasped. 'You *are* a bloody lunatic!'

Believing his short career to be well and truly over, Robert went to hand him the reins, then was thrilled and delighted when the fat man laughed. 'I'm buggered if you're not a born driver. Blimey! Just when I thought we were both goners, you got us out of a bad spot and you never once panicked.' He pointed to the road ahead. 'Take us back as quick as you can,' he said. 'I reckon I've wet me bleedin' pants!'

On the way back to the depot, he confessed a thing or two to Robert. 'There ain't one manjack of us drivers who hasn't at some time or another run into a brick wall, or trapped the front wheels of a carriage into the tram-ruts . . . so deep you could see the tram bearing down before you'd got but a minute to escape.

One fella went into the canal – lost the horse, carriage, passenger an' all! Thankfully, both driver and passenger were got out, though the driver were soon sent packing. Like the boss said, it's understandable to lose a wheel or two now and then, but to lose the whole bloody boilings is downright neglectful.' He laughed uproariously at his own joke.

'What will you tell the boss when he asks how I got on today?' Robert was still anxious.

'Why! I'll tell him the truth,' came the answer. 'I'll say as how that damned cat ran across the front of the horse and sent it into a frenzy.'

'But there weren't any cat!'

'Aye, but *he* won't know that, will he?' Stan gave a knowing wink. 'Then I'll say as how you got us out of a tricky situation without so much as turning a hair.'

Robert laughed. 'Trying to kill half the workforce in the warehouse wasn't a good way to start off though, was it?'

'Huh! You ain't seen nothing yet, me laddo.' He laughed so loud he made the horse skip forward. 'Hey, that's enough o' that!' he yelled. 'We've had enough excitement for one day!'

As they drew into the yard, Robert felt content. At long last he was making a comeback, recovering his self-respect and earning a wage into the bargain.

He had a good feeling, that it wouldn't be too long before his search for Nancy and Jack would bear fruit.

During the next two weeks he was kept working so hard and for so long that he had little time to continue his enquiries. Up early in the morning and home late at night, he was always bone-weary and ready for his bed. 'You're doing fine, son,' Mortimer Jackson always said, and never tired of telling his colleagues and friends how he had 'taken on a much-promising fellow in Robert Sullivan'.

Every trip he did, be it across town to collect a man going to his business, or taking a family home from their shopping, Robert kept a keen eye out for anything and anyone he thought might help him trace his children. One day he thought he saw Iris handling some cauliflowers outside a fruiterers, but when she turned it wasn't her at all. Another time he picked up two women who talked so loud to each other he thought they must be deaf, but what they had to say caught his attention . . . 'There's talk they might be shutting down the children's home,' said one. 'Oh, they'll never do that,' answered the other, 'else where would the poor unfortunates go?'

The sorry truth not only compounded Robert's guilt but also made him think that it was a sad thing if that place was the only home some children might ever know.

On the second Friday afternoon, Mortimer Jackson let him leave early. 'You've passed with flying colours,' he told him kindly. 'You're on full wages from today, though bear in mind you're still on trial until I say you're not.' He was never one to give anything away without a man having to fret over it. But Robert thanked him, and said as how he was enjoying the work more than he could ever have imagined.

Rushing home, he had an errand he needed to tend. So he washed and changed in good time and went at the double to the town hall where, with only five minutes to spare before they closed the doors, he hurried to the desk, bitterly disappointed when he saw that it was a man in attendance. 'There was a young woman behind the desk the last time I called.' He described her to the clerk. 'Is it possible I could see her?'

The bony-faced clerk shook his head. 'You mean Anne Moore. I'm sorry, Miss Moore's been away these past few days with a touch of influenza. You might come back next week some time,' he suggested. 'I'm sure it won't be too long before she returns to her work.' He gave a stiff, dutiful smile. 'Can *I* help at all?'

Robert thanked him, but said, 'No. It's your Miss Moore I need to speak with.' Another disappointment, he thought. And who knew when he might have the opportunity to call here again.

Disillusioned, he went away.

Outside in the cool of a lovely evening, he toyed for a minute with the idea of going to the children's home but then thought better of it. If they wouldn't give him information last time, they'd be even more tight-lipped if he turned up again. More to the point, that devious manager might carry out his threat and have him thrown into jail. That would be the end of his search for Nancy and Jack. No! He had to play it different. He had to try and be as cunning as them. Besides, there was still Iris Dayley, if only he could get a sighting of her – but she was like a will o' the wisp. Many people knew of her, but nobody seemed to know where she lived. But there was still the chance of coming back to the town hall next week, so all was not yet lost.

With that in mind, he went to the pub and spent a shilling on a quiet evening, sitting in the corner, watching and listening, hoping he could pick up a snippet of useful information. But he neither heard nor saw anything that was of any use to him.

At a quarter past ten, he said good night to the landlord and made his lonely way back to the lodgings, where he drank a welcome cup of cocoa in the company of two equally lonely salesmen down from the North.

The next day being Saturday, he took himself off to stroll round the market; a colourful, noisy place, it took his mind off the many matters pressing hard on his mind – not least of all Mary, the woman he had loved like no other. The market was a lively place, heaving with people and noise. If only for a short time, it was good for him to lose his thoughts in all of that.

He took a leisurely interest in anything and everything that was on offer. At one stall, he bought a pair of smart brown shoes that fitted him to a T. 'They've only been worn the once,' the stallholder told him. 'Belonged to a fellow of means, they did. Only now he's got gout and his feet are growing misshapen. Apparently he has to have his shoes specially made these days . . . or so his manservant tells me.'

The stallholder looked like a fellow who could tell a tale or two, so Robert didn't know whether to believe him or not. Still, what did it matter? The shoes were of excellent quality; they fitted well, and they were the most comfortable he'd ever had on his feet. 'How much?'

The man pulled a face and made a noise and gave his price. 'Two bob, mate.'

Robert put the shoes back on the stall. 'Too much.' He started walking away.

'Hey! Wait on!' The man called him back. 'All right, then . . . one and ninepence, but I'll be doing meself down at that.'

Smiling to himself, Robert walked on. He had better use for his money.

'All right – one and six, and that's me last argument!'

Pausing, Robert turned. 'One and tuppence – it's all I can afford.'

'You're a damned robber, that's what I think!' The man made another face and pulled his mouth this way and that. He groaned and sighed and rolled his eyes to the skies. 'Bloody hell, I'll go broke at this rate!' He gave another, heavier sigh and nodded his head. 'All right, but you're a hard man to do business with.'

Robert paid the money and walked off, happy with his almost new pair of expensive shoes. They would last him a good many years to come.

Unbeknownst to Robert, as he walked away in one direction, Alice Compton entered the market from another.

Having fulfilled her dream of having a child, Alice proudly

pushed him along in his perambulator; a fat little thing was Johnnie, with dark wispy hair, wide-awake eyes and chubby cheeks. 'Morning, missus.' The stallholder was a rounded motherly sort whose innocent, ready smile belied the sharp business mind beneath. 'Look here. I've some pretty crocheted coats that will look a treat on that babby o' yourn.'

She had seen Alice about the market on many an occasion and, providing she had time and there weren't too many customers waiting, she would often engage her in a conversation. 'Go on! Have a look,' she urged. 'See what lovely work it is.'

Draping one of the blue matinee jackets over her arm, she showed Alice the way the tiny buttons looped into the fasteners, and how the jacket was long enough to, 'Keep its little arse warm, so it will.'

Alice liked what she saw. 'Go on then,' she said and parted with a sixpence. 'But I don't want anything else,' she warned, pointing to the baby. 'He had a bad night, so none of us got any sleep. I only came out for a bit of fresh air. I hoped it might send him off, but no, he's still wide awake.' She gave a long, lazy yawn. 'Excuse me, but I'm that tired, I've half a mind to climb in beside him.'

'You look bright enough to me.' The woman had always thought Alice to be a plain-featured woman, but homely and quietly pleasant. 'Keep the little bugger out as long as yer can an' he'll sleep like a top tonight.'

Alice yawned again. 'I hope so.'

When a second customer showed interest in her wares, the stallholder turned her attention away from Alice. 'Mind how you go,' she said, and Alice assured her she would.

She hadn't gone too far when she heard someone call her name. 'Alice! Alice Compton! Hang on a minute!'

By the time she had swung round to see who it was, the young woman was already by her side, puffing and panting and tickling the baby's chin. 'My! I didn't know you'd had a baby. Isn't he beautiful! What's his name?'

Alice was surprised to see that it was Anne Moore who had called out to her. Having left her job a long time ago now, she was always pleased to see someone from the town hall. 'He's called Johnnie. Anne, how are you?' She couldn't help but notice how the younger woman seemed to lean heavily on the baby's perambulator. She could also see how Anne's face was peaked and thin, whereas it had always been pink and glowing before.

'I've been laid low with the dreaded influenza,' the young woman told her, 'so I mustn't get too close to the baby. I'm feeling much better now, but the doctor says I can't go back to work for at least another week.'

'Should you be out then?' Alice was concerned. 'Shouldn't you be resting in your bed?'

The younger woman rejected that idea. 'I couldn't abide another day without coming out in the fresh air.' Taking Alice aside, she told her, 'I'm glad I've caught up with you though, because I promised somebody I'd have a word with you the first chance I got.'

'What about?'

Anne explained. 'Before I got took ill, a man came into the town hall – asking for you, he was. Said as how you were there the night he left his children. Said as how he came back but the gates were shut, and how, through no fault of his own, he couldn't come back again, and now his children have gone and he doesn't know which way to turn.' She would have babbled on, but Alice stopped her.

'I think we'd best go and sit down somewhere,' she suggested. 'You look done in. Tell me all about it over a cup of tea, eh?'

Thankfully, Anne nodded in agreement and they set off, unaware that if they had walked on just a few more yards, they would have bumped into Robert himself.

It took only a few minutes to reach the café and another few to have their tea and toast in front of them. 'Now then, what's this all about?' Alice asked curiously.

'Well, like I say, this man came into the Town Hall and asked for you – described you to a T, he did. He said his name was Robert Sullivan, and that he was looking for his children.'

Alice was puzzled. 'I've never heard of anybody by that name. And what makes him think *I* might know where his children are?'

The younger woman shrugged her shoulders. 'He seemed really nice,' she explained. 'He was worried out of his mind, even I could see that.' In great detail, she went on to tell Alice Exactly what Robert had told her. 'He was very pale – as though he'd not been outside for a long time. At first I thought he might have been in prison, but somehow that didn't seem right to me. He looked kind of sad inside himself, if you know what I mean? Then as he walked away, I saw he had the slightest limp. I couldn't help but wonder if he'd been in some sort of accident and been laid up in the Infirmary. Whatever the reason, he couldn't come back for his kids, and now, he's like a haunted man.'

'What did he tell you about the children?' Alice was beginning to get the picture. 'Did he describe them to you?'

'Not Exactly. He just said they were a boy and a girl . . . Nancy and Jack, that's what he said.'

'Oh, my God!' Instinctively, Alice caught at her throat. 'I knew those children.' Tears filled her eyes, and it was a moment before she could talk.

'What is it, Alice? What's wrong?' Like many others, Anne had heard murmurings about the underhand dealings at the children's home and now, she, too, was concerned. 'Did something happen to them?'

Alice composed herself. She had never forgotten Nancy and Jack. Like their father she had been haunted by the idea of them being unhappy and isolated, and all through no fault of their own. 'The truth is, they got sent away.'

'Where to?'

'The boy was so naughty,' she revealed. '"Bad Boy Jack" they called him, but he wasn't really. He was just so confused and frightened, he hit out at whatever and whoever he could.' She made a confession. 'I wanted them for myself, you know,' she said softly. 'I really wanted to take them home, Jack and his little sister, Nancy.' Gulping hard she went on, 'She was such a pretty little thing, quiet like, with these big blue eyes . . . oh, Anne! She looked like a little doll, so she did. And the boy was so loving and protective towards her.'

'What happened to them?' Anne whispered.

'I'm not altogether sure,' she admitted. 'But one afternoon, when Ennington was called out to deal with a rebellious child, I sneaked into his office and took a look at his private ledger.'

'Crikey!' Ennington was known for his fiery reputation. 'He didn't catch you, did he?'

'No, but I found a few things out,' she confessed cautiously. 'The boy was sent to a farm somewhere in the North. That seemed to be a genuine placing, because it was in the *official* ledger as well. As for the girl, Nancy, I've always suspected she was sold. There was an entry made on the very day the children were sent away. It related to "the girl". It seemed money did change hands at some stage, but whether it was directly to do with Nancy, I couldn't be sure.'

'Bloody hell, Alice!' Anne Moore, like so many others, had heard rumours of shady dealings going on inside the Galloways Children's Home. 'It's a wonder he didn't find out and have you flogged to the bones.' She felt frightened just listening to what Alice had done. 'Did you tell the authorities?'

Alice shook her head. 'No, I didn't, much to my shame. I had thought of it, and I probably would have told, but the next time I sneaked into the office, Ennington's private ledger was gone.'

'Ah, well, he's such a cunning devil, he probably suspected somebody had been at his books.'

'That's what I thought. So now, there was no way I could prove it. I thought about it for a long time, but I wasn't sure what to do for the best. If I went to the authorities, how was I to know whether or not he didn't have them in the palm of his hand as well? On the other hand, if I *didn't* report him, how many other children would be sold on?'

She took a deep, calming breath. 'Apart from not knowing if the authorities were in on it, there were two things that stopped me from reporting him.' Her gaze went down to her own son, now fast asleep. 'I found out I was carrying him. And, according to Ennington's private ledger, the girl, Nancy, was not sent for any ill-usage, or I would have told there and then, whatever the consequences. No, thankfully, she was sent to a respectable, wealthy family, to heal a poor woman's breaking heart after losing her own child. In fact, I actually saw the gentleman who took her away. He seemed kind enough, and obviously well-to-do. In the end, I convinced myself that she would be taken good care of.'

Anne nodded approvingly. 'I think you did right to say nothing. Like you said, he might well be in partnership with somebody in authority, and there'd be no telling who it could be. There are so many rotten apples in the system, you can't know who you can trust from one minute to the next.'

In her mind, Alice recalled that night. 'It was awful,' she admitted. 'They should never have separated them two young 'uns. The boy was distraught . . . they both were, though the girl was only a babby really and didn't fully understand what was happening. But oh, if you'd seen young Jack's face when she was driven off, thinking she never wanted to see him again. I've never seen such unhappiness. Yet for all that, he was thinking of her well-being the whole time, putting her before himself. He knew she'd gone somewhere where she'd have a good life, and though it broke his heart, he accepted that; even though he believed she'd turned her back on him.'

'Why would he think that?'

'Because she didn't see him as she was being driven off. She couldn't, you understand? Because not only was the carriage window too high for her to see out, but the gent had brought things with him to entice her away without a fuss. She got caught up in his cunning, and for that minute or two when she was being driven out of sight, she forgot to turn and look for her brother.'

Alice could see Jack's face now and it tore her apart. 'He was like a soul destroyed,' she recalled. 'He believed that he was her protector, and he'd let her down. But when she forgot to turn and wave him goodbye . . .' She slowly shook her head. 'Soon after that, he was gone an' all, to a farmer, if I recall. I reckon he went to a good home, but who knows? All I do know is, they should *never* have been separated.'

'What about the man – their father? He's bound to come back. What will I tell him?'

'When is it you go back?'

'Another week, the doctor said.'

'Then I've got a week to think it over. I'll come to you at the town hall next Monday morning. Until then, it's best not to say anything.'

They talked some more, about Robert Sullivan, then about children and marriage and all the things women find fascinating. A short time later they parted and went their separate ways. 'I'll not tell a soul,' the young woman promised as she went. 'I'm glad I saw you though, 'cause it were playing on my mind.'

Alice thanked her, and was soon on her way home with the baby. She had a lot to think about. And a burning need to talk it over with her good husband, Anthony.

* * *

'You mustn't get involved!' Having listened to what she had to say, Anthony was anxious. 'For a start you don't know this bloke from Adam. How can you tell he's really the kids' father?'

'It all sounds so right.' Alice herself had no doubts. 'He knew their names and he knew them by description. He also described how they were left at the town hall. And if that isn't enough proof for you, I think I recall the man who sat there with the children before he disappeared. The way Anne described him, I'm convinced it's the children's father.'

'So, what will you do?' Pacing the floor, her husband flung his arms out sideways. 'Will you go to Ennington and demand to know where the children are? Tell the town hall authorities and hope they can get to the bottom of it all, when half the time they're probably mixed up in it themselves? And what about the children? Even if they were found, what if they're content? What if they don't want a father who deserted them – have you thought of that? Christ Almighty, Alice! It's been *six years and more* since all this happened!'

It struck Alice that this was the first row they'd had in many a long while, but it was important for her to voice what she felt, whether her husband liked it or not. '*Somebody* should tell him,' she argued. 'He has a right to know.'

Anthony disagreed violently. 'He has *no* rights at all!' He began to yell. 'Don't forget how he ran off and left them poor little mites and now he expects to pick up where he left off, just like that – as if it never happened.'

'But he came back, and the town hall was shut against him. He told Anne he couldn't come back after that, through no fault of his own. And I believe him. I saw him on the bench with those children and if ever a man loved his kids, *he* did. It was in his eyes and the way he cradled them both in his arms.'

'So why would he desert them?'

'I don't know the answer to that question,' she admitted. 'All I know is, if I don't tell him about the ledger and the information I found there, I won't be able to live with myself.'

'I FORBID IT!' Clenching his fist, Anthony smacked it hard on the table top. 'I don't want you to have anything to do with it, do you understand?'

Shocked and angered by the tone of his voice, Alice turned away, but suddenly he was there, holding her back, pleading with her. 'I'm only concerned about the consequences of you getting involved in summat like that. It's too dangerous! Remember how that housekeeper was attacked after some bloke kept asking her questions? Everybody knows there's funny business going on at that place.' He held her to him. 'I just don't want you caught up in it, that's all.'

Holding her away he asked softly, 'And what about our own baby?'

Fear stalked her voice. 'What do you mean?'

'I mean, if they'd beat up an old woman, do you really think they would stop at hurting a child?' He shook her gently. 'Think about it, Alice! Think of the years we tried for this beautiful babby. Look, sweetheart, we have a good enough life. We've got the family we always wanted, and we're happy enough. Why risk all that, for some bloke who deserted his kids?'

Alice's blood ran cold. 'Our Johnnie? I never thought of it like that.'

'Then you'd best think now, before you do anything silly.' He breathed out a sigh. 'Please . . . just leave it be. If this man wants his kids badly enough, he'll find them without your help.' He tilted her face to his. 'You do understand what I'm saying, don't you?'

'Yes.'

'Good!' The relief showed in his smile and in the gentle, appreciative way he kissed her. 'I'm sorry if I shouted at you.'

'It's all right.' She was glad when suddenly the baby started crying. 'I'd best go and see to him.' Without delay, she hurried away, up the stairs and into the baby's room. By the time she got there he was whimpering quietly.

After changing his wet napkin, she then laid him back in his cot; her face melting with love as she gazed down on him. 'What would he do if somebody took *you* away?' she mused. 'He'd move heaven and earth to get you back . . . we *both* would.'

As she watched, he closed his eyes and drifted into a gentle sleep. 'Goodnight, sleep tight, sweetheart.' She bent to kiss his forehead and afterwards went to the window, where she stood for what seemed an age, just looking out at the darkening skies.

She thought of what Anthony had said just now, and what Anne had said earlier, and her head began to spin. 'What am I to do?' she whispered.

One thing was certain. What her husband had said just now had made her think, and he was right. What kind of mother would she be, if she put this beautiful babby at risk?

A moment later, as she passed the cot she leaned down to tuck him in, lingering at his side for another minute or two. 'It breaks my heart to leave that man agonising after his children,' she murmured, 'especially when I might be able to help him.'

As she closed the door, she took another peep at her son. 'You're too precious for me to risk anybody hurting you. But if there was a way I could do it without folks knowing it was me, I might think about it.' The idea that her baby could be hurt sent a shiver through her. 'No! It's too dangerous.'

She returned to the sitting room where Anthony was reading his newspaper. As she walked in, he began commenting on various items of news, in particular the newly created Commonwealth, and the implications of Marconi's experiments with radio transmissions. 'It's all moving too fast,' he said, looking up from his newspaper. When she agreed, he answered that he was happy she had decided, 'not to get involved in that bloke's business with the children'.

Alice smiled and nodded, but she herself was not happy at all.

So, while he read his newspaper, she sat sewing and thinking, rocking in her chair and mentally going over every word Anne had said, about how Robert Sullivan was a haunted man. Then she thought of Anthony's argument, and it made her stop and think of the consequences, if she decided to reveal any information she had on Ennington, and Robert's children.

She believed with all her heart that Robert Sullivan deserved to be helped. But then again, was she prepared to put everything she loved at risk, in order to assist this man – a stranger, after all, who had deserted his children?

She looked at her husband and roved her gaze round that cosy room. She glanced up towards the bedroom where her son lay sleeping. For a moment her mind was wick with all manner of thoughts.

Then she took up her sewing, settled back in the chair, and thanked the good Lord for all her blessings.

Part Three

DECEMBER 1901

CHANGES

Chapter Seventeen

1901 had been an eventful year; the Boer War was still ongoing, and many families could not settle until their loved ones returned. At home, the rumours heightened about Queen Victoria being in ill-health. It was a changing world, which in turn created an uneasiness throughout the land.

'With so many men away fighting, I consider myself fortunate to have been so far left alone.' Paul had already lodged his situation with the authorities, stating that he had a 'nervous' wife who had still not yet fully recovered from losing her child, and an aging aunt who relied on him totally. Moreover, he had in his employ some twenty men, who otherwise would not have work or wages to support their families.

So far it appeared to have done the trick. Not only that, but the Old Palace Hotel was renovated in good time, with the help of further finance and a recruitment of men from other towns.

Now, on this New Year's Eve, the hotel – renamed 'The Regency' – was thrown open to its guests for a night of celebration and thanksgiving.

It was a New Year's Eve they would never forget!

The sea heaved along the shoreline, the falling snow billowed into drifts along the hedgerows, and the ground underfoot was treacherous after the previous frost. As the evening wore on, the wind that had started earlier as a gentle breeze continued to grow in strength until now it rattled the windows, and bent the avenue of trees along the promenade.

Paul was devastated. After almost two years of hard work and dedication in restoring the hotel to its former glory, it looked as if his planned celebrations would not happen – at least not with this kind of weather blowing up.

'Nobody's going to attend a party on a night like this,' he groaned. 'If they've got any sense, they'll stay inside, next to a nice warm fire.'

Mary fully understood how he must feel. 'It's early yet,' she reminded him. 'The invitations said eight thirty, and it's only just quarter past.'

He gave a wry, disbelieving nod. 'Maybe, but you'll always have one or two who like to be early, and there's no sign of that.' He continued to look out of the window, hoping against hope that the guests would brave the elements; yet with every passing minute his hopes diminished.

Mary, however, was more optimistic. 'There's still time,' she insisted, coming to his side. 'Anyway, if the party doesn't happen tonight, there'll always be another night.'

Paul turned to gaze on her. 'It looks like it might be just the two of us, and what man could resist you as you are now?' His avaricious eyes roved her from top to bottom, from the sleek, short bob of her fair hair, to the slinky dress with its décolletage and swinging skirt, and those pretty shoes that showed her ankles to a treat. 'You're so lovely.'

It wasn't just the hotel he wanted to show off to the guests; he wanted them to see what a lucky man he was, to own a wife like Mary.

Looking into her quiet, nutmeg-coloured eyes he bent his head to kiss her. 'And you're right.' In the light of her enthusiasm, he began to buck up. 'Happen they will come after all, and if they don't, you and me will celebrate all by ourselves.'

Sliding an arm round her waist, he turned her towards the room. 'I can't believe we got there in the end,' he said. 'I don't mind telling you, there were times when I really began to think it would never happen.'

Mary had no such qualms. 'I always knew you would do it,' she remarked softly. 'You're not a man to give up easily.'

It was strange though, the way he had shut her out, almost without meaning to. The Regency was all Paul's hotel, not, as he had promised, hers. She had had no part in it, not even in choosing the colours for the tablecloths, though to her surprise she *had* been consulted on whether she thought round or square tables would be more fitting. She had suggested round, though in the end he went against her and chose to order square ones.

She knew he didn't mean it to be a snub or a slight on her intelligence. It was just the way he did things; like most men, he had his own territory and she had hers.

Yet she had to admit, 'It all looks so wonderful.'

This particular room was the main dining room, where guests would enjoy their meals, be it breakfast, lunch or dinner. Tea and snacks would be served in the smaller, adjoining room, equally pretty and with the same panoramic views of the garden.

This larger, more spacious room had been created out of three smaller ones. With its wide windows and high ceilings, it was a bright sunny room in summer and wonderfully warm in winter. The uninterrupted seaview to the front and vast, landscaped gardens to the rear, seeming almost to sweep into the room itself, made it a place most people would want to linger.

Keen to have her approval he asked, 'Do you really think I got it right? The colours and décor, I mean?'

She gazed round, at the cream-coloured walls and the panels of darker shade with a picture hung squarely in the centre of each one. She noted the wall-lights of crystal and chrome and there in the ceiling, two great chandeliers to match. 'You did a good job,' she said truthfully, though the square tables grated on her senses.

Albeit too formal for her liking, she had to admit they did look splendid, dressed beautifully with white tablecloths under a square of sage-green linen. Each table was set with the best cutlery and crystal wine glasses, and beside every setting was a small present for each guest to mark the occasion.

'No one could have done better,' she told him, and he smiled, like a schoolboy with a new toy.

He seemed to grow in stature before her eyes. 'Tomorrow will be the start of a brand new year, the real beginning of the twentieth century,' he declared proudly, 'and I can't wait for it all to happen.' Suddenly his mood darkened. 'It's a pity I haven't got a son to hand it down to.'

When he saw the shock on her face, he was mortified. 'Oh sweetheart, I'm sorry!' He drew her to him, not seeming to notice when she stiffened against him. 'That was a thoughtless thing to say. I'm so sorry. How could I have been so bloody stupid!' Groaning from the pit of his stomach, he tried hard to rescue the situation. 'I know how much you wanted to give me a son. I'm just grateful that the fall down the stairs didn't take *you* from me as well.' Pressing her close he babbled on, 'We're young and healthy. There'll be other times. We just have to be patient.'

At that moment, enclosed in his arms, Mary felt nothing for him.

She wondered what he would say if he knew it was Agatha, his precious aunt, who had caused the fall that cost him his son?

Suddenly, much to her relief, the clattering of wheels could be heard outside. Letting go of Mary, he rushed to the window. 'There's a carriage!' he cried excitedly. 'Oh, and another! Come and see, darling. Come and see!'

Momentarily drained of enthusiasm, Mary went to see, and

sure enough, the guests were beginning to arrive.

Paul all but danced on the spot. 'It's happening!' he said joyfully. 'Quick, Mary, summon the waiters. I'll make my way to the door . . . we'll greet them together. Quickly! We mustn't be seen to be disorganised.'

So, while Mary hurried away to summon the waiters, Paul quickened his pace to the front door, which he swung open in anticipation, being almost blown off his feet by the cold blast of air that swept in. No sooner had the first couple mounted the steps and presented themselves, than Mary was there to greet them, every bit the dutiful wife alongside her husband.

The first pair was a Mr Lattimer and his son, hoteliers themselves, come to weigh up the competition. The second couple to arrive was Mr and Mrs Horace Burnley – old, fat and disgustingly wealthy. Long experienced in the business of financing, Mr Burnley had Paul in the palm of his hand, at least until he could begin paying back the sizeable loan made to him.

'It's going to be a real success after all.' As the smartly dressed waiters moved amongst the guests with trays of wine and dainties, Paul was beside himself with excitement, especially when the four guests quickly swelled to six, then to eight.

And still they came, arriving in their carriages and vehicles, all done up in their party best, and looking forward to an evening of eating and dancing.

The last to arrive was Agatha, with the lovable Emily by her side. Never was there a greater comparison than these two; the servant in a homemade flowered dress with long brown coat and small-brimmed hat; then old Agatha wrapped in furs and velvet, her grey hair swathed in a creation of feathers and tulle, and the most enormous handbag dangling from her arm.

'Silly old fool! She looks ridiculous,' murmured one brave soul. 'Oh, but I wish I could carry myself like she does,' sighed another. A moment later the two women scurried away discreetly to the cloakroom, to see if they could improve their own appearance.

Mary watched it all impassively. She heard the varying conversations going on about her; some were angry about the soaring price of potatoes . . . 'my housekeeper tells me it's now tuppence for half a dozen where once upon a time you could be sure of a bag full for the same money'. The ladies discussed household matters, while the men seemed more excited about the new petrol-driven vehicles that were slowly beginning to appear on the streets.

Mary took it all in, though she kept a watchful eye on her husband, Paul, noting how he loved to be in the centre of attention. In the time they'd been married she had come to know him inside out, and had quickly learned that as well as being a polite and gentle man, he was also spoiled and sulky when things did not go his way.

Yet on this night as always, she did him proud. This was Paul's night – the night when his long-held dream came true. After an age of structural work, renovations and decorating, his hotel was open at last. It was a notable achievement, and one he justly deserved to celebrate.

Sparing no expense, he had laid on more than a feast. He'd hired a pianist to play in the background through their lavish dinner, paid a pretty painted singer to entertain them over coffee, and arranged for a musical trio to set their feet a-tapping and get them up on the dance floor afterwards.

The guests loved every minute of it. Their nostrils assailed with the aroma of good food, and in their ears the heartening echo of tinkling wine glasses, they allowed themselves to be pampered and cosseted and were happy to be so.

For a while, during which time Paul mingled and smiled and wallowed in all the compliments, Mary sat with Emily at her table; they watched the couples dancing in each other's arms and

Emily sighed and smiled wistfully, and wished she was thirty years younger. 'It's a lovely, *lovely* party,' she said. 'I can't recall ever enjoying myself so much.'

Mary agreed. For all that she had not been allowed too much of a part in the preparations, she could not help but admire Paul's business skills.

'He's worked long and tirelessly for this night,' she told the other woman. 'I hope and believe he's got himself a hotel that people will want to come back to time and again.'

'I'm sure you're right,' Emily agreed, and pointed to Agatha, who was tagging along behind Paul as he chatted to each guest in turn. 'Look at her! When will she ever learn not to poke her nose in.'

As always when with Emily, Mary spoke her mind. 'Paul should be more forceful with her.' Her voice dropped almost to a whisper. If he could only see what she was capable of, he'd soon be rid of her!'

Glancing at Mary, who was suddenly lost in her own dark thoughts, Emily saw the hostility in her face. Stirred by her own suspicions, she leaned closer. 'If I ask you something, will you be truthful with me?'

At once concerned that she might have betrayed her innermost feelings, Mary replied, 'I've always been as honest with you as I can be. So, what do you want to know?'

Her eyes shifting to the old lady, who was deep in conversation with Horace Burnley, she asked in a whisper, 'You would tell me, wouldn't you, if *she* had had anything to do with you losing the baby?'

Eyes wide with shock, Mary stared at her. 'What makes you say a thing like that?'

Emily laid a hand over hers. 'Because I've seen how you've changed since that night. I've sensed something about Agatha that I don't much like, and I've seen the way you are when she's about. It's as though there's something really bad going on between the two of you, and it isn't just the old rivalry, with her fighting you for Paul's affections. It's summat deeper than that. I can feel it.'

Mary looked away. 'We don't get on, that's all,' she muttered. 'We never have. From the first minute she laid eyes on me she was determined not to like me, and there's nothing I can do about that.'

Emily was not convinced. 'Mary – look at me!'

Nervous, Mary looked at her.

The servant told her what was on her mind. 'I've looked after that sulky, miserable old woman for a long time now, and I dare say I'll go on taking care of her, despite her nasty, selfish ways.' Her voice hardened. 'But if I ever thought she had a hand in you losing that child, I swear to God, I'd turn my back on her for good.'

Half-heartedly, Mary protested, 'You're not to think such things.'

But Emily had already seen the truth of it in Mary's sad eyes. 'My thinking is this,' she began. 'If she *did* cause you to fall down them stairs, when you were six months with child, you wouldn't tell, because you're more concerned about other folk's feelings than you are about your own. I know you well enough by now, my girl! You'd keep quiet for Paul's sake. You'd not want to upset the apple cart, because for all her idiot ways, Paul cares a great deal for his crusty old aunt.'

Something else suddenly occurred to her. 'Unless that old bugger made some kind of a threat to keep you quiet! Did she? Did she threaten you, or frighten you in some way, so's you'd keep your mouth shut?'

Hating herself for lying, Mary shook her head. 'You're wrong,' she answered weakly. 'It was an accident. Please, Emily, let's leave it at that.' And, much to her old friend's frustration, she would not be cajoled into saying another thing.

But it was already too late. Emily knew then, without a shadow of a doubt, that Agatha had been at the root of Mary losing that poor unborn babby.

'Look, love, I know how bad it is for you, living in the same house as *her*, and even sometimes taking second place. I know she's never accepted you, and I've seen how Paul has grown more and more dependent on her. Y'see, folk like Agatha are never satisfied unless they're controlling people. They're cunning and persistent. They can worm their way into a person's soul almost without them knowing. She's done it with Paul, and like you, I've seen it happening and been powerless to do anything about it.'

Raising her eyes, Mary turned to look at her. 'You're such a wise kind soul,' she murmured, deeply touched. 'You seem to know everything and everybody. Is there anything you *don't* know?'

Emily gave a chuckle. 'I don't know why my glass is empty,' she said pointedly, at which Mary got up and went to the bar.

Having chatted to a few guests on the way, she then returned with a full glass for Emily. 'I need a breath of air,' she said. 'I'll be back soon,' and she hurried away.

Averting her eyes, Mary hurried out of the room and dashed upstairs, where she hid in a boxroom, out of sight of the guests. There she wept, until the hurt began to flow away. A few minutes later, she almost leapt out of her skin when Emily's voice sounded behind her. 'I won't say anything to either of them, if that's what you're worried about, pet,' she promised, 'but I hope you can bring yourself to tell Paul what really happened. It's time his eyes were opened as to what evil *she's* capable of.'

Realising there was no fooling her old friend, Mary thanked her, but said sadly, 'It's all water under the bridge now. There's no use me getting into a fight I know I can't win. He would always take her word against mine and that would only put me in an even worse situation than I already am.' There! She had spoken her true feelings and from the look on her face, Emily was not surprised.

'You're still dreadfully unhappy, aren't you?' Emily had come to love the young woman like her own daughter, and it hurt to see her like this – especially after she herself had half persuaded Mary to believe that life with Paul might not be so bad, what with the child coming an' all.

Mary gave a wry little smile. 'I've never been so unhappy in all my life.' It was good to have someone to confide in. She wished now, that she had opened her heart to Emily sooner.

'Is it because of the babby that you're so unhappy?'

'Yes, and the way it is with Agatha. You're right when you say she's wormed her way into his affections. It's got so Paul will always consult her on matters, where he would never consult me.'

She gestured to the hotel and the room where everyone seemed to be on the floor, dancing and laughing, and making the occasional complimentary comment about Paul and his wonderful new venture. 'Take this hotel for example,' she went on. 'Oh, Emily! I would have loved him to trust me enough on small matters, such as the crockery, or curtains or even the colour of the cloakroom walls. But he never asked my opinion and if he did, he then totally ignored it.'

'And you blame her for that, do you?' Emily knew well enough who the villain was here.

'I hope I don't sound jealous or petty, but if I'm truthful I felt really let down when I found out she'd been consulted about the colour and emblem on the hotel linen. Oh, I know she made a good choice in that lovely emerald green, but it would have been so nice if I'd had a part to play in Paul's dream. I don't think it's too much for me as his wife to ask, do you?'

Emily was angry. 'If it was me, I'd have raised the damned roof! All right, I expect she's probably invested some capital in the hotel, but it doesn't give her – or Paul, come to that – the right to overlook you. You're his wife, for goodness' sake! No! It's high time Paul stood up to his aunt. Surely he can see what damage she's doing?'

But Mary had already lost heart. 'I think it's too late for that. First of all it was losing the bairn, then it was Agatha's constant niggling away at the both of us. The truth is, she's lowered his opinion of me, until now I imagine he wonders if he did right in marrying me.'

This time Emily was really shocked. 'No, surely not! He still loves you as much as ever . . .' Suspicion crept in. 'He *does*, doesn't he?'

'I don't know any more. I think, deep down, he blames me for losing the baby – the son he so desperately wanted. He seems to have shut me out. In fact, I'm beginning to wonder if I'll ever really be a part of Paul's life.'

'You *must* tell him the truth about the miscarriage.'

Mary laughed bitterly. 'How can I? How can I tell him that his old aunt blocked my way up the stairs, pressing me backwards with the force of her own body as she argued and bullied, trying to make me admit that it wasn't Paul's child, that it was another man's bastard. She claimed I was a fortune-seeker and that I didn't have a single jot of feeling for her nephew. "It would be best if you and the brat were out of his life altogether", that's what she kept saying, over and over!' A torrent of tears fell down her face as she relived the terrifying scene.

The events would live on in her mind for as long as she breathed; the sense of helplessness when she lost her foothold, the jubilant look on the old woman's face as she watched her hurtling backwards down the stairs, the sudden, searing pain and the blood – so much blood.

Emily had stopped listening on Mary's first damning words. 'Is that what she did – block your way on the stairs?'

'If only you'd seen her, Emily. She was like a crazy woman! I was on my way up, and she came down towards me. Suddenly she was yelling and cursing, and then she seemed to lunge at me. I didn't remember anything else until I woke up in the Infirmary.' Now, with the thought of that tiny life that was lost, she let the tears fall once more.

Emily held her until she was quiet again. 'The wicked devil!' The older woman wanted to go to Agatha there and then, to accuse her in front of Paul, but she knew she could not. It was up to Mary and no one else, to show the old bitch up for what she was. 'He has to know what she did, my love. You *must* tell him – tell him how she pushed you down the stairs, how she was the one who cost him his son.'

Mary refused. 'I can't be sure she did it on purpose,' she admitted. 'Yes, she was yelling and screaming at me, and she did seem to come at me for a minute. But I couldn't swear on the Bible that she deliberately pushed me.'

Yet in her mind's eye she saw again the triumphant look on the woman's face as she fell. 'I've no doubt she was glad to see me falling, but I wouldn't want to accuse her, if it really was an accident after all.'

Emily grew calmer. 'She's always been a jealous, possessive old biddy, especially where Paul is concerned. I've seen the change in her since you and Paul got wed,' she confessed, 'and I don't doubt for one minute that she's capable of doing something as callous as sending you down the stairs, babby an' all.'

Common sense prevailed. 'But I do understand what you're saying, and if you're really not sure that she did it on purpose, then you're right to say nowt.' She had a warning. 'All the same, pet, you must watch her like a hawk from now on.'

Mary assured her she would.

These past few months, the young woman had been rethinking her life. 'I feel like a stranger in the house. I'm not content, Emily. When I think on it, I haven't really had a minute's happiness since Paul took me for his wife. He's a good, kind man, but he's changed. I'm not sure there's a future for us any more.'

Torn apart by Mary's confession, Emily asked, 'Is there no love in your heart for him?'

'No, Emily, there isn't – not in the way you mean.' She wished she could change the way she felt, but it was not possible. 'The truth is, I should never have agreed to be married. I was only thinking of the baby. It seemed the right thing to do at the time, but now…' She paused to think, her heart heavy as she whispered, 'I've tried so hard, but I've never really been able to love him as a wife should.'

'And the other man,' Emily said, just as softly, 'Robert, was it . . . do you still think of him?'

Mary gave a forlorn smile. 'All the time.' In fact, every minute of every day and night, even in her dreams. 'God forgive me, but Robert was the only man I have ever truly loved. But that's all gone now. I lost him long ago.'

She could see his face in her mind as clear as if he was sitting here beside her. 'Like a fool I deserted him, Emily, and here I am thinking of deserting Paul, for reasons not too different.' The sigh she gave came up from her soul. 'Sometimes I think being unhappy and losing the baby, is all part of my punishment.'

The older woman's heart went out to her. 'No, pet. We all do what we can in life, only sometimes it's never enough. In the first place, you left because you had no choice. And now it seems to me that you're caught up in another heartache.'

Regretting having burdened Emily with her troubles, Mary feigned indifference. 'No matter,' she said casually. 'I have made my bed, and I'll have to lie on it.'

With that the pair of them went back downstairs, where

Agatha commandeered the reluctant Emily to help her. 'I've come undone at the back,' she complained. I've been looking for you everywhere. You know very well I wouldn't want anybody else messing with my corset!'

As she obediently followed her into a cloakroom, Emily turned to glance at Mary, who was watching them. She winked and smiled, and Mary knew she was keeping in with Agatha for a purpose. I know what you're up to, she mused. You mean to catch her out one way or another. But you won't get the better of her; she's too cunning by half for the likes of us.

Mary was right in her deductions, because that was exactly what the servant intended . . . to catch her out. She was half-tempted to tackle her about Mary and the miscarriage right there and then. But, like Mary, she had to be sure before she started making accusations. Yet, she knew how the old woman liked her drop of gin of an evening, and when she drank, her tongue got loose. Maybe one night, with a bit of encouragement, it might loosen enough to betray the truth of that night.

So, for now she helped the old woman and said nothing. She had been a good friend to Agatha, but if the day ever came when she could prove that Mary had been deliberately pushed, she would show her no mercy. Badness like that must not go unpunished.

That night, Mary made her excuses once the guests had departed and went to bed, leaving Paul and his aunt downstairs discussing the hotel and how it was bound to be a great success.

An hour later she was still wide awake; she couldn't sleep. Instead she lay there reminiscing about the past, alone in that big bed with nothing to keep her warm but her thoughts. Tonight, Emily had awoken memories she had tried so hard to keep away . . . memories of her and Robert, kissing under the mistletoe at Christmas; laughing at the slightest thing, not because it was hugely funny, but because they were so content in each other's company. She remembered their long walks in the park, holding hands and making plans for the future.

The memories made her smile, they made her sad. Most of all, they made her lonelier than ever.

Now, as she heard Paul coming along the landing, her heart sank and she quickly turned over. She couldn't face him. With a bit of luck he would climb into bed and go straight off to sleep.

'Mary, love?' A few minutes later, after stumbling about in the half-light and still excited by the evening's events, Paul climbed into bed beside her. 'Are you awake?' Leaning over her shoulder he whispered in her ear, 'Sweetheart, are you awake?' His hand reached down to fondle her breast, and his voice trembled in her ear. 'Mary, wake up, dear. I need to make love.'

Repulsed, Mary lay as still as she could, pretending to breathe deeply, hoping against hope that he might leave her alone.

Undeterred, he persisted. His fingers toyed with her nipple, then his hand slid from her breast down towards the warmth of her thighs. When after a moment or two of probing he found the softness between her legs, he stroked and played with her until she could feel the hardness of his member in her back. 'Mary!' He pulled gently on her shoulders. 'Quick, turn over!'

Suddenly he had her on her back. Climbing on top of her, he lifted her nightgown high to her neck. He then leaned down and with his mouth drooling against her face, he thrust deep inside her; he drew out twice, then gave another great invasive push and it was over.

Laughing softly, he rolled off. 'It's been the best evening ever!' he told her. Then, with a sigh he fell asleep and was soon snoring.

Shamed, Mary drew her nightgown down and getting out of bed, she ran to the bathroom where she frantically doused herself clean.

For a long time afterwards she sat on the edge of the bath, hating him, hating herself; desperately wondering how she could ever escape from this impossible situation.

Chapter Eighteen

It was early July, and after a long hot spell of sunshine and dry weather, the crops were ripening in the fields. The corn had been harvested, and the stooks were now ready for gathering. It was the season Jack loved the most. Up with the lark and out in the fields, he found nothing more gratifying, unless it was the sight of Lizzy running through the countryside, skirt dancing and the wind in her brown, shoulder-length hair; or when she was riding old Maisie across the brook, kicking up the water behind her and laughing as she went.

'Come on then, son.' Wide awake and eager, Justin had the horse and high-sided farm cart at the ready. 'Let's be 'aving yer.'

From the window, Lizzy's frantic call caused them to look up. 'Wait for me!' One minute she was there and the next she was gone, and before Jack had time to climb aboard the wagon she was running down the path towards them. 'Hey, you two! Don't go without me!'

Reaching down, Jack helped her on to the wagon. 'We wouldn't dare,' he laughed.

Holding up the bag she was carrying, Lizzy gave a mischievous grin. 'It's just as well, because if you *had* gone without me, you'd have gone without this as well.'

For a minute Jack was puzzled, then he realised. Taking the bag, he showed the contents to the old man. 'We very nearly went without our lunch. Look here, Dad.' Calling the old man 'Dad' was second nature to him these days. His own father was not forgotten, but if he was to have any peace in his life, Jack knew he would have to put Robert Sullivan to the back of his mind; after a long, agonising time, he had finally managed to do so, though not altogether happily.

As far as his sister Nancy was concerned, he thought about her all the time, though it broke his heart to recall how she had left him behind without a backwards glance.

Justin laughed out loud. 'An' there was me,' he tutted, 'thinking we might sneak off without fetching some nuisance-woman along, an' all the while she's got our grub.' Winking at Jack he then turned to Lizzy. 'Thank you very much, young lady, and now if yer please, yer can get off my wagon and leave us to do men's work.' Much to Jack's amusement, he deliberately brought the vehicle to a halt, and appeared to be waiting for his stepdaughter to climb down before moving on again. 'Come on, lass, I ain't got all day.'

Lizzy was horrified, but when she saw the pair of them giggling, she playfully pushed the old man in the back. 'Oh you!' she laughed. 'You couldn't afford to leave me behind. Who'd help Jack collect the sheaves while you drive the wagon, eh?' Coming up to fifteen, she was an integral part of the working team and they knew it only too well.

The old man tutted and sighed and, winking at Jack, pretended to have been outwitted. 'D'yer know, lad, she might be right. I know she's not much good at throwing them sheaves up, but a little help is better than none. What d'yer think, lad? Shall we tek 'er along?'

Jack could hardly contain his laughter. 'I don't suppose it would hurt, just for this once.'

As they ambled down the lane, their merry laughter echoed across the morning fields.

Jack glanced at Lizzy, with her ready smile and pink, glowing cheeks, and he thought he had never been happier in the whole of his life.

It took a good twenty minutes and more to reach the bottom field. They then crossed the shallow part of the brook into the hay meadow, and then went on into Major's Field, where the corn had already been cut by farm labourers hired and paid by the day. 'Look at that!' Justin's delighted gaze took in the many sheaves, all made up in stooks, bound and left to dry some three days before. 'It's a sight for sore eyes, so it is.'

Once the sheaves were gathered and stored it was like money in the bank.

It wasn't a huge crop by most farmers' standards, since the field was relatively small, but it brought in enough money to feed the animals, pay the vet's bills, and set the field again for the next year.

Justin was never looking for a profit. If he made enough to live on, he was content. That was the reason he'd strongly resisted the many developers who, time and again, had offered him money to purchase acres of his land. The thought of this beautiful place being covered in bricks and mortar filled him with dread.

Having arrived, he now drew the wagon to a halt where, from his lofty perch he surveyed the sea of golden corn-stooks. 'It's a good crop,' he announced, taking off his cap and enjoying the warm, gentle breeze. 'I'm thankful we didn't get no rain in the night.'

Climbing down from the wagon he stretched his legs and racked his back. Then he took out his pipe and lit it with a wad of baccy. 'Mind you,' he puffed and blew and created a smokescreen all about himself, 'while a heavy downpour can ruin a whole year's work, there's nowt better than the smell o' ripe corn when it's been gently washed with a drop o' rain – though only just enough to mek it taste sweet, eh?'

Having been a part of this life long enough to know, Jack could only agree. 'I'll fetch Maisie's water.' Collecting the bucket from the wagon, he went to the brook, a moment or two later returning with it filled to the brim with delicious cold water. There y'are, me old beauty.' There were some who claimed lightheartedly that Jack had grown into Justin's way of speaking, though not yet into his bad habits, with the smoking and the swearing. That said, there wasn't a manjack among them who didn't love the old man.

'This'll keep you going for a time.' Jack held the bucket in his arms while the old mare had a long, noisy drink, then he hung the bucket alongside her from a hook in the wagon. 'You'll get another when we stop,' he promised, and the old mare seemed to know what he was saying, because she gave him a surprisingly wet, sloppy kiss with the whole length of her tongue.

Taken by surprise, Jack leapt aside. Lizzy laughed out loud. 'You're the first boy I know to run away when a girl gives you a kiss,' she joked.

Justin had been chuckling, too, but now he stared down at her. 'An' what, might I ask, do *you* know about giving kisses, young lady?'

'Nothing!' The pink flush began in her neck and spread right up to her cheekbones. 'I were only saying, that's all.'

'Mmm!' He winked aside at Jack, who himself had been wondering about her remark. 'I reckon she's been a-kissin' the boys, don't you, son?'

Jack was momentarily lost for words. The idea of Lizzy anywhere near another boy was enough to make him go cold. Still, as he knew Justin was only teasing, he played along. 'Some pimply little fella, I expect – fancies his chances 'cause she's the prettiest girl in school.'

Embarrassed to her boots, Lizzy gave them each a warning glance. 'I haven't been kissing *anybody*. And if that's all you want to do, tormenting me, then I'd best get started on the work, or we'll not get any done today!' With that she walked on, head high and a rebellious bounce to her step.

'I'll tan his hide if I catch up with him!' Justin was in good humour. 'You see if I don't.' He gave a low chuckle. 'I'll tell you what,' he told Jack, 'if there ain't no lad approached her for a kiss yet, all I can say is . . . there must be summat wrong with the buggers!' In fact his dream was for Jack and Lizzy to get together. That would be perfect.

Jack merely nodded. Until now he hadn't given it a thought, but suddenly he knew that if any lad was to approach Lizzy, he wouldn't like it, not one bit he wouldn't. In that minute something took hold of him and wouldn't let go. *He loved her!* The revelation was like a knife cutting through his very soul.

For now though, and for a long time to come, he must keep his feelings to himself. But it would be awful hard, he thought. Something like that needed telling. It needed sharing. But not yet. After all, they were both still very young.

The routine was to start at the top of the field and work their way back, and that was what they did, with the old man atop his wagon, puffing and blowing on his pipe and bursting into song in between, while the youngsters ran ahead to prepare the stooks for loading. The sheaves were best separated to make it easier. In the first instance, Lizzy would climb on board and Jack would hand them up for neatly stacking. Next load it would be Jack on the wagon and Lizzy handing them up.

As the morning wore on, the sun began to blaze down and the work grew more demanding. Wanting to get the majority of sheaves stacked on the wagon before the heat brought them to a halt, they kept going, pausing only now and then for a drop of water from the flasks put up by Viola. When the three of them had a drink, so did the old horse.

Come midday, the sweat was trickling down their backs and their arms ached from shoulder to wrist. But there was no stopping, not for a while anyways, not if they were to get the whole lot home and dry before night fell.

Two o'clock came and went; the wagon grew heavier and the horse grew weary. But still the sheaves were piled on, and nobody complained; not even the horse. By three o'clock they were a quarter way down the field and the wagon was almost fully loaded. Its wheels had begun to sit in the many ruts, and the higher it was loaded, the more the work slowed down.

'That'll 'ave to do for now!' Justin called a halt. It's time we stopped for us dinners.' Taking out his wad of baccy, he began to stuff his pipe, while nearby Jack and Lizzy fell to the ground, legs stretched out and faces to the sun. 'By! Bless yer 'earts, you've worked like two good 'uns.' Justin was always happy when the harvest was in. 'I reckon we should 'ave it all away by nine o'clock.'

Having taken a minute to recover from the searing heat, Jack got to his feet and collecting the hamper from the wagon-shaft where he'd tied it earlier, he set it to the ground. 'I'd best see to Maisie,' he said, and began untying her bag of hay from the side of the wagon.

Clambering down, Justin went to Maisie. 'The poor old bugger's done in,' he said, stroking her neck, 'Aw, but she's a good 'un . . . aren't yer, eh?' She wasn't a handsome mare by any means, but she had a big heart and a fond nature. For Justin, that was more important then being pretty. Since Samson's dramatic birth – the foal was now a dashing young stallion – he'd made sure Maisie was well looked after and her workload halved.

Thinking how fortunate he had been in his life, he looked at Lizzy, who was unpacking the hamper on to the blanket, and

Jack, who was making his way down – a fine, strong figure of a young man, with his face dirtied by dust and his arms browned by the sun – and his old heart swelled with pride. 'We're a good team, the three of us,' he said, cocking his head and smiling. 'I reckon we could turn the world upside down if we'd a mind!'

Jack laughed at that. 'I don't think so,' he disagreed. 'If you hadn't stopped just now, I reckon I'd have been on my knees.'

'Never!' Like Lizzy, Justin knew different. 'It'd tek more than a field o' corn to bring *you* to yer knees.'

Lizzy called them over. 'It's ready,' she said. 'Come and sit down.'

First, Jack strapped the hay-bag round Maisie's neck. 'You've earned that,' he said, and much to the others' amusement, dodged out of the way before she could wash him with her tongue again.

When they were all sat down, enjoying the sandwiches fattened with ham and cheese, and seasoned with a sprinkling of herbs, Justin remarked on how, 'We should get top price for this little lot. It's good corn – some o' the best I've ever seen.' Dropping a sliver of ham down his chin he wiped it away and stuffed it in his mouth, afterwards licking his fingers. 'I might even be able to afford the pair of youse an extra tanner.'

Both Jack and Lizzy nonsensed that idea, but he insisted. 'You're not little kids any more,' he pointed out. 'Here's the both of youse, nearly growed up. You'll find plenty of use for an extra tanner, and I'll hear no more of yer arguments.'

Replete and sleepy now, they finished their meal. Afterwards, Lizzy washed at the brook, splashing her face and hands, while not too far away, Jack took off his shirt and swilled his top half. From the corner of her eye, she watched him, thinking how handsome he was, and that if anybody should be kissing her, it shouldn't be no 'pimply young fella', because she would much rather it was Jack.

Suddenly, while she was watching him, Jack turned and

caught her gaze and try as she might, she couldn't look away. A feeling of pure wonder flowed between them. It was the most amazing experience, and one which neither of them would ever forget. It was as if, in that brief, fleeting minute, their love for each other had suddenly blossomed into a real, physical presence.

'I'd best get back.' Rushed and nervous, Lizzy ran off, leaving Jack looking after her, his insides shaking and his heart beating fifteen to the dozen.

When they returned, first Lizzy then Jack, oddly subdued and not daring to look the other in the eye, Justin caught the mood between them and was thrilled. 'I reckon we've just seen the beginnings of love,' he told the old horse. 'With a bit o' luck and a gentle push in the right direction, there might even come the day when we see them as man and wife.' It had always been his secret ambition. 'There's nowt I'd love more in this life.'

With that in mind he began his merry whistling. But neither Jack nor Lizzy seemed to hear.

Instead they were only aware of each other; Lizzy unsure and afraid of the feelings inside her, and Jack, burning with love, aching to hold her, but realising she was too young. It was a torment. But one which he would have to endure, until the time was right to tell her how he felt.

Just as he had promised, with the last few sheaves thrown atop the wagon, Justin headed old Maisie home a few minutes before the stroke of nine. 'I don't know about you two,' he said as they climbed up, 'but I can't wait to get me feet up, an' a hot brew inside me.' He gave a cheeky wink. 'I'd not say no to a plate o' cottage pie an' fried taters neither!'

The two youngsters sat side by side, each afraid to glance at the other, and their hands only a heartbeat away from holding.

As they came out of the meadow and across the brook, the wagon hit some hidden stones, sending the three of them crashing into each other. 'Whoops-a-daisy!' Justin fought to right himself while, beside him, Jack protected Lizzy with his body.

Finding herself suddenly enclosed in Jack's arms, the girl blushed deep crimson. 'I'm all right now,' she said as the wagon climbed on to the bank. But she really wouldn't have minded if Jack had held on to her for ever.

So, for the remainder of the journey, they sat quiet, acutely aware of the other's nearness. Up front, Justin whistled and sang, puffing his pipe and seemingly oblivious to it all.

As they neared the cottage, Jack wondered if he and Lizzy would ever be as close as this again. In a fit of fear and uncertainty, he slid his hand over hers. When to his great delight, she curled her fingers round his, he felt his happy heart turn somersaults.

But then all too soon, they were coming up the path and Justin was heading for the rickyard. 'Right then, you two . . . it's time to offload.' He halted the ensemble and, in spite of Jack and Lizzy's protests, helped offload every single sheaf.

By ten thirty the wagon was emptied and Justin clapped his hands. 'We'll give 'em a week or so to dry out proper, then it's time for the threshing and chaff-cuttin' and we'll swap the bags o' grain for hard cash.'

As they walked back to the cottage, wearied and dirty, Jack couldn't help but notice how breathless Justin was. 'Are you all right, Dad?' He tried to slow the pace but Justin kept pressing ahead.

'Course I'm all right, son. Why shouldn't I be?' He felt unusually weary, and his every bone ached inside him, but in front of the two young 'uns, he quickly laughed it off. 'I'm after me brew,' he told them, 'an' a generous helping o' that meat pie I saw our Vi mekkin' last night.' With that he quickened his steps and went into the cottage at a rush. 'Evenin', wife!' he called out. 'You've three hungry folks to feed, so come on, let's be 'aving yer!'

Viola appeared at the kitchen door. 'There's nobody sitting at my table,' she answered harshly, 'not without they're washed and changed first!'

So, while Lizzy washed at the sink, and Justin after her, Jack collected clean clothes from his room. Taking them out to the pump, he jacked the handle until the water gushed out freely, and there he washed and changed; some fifteen minutes later presenting himself at the table, where Lizzy and Justin were already seated. 'By! You're so clean and shiny, I'm buggered if yer don't look like a pair o' strangers.' After looking from Lizzy to Jack, Justin called his wife, who was on her way in with the dish of meat-pie. 'Look 'ere, wife – we've a couple o' strangers at the table.'

Viola feigned a good-humoured smile. 'They can't be as strange as *you*!' she answered, which set Justin off laughing, though he took a coughing fit and on her instructions, had to leave the table until he recovered.

Deeply concerned, Jack watched the old man throughout the meal. He saw how, in spite of being hungry, Justin merely toyed with his food. He saw him growing paler and sicker and when, some half hour into the meal, Justin excused himself, Jack went after him, much to Viola's annoyance. 'You stay right where you are, my girl!' she ordered Lizzy. 'If the men see fit to waste a good meal, it's up to them, but I'll not have *you* going hungry after working all day long.'

In order to keep her from leaving, she got out of her chair and came to sit beside her daughter, where for the next while she kept her busy in conversation; Lizzy, however, paid little heed, keeping her eyes on the door, waiting for them to return.

Outside, Justin sat on the wall with Jack beside him. 'I've overdone it, son,' he told him with a weary smile. 'I'm a silly old bugger who thinks he can keep up with the young 'uns.' He patted Jack on the back. 'I'll be all right,' he promised. 'It's just that sometimes I forget how old I am.'

Jack wouldn't have that. 'You're not old! You've just finished a long hard day with the sun blazing down on you. *Anybody* would feel exhausted after that.'

'Mebbe, but I reckon from now on, I'd best let *you* do the man's work, eh?' Now as he smiled, there was a terrible resignation in his face, as though already he was giving in. Looking into Jack's face, he said softly, 'When yer get to a certain age, son, yer make the mistake o' thinkin' yer can live for ever. But then yer bones start to ache and it teks longer to do the same job yer did in half the time when yer were younger.'

He gave a long, drawn-out sigh. 'Aye. It's time I turned it all over to you.' Again there was that winning smile. 'What would I do without yer, eh?'

Jack was glad to see him smile, but then Justin would smile whatever ailed him, or however bad he felt. But there was something else, too. The old farmer was heartbroken to think he had come to the end of the road.

Jack heard his words and he saw the smile, and he knew it was all show. So he gave the old man back his pride. 'I'm not quite ready for you to turn it all over to me yet,' he lied. 'There are still things you need to show me – a lot I've yet to learn. So don't go thinking I'm a better man than you, however old you are, 'cause I never could be.'

On his last words he smiled reassuringly into the old man's face, and slowly but surely, there was that smile again on the homely old features, but this time it was filled with hope, and gratitude. 'You're a grand lad,' he murmured. 'Yer seem to understand me better than anybody. An' I'm a lucky man to 'ave yer for a son.' Swallowing hard so the tears wouldn't fall, he held his head up. 'Right then! Let's finish us supper, eh? If we're to get on with all that needs doing, we'll want us strength, won't we?'

Draping his arm over Jack's shoulder he walked with him

back to the cottage. 'By! Smell that meat pie, lad! Ooh, I can feel me appetite comin' back. D'yer know what? I reckon I could manage *two* helpin's now!' And the two of them went inside laughing with the sheer joy of relief, and being content, as ever, in each other's company.

Lizzy was greatly relieved to see them come back in good spirits; she asked her daddy if he was all right and Justin told her he felt grand. On his answer her gaze went to Jack, who was already peeping at her and thinking how lovely she was. They exchanged smiles and broke into conversation about the day, with Justin uplifted and laughing, and full of new life.

Viola was none too pleased to see how the old man appeared to have rallied. When he had tottered out of the door, she had hoped against hope that he was on his last legs. Now though, she could see how that damned boy, Jack, had given him the strength to go on.

And she hated him all the more for it!

The following weeks were a joy. The good weather held and all the harvest was got in. 'By! Them are some o' the best apples I've ever grown,' Justin declared as they took the last basket into the barn. 'We should get a good price for 'em at market.' The plums were fat and juicy, and the raspberries positively burst with goodness. By the time they had gathered the harvest, it was time for celebration. As always, Viola Lyndhurst put on a fine spread and the neighbours, six in all, came to share in their good fortune.

It was a pleasant evening; the sun shone and the birds chirped in the trees, and everyone ate to their hearts' content. Afterwards when the elderberry wine began to flow, Justin played his old fiddle and Lizzy sang, and when it was over, they went to their beds worn out but content – all but Viola, who hadn't got over how her husband had rallied and gained new strength. 'Damn the man!' she muttered as she watched him play the fiddle, laughing and singing along and tapping his feet as the others clapped to the tune.

After a while she couldn't bear to watch and hid in the kitchen to sulk.

All too soon there was more work to be done on the farm. 'We'd best tackle the outdoor jobs now. We mustn't wait till winter catches us out.' Justin knew this only too well. He had only ever been caught out once – and that was the worst winter he had ever experienced. Two of his best rams were lost, and one of his barns collapsed under the weight of the heavy snow. 'We'll mek a start on the old barn,' he decided. 'It needs shoring up at one end, and a new roof. We've already got the timbers.'

The wood had been piled in the rickyard these past two months, only what with one thing and another, there had never been the time to deal with it. Now though, with the harvest out of the way, it was time to tackle these important jobs.

For the next few weeks, the work was incessant, though all the time Jack watched the old man so he didn't overdo things. He carried the timber up before Justin woke in the morning, and he set out the day's work two hours before it was begun. So, while he was doing all the heavy lifting, Justin was still in charge.

It was a good plan that suited them both. The farmer knew what Jack intended, and though neither of them mentioned it, each accepted the way of it. So, as planned, Justin kept his pride, while Jack satisfied himself that he was doing all he could to minimise the old man's workload.

By the middle of October, the work was done. The yard was tidied up from one end to the other; the thatching was finished on the back of the cottage; the outside privy was painted and a new door put on. The old barn was like new, and the big shed was lined from top to bottom. 'By! That'll be warm as toast for the beasts when the bad weather comes,' Justin declared.

Proud and tired, the two of them stood back to see the work they'd done. 'There's just the fields to be tended now.'

Ploughing and seeding was always a favourite job with the old man. 'If we get another rich crop like this year's, I'll not be disappointed.'

Sitting on the bench to smoke his pipe, he watched as Jack put away the ladders and tools. With immense pride, he noticed how Jack had come on this last year. Always a strong lad, he had grown taller, his muscular body had filled out and suddenly, as Justin observed him, he realised that Jack was no longer a boy. He was a man. Almost without him noticing, Jack had matured and grown – already showing signs of the good, contented man he would be in years to come.

As the day wore on, the old man glanced up to the evening skies with their melting lights and incoming cloak of evening. 'Thank You, Lord,' he murmured. 'You couldn't have sent me a better son than Jack. When my time comes, I know I can leave all this to him and rest easy, knowing it'll be loved, and tekken care of.' That thought was a great comfort to him.

Under the old man's supervision, Jack soon learned how to plough and seed. Not wanting him to think he could master everything at once, Justin told him he was 'almost' a farmer and, thanking him, Jack revealed how he never wanted to be anything else *but* a farmer. That put a smile on Justin's face, and a song in his old heart.

On this particular day, at the very minute when Justin was giving Jack a hand to scrape clean the plough, Lizzy brought them some refreshments. 'There's ham sandwiches, and cider to drink.' She set the tray on the wooden-slatted table. 'There's fruit, too,' she said. 'A basin of stewed spiced apples but there's no cream. That ginger stray got in the window and stole the lot.'

Justin threw his arms up in despair. 'That bloody cat! I've lost chickens to it, it's been in the barn again and shredded all me hessian sacks, and it's piddled so often in the raspberry patch it fair meks yer eyes water!' He shook his fist in the air. 'I swear I'll wring its scrawny neck if I catch it round 'ere again!'

Jack laughed good-humouredly. 'I've lost count of the times you've threatened to wring its neck,' he reminded the old man. 'You know very well you'd never harm a hair on its furry head.'

Knowing the truth of Jack's words, the old man sighed resignedly. 'The trouble is, I'm too soft for me own good.'

While the men washed their hands in the trough, Lizzy set out the food. 'Hurry up before the flies get it!' she urged.

A moment later the three of them were seated round the table; Jack and the old man tucking into the chunky sandwiches, and Lizzy happily tasting a spoonful of the stewed apple. Content in each other's company, they chatted about the work they'd managed to complete between them. Justin said how pleased he was that they'd got so much done in such a short time but, as he told them, 'I reckon we'll knock off early today.'

Jack didn't like the sound of that. 'Are you feeling all right, Dad?'

Suddenly his thoughts were shattered when the old man answered Jack's pointed question. The answer was given with a bright smile and a gentle chiding. 'Course I'm all right, son. I fancy an early night, that's all.'

The truth was, he had not been feeling too well all day, but he wasn't about to worry the ones he loved, so he skilfully back-tracked. 'Mind you, by the time we've finished off, I dare say we'll not be away any earlier than usual.'

Shivering inside and suddenly feeling a cold chill through his thinning hair, he put on his flat cap and smiled from one to the other. 'Lizzy, lass, when yer get back, ask yer mam if she can boil up the copper. I've an idea I might light a fire in the outhouse and enjoy a long, lazy soak in the bath.'

Lizzy said she would, and went on to mention how she would be glad when school was finished for good, because she so much enjoyed helping around the place, and there never seemed much time in the week, what with the work she had to do for the teacher. 'I'll be fifteen in another six weeks,' she reminded him.

'I know it only too well, lass,' he answered. 'You'd best soon tell me what it is you're after for yer birthday present, 'cause as yer know, I'm useless at thinking up summat useful, especially for a young lady such as yersel'.'

Lizzy wiped a juicy drop from her chin. 'I'm not bothered about a present,' she admitted. 'I'm only too glad to be leaving school at last.'

The old man looked up. 'Who said you could leave school?'

'*You* did!' She grew pale. 'You said if I continued to take lessons, and work hard up to the age of fifteen, I could leave and take on a clerical position.'

'Mmm.' He chewed her reply over for a minute, along with another ham sandwich. 'Oh aye, lass, so I did.' He tore off another piece of his ham sandwich and almost choked on it. 'Now then, are yer sure it's what yer want, 'cause it's a hard world out there, an' the more you can learn now, the better it'll stand yer in good stead for later on.'

The girl was adamant. I've stayed at school too long already,' she argued. 'Anyway, I'm not learning much these days. The teacher has me helping *her* most of the time. All the children are younger than me and there's more coming to school.'

'Aye well, happen she thinks *you'd* mek a good teacher an' all, eh?'

'I don't want to be a teacher. I want to work outside, with grown-ups.'

'Oh aye, doing what?'

'Like I said, clerical work maybe. There's a position going at

John Williams' warehouse, I heard them talking about it in the cobbler's the other day. It would be interesting to keep books and write out worksheets for the men. Besides, I'd be independent, instead of you having to pay out to keep me in school.'

'Oh now, it weren't paying out as such.' He tapped his nose on imparting the truth. 'It were more like a little private enterprise, such as doing odd jobs round the place and providing the governers with produce and such.' He had thought it a small price to pay for his stepdaughter's ongoing education. 'Millie Martin's dad did the same, and you'll not hear *her* complaining.'

'She does, all the time, and now the teacher's got us both helping her. Don't think I'm not grateful, Dad, but I really want to go out to work and that clerical position at the warehouse sounds just right.'

'I'm not 'aving no daughter o' mine workin' in a ware'ouse!'

'Then I'll find something else.' Glancing at Jack, she tried to recruit him into the conversation. 'What do you think, Jack? What sort of work should I be looking for?'

All this time Jack had kept out of the argument. After all, it wasn't something he felt he should interfere in, but now that Lizzy had asked, he gave her his honest answer. 'First of all, in my opinion there's nothing wrong with working in a warehouse. It's good honest work and there's many a man who's raised his family from such a job. But, somehow I don't think you'd be happy. You're too used to the outdoors and fresh air. Anybody can see, you'd be like a bird in a cage. What you should do is take your time and see what suits.'

'And secondly?'

'You're a sensible, intelligent girl, Lizzy. Whatever me and Dad says, you'll do all right. But you need to be sure you're going into the right kind of work – something that makes you feel good inside. Something that makes you want to get up in the morning, winter or summer.'

Lizzy was deeply moved by what he had said. 'Thank you, Jack. I'll bear all that in mind.'

Justin, too, had been sobered by Jack's comments. 'I couldn't 'ave put it better mesel',' he remarked. 'It's a pity we couldn't have kept the pair of youse on with the learning.'

Jack shook his head. 'I'm learning all I need to,' he said quietly. 'I'm like you, Dad. I love the land more than anything,' – except Lizzy, he thought. 'As long as I live, I know I'll never want to do anything else.'

Proud tears trembled in the old man's eyes. 'By! You're a fella after me own heart, so yer are.' He raised the mug of cider to toast their health. 'Here's to my young 'uns,' he said. 'May they find all the love and happiness in the world.' With each other, he thought, because he believed in his heart that that was where they would find their contentment.

With that he stood up, settled the cap squarely on his head and wended his way to the barn. 'He's so proud of you, Jack.' Lizzy felt all kinds of pleasure glowing inside her.

Jack gave her a kindly wink. 'An' I'm proud *of you*,' he said before, like Justin, he strode off to finish the day's work.

Later that night, when they were sat round the table in the kitchen, Justin was unusually quiet, until his wife grew impatient with him. 'Have you gone deaf, or what?' she asked rudely.

Startled, Justin looked up. 'I'm sorry, dear. I were miles away. What were yer saying?'

'I was saying as how I've boiled the water in the copper,' she told him. 'You'll find the tin-bath hanging where it's allus been. And mind yer don't use too much water, 'cause I've a pile o' dirty laundry waiting to go in.'

He nodded. 'Oh aye, right. I'll go an' light the fire . . . give it half an hour or so to get warm in there.' Excusing himself, he stood up. 'That were a lovely meal, thank you.'

'Hey!'

He paused. 'What now?'

'You've not finished.' She pointed to his half-emptied plate. 'After all my hard work getting you a decent meal, you've hardly touched it. What's wrong with you?'

'There's nowt wrong, lass,' he said wearily. 'I ate too many o' them lovely sandwiches yer sent, that's all.'

She had no real argument to that. 'Aye, well, I'll not make such a big dinner for you in future,' she answered curtly. 'Or I'll not send so many sandwiches, not if it's going to spoil your appetite for the evening. Go on then! Be off with yer, and mind you save me plenty of water for the laundry.' With that she bent her head to finish her own meal, afterwards wiping the plate clean.

By the time she looked up, Justin was gone, and the others were toying with their food. 'Either eat up or leave the table,' she told Jack angrily. 'I'm sure I don't know what's got into the both of you!'

Jack apologised. 'It's like Dad said. The sandwiches were lovely, very filling, too.'

Incensed by his referring to Justin as 'Dad', she snapped, 'There's logs to be split. If you don't want my food, get off and do that!'

When he stood to excuse himself, so did Lizzy, but she was soon told, albeit in a cajoling voice, 'You sit down, my lovely. I'm sure you'll not want to waste all your mammy's hard work in getting such a meal together. Besides, we can talk about what you've been doing out there in the fields. I know how much you love being out there, though God only knows, there are times when I wish you didn't!'

She kept her there through the apple pie and custard, then through the pot of tea, and she still had her there twenty minutes later when Jack came running in, his face white and the fear alight in his eyes as he cried for Lizzy to, 'Get blankets, quick!' Addressing Viola he ordered, 'I need your help. Dad's collapsed. We have to get him into bed. Hurry! Please, HURRY!'

While Jack ran back to the outhouse, Lizzy was rushing upstairs to fetch blankets. It took another minute before Viola herself went after Jack, and even then she didn't rush. Instead she ambled down the path as if she was on the way to hang out her precious washing, and all the while there was a smile on her face and hope in her heart, that when she got to the outhouse, she might find it was all too late.

Having dragged him out of the bath and dried and dressed him as best he could, Jack already had the old man on his feet, though he was shivering and obviously very poorly. 'Cling on to me,' Jack told him, and he did, because he had no strength to do otherwise.

Lizzy was the first to arrive; wet-eyed and fearful, she tried not to show it. 'You'll be all right, Daddy,' she kept telling him, and he smiled back, though compared to his usual bright, merry smile, it was a weak and feeble effort.

When Viola came in the door, Jack asked her to hold her husband steady while he tied the blankets round him. As he did so, he whispered to Lizzy to, 'Run for the doctor. Tell him that Dad's collapsed and he needs tending straight away!' The girl didn't need telling twice. She was out of the door almost before he'd finished speaking.

Between them, Viola and Jack got the old man to his bed; though he continued to shiver uncontrollably and found it hard to talk. For the next few minutes, while the big woman stood back, Jack collected a blanket from his own bed. Throwing it gently over the old man, he made him comfortable. 'We need a fire in here,' he said.

Even though the sun was still shining through the window, it brought no heat, not at this time of evening. 'If you could fetch paper and kindling,' he asked of Viola, 'I'll get a fire going.'

When she was slow in responding, he told her to, 'Keep an eye on Dad!' While he ran down to the shed, she remained by the door, her eyes glued to the old man; she saw how he gasped at his breathing and how his gaze tried to seek her out, and she saw the weakness taking him from her. But his sorry plight brought no compassion to her hard heart. All she could think of was how soon it might be before she could take charge – and when that happened, one of her first jobs would be to throw Jack out on his ear.

The boy was back in no time at all. First making sure the old man was all right, he then knelt by the grate and making a pyramid of the paper and kindling, he took the matches from the mantelpiece and set light to it all. Soon the wood caught fire and the heat began to waft into the room. 'That's better.' He then returned to tend the old man. 'The doctor will be here soon,' he told him, and nodding appreciatively, Justin reached out to take hold of his hand.

'Thank you, son.' His old eyes shifted to the back of the room, where Viola was standing. For the briefest of seconds their eyes met, and in that moment he knew her secret thoughts, and it was a devastating revelation to him.

She wanted him out of the way so she could domineer and dictate, and ruin everything he had worked for all his life.

Then, seeing how he half suspected, she smiled and reassured him, and he wondered if, in his fever, he had got it all wrong.

Soon, the room was warming through, and the old man ceased shivering. In no time at all, the doctor arrived and asked them to wait downstairs while he examined his patient; which they did, though Jack and Lizzy couldn't rest, while Viola sat calmly in the rocking chair, pushing it back and forth and secretly contemplating the consequences of this night.

In her mind's eye she could see the land and property coming to her. She could see herself talking with the same property developers who, time and again, Justin had turned away. But he was in no fit state to argue now, she thought. With him gone, it would all be hers, sooner than she had realised. The prospect was exhilarating.

A short time later the doctor came to convey his findings. Jack and Lizzy were somewhat relieved by what he had to say, though Viola's hopes were cruelly dashed. She felt horribly cheated and resentful, but being a cunning devil, she managed to smile over the bitterness. 'So he'll soon be as good as new, will he, Doctor?'

'He's been working too hard – overdoing it as usual. He's a cantankerous old devil at times and won't be told that he needs to slow down. Too proud by half, that's his trouble.' Taking a writing pad from his black bag he produced a prescription. 'Get him this – it's a tonic. I've confined him to bed for at least a week, and no work at all for another two weeks after that.' He tut-tutted. 'You'll need to watch him, mind. You know better than me what he's like.'

'Can we go up and see him now?' Jack, like Lizzy, was anxious.

'I don't see why not.' As they went towards the stairway he warned, 'Try not to tire him though. He needs to sleep.'

While the doctor began talking to Viola about the need for a special nourishing diet, the two youngsters made their way upstairs to the sick man. 'The doctor says you've been overdoing it. You need to have at least three weeks off work, and no argument!' Lizzy told him in no uncertain terms.

The way he felt, Justin had no intention of arguing. He grinned at her, and growing sleepy, promised he would do as he was told. 'A man never knows when he begins to grow old,' he said, and no sooner were the words out of his mouth, than he was fast asleep.

Lizzy cried softly, more with relief than anything else.

Subdued by the incident, Jack kept hold of the old man's hand a while longer. 'You gave me a real fright,' he murmured, gazing down on that familiar, beloved old face. 'From now on, *I'll* be your strength.'

Hearing his words, Lizzy loved him all the more. Jack was very special, and so was Justin. They were two of a kind and she could never imagine a life without either of them.

Chapter Nineteen

The following day, Justin seemed to perk up; threatening how now that he'd rested, he felt good enough to get out of his bed. Jack and Lizzy dared him to, and because he could see how concerned they were, and what with his legs feeling a bit like jelly, he decided that he might stay in bed after all. 'You're a terrible pair o' bullies, so yer are!' he chided them.

The second day in bed was not so good. He slept for most of the time. 'He doesn't seem to be getting any better,' Lizzy told her mother.

Jack, too, was beginning to grow concerned. 'Happen we should get the doctor back,' he suggested, much to Viola's horror. 'Dad's so weak, and he's tired all the time.'

'It's nothing to concern yourselves about.' The big woman gave the broth she was making another stir. 'The doctor told me he would grow weak before he gets stronger. That's why he confined him to his bed for all that time.' Taking the pan off the fire, she poured a generous helping of the thick, meaty soup into a small earthenware bowl; the aroma was wonderful. 'All good stuff this,' she said, full of her own importance. 'Once he gets this broth down him, he'll soon start to perk up.'

Lizzy offered to take it, but was told, 'It's best if I keep an eye on him – make sure he drinks every last drop. I'd appreciate it though, if you'd take the washing out of the copper and peg it on the line for me? What with running up and down the stairs for most of the day, I haven't had time to do it.'

While Lizzy did as she was bid, Jack went out to the shed to load eight full crates on to the cart; two of plums; one of eggs; one bursting with cauliflowers, and the remaining four filled to the brim with delicious, juicy apples. 'I'll be off to market now,' he told Lizzy through the door of the outhouse. 'When I get back, we can sit with Dad for a while.'

Lizzy so much wanted to go with him. 'Wait ten minutes and I'll be finished,' she pleaded. 'I expect Dad will sleep for a while once he's had his broth. He won't even know we're gone.'

Jack was only too delighted to have her along. 'I'll wait by the gate,' he answered, and as he went away she sang softly to herself.

She had never met a boy like Jack, and though he called her father 'Dad' and was supposed to be like a brother to her, she had never really seen him in that light. He was more than a brother, more than a friend. In fact, he had come to mean so much to her, that she could not fully understand her own feelings. All she knew was, when they were apart, she felt desperately lonely.

Soon they were on their way, chatting as they went – about Lizzy soon being able to work and earn, and Jack reassuring her about how he was sure Justin would soon be strong and healthy again. 'I know he's not my real father,' he said, 'but I love him as though he was.' A sense of bitterness coloured his voice. 'I can never imagine Justin deserting his children!'

Lizzy sensed the deep regret in him. 'Look – Justin isn't my real father either, but I love him just as much as you do. I can't remember my real father. He died when I was little. I know how much you love being here with us, and I'm glad every day that Justin found you,' she told him affectionately. 'But you still miss them, don't you, your real father and your sister?'

'Mebbe.'

'It's only natural. They are your flesh and blood, after all.'

'My real father, as you call him, went away and left us with strangers. We might have been sold on the street for all he cared! As for my sister, who I would have died for, she couldn't have thought any more of me than *he* did. When this fine, wealthy gent took her away, she never looked back, not once. She forgot about me. By now, she probably doesn't even remember my face.' Overcome with emotion, he fell silent.

'Jack?'

'Yes?'

'It's all right to be angry, but she was so young. You can't know she didn't love you.'

'If you say so.'

'Do you think you'll ever want to find them – your sister and your real daddy?'

'No. That part of my life is gone for ever. Best to let it be.'

'You might never see them again. Doesn't that worry you?'

Gently smacking the reins against the horse's rump he rounded the corner. 'It didn't worry them not to see *me* again, so why should *I* care?' But he did. So much so, the older he got, the more he seemed to wonder about them. 'Besides, I'm really happy here, Lizzy – with you and Justin.'

She smiled at that. 'I'm glad.'

He gave a chuckle, though there was little mirth in it. 'Your mother has never taken to me though. I reckon she wishes she'd never clapped eyes on me.' Though the feeling was mutual where he was concerned. But, if he had to suffer her to enjoy his life here, he could put up with that, he thought.

Lizzy tried hard to excuse her. 'It's just the way she is. She's never liked strangers.'

'Is that what I am – a stranger?'

Reaching up she gave him a kiss on the side of his face. 'No,' she said tenderly. 'You're part of the family, and I love you.'

A great well of emotion rippled through him. He gazed down on her and just then, while the two of them were looking into each other's eyes and wondering about the powerful feelings inside them, the horse stumbled and a crate of apples went rolling off the back of the cart.

As it went careering down the lane, Jack drew the horse to a halt and together with Lizzy he scrambled down to recover the crate. 'That'll teach me to look where I'm going!' he cried as they ran back along the lane. But he was so incredibly happy, what did it matter if they lost one crate of apples? He could always pay Justin out of his wages.

The apples had tumbled all over the lane, but only two were bruised beyond redemption. 'I'm sure old Maisie would appreciate these.' And Jack put them in his pocket for the horse.

By the time they got back to the cart with the crate, the horse was beginning to fidget. 'All right, Maisie girl!' Jack reached into his trouser-pocket for the apples, only to find they'd mashed to a pulp when he'd lifted the crate on to the cart. 'Ooh, it's horrible!' Jack scooped it out, while Lizzy laughed out loud at the look of revulsion on his face.

Seeing the funny side of it all, Jack, too, burst out laughing.

The pair of them giggled all the way to market, while Maisie made the best of the mashed apple she'd been given, licking her lips and trotting along the lane 'like a good 'un', as Justin would say.

Behind them in the cottage, Viola stood by the bedroom door for an age, the bowl of soup in her hands, and her ear to the door, listening for any sound from inside. When after a time she was sure he must be fast asleep, she opened the door gingerly and peeped in, only to see him peeping back at her. 'How are you feeling?' she asked, slightly shocked.

'Tired,' he answered. 'An' a bit hungry.'

'I'll go and make you some broth then.' She held the bowl of soup out of sight. 'I'll not be long. Meanwhile, you get some sleep.'

He nodded, and she closed the door, a wicked smile on her face.

Elated by her own trickery she went downstairs and out to the vegetable patch where slowly, as though savouring every last drop, she poured the broth in amongst the compost. That done she looked in at the bedroom window, gave a smile and calmly went back inside, where she washed the dish and saucepan, and put them both away.

For two more days, the same scene was enacted; Viola would make her husband's food, and either Lizzy or Jack would ask if they could feed it to the old man, who was weakening by the day. She would refuse, insisting that she had to entice him into eating every last drop. Then, while the two of them were busy elsewhere, she would take the food upstairs, hide it behind the chair on the landing and go inside to ask how he was. 'I reckon I could fancy some o' that lovely broth yer mek so well?' he would whisper, and she, acting the loving wife, would promise she'd be back in a minute with it.

Fading fast, the old man would fall asleep while, congratulating herself that she had found the solution to her and Lizzy's future, his 'loving' wife would take the food out to the compost heap and pour it all away. And nobody was any the wiser.

Every evening when he and Lizzy went in to see how Justin was, Jack would grow desperately worried about the old man's plight. This evening was no exception. 'Drink it gently now.' Holding the glass of water to the old man's lips, he and Lizzy helped him sit up, far enough so as not to choke on the water. The old man would take a sip or two and fall back on to the pillow, unable even to raise his arms.

Knowing how she could not stop them from going in to see her husband, Viola had left only the smallest measure of water by his bedside. Afterwards she would follow Jack and Lizzy in, to remove what was left of the water; though neither they nor Justin knew of it.

'I think we should get the doctor back.' Jack came down the stairs to tell her how worried he and Lizzy were. 'He seems so weak.'

'He doesn't need a doctor,' Viola retorted. 'He needs rest, and the two of you worrying him every evening doesn't help.'

'But he's so poorly, Mam,' Lizzy argued. 'Why not let the doctor just come and take a look at him?'

'*No*. It'll only make him worse. You know how your father hates the doctor round him. And besides, he's eating well enough. I take him porridge in the morning and broth later on, and he eats every last drop. He'll be fine. He'll rest and grow strong. Stop your fretting.'

On the Saturday morning, Jack was kept busy with nailing wooden sides on to the small market cart, so they could stack the crates without fear of them falling off in future.

On her mother's instructions, Lizzy was getting ready to go into town with her. 'Bring a basket!' Viola called up. 'We've a fair bit o' shopping to do round the market.'

On leaving, she told Jack, 'Stay away from Justin, and try not to make too much noise as you go about your work. He's had his porridge and now he's resting. It's what he needs . . . plenty of sleep. '*I'll* see to him when I get back.' With that she flounced off, with Lizzy trailing reluctantly behind, thinking how she would much rather have stayed with her two favourite men.

Later on, with the cart-sides fixed and working well on the hinges, Jack stood back to inspect his handiwork. 'Not bad, eh, Dad? I reckon you'd be proud of me.' He gave a half-smile. 'When we get you back on your feet again, you'll see how much easier it is to stack the crates and not be frightened of turning a corner in case you lose the lot in the ditch.'

Ever anxious, he glanced up at the bedroom window. 'What's happening to you, Dad? Why can't you rally round?' It wasn't like Justin to give in like that.

Remembering Viola's words: 'Stay away from Justin. *I'll* see to him when I get back,' he felt a rush of defiance. But then he remembered how the old man must need his sleep and, against his deeper instincts, he found all manner of work to be getting on with.

It was two o'clock when he stopped for a break. He looked up at the bedroom window and wondered if the old man had slept long enough for him to go and see how he was. He decided enough time had elapsed and it would be all right. He should have had a good rest by now.

Running to the cottage he dropped his boots off at the door and went softly up the stairs. At first on opening the door he thought the old man was asleep, but as he went to close the door he heard him call out, 'Is that you, Vi?'

Relieved, Jack went inside. 'No, Dad, it's me.' Coming close to the bed he was horrified by Justin's appearance; his face was gaunt and his hair seemed overnight to have been drained of colour. 'I've come to see how you are,' he said, kneeling down so the old man could see and hear him clearly. Taking hold of his hand, he told him, 'Lizzy's gone into town with her mam. They've some shopping to do.'

The old man nodded, but didn't seem to be closely listening.

'And I've been working on the cart we use for market,' When he saw how Justin seemed suddenly alert, he explained excitedly, 'I've fixed some high sides on it, so it'll take double the load, and keep it secure into the bargain.'

Realising he should have asked permission, he apologised. 'Is that all right, Dad?' he asked now. 'If it's not, I can always take the sides off again. I've made it so they clip off and on, with those big heavy hinges. You remember the ones you said you might sell, 'cause we didn't have no use for 'em?'

Suddenly the old man was smiling, his eyes brighter than Jack had seen them for a long while. 'So, it's all right then?' he asked. 'You're not angry?'

'No.' Raising his hand he patted Jack like he used to. 'It's good.'

With tears in his eyes, Jack realised how talking about the work and such had kindled a spark of interest in Justin. 'Is there anything I can get you?'

The old man licked his lips, but as Jack went to give him a drop of water he realised there was none there. 'She must have forgot,' he assumed. 'I'll go and get some.'

The old man kept his hand over Jack's. 'I'm . . . hungry.'

Jack was astonished. 'By! You must be getting better. You've had a huge bowl of porridge and it's not even teatime yet, and already you're hungry again. That's wonderful!'

For a minute, Justin looked puzzled. He couldn't understand what Jack was saying so, in a quiet voice, he told him again, 'I'm hungry.'

'All right. You rest easy, Dad.' Jack squeezed his hand before letting it go. 'I'll be quick as I can.'

Losing no time he ran down the stairs and into the kitchen. Discovering a half loaf of bread in the larder, he sliced off two thin pieces and laying them in the bottom of a small dish, he then left them soaking in sugar; meanwhile he warmed the milk in a saucepan and poured it over the sugar and bread, until the bread sucked in all the milk and it took on a soft, palatable texture.

That done, he waited for the milk to cool a little before taking it upstairs. 'It's only milk-pobs,' he told the sick man. 'It's filling, but not too heavy.' He chuckled. 'Besides, it's the best I could do.'

Easing the patient up, he placed a pillow under his back so as to prop him forward a little and then began to spoonfeed him, watching as each tiny piece of melted bread was taken and swallowed, though after two or three pieces, the old man could only manage to drink the rich, warm milk – at times, and to Jack's deep concern, almost lapping at it like a hungry cat.

After a while, growing exhausted, he let Jack make him comfortable again. 'You've done well,' the boy told him. 'Happen now you'll get stronger, eh?' He used a measure of cunning blackmail to entice him. 'Oh, I didn't tell you, did I?' he began. 'I've got a problem with one of the hinges.' Having now got Justin's attention he went on, in a serious voice, 'The side won't fix tight, and however hard I try, I can't seem to get it right. Happen you'll help me when you're better, eh?'

Suspecting Jack's motive for fibbing, and knowing how he had the ability to mend anything, however difficult, the old man smiled. 'Aye, 'appen,' he said with a slow, knowing smile. Raising his hand he laid it over Jack's fist. 'Good . . . lad.' Then, seeming more content than he had done this past week and more, he turned away and was soon fast asleep.

Delighted that Justin had somehow begun to turn the corner, Jack carefully washed the pan and the bowl and replaced them where he'd found them. That done, he went down the garden whistling. Suddenly the day seemed brighter, the sun was even warmer, and there was a kindling of hope that Justin would begin to get well again. And that was something to whistle about!

From the bedroom, the old man heard him and smiled, thinking not for the first time what a fortunate man he was, to have such a caring son as Jack.

Two hours later, Lizzy and her mother returned, Lizzy pleased with the small present she'd got for Justin, and Viola moaning and complaining about everything in general – the heat, the price of things, her poor aching feet and the many shoppers, 'Getting in my way everywhere I turned!'

Still grumbling, she shuffled inside, while Lizzy stayed behind to show Jack the baccy tin she'd bought for their father; a small oblong thing it was engraved with the head of a Labrador dog. 'We had a dog like that here, once,' she told him. 'Only it got run over on the lane and broke Daddy's heart.'

Jack remarked on how handsome the tin was, 'He'll love it,' he promised. A moment later, he watched her as she went inside. 'No more than he loves *you* though,' he murmured. 'No more than *I* love you.' Glancing about, afraid even the sparrows might overhear his confession, he quickly entered the barn and, stripping off his shirt, went about his work.

It wasn't long after, while he was climbing the ladder to the loft, that he heard a lot of yelling and shouting. 'What the devil's going on?' he said aloud. Anxious, he began scrambling back down the ladder, being almost three-quarters of the way down when Viola came rushing through the door. 'You interfering bastard, you!' Grabbing the horse-whip from the door-hook, she ran at him like a crazy thing. 'Did you think I wouldn't find out what you've been up to?'

With every word she hit out, splitting his back wide open as the tail end of the whip licked into his skin, to send the blood splattering in all directions. Shocked and in agony, he couldn't turn round and he couldn't escape. 'I know *exactly* how I leave my dishes and pans. You fed him, didn't you?' This time when she brought the lash down, it cut across his neck, making him cry out. 'You went against my orders,' she screamed. 'You took him food, didn't you?' The tail end of the whip lashed round his waist, then the middle of his back, again and again, until he was dazed and sick with pain.

And still she went on, giving him no time to recover or protect himself. 'By the time I've finished with you, you'll wish you were back in that filthy orphanage!'

Breathless and redfaced, she took the whip to his legs, excited by the sight of crimson blood running through his trouser-bottoms. Her wickedness knew no bounds. 'If only you knew how much I hate you! You've wormed your way in with him and now my daughter. But no more. It's over.' She paused to gather strength, 'I should have given you a hiding long ago!' Raising her arm she brought the whip down hard and caught him under the armpit, making him cry out. When at last his grip loosened on the ladder, she began to laugh – loud and raucous it was, like someone who'd taken leave of their senses. 'You've haunted me long enough. I want rid of you, once and for all!' Sensing that he was near unconscious she raised her arm yet again, ready to strike the final blow.

'NO!' Suddenly, Lizzy was there. 'LEAVE HIM ALONE!' Crying and frantic, she hit out at her mother, begging and pleading. 'Leave him alone! *You're killing him!*'

Too far gone for reasoning, Viola lashed out with the length of her arm, sending Lizzy flying across the floor. When at that moment Jack slithered to the ground she went to whip him again, but the sudden, startling sound of a shot ringing out made her turn, and what she saw shocked her to her roots. *Justin!*'

Leaning on the door-jamb, his face whiter than chalk and his eyes big as saucers in his gaunt face, he kept the shotgun aimed at her chest, his voice shivering with hatred as he warned her, '*Raise that whip once more and I swear to God, you'll never raise it again.*'

Like the coward she was, Viola pleaded with him. 'Listen to me, Justin, he went against the doctor's orders. I was told you mustn't eat just yet, and he took it on himself to feed you. What was I to do?'

When Lizzy ran to help Jack, Viola screamed a warning. 'Let him lie there. It's only what he deserves!'

Ignoring her words, the girl cradled Jack in her arms, softly sobbing into his hair. The sound of her sobbing delighted her mother, for she believed it meant Jack might be past all help. 'Leave him,' she snapped. 'There's nothing you can do for him now.'

Aiming the gun higher, in line with her forehead, Justin stared at her in disbelief. Suddenly he did not know this woman who was his wife. 'Put the whip back where you got it from!' he ordered gruffly.

'No, listen to me, Justin – he's no good. I don't want him in my house any more.'

Clicking the safety catch off he ordered her again. 'Put it back – NOW!'

Seeing a side to him that she never knew existed, and fearing for her own worthless self, the woman scurried to the door-hook and quickly replaced the whip on its peg.

He wasn't finished with her yet. 'Mark what I say,' he told her. 'This is not *your* house. It was never intended to be yours. Everything I own was always meant for Lizzy. Now, I also have a son, and that puts you nowhere.'

Realising she had gone too far, his wife tried to cajole him. 'You don't understand, dear. He's bad. You said yourself when you first brought him to this house, how they told you he was bad. Bad Boy Jack, that's what they called him, and now you can see why.'

'Get out of here, Viola.' There was a terrible calmness to his voice. 'Get out, and never come back.' He felt the strength ebbing from him, but he dared not let her see. Instead he took a deep, invigorating breath. 'As long as I live, I never want to see your face again.'

Seeing the whites of his eyes she grew frantic. 'Come on, Lizzy!' she called out. 'He's gone mad . . . we have to go.' Turning to Justin she warned, 'I won't let you get away with this. I have rights!'

His answer was to fire a shot at her feet – not to injure her, but just enough to make her scream and run for the door. 'Lizzy!' she implored. 'Quick! For mercy's sake, leave him!'

Clinging to Jack, her clothes splashed with his blood, the girl shook her head. 'I won't leave him. I won't!'

'What are you saying, child? Have you lost your mind?'

'I don't want to go with you. It's *you* that's bad, not Jack. Never Jack.'

When Justin fired another shot, Viola almost tripped over in her haste to get away. 'I warn you,' she yelled as she ran, 'I'll make you pay for this!'

With the last breath before he collapsed against the hay bale, Justin gave *her* a warning. 'You've got ten minutes to pack and be gone. Or I won't answer for the consequences.'

Calling weakly out to Lizzy, he told her, 'Leave him now, child. Go and fetch help, there's a good lass.' Then his legs folded beneath him.

Laying Jack gently against the hessian sacks, Lizzy whispered brokenly, 'It'll be all right, Jack. I promise it'll be all right.' There was no reply, no sign of life except for the trembling that involuntarily rippled from every corner of his body.

Justin knew how desperate the situation was. 'Hurry, my lass. Fetch help. Run like you've never run before.'

And that was what she did. But not before she had made Justin comfortable. As she went like the wind across the fields, she gave up a small prayer. 'Help them, Lord,' she asked. 'Please, let them be all right.'

Not once did she think of her mother.

In the young girl's desperate thoughts, it was as though Viola had never existed.

Part Four

NOVEMBER 1904

OLD ENEMIES

Chapter Twenty

When Robert was called to the office he thought he must have done something wrong. 'You're in trouble now, me boyo!' After working for Mortimer Jackson for more years than he cared to remember, the jolly redheaded Welshman called Geoff knew the way of things. 'When the boss calls you inside, it's either because you're for the chop,' sliding a stiff hand across his throat he made clear his meaning, 'or you're about to be rewarded.' He wondered aloud, 'What can you have done, that might fetch a reward?'

Robert could think of nothing. 'So that must mean I'm for the chop,' he said worriedly.

'Well, there's only one way to find out. You'd best get inside and take your medicine.'

Feeling somewhat apprehensive, Robert straightened his tie, back-raised his feet to shine his shoes one on each trouser leg, and with a lengthy sigh, he tapped on the office door. 'Come!' The deep, gruff voice summoned him inside.

'You sent for me, Mr Jackson?' Not sure what to do, Robert lingered by the doorway.

'Come in. Sit yourself down.' Gesturing to the chair facing him across his desk, the big man waited until Robert was seated. 'I suppose you know I had to finish Lennie last week?'

'I do, yes.' He began to suspect that it might well be *him* who was next to be 'finished'.

'I expect you're all wondering why I got rid of him. Well?' When Robert didn't answer, Jackson waved his hand impatiently. 'Come on, Sullivan. What's been said?'

'Well, there has been talk, I'll admit.'

'What kinda talk?'

'The others are saying that you are cutting back on staff, and none of us know who'll be next.' He swallowed hard. 'I expect that's why I'm here. Last in, first out – that's the way of it, I suppose?'

'Hmh!' The big man leaned back in his chair, making it creak and groan under his considerable weight. 'Well, you suppose wrong!' Now as he got out of his chair it seemed to sigh with relief. 'First of all, I'd like to know why I'd cut back on staff when my order books are stuffed full. On top of that, I'll be taking delivery of two brand new motor-cars any day now.' His smile enveloped his face. 'Now then, what d'you think to that, eh?' His chest swelled so large with pride, it was almost fit to burst.

'That's wonderful, Mr Jackson. But it's only what you deserve. The men say as how you started from nothing and soon worked your way up to being the biggest company of its kind. That doesn't happen all by itself, sir. It takes hard work and dedication.' Robert dared to add, 'One of these days, I'd like to try and do the same.'

The big man considered that for a minute. 'Mmm! So, you've a mind to take me on at my own game, is that what you're saying?'

'No, sir. Not necessarily. Though I'd be a liar if I said I didn't enjoy the work, because I do – and I find it gratifying. I'd also be a liar if I didn't admit that I would like to be my own boss one day, though I can't see it happening for some long time to come. As for taking you on at your own game, I dare say I might well look at *other* businesses, once I've saved the capital – and that could take me years.'

'I see!' He walked about a bit, occasionally glancing at Robert and then looking back out of the window at his fleet of carriages and motor-cars. Suddenly he was standing in front of Robert and telling him, 'I don't believe you, Sullivan!'

Robert was startled. 'What do you mean, sir?'

'I don't believe you'd look at other businesses if you could afford to start up in my kind of work. I reckon you've already made up your mind. That's why I called you in here.' When Robert went to protest, he put up a staying hand. 'No, sir! Bide your time and hear me out.'

Clearing his throat and walking about a bit more, he went on, 'First of all, *nobody's* job is on the line, and I shall make it my business to let the men know that, I've had more men through this yard than I care to remember, and I've only ever had two bad apples; one I got rid of a bit quick, and the other was more cunning, using my vehicles to do work on the side . . . doctoring his returns and cheating me at every opportunity. Oh aye, it took me a bit longer to pin that canny devil down, but I did, and now he's gone, and we'll say no more about it.'

He looked at Robert out of the corner of his eye. 'You'll know your answer now, won't you, eh? Lennie weren't got rid of because I were cutting back on staff. He were got rid of because he was a cheating, lying, thieving bugger, and I shall see to it that he doesn't get work within a hundred miles of here, damn and blast the man!'

Seeing Mortimer Jackson rise to anger was like witnessing a rhino in full charge. The sight of it made Robert sit up smart. 'Yes, sir. I can see you did right to be rid of him. I'd have done exactly the same, I'm sure!'

For a long minute there was an uneasy silence, during which Robert reflected on the exchange of words between himself and

Mortimer Jackson. Slowly now, the big man calmed down. 'Now then, I've a proposition to make.'

Surprised, Robert looked up. 'A proposition? What kind of proposition?'

'One you'd be a fool to turn down.' Coming to sit on the desk in front of Robert, he went on in serious tone, 'First of all, I reckon *I'd* be the fool, if I let a man like you loose to compete against me. No matter how much you may disagree, I still reckon it won't be too long before you find a way to set up on your own. You're too much like me, Sullivan. You're ambitious, and you're a grafter. You're not afraid to work hard and long, and should you get a carriage of your own, it wouldn't be too long before you got another, and then another.'

Robert was flattered. 'If you believe that, you see more in me than I see myself. For one thing, I spend nearly all I earn trying to buy information about my children. Besides which, I've recently moved out of my former lodgings and now rent a small place in Harpur Street.' He gave a wry little chuckle. 'After that, it doesn't leave much for starting up a business.'

'Ah, but there's men who would willingly back a fella such as yourself . . . hard-nosed businessmen who would give a year's takings to see me go under. Oh aye, there's ways and means when the play gets dirty, and if a man is desperate to set up on his own, he'll take any help that's given.'

'But I'm *not* desperate.' Robert wondered where all this was leading.

'Ah! Not yet, mebbe, but mark my words, you *will* be. You're not a man to be content working for somebody else for too long. Oh, no! We're too much alike, you and me.' Leaning forward, Jackson spoke with admiration. 'I don't mind telling you, you're the best worker ever been in my employ.'

'Thank you, sir. That's very kind.' Robert was so taken aback, he didn't know what else to say.

'Kind be buggered!' The big man laughed out loud. 'I'm as cunning as a sackful o' monkeys, that's what I am. So, to save my business from being put under pressure from such as yourself, I'm offering you the best chance you're ever likely to get.'

Watching Robert's face for a reaction, he told him in a rush, 'I'll give you your first carriage and I'll set you up in your own yard. On top o' that, I'll hand over a certain number of customers but, in return for all that, I'll want a sound legal contract drawn up between the two of us.'

Robert was overwhelmed. 'I can't believe it! Why would you do such a thing?'

'I've already told you – I'm only doing what any other clever businessman would do, given the chance. You see, *this* way I get to keep you under my wing, and *you* get to run your own business. You'll be free to find your own profit level and build up the concern to as large as you like. That way, you'll not be tempted if anybody else should approach you.'

Robert was puzzled. 'It sounds like a dream come true for me,' he pointed out, 'but what do *you* get out of it?'

'Two things. Firstly, you'll be operating under the company name of Mortimer Jackson, so as you build up your own reputation, you'll be building mine along with it. Secondly, I shall expect a percentage of everything you earn – not exorbitant, mind – just a fair return for my investment. Moreover, the establishment shall stay in my ownership, until such a time as you can buy me out – but then only if I agree to it, you understand?'

Robert was beginning to see the shrewdness of his employer's mind. 'And all that will be written down in the contract, will it?'

'Under the witness of a solicitor, yes.'

There was a twinkle in the other man's eyes. 'You've not told me everything,' Robert remarked knowingly. 'There's something else, isn't there?'

Mortimer Jackson thought how this was the reason he trusted this man above all others; he had an honest nature, and a quick mind. 'Well, as a matter of fact,' he admitted, 'I've been tempted for some time to concentrate on the motor-cars; more and more people seem to be asking for them these days. The trouble is, if I move out of carriages altogether I might be shooting myself in the foot. On the other hand, it would be increasingly difficult to run the two side by side, since motor-cars need different facilities from horses.'

The thought of his new venture put a self-satisfied grin on his face, but it faded as he went on soberly, 'If the new idea went well, I'd need to be looking for larger premises, and a good man to run it all. All that costs time and money and I'd much prefer to stay where I am.'

He smiled craftily. 'The truth is, I'm coming up to sixty-two, and I don't feel like launching another business – and that's a private matter, you understand. I've always kept my age close to my heart! We don't want the men thinking I'm past it, do we, eh? Secondly, why should I take on the risk and expense of two separate businesses – splitting my time and energy – if I've a man who can take all that responsibility off my back; a man who I feel will treble my investment in good time; a man who I feel I can trust?'

Robert smiled. 'Oh, now I'm beginning to see your way of thinking,' he remarked with a wry little smile. 'You set me up with the carriage and as I build up the business, you sell me more of your carriages, while at the same time you're building up your fleet of motor-cars. So, in effect, you've got the two businesses running tandem – both in your name still, and supplying two sets of customers, them as wants to ride in a carriage, and them as wants to ride in a newfangled motor-car. And while I spend all my time and energy, it will be on your account, not mine.'

Mortimer had no qualms about his plans. 'In a nutshell!' He was proud of his thinking.

'So you'll be doubling your profits, and in a year or two, maybe sooner, I'll be working all the hours God sends, and you'll be taking the lion's share of the profits. Am I right?'

'A fair share, that's what I said, yes.'

'So, there may never come a day when I'll have my own name over the door.' Robert wanted the terms changed. 'If, as you say, it will be legally binding that I cannot buy the business, unless or until you agree, by that time I may have doubled that business, so that when it comes time to value it, I might well have to pay a small fortune to buy the very business I've worked so hard to build up. If you ask me, *that* will be like shooting myself in the foot.'

Put like that, Mortimer had no answer. Instead he hummed and hawed and coughed and finally conceded, 'We could always amend that bit in the contract, to say something like . . . you will have a right to buy the carriage business after a period of time to be agreed, for a fair price mooted by an arbitrator . . . and your input to be taken into consideration. However, I must insist on a clause to prevent you from setting up with motor-cars, at least for a given period of time, and after that, you must not enter into any such business within a certain radius of this vicinity. Agreed?'

Robert agreed, but with his own proviso. 'That if at any time in the future you are looking to sell your business, be it for retirement or otherwise, I will be given first refusal.'

Mortimer gawped, then he smiled and now he was chuckling. 'By! It's as well I'm taking you under my wing, Mr Sullivan,' he gasped, ''cause you're far too clever and devious a fella to be let loose out there.'

'So you agree?'

'Yes, why not? If ever I thought of retiring, or needed to sell for whatever reason, I'd as soon sell to you as to the other jackals.' He blew out his cheeks and shook his head. 'I were right about you,' he said. 'You've the makings of a canny businessman. I'll bet within the last three years, you've made me twice as rich as I was before.'

Robert liked the sound of that. 'I hope so,' he answered. 'It's the least I could do to repay you for giving me such a marvellous opportunity.' Smiling and satisfied, he stood up to shake the other man's hand. 'If I'm only half the businessman you are, I'll be better than the rest.'

'This opportunity is no more than you deserve. Remember that. Remember, too, that you'll have little life of your own while you're building it up. You'll find it eats into your day and night, without mercy.'

'All the same, you've done me proud this day,' Robert answered with sincerity. 'Rest assured, sir, you won't regret it.'

Again, Mr Mortimer hummed and hawed and enquired, 'Have you had any luck in tracing your children?'

Robert's heart sank. 'Not as much as I'd like,' he confessed. 'Wherever I turn, every door seems slammed shut against me. I've managed to discover from different sources that the transaction for Nancy was a private one between foster-parent and management. As far as Jack is concerned, it appeared to have been done through the proper channels. Nobody seems willing to part with any more information than that, or they simply don't know – and if they do, they're keeping it to theirselves. Another thing one of the minders told me – at the cost of half my wage, I might tell you – was that she had an idea Jack was sent North . . . somewhere near Burnley in Lancashire, she thought, while Nancy went close to home – but she couldn't be sure.'

'Ah! So that's why you begged a week off – to travel around and see if you could find them. And you had no luck, I take it?'

'None at all. I went to four different towns and spent the whole week trudging from one place to another. I even had a private detective helping me, but I know from experience they cost a fortune, so I wasn't able to keep him on after a couple of days. I pinned adverts in shop windows and visited every office that might have been able to help, but none of them could. I even stopped people in the street until they thought I was a madman. But I'm not through yet. I'll find them if it takes the rest of my life!'

'It's been a good many years since they were taken, has it not?'

'Yes, sir. Nancy must be coming up to twelve now. As for Jack, he'll be a young man – sixteen if my memory serves me right.'

'Good God, man,' his employer burst out, 'don't you think it's time you let it go? If you haven't found them now, after all these years, you could spend the rest of your life on a lost journey.'

'No, sir. I can't let it go,' Robert replied with vehement sincerity. 'It's my fault they were sent to strangers. I have to know they're well cared for and content. Once I'm assured of that, I might be able to rest easier.'

'I see.' This was the calibre of man whom he had taken on, and Jackson expected no less of him.

'What haunts me is that the two of them were separated – Nancy going one way and Jack going the other.' He groaned. 'That must have destroyed Jack, because he idolised his sister. Dear God! That bastard Ennington has a lot to answer for!'

'Ah, well now, that's the reason I've been inquisitive.' Jackson gave a smart little grin. 'You'll be pleased to know He's been arrested.'

Robert was thrilled. 'Arrested? When did this happen? What was he arrested for? As if I didn't know!'

'It seems the authorities caught up with his underhand dealings. There's an investigation going on as to where all the children were sent. According to my reliable source, Ennington placed just enough genuine transactions to ward off suspicion; while the rest of the children were sold for private profit.'

A moment later, opening the door for Robert, he confided, 'It was an old woman – an ex-employee – who shopped him. Apparently he had her beaten up so badly, she knew she would never recover. She confessed it all before passing away, and the authorities collared him red-handed, with all the evidence intact.'

Robert was beside himself with relief. 'So, he got his come-uppance after all?'

'Seems like it. Moreover, there's talk that Galloways Children's Home will be closed, refurbished and then reopened under completely new management. The local council are going to keep a much closer eye on it in the future – inspections and the like.'

A thought struck Robert. 'If, as you say, they caught this Ennington with the evidence, there must be a chance of me finding out where Jack and Nancy were taken!'

'That's what I thought, but you never know when you're dealing with the Establishment. Tight-lipped, arrogant buggers they are!' He slapped Robert on the back. 'All the same, I wish you luck,' he said. 'Now look – whether you find them or whether you don't, we have an important deal going, and while I sympathise with your dilemma concerning the children, I need to know you won't lead me a merry dance. I expect it all to be finalised before the end of the week. All right?'

'Yes, sir. I'm looking forward to it.'

There was a moment of discussion about timing and such, before they parted company; Mortimer to straightway get on to his solicitor, and Robert to convey the welcome news to the men that their jobs were safe after all. As promised, he was careful not to divulge anything about their business transaction.

'What exactly went on in there?' the Welshman wanted to know. 'I must say, you've come out in a state of great excitement. Is there something you're not telling us?'

Too thrilled and gratified to keep it to himself, Robert told them about Ennington's arrest and the discovery of the secret ledger; now, at long last, there was a real chance he could trace Jack and Nancy.

Some of the men were as pleased as Punch, but one or two were more sceptical. 'You wouldn't even know what they looked like after all this time,' said one. 'Happen they'd not want to know you,' said another, gloomily. 'They might not understand why you did what you did. Perhaps they'd soon as spit in your face than talk to you.'

'He's right,' someone else said self-righteously. 'You'd be best off leaving 'em to get on with their lot. If you go poking about now, you'll only upset the apple-cart. Let 'em be, man, why don't you? It's not fair to turn their lives upside down a second time. Nor your own, come to that.'

One thoughtful, kindly man suggested, 'All these years, you've been tearing yourself apart. Don't you think it's time to set it all aside and think as how they might be well settled now. For pity's sake, give yourself a life, man! Look at you . . . alone and unwed, and every spare minute spent living in the past. Give it up, for your sake as well as for theirs.'

Later that week, Robert was made to reflect on this man's wise, well-meant words.

On Friday afternoon, he met with Mortimer Jackson to sign the contract. The solicitor witnessed both signatures, and the deal was done. 'Leave the rest to me now,' the big fella told him. 'I've already got some premises in mind, but until I'd found the right man for the job, there was little point in securing them.'

Unable to believe his good fortune, Robert thought he might celebrate. After work he hurried home to wash and change, then as it was a pleasant evening, he walked the mile to the pub near the children's home, where he bought a jar of ale and two meat pies. 'It's been a while since we've seen you.' The landlord had not forgotten him.

Robert explained how he'd been up to his neck in work.

Sitting at the corner table, sipping his ale and tucking into his pies, he reflected on the happenings of these past few days. He was to be his own boss! Even now he couldn't believe it. He thought of what his colleague had said, about it being time to let the children go, and how he had torn himself apart, and he pondered at length on his words. He had to admit there was some truth in them. Moreover, what if Jack and Nancy *were* happy? What if he came along and spoiled it all for them? What if they had never forgiven him and he was the last person on God's earth they wanted to see? These were daunting questions that could only be answered on coming face to face with his children.

Deep in thought, he didn't see Anne Moore, the clerk at the town hall, come in through the door, nor did he see her approach until she was right beside him. 'Penny for them,' she said, sitting opposite him with a smile lighting up her pretty face. 'But then I can guess what you're thinking about, can't I?'

Gesturing for her to sit down, he smiled back. 'Can you?' He and Anne had grown closer since their first, long-ago meeting at the town hall.

She had hardly sat down when the landlord came across. 'What can I get you, miss?' During this past year the men who frequented his pub had grown used to the odd woman coming in for a drink, although they didn't care for the idea, not one jot.

'Sarsaparilla, if you please,' she replied, and away he went.

'Them two seem to be getting to know each other very well, don't you think?' one of the bar customers remarked.

'Nothing to do with me,' replied the landlord cautiously. 'I serve drinks. I don't pry into other folk's relationships. In my experience, it can only land a man in hot water.'

Having talked together at the town hall more times than he cared to remember, and all to no avail, Robert and Anne Moore had become friends. Robert saw her as someone he could confide in, and confide he did – until she knew almost as much about his life as he did himself. Nevertheless, they had never talked outside the town hall, which was why he was surprised to see her now. 'What brings you here?' he asked. 'I'm sure this isn't the kind of place you usually frequent?'

Anne thanked the landlord for her sarsaparilla, which he put down and hurried away, though keeping his ear cocked to their conversation as he went.

'You're right,' she answered. 'I wouldn't normally dare come into a place like this, only I recall you saying as how you often come in here when you need to think, and I tried it on the off-chance you'd be here.' She gave him an understanding glance. 'I can't say I'm surprised you find a certain belonging to this particular inn though, being as it's near the Galloways Home, where your children were sent.'

'It's somewhere to go,' he replied soberly. 'It's not much fun being at home on your own.'

'I know the feeling,' she confided. 'I rowed with my parents some time ago, got engaged too soon, and it was all over before I even got to know my fiancé properly. It's a lonely life when you've no one to talk to, though of course, we've both got workmates, and that's a measure of consolation.'

Robert agreed, but at the minute he was more concerned about her reason for being here. 'If you don't usually frequent places like this, why did you come here tonight?' he asked pointedly.

'I came to find you.'

At once he was sitting on the edge of his seat, eyes wide with excitement. 'Oh, my God! Have you news of Jack and Nancy?'

She shook her head. 'Not directly, no. But I thought you'd be interested to know that the Galloways Children's Home has been shut down. Clive Ennington's been arrested and the authorities are at this very minute preparing a case against him; there's them as say he'll serve a long stretch in jail for what he's done. It seems they've got *both* his ledgers; the "official" one, and the other one, which he kept locked in his desk.'

When she saw that he was not altogether taken aback by the news, Anne suspected he'd been given it beforehand. 'You already know, don't you?'

Disappointed, Robert nodded. 'The boss told me today. He heard it from one of his acquaintances.'

'I'm sorry I couldn't bring news of your children,' she apologised. 'But don't you see what this means?'

'I *was* hoping it might mean that I could find out where Jack and his sister had been sent, but it seems it isn't that easy.' He took a great gulp of his pint. 'It never is!'

Sipping at her sarsaparilla, she discreetly observed him; that noble handsome face and the shock of dark hair that gave him that brooding look. In all the many times he'd come to the town hall in search of information, she had grown used to his familiar figure, coming towards her, giving her that lazy, somewhat shy smile as he asked her the same questions over and over. 'Robert?'

He put his pint down and looked up. 'Yes?'

'Can I ask you something?'

'Ask away.'

'I know you love your kids, and I know you feel guilty . . . but you shouldn't. It wasn't your fault, not really.'

'How do you know that?' A certain bitterness crept into his voice. 'You weren't there.'

'No, but you've told me the story often enough – about your wife and the heartless manner in which she deserted all three of you for her own selfish ends. I know about the woman called Mary, and how she left you when the going got tough. You've told me many a time how much you loved her, and how devastated you were when she left. You were trying to hold down a demanding job and keep your family intact at the same time. I can imagine how you began to sink into despair, until it felt as if there was no point in going on . . . that the children might be better off without you . . . that they might find a family – a mother to care for them if you let them go.'

He gave a deep, shameful groan. 'My God! Did I tell you all that?'

'You also told me how you went to throw yourself off that bridge, but that someone rescued you. And then, thinking of your children, you changed your mind and ran back to get them, but they were gone and the doors were locked. By the next morning, you had been in that terrible accident, so you couldn't go back for them.'

Robert was mortified. 'You must be a good listener.' He looked her in the eye; such pretty eyes, he thought, much the same colour as Mary's. 'Look, Anne, I'm sorry to have burdened you with all that. I had no right to.' He felt the shame burn deep inside himself. 'Just now when you reminded me of how it was, I realised again what a terrible coward I must have been to even think of leaving them behind. I'm their father, for God's sake! It was *me* they needed, not some stranger. I let them down badly. I can never forgive myself for that.'

She asked him something then, that made him think long and hard. 'Listen to me, Robert.' She paused, hardly daring to ask, but she had to, for his sake. 'Tell me . . . would it break your heart now, if you were to let the children go?'

'Why should I do that?' He took another gulp of his pint.

'Because if you don't, you'll destroy yourself as sure as if you really *had* thrown yourself off that bridge.'

He fell silent, the echo of his colleague's voice reverberating in his mind. *All these years you've been tearing yourself apart . . . alone, unwed . . . for pity's sake, give yourself a life, man.* He heard it in his head, over and over, and he knew every word was the truth.

'Robert, did you hear what I said?'

'Yes, I heard.' He could not bring himself to look at her. Instead he finished his drink and ordered another.

Gently, she persisted. 'You shouldn't be sitting here, filled with regrets and useless hope.' She was harsh but believed it was what he needed to hear, to bring him to his senses. 'Aren't you lonely, Robert? Don't you wish you could go home to a warm fire of a night, and a wife who would be proud to take care of you?'

'What man wouldn't?' he replied. 'It would be good, yes, I'll not deny it.' In his mind he could see Mary, slim and pretty, with her laughing eyes and long, fair hair. 'I've always been a family man at heart.'

'Then why don't you give up the chase? God knows you've tried every which way to find them, and in the meantime you've grown older, more tired and worn. Time won't always be on your side.'

'There you go, sir!' The landlord set the pint down on the table, and ambled away.

'And what about children? There's still time for you to start a new family. Your two must be almost grown now. Are you sure they would even *know* you?'

Raising his pint of ale he drank hard of it. 'I can't be sure of that.'

'I know what it's like to be lonely, Robert.' She felt shy, ashamed. But she so much wanted him to like her, perhaps even enough to ask her out now and then.

He laughed. 'It seems we're two of a kind.'

'We could be friends . . . if you like?' The suggestion was given nervously.

Setting his pint down he stared at her through new eyes. Whenever he had gone to see her, it was to ask after his children, to find out if she had anything new to tell him. He had never thought of her as a *woman*. But he thought of it now, and could see how it might provide an answer to both of their lonely lives. 'You're very pretty, Anne. Did anyone ever tell you that?'

Blushing, she smiled at him from under fluttering lashes. 'My fiancé did, but then we never really got beyond that. He went away, you see, and he never came back.'

'I understand.' Looking away he took another drink of his ale. 'All I can say is, he must have been a bloody fool!'

'There you are then.' Encouraged, she could see them getting together. 'I was deserted, just like you. That's something else we have in common.'

Alarm bells began to ring. He liked her, but not in the way she wanted. 'I think I'm getting too drunk.' Shaking his head like a dog out of water, he slammed down his pint. 'I need to keep a clear head,' he laughed, 'and here I am, getting pie-eyed!'

'Why do you need to keep a clear head?'

'Two reasons. One because I'm beginning to fancy you, when I should know better. And two, because for the first time in years I can see there might be a chance to find out where Nancy and Jack are now. If the authorities have the ledgers, it's up to me to approach them – which I intend doing first thing on Monday morning. I shall have to ask the boss for time off, but somehow I don't think he'd begrudge me that.'

Without further ado, he got out of his seat and taking hold of her arm, said sternly, 'Now then, young lady, I'd best get you home.'

After settling his dues with the landlord, he escorted Anne outside. 'Which way?'

'I've got a flat along the embankment.' Stretching her neck to see up the street she cried, 'Look! There's a cab!'

One glance at the bright green livery told Robert that it was one of their competitor's vehicles. 'I wouldn't soil my shoes going in that contraption,' he said proudly. 'Besides, I think it might do us good to walk.' He finished on a hiccup.

She laughed. 'How much ale did you have before I arrived?'

'Too much.' Taking her arm he walked her along the street and down towards the bridge. 'How far is it to your place?'

'Twenty minutes at a brisk pace; half an hour if we walk steady.'

'Then we'll walk steady,' he decided. 'That way I'll be more sober by the time we get there.'

So they set off at a slow pace and were soon walking along more briskly. 'Back there, you said you were lonely,' she reminded him.

'You're right. I did . . . and I am.'

'*How* lonely?'

He walked a short distance before he knew the answer to that. How lonely was lonely? he thought.

'I'm the loneliest man in the whole wide world,' he conceded. 'Did you know that you're the second person today who's told me that I haven't got a life – that I don't have a wife or a family?'

How true that was, he thought. He *didn't* have a life of his own; no friend outside of work, and no woman to keep him warm. On top of that, every spare shilling, every minute of every day, and most nights after work, he was living for Jack and Nancy, when maybe, God willing, they had a good life somewhere, and had forgotten him long since. It was a sobering thought.

They arrived at the flat some twenty-five minutes later, just as the town hall clock struck eleven. 'This is a nice spot,' he commented as they walked the short path to the front door. 'I wouldn't mind a place along the embankment myself.'

Pausing on the path he looked back, taking in the river and the pretty arched bridge, and the many flower beds shimmering in the moonlight. 'I dare say it costs you the best part of your wage to stay in a place such as this?'

'It does, yes, but what else have I got to spend my money on?' The comment was so caustic it pulled him up sharp.

'That's a sad thing to say,' he remarked. She looked so attractive in the moonlight, he had a sudden urge to hold her. Instead he looked up at the house, a beautiful old place; painted white with timber gables it spilled over into expansive, beautifully kept gardens.

He saw her to the door and when she had turned the key in the lock he told her, 'You'll be safe enough now. I'd best be off. No doubt you'll let me know if you hear anything – about Ennington, I mean?'

The disappointment showed in her face. 'Won't you come inside?'

He declined gratefully. 'Best not, eh?'

'I make a good cup of cocoa,' she enticed.

He thought for a minute. What harm would it do? They were both adults and he had no one to go home to. Besides, it would while away a half hour or so. 'Go on then!' He followed her inside, then up the stairs and into her flat; small but nicely furnished, it was a homely place. 'You keep it nice, I must say.'

She showed him from room to room; the kitchen and bathroom were each tiny, but had been fitted out with all that was necessary. The sitting room was long and narrow, bedecked with rugs and pictures and a whole collection of animal ornaments. 'I see you've a love for china dogs,' he observed, and she answered, 'I'm not allowed a real one here, so I have to settle for what I can get.'

The one and only bedroom was surprisingly large, with a long rug either side of the bed, crimson in colour, with an eider-down and lampshade to match. He was surprised. Somehow he did not relate that strong vibrant colour to this small, pretty woman.

While she seemed to want to linger in the bedroom, he turned to leave. It was only a moment but suddenly she was whispering his name, and when he turned he couldn't believe his eyes;

standing before him she slipped off her dress, and there was nothing beneath, except a naked, perfectly formed, beautiful woman.

He felt all manner of passion rush through him – anger, disgust, and a deep-down yearning to hold her in his arms. She looks so much like Mary, he thought, and when she took hold of his hand and placed it round her breast, soft and sensuous, his senses reeled.

Then she moved his hand down, to the furry triangle between her thighs. 'You do want me, don't you?' she sighed, touching his neck with the very tip of her wet tongue. 'I want you . . . I've always wanted you,' she murmured.

Suddenly they were on the bed, his shirt lying on the floor and his trousers pulled down to the ankles. There was no time to get them off, before she was arching her slim body, teasing his hardened member to easily find its way. When at last, with a cry he slid into her, she groaned and whimpered, giving herself freely. Wrapping her legs round his thighs she would not let him go, even if he wanted her to, which at that moment in time was the last thing he wanted.

It was a long time since he had been with a woman and now, all the pent-up passion of these past years flowed away, in a blinding rush.

The loving, the kisses, even the small talk afterwards, was not for her. It was for Mary. But Anne did not know that, nor did she care. 'You were wonderful!' she sighed. 'Better than any man I've ever been with.'

Fastening his trouser buttons, he asked curiously, 'How many men is that?'

She laughed. 'Four . . . five, I've lost count. I'm a woman who needs company.'

Fired with a peculiar mix of emotions, he took his leave.

'We'll see each other again, won't we?' she called after him.

He didn't answer. He was already gone; like a fleeting shadow, he melted into the night.

Not long after, hunched on a seat overlooking the river, he heard the town hall clock strike midnight, then the half hour and after a while, when his head had cleared and his bones began to stiffen with the cold, he thought it best to make his way home.

At the top of the river was a narrow alleyway which cut through to the main street. He was almost at the mouth of the alley, when he heard voices; it sounded like two men laughing and talking. Been out boozing, he thought, and smiled. It was a poor substitute for going home to a family.

Suddenly one of the men said something in the midst of laughter, that shook him through. 'Remember the last robbery we did, when that Geordie fella thought he could make off with his share o' the money? We soon put paid to him, didn't we, eh?'

Horrified, Robert hid himself round the corner and listened. The conversation continued; he could hear them discussing a robbery they'd just committed. Now they were gloating of their past exploits – one of them being the murder of a man who had been Robert's friend to the last.

Thinking he recognised the voice of one of the men, he dared to peep round the alley, and at once his suspicions were confirmed. '*You!*' Throwing himself at Geordie's old partner he screamed out, '*So you're the bastard who killed Geordie!*' As long as he lived, he would never forget the man who had stolen years out of his life, and lost him his children into the bargain.

Taken by surprise, Marlon tried to defend himself, but there was no stopping Robert, who was so incensed, he became like a wild thing. Gerry Reynolds, the thug's partner in crime, leapt on Robert's back, but such was the older man's deep-seated rage it seemed he had the strength of ten.

He soon had Gerry on the ground, dazed and trembling, watching with terror as Robert dragged Marlon to the river and there held his head under the water, all the time yelling at him. 'You might as well have killed me straight off!' he cried. 'You took years from me – and now, thanks to you, I've no family left. The only friend I had was Geordie, and he was a better man than you'll *ever* be, but you had to kill him, didn't you? You tainted him with the same filthy brush as yourself, and then you killed him! Well, now it's *your* turn!'

Rolling to his feet, Gerry seized hold of Robert from the back, trying his best to make him release the other man who by now was beginning to give up the struggle. But Robert was not about to let go; until Reynolds hit him hard across the head with some stick or pole he'd found lying close by.

Dazed and hurt, Robert fell away, while Reynolds dragged his pal out of the water.

Suddenly Marlon was on him, kicking and screaming, and saying as how, 'Geordie deserved what he got! He turned tail and ran, like the coward he was. He went soft on me, because he felt guilty about what happened to you. *Well, I don't feel guilty an' it were me as pushed you under that carriage! To hell with the pair of you!*'

Turning to Reynolds he shouted, 'Get hold of his legs, Gerry. We can watch him drown afore we take off.'

But Robert was ready for them. Grabbing hold of Marlon, he slammed him hard against the wall, sending him crashing to the ground, cut and bleeding; and while the man was lying there, groaning and crying, Robert dared Reynolds to come and get him. 'Come on! Let's see what you're made of!' Foolishly, he turned his back on Marlon, who he thought was near-unconscious.

Without warning, Marlon got up and launched himself at Robert; he fought back and the pair of them fell into the river, where the furious battle continued.

From the shore, Reynolds grew frantic; he saw them hitting out at each other, then they were under the water and he was sure they'd drowned. Then they were up again, choking, still fighting, punching at each other, looking like they each had murder in mind. Suddenly, Robert had his hands round the other man's throat and was pushing him below the water. A minute later, Marlon raised his head. '*Help me!*' he gurgled at Reynolds who, like the coward he was, took to his heels and ran.

'There's nobody to help you now, you bastard!' Robert panted. With Geordie's face large in his mind, he meant to pay kind for kind, so when he held him under for the third time, there was no mercy in Robert's heart.

Out of the darkness, he could hear police whistles and the sound of running feet. With a groan he let the other man loose and when he came to the surface he told him in a voice trembling with rage, 'I'm not done with you yet. I'll search you out wherever you are. You might have escaped tonight, but make no mistake on it . . . *you're a dead man*!'

As the police closed in they scrambled out of the water; Marlon going one way and Robert the other. And he didn't rest easy until he'd closed his front door. Soaked to the skin and breathless from the running, he stripped off and washed, then got into bed, where he fell into an uneasy sleep.

Back at the warehouse where they lived, Marlon gave Reynolds a thorough pasting. 'You cowardly bugger, what use are you to me, eh?'

Reynolds was shaking with terror. 'There were no stopping him! He's out of his bleedin' 'ead! Who is he, for Chrissake?'

'He's a maniac, that's who! Some years back I had a run-in with him and threw him under a carriage and four. He can't be human. He should never have survived what happened to him. When they scraped him off the ground, he must have been mangled like pulp.'

'Jesus! No wonder he wants to kill yer.'

'He's the one I told you about before – the one Geordie made up to. And you're right. The years in hospital have sent him off his head. Christ Almighty! He meant to kill the pair of us. As sure as I'm standing here, he'll search us out and kill us. One dark night when we're not looking, he'll come up behind us and slip a knife in our ribs.'

Nervous, Reynolds glanced at the door. 'What are we gonna do?'

'I'll tell you what we're gonna do.' Grabbing at the young man's arm, he demanded threateningly, 'We did all right tonight, didn't we? It must have been the best robbery yet.' He looked at him through narrowed eyes. 'You've got the money safe, I hope?'

Running across the room, Reynolds took up a floorboard and plucked the sack out. Filled with money and silver artefacts, it was worth a tidy sum. 'It's all here,' he promised. 'What's your plan?'

Marlon grinned. 'Simple,' he answered. 'The bugger can't get us if we're out of his reach, can he, eh?' Taking the sack by its tail, he tipped the contents out on the table, and began sharing it. 'We'll have to split up. It's the best way.'

Driven by fear for their very lives, that was what they did; with Marlon heading south, and Reynolds taking the road north.

'I don't need nobody!' Reynolds muttered as he went. 'I'm smart enough to make my own way.'

He thought about the children's home and the way he had ruled the roost there. To his reckoning, the big outside world was no different. The North seemed as good a place as any to start afresh, and far enough away from that madman, for him to be safe.

As far as the decent people of Bedford were concerned – and Robert Sullivan especially – it was good shuts to them both.

Chapter Twenty-one

Nancy liked nothing better than to sit in the kitchen and chat to the cook at Paisley Hall. Ever since poor Mrs Bellamy's shocking murder, the Cornwell family had employed a treasure of a woman called Mrs Lamb. She cooked like a dream, and was a comfortable sort of person who rarely lost her temper. Now, after more than five years in their employ, she had become an integral part of the household.

Rising fourteen now, Nancy still enjoyed watching Mrs Lamb making the bread, and the other day she had been allowed to help when the trays of jam tarts were taken out of the oven. The girl loved the warmth and the delicious smells in the big basement kitchen. Apart from that she had come to look on Cook as a friend.

Sometimes she would confide in Mrs Lamb when she could not bring herself to confide in anyone else – not even David, who meant the world to her. Today was no exception. With so many things playing on her mind, she was unable to sleep, and now, after having lain awake for an age, she put on her dressing-gown and tiptoed downstairs.

Though it was only 5 a.m. Cook was already up and about in the kitchen. 'Good grief, child! Whatever are you doing out of yer bed at this time of a morning?' She was amazed to see Nancy come through the door.

'I woke up in a start and can't get back to sleep. I keep hearing noises,' Nancy told her, 'like somebody walking about. There were doors opening and closing, and somebody was talking to themselves.' She shivered. 'It was really scary.'

Careful not to alarm the girl, Mrs Lamb said, 'You must have been dreaming, love. If there'd been anybody creeping about, I'm sure I would have heard, because I'm a light sleeper – allus have been.' Turning from filling the kettle, she asked softly, 'You ain't been having them nightmares again, have you?'

Nancy sat herself down at the table. 'They won't go away,' she said worriedly. 'It's always the same dream, and I can't understand what it means.'

Sensing something untoward, Cook glanced over at her. Seeing how the tears were flowing, she put down the tea caddy and sat next to the weeping girl. 'Aw, look, you're not to upset yerself, pet,' she said kindly. 'It takes a lot to make you cry, so there must be something you're not telling me.' Giving her a gentle shake she prompted, 'What is it? What can be playing so heavy on your mind that you can't sleep?'

Wiping away the tears, Nancy confessed, 'I can't seem to get all the pictures out of my head. Sometimes they won't let me go to sleep, and when I do sleep, they're still there.'

'I see. Well, I'd be thankful if you were to tell me all about it. So, you just sit right where you are an' I'll mek us a nice cup o' tea in a trice. I've time to sit with you afore the day begins proper.'

Then Mrs Lamb got on with the business of making a pot of tea. As good as her word she was back in no time; with the fire already burning in the hearth and the kettle at the ready, it soon boiled and the tea was made. With it she brought a toasted muffin and a dish of homemade strawberry jam. 'There now. We've time enough for a little chat,' she said, carefully offloading the tray and giving Nancy her tea and muffin.

'I'm not hungry, thank you all the same.' The last thing Nancy felt like at this time of morning was eating. But the tea was welcome and she took an invigorating sip.

Settling herself into the chair, Cook took back the muffin. 'Waste not, want not,' she declared and tore off a sizeable chunk. 'Now then, I want to hear all about these "pictures" you keep seeing.' She reminded Nancy, 'I've known long enough that you've been suffering from nightmares, but you never would talk about it, so there was nothing I could do. But I'm here to help if I can, so tell me now, what's it all about, eh?'

Nancy told her, hesitantly at first, then with more confidence as she saw how the woman was genuinely concerned. 'It's always the same,' she confided. 'There's me, with this boy, we're sitting on some steps, but I don't know where. Then there's a man. Then the man goes away. Afterwards, me and the boy are taken to this big, dark place.' She shivered, folding her arms, as she went on in a hushed voice, 'I didn't like it there, so when another man comes to take me away, I feel happy to be going.' Her voice broke before going on more softly, 'But the boy never came with me, and that was a sad thing.'

Cook realised how the girl was beginning to remember. 'The man who takes you away . . . that would be our Mr Cornwell, your daddy?'

Nancy nodded. 'He's not my real father though, is he?'

Mrs Lamb frowned suddenly. 'Has that Pauline been going on at you again, about how you were plucked out of the orphanage and brought here – telling you that you don't belong! I've heard her say all these things to you before, and I'm not surprised you're having nightmares.'

'Well, it's true, isn't it?' The older Nancy grew and the more Pauline kept reminding her of her roots, the more Nancy seemed to be remembering, and the more unsure she became. 'It's right what she says – I *haven't* got a mother or father. I'm only here to replace Pauline's drowned sister. I'm only lent to this house until my real parents come to get me. But what if they don't? What will I do then?'

Cook stiffened with anger. 'You'll always be wanted here. You mustn't take any notice of Pauline. She can be a nasty, spiteful creature when she puts her mind to it. To all intents and purposes, Mr and Mrs Cornwell *are* your parents, and they have been for a good few years. Why! The mistress positively dotes on you, and all right, I know Mr Cornwell doesn't have much to do with you, but he's a busy man. He doesn't even have time for the other two, so it's not a personal thing. I'm sure he loves you, every bit as much as the rest of us do.'

Cupping Nancy's face between big podgy fingers she gave it a smack of a kiss. 'I'll tell you something else, Sara-Jane,' she said. 'You're a lovelier person than Pauline will *ever* be, and that's why she's so jealous of you.'

Nancy had stopped listening. Now she looked Mrs Lamb in the eye and though her voice began to quiver, there was also a degree of recrimination in it. '*You called me Sara-Jane!*'

Caught between the devil and the deep blue sea, Cook didn't quite know what to say, so in the end she stated the obvious. 'But that's the name we've been ordered to address you by, child. It's the name you've been given, and it's how you're known now. Oh, I know you're not happy about that, but I can't be seen to go against Mrs Cornwell's wishes – you know that, don't you?'

Nancy understood. 'Yes. But it still isn't my name. It's the drowned girl's name. Pauline tells me her mammy wants me to become the other daughter . . . the one she lost. But I can't! How can I, when I'm *Nancy*?' she cried. 'And it isn't just that. She used to make me wear Sara-Jane's clothes – she still would, if only I hadn't grown.' She bowed her head. 'Sometimes I think I'll run away and look for my real daddy.'

'Have you spoken with David about all this?'

Nancy shook her head. 'It wouldn't be fair to worry him. There's nothing he can do anyway.'

'Look, my love, I know how disturbing all this has been for you, and what with Pauline tormenting you, it doesn't help . . . that much at least you could speak to your mammy about. She can put a stop to it, you see.'

'No! I can't do that. She's been so ill recently.'

'Then if there's nobody can help you, you've to help yourself. You're fourteen now, and it won't be long before you're a grown woman, with a certain amount of freedom. If you're still of a mind to find your real daddy, then you'll have time enough, I'm sure. Until then, I think maybe you should try and put all this business of not belonging out of your mind. Whether you believe it or not, you *are* part of this family, and you must never doubt that. As for the nightmares, once you make up your mind to forget about the boy and the man, and the place you were taken to before the master came for you, the dreams will stop all by themselves.'

Nancy took all that in, but still she couldn't shake off the ache in her heart, or those vivid pictures in her mind. 'I've always known there was someone belonging to me,' she said now. 'Only I had forgotten their faces.' Her voice broke. 'That little girl and the boy . . . I know the girl is me, but I can't think who the boy might be.' It was beginning to haunt her. 'I think the man must be my real father, but I can't be certain. Maybe the boy is my brother . . .' Her voice trailed away and her face began to crumple, and suddenly she was sobbing. 'Oh Cook, who am I really? Where do I belong?'

'Come on now, yer mustn't torture yourself.' Taking Nancy into her fat arms, Mrs Lamb held her close, her own tears rolling down her cheeks to plop on to her starched white collar. 'It's true you were brought here from the children's home – that's no secret. But none of us know why you were there, or who your family was afore. If yer ask me, you've to try and put it all out of yer mind. It were a long time since, and folks move on. Sadly, nothing in this world stands still, and sometimes it's bad to look back. But, you've a family here now, and lots o' folk who think the world of yer. Perhaps you'll need to think yourself luckier than most, and settle for that.'

While Mrs Lamb got on with her chores, de-rinding the bacon, peeling mushrooms and rinsing kidneys for the big family breakfast, they chatted about this and that in a calming fashion, until Cook believed she had persuaded the girl to forget the past. 'Concentrate on what you've got, my girl,' she advised her. 'You've a family who take care of you, and all the education any girl could want. You've a fine home and pretty clothes and a mammy who wouldn't swap you for the world. And think on – you'll not always be a child. When you're grown, you'll have choices.' She chuckled. 'Whether you believe it or not, you might even make a wonderful pianist and conquer the world.'

That brought a smile to Nancy's face. 'I don't think that will ever happen,' she giggled. 'In fact, I've been thinking of asking Mama if I can give up the lessons.'

'Oh, yer mustn't do that!' Cook often heard her playing the piano; she thought it very soothing. 'Then there's David, who worships the ground you walk on. How would he feel if he knew you were upsetting yourself like this, eh?'

The mention of David brought Nancy up sharp. If there was any member of this family she would be loath to leave behind, it would be David. Her mummy was kind and attentive and Nancy did love her, but there had never been that special something between them. Not like there was between herself and David, Right from the start, he had been the light of her life.

'Now, you will try to be content, won't yer?' Cook pleaded. 'Try and put them pictures out of yer mind. An' if it all becomes too much, you must come down here and we'll have another chat, and another . . . until we've talked away all your worries.'

Another embrace, then: 'Will you try for me, and for your own happiness? Try an' forget what happened all them years ago. 'Cause it'll do no good, to keep dwelling on it.'

Not wanting to seem ungrateful, Nancy promised she would try.

Just then Meg came in, scratching her head and yawning. 'One o' these days I'll run off an' marry a rich man,' she said.

Mrs Lamb laughed heartily at that. 'Huh! If any rich man were to see you now, *he'd* be the one to run off an' no mistake!'

Smiling at their antics, Nancy bade them cheerio. 'I'd best get washed and dressed,' she told Cook. 'David promised he'd take me ice-skating today.' Excited by the idea, she tried hard to push the pictures and images out of her mind. Maybe Cook was right. If she was to have any peace at all, she'd have to forget the past, and whatever it was that had brought her here to this house, and this troubled family.

All the same, even as she ran upstairs, the image of Jack's face came into her mind. 'Was he my brother?' she murmured.

Maybe she would never know.

Later, when the household was seated over breakfast, Edward reminded his wife, 'Don't forget, I'm leaving for Paris this morning.'

'I haven't forgotten,' she answered. 'Your bag is all packed and ready in the hallway.' Rosemary had instructed the servants earlier. 'What time will you be leaving, do you think?'

'Well, let me see. There are a few things I need to do at the office before I go, then I have a client to call on. But that won't take long. I imagine I should be able to catch the eleven a.m. train. If all goes well, I should be back in three days. It's not something I'm looking forward to, but this business has been dragging on far too long. The merchants are holding out for a bigger price and our people have ships waiting to take the merchandise abroad. The deal has to be tied up soon or we'll lose our investment.'

Rosemary hated it when he had to go away. 'I do wish you could leave it to one of the partners,' she said wistfully.

'Nonsense, dear! You know nothing of business matters.' Wiping the napkin round the corners of his mouth, he stood up to leave. 'If you want something doing properly, you must do it yourself. I've learned that from experience.'

'All the same, I do miss you when you're not here.'

'Good grief, woman, we're not love-struck children.' There was a cutting sarcasm to his voice. 'I'm sure you've enough to occupy your mind round this house, without worrying about me.'

Embarrassed and angry at this callous, off-handed treatment of his wife, Nancy excused herself from the table. There were times when she truly did not like Edward Cornwell, and this was one of those times.

David remained, with a word or two to say to his arrogant father. 'There's no need for you to worry,' he remarked in a cool meaningful tone. 'Mother will be fine. I'm sure you'd want me to look after her in your absence.'

The words struck home, because now it was Edward Cornwell who was embarrassed. He hummed and hawed and coughed into his handkerchief. 'Of course, my boy. Yes. Yes! You make sure you do that.'

As he went out of the door he turned to address David with a proud smile. 'I've left instructions that you are to take over my smallest portfolio while I'm away. I believe it's time you had your own portfolio, and when I get back I intend seeing to that. Meanwhile, you'll find progress to date and other important information all outlined in the ledger.'

David appreciated the confidence being placed in him. 'Thank you, sir.'

'Don't worry – there's nothing too taxing in there. Small, routine issues compared to my other transactions . . . a matter of Mr Linden's accounts, and the monitoring of a certain stock purchase – oh, and there's an outstanding debt to be recalled. Nothing you can't handle, I'm sure.' He looked from David to Rosemary, gave a curt nod, and was quickly gone. He completely ignored Pauline, who had witnessed the whole scene from the opposite side of the table.

The next they heard of him was when the door slammed shut and the carriage outside moved away.

Moments later, David kissed his mother goodbye. 'I'll try to get away early if I can,' he told her, and was rewarded with a grip of the hand and a watery smile.

'You'll do your father proud, I'm sure,' his mother said fondly.

While he went away to find Nancy, Pauline observed her mother with concern. She saw how ill Rosemary looked and was filled with a seething rage. 'You'd have thought he might have postponed his trip to Paris,' she said scathingly. 'He knows how ill you've been and he doesn't seem to care one bit, as long as he's swanning about the world!'

'You're quite wrong, dear,' Rosemary chided. 'Your father has never liked to travel for his work. It's very tiring, but he has no choice.'

Pauline fell into a sulk, and her mother, knowing how difficult she was to reason with, thought it best to divert her attention. 'I understand that nice Peter Carstairs has asked your father if he might be allowed to call on you?'

Rosemary was thrilled. Pauline was never one for the opposite sex, but she seemed to have taken a liking to that young man. It was most gratifying that someone of Peter Carstairs's character and background had shown an interest in her daughter; especially since Pauline was not the prettiest of creatures, bless her heart. Then there was her often surly, disagreeable nature.

'You do like the young man, don't you, dear?'

'He's better than most, I suppose.'

'Indeed he is . . . *and* wealthier. His father runs a fleet of merchant ships, or so Edward tells me.'

'He tells you right.'

'When will you see him again, do you think?'

'He asked Father if he might take me to the park this evening.'

'And will you go?'

Pauline feigned indifference. 'I'm not sure. There's a keen March chill. It might not be pleasant to be walking out just yet. I might decide to come ice-skating with you and the others this evening.'

'Well, you're most welcome, my dear, you know that.'

'I wish it could be just the two of us though.' A dark mood took hold of Pauline. 'I hate the way Father treats you, and I hate sharing you with all of them!'

'Don't be silly, dear. Families are renowned for having their ups and downs. We're no different from most.' She was always unnerved when Pauline fell into one of her moods. 'I'd best go and get ready.'

'Where are you going?'

'Oh, my dear! Surely you remember?'

'Oh yes.' Pauline had not really forgotten. How could she? 'It's March the sixteenth.' Her voice was hard, angry – and yet on her face there was the semblance of a smile.

Rosemary nodded appreciatively. 'Twelve years to the day we lost your sister,' she affirmed. 'I shall be paying a visit to the churchyard. Sara-Jane is coming with me and, of course, I would like you to be there – if you have no other plans, that is?'

Pauline had her own reasons for wanting to stay behind. 'To tell you the truth, I have a blinding headache, Mama. I thought I might lie down until it goes, if that's all right with you?' She passed her hand over her forehead, as though in discomfort. 'I hardly got any sleep at all last night.'

'Of course, you go and lie down and I'll come up and see you when I get back.'

While these two were discussing whether Pauline would be well enough to go skating in the evening, David was saying goodbye to Nancy at the front door. 'I wish I was coming with you,' she said. 'Instead of going to the churchyard.'

He understood her reasoning. 'Mother is fanatical about the date,' he warned. 'It was a terrible tragedy. When it happened she was overwhelmed with grief. She's never got over it.' He lowered his voice to a whisper. 'You will keep your eye on her, won't you?'

Nancy assured him she would. 'But don't you think it's strange that she's never asked me to go with her before?'

'No. It's always been a very private thing for her – taking the flowers . . . remembering. It isn't easy for her.'

'I understand, and don't worry, I *will* keep an eye on her. You'd best go, or you'll be late.'

'Don't forget, I'll be home in time to come skating with you.'

They said their goodbyes and he hurried off to his father's office – a twenty-minute carriage-ride into the centre of Woburn.

At nine thirty, Rosemary left to collect the flowers. 'Tell Sara-Jane to be ready by the time I get back,' she instructed Meg. 'I won't be above half an hour.'

Meg did as she was told, and by the time Rosemary returned, Nancy was ready and waiting. 'You look nice, dear.' Observing Nancy in her ankle boots and dark blue two-piece with long, straight skirt and smart fitted jacket, she couldn't help but say with pride, 'You look so grown up and pretty these days – but then you've *always* been pretty.'

Nancy gave her a kiss and a hug. 'Thank you for the costume,' she said. 'It's my favourite.' She thought Rosemary looked quite smart, too; the burgundy long-coat and matching hat with its small, curled brim was very attractive.

Rosemary loved to be fussed over; she never got kisses and hugs from her husband nor her eldest daughter, though her son David was always attentive, and this child was naturally affectionate. That was why she loved them so much. 'Time we left, my dear.' She instinctively tucked a stray lock of Nancy's hair into place. 'Normally we could walk to the churchyard, but it's quite a way and there's a cold wind blowing, so I thought it might be best if we took a cab. I have one outside ready and waiting.'

A moment or two later, as they climbed into the vehicle, Rosemary gestured at the huge bouquet of flowers and the tiny posy lying alongside it. 'As it's such a nasty, dull day, I've chosen bright colours,' she pointed out. 'What do you think?'

Nancy looked at the enormous bunch of spring flowers, all held together with an extravagant pink bow, and alongside it the posy of bright tulips and narcissi, and she could see how very much this woman must have loved her poor, lost daughter. 'They're beautiful!' she gasped, and thought she would never again see such a magnificent bouquet of flowers.

Pauline watched from the window as they left. 'What makes you think I want to go to the churchyard to see *her*!' A look of disgust darkened her features. 'I've got better things to do.'

When at that moment the grandfather clock chimed the hour of ten, she quickly ran upstairs to her room, where she cleaned her teeth and brushed her hair. Running back downstairs, she pulled on her black beret and brown long-coat, and went rushing out, softly closing the door behind her.

Meg was in the dining room by this time, clearing away the breakfast things. Hearing the front door click shut, she went to the window and looked out, to see Pauline going down the street, half walking, half running as she crossed the road. 'Wonder what that young madam is up to?' she murmured. Having been at this house long enough to know the characters of each and every member of the family, she had come to expect the unexpected of that one in particular.

Meg couldn't wait to carry the news to Mrs Lamb. 'I heard her tell her mammy that she was going back to bed – got a headache, she said. And the minute the others have turned their backs, here she is sneaking off, running down the street as if Old Nick himself was on her heels.'

Cook was deeply concerned. 'She's a strange, secretive one and no mistake.' Like her predecessor, she had a bad feeling that something was about to happen; as it always did when Pauline got one of her moods on.

'What's she up to, d'you reckon?' The kitchenmaid was beside herself with excitement.

Cook could see nothing to get excited about. 'You get on with your work,' she told Meg. 'Or *I'll* likely get excited and swipe you one with this rolling-pin!'

Meg poured boiling water on to soda crystals in the sink and began dumping the greasy plates in to soak. 'I were only saying!' she grumbled.

'Yes, well, "saying" is what gets people into trouble, and never you forget that.'

While Meg set off to finish clearing the dining room, Mrs Lamb laid down her work-tools and sat heavily in the chair, her face a study in worry. 'There's something fishy going on,' she murmured. 'Lying to her mammy, sneaking off the minute their backs are turned. What in God's name is she planning?' She thought of all the women who had been murdered, and how the master was off on his travels again, and suddenly it all began to add up. 'No! I'm saying nothing to no one!' she decided. 'I've got enough to be going on with, without getting tangled up in something like that!' For some reason, she remembered the terrible end of her predecessor; no one had ever been arrested for the savage murder of Annie Bellamy. A shiver ran down the cook's spine and she was glad when Meg came trotting back to the kitchen and made everything seem normal again.

When Meg returned from cleaning the dining room, she was amazed to see how much work Cook had done, with new-made loaves laid out ready, trays of jam tarts and muffins all lined up like soldiers, and the smell of fresh coffee brewing in the pot. 'You've been busy,' she remarked. 'I've only been gone what – half an hour? You must have worked like somebody driven!'

Impatient and worn, Cook told her to pour out the coffee. 'It's time for a break.' But Meg had been right just now, she thought. 'Driven' was exactly what she had been. Driven by the fear of not knowing what was going on, and driven by the fear of ever finding out. 'I'll have one o' them jam tarts with my coffee, if you please,' she said, and fell into the chair, to await her refreshments and to mull over what that mad creature, Pauline, was up to, right at this minute.

Having waited for what seemed an age, Pauline stayed well out of sight of the travellers, yet from her vantage point she could see right the way along the platform. Impatiently, she glanced at the clock on the wall. 'Another ten minutes and the London train will be here,' she mused. 'Where the devil is he?'

Five minutes passed, and she began to wonder if she had made a mistake. Then, just as the train pulled in, she thought she saw him – but the steam from the engine billowed all over the platform, momentarily shrouding the passengers from her sight.

Suddenly it cleared and she could see her father. He was climbing on board. There was an attractive, dark-haired woman just ahead of him and for a minute Pauline couldn't make out whether they were together or not; until he raised his arm and patted her suggestively on the backside. The woman turned and smiled, and as the train drew away, they could clearly be seen, seated together, blatantly kissing, obviously embarking on a romantic, three-day trip. 'Bastard!' Pauline spat out the word. 'You never learn, do you, Father?'

When the train was gone and out of sight, the girl stayed where she was for a while, her fists clenching and unclenching, and her eyes closed as if she was in great pain. Eventually she made her way off the platform, inwardly seething, her face set like stone as she thought of her father and that woman. 'He'll be punished,' she muttered madly. 'They *both* will. And it will serve them right!'

At the churchyard, Nancy felt curiously moved by Rosemary's obvious devotion. She saw how tenderly she laid the flowers beneath the headstone, and she saw the tears fall. 'It was such a terrible thing,' she murmured. 'Sometimes I wonder if Pauline did all she could to save you?'

To Nancy's mind, it was a shocking thing for a mother to say. But she put it down to grief.

Afterwards in the church, she prayed before the altar and asked that the good Lord would help this woman who had taken her on and been so kind to her. 'She's very sad,' she whispered, and glanced across at Rosemary who was lighting candles. 'I wish You could take away the hurt.'

Later, she also lit a candle, and together, in subdued mood, they made their way to the market, where Rosemary intended buying more embroidery thread to complete her tapestry. It was a fond pastime of hers – one of the few things that gave her a measure of contentment.

That evening, the entire family – with the exception, of course, of Edward – enjoyed an evening of skating. Just as she was talented at the piano, Pauline showed exceptional skills on the skating rink. She twirled and dived and looked splendid in her dark outfit and shining boots.

Rosemary watched on proudly. 'She has a natural talent,' she told Nancy. 'Go on, dear. Show me what you can do.'

Nancy had only ever been on the ice-rink twice, and this time was as disastrous as the last. Falling all over the place she picked herself up time and again, until laughing, David took her by the hand and escorted her round the rink. 'You're tensed up,' he said. 'The trick is to relax.'

Nancy laughed at that. 'Of course I'm tensed up,' she cried. 'I'm aching in every bit of my body!'

Several times Pauline swooped by, glancing at them as if they were the dirt under her feet, until a moment later she was brought down by a child crossing her path. Furious, she marched off the rink, and never came back.

Nancy, however, persevered. Under David's patient guidance she managed to go the whole way round once without tumbling. 'Well done!' Rosemary called out, clapping with enthusiasm.

While behind her, Pauline was in a deep sulk.

She remained that way – all night, and afterwards as they made their way home; once there, she went straight up to her room without a word to anyone.

The weather took a sudden, gentle turn. By the time Edward arrived home after three days without word, the March wind had lessened to a lighter breeze; though still quite cold it wasn't the bitter chill that had previously swept the land.

Delighted to see him home, Rosemary rose from the dinner table to greet him. 'How did you get on, dear?'

Edward dropped his travel-bag on to the table. 'Hard work, but gratifying,' he replied cagily. 'Let's just say I'm very pleased with my trip. It went exceedingly well.'

Pauline noticed his smug, self-satisfied grin and the anger she had tried so hard to suppress, began to surface. 'I'm going to my room,' she announced and swept by him without a word.

'Got another of her moods on, has she?' Edward's jubilant manner faded. 'Meg . . . MEG! Where the devil are you?'

The servant came rushing in, breathless and red-faced. 'I were just on me way, sir.'

'I'm ready for my meal now, if you please! Oh, and I'll have extra potatoes,' he demanded. 'The journey appears to have increased my appetite.' In fact, it was the thought of tonight and seeing his woman again that had increased his appetite – and it wasn't an appetite for food neither, he thought slyly.

Meg gave a tight little curtsey. 'Straight away, sir.'

'Oh, and get rid of that.' Reaching out to the travel-bag, he swiped it off the table.

Thinking what an unbearable swine he was, she collected the bag from the floor. Then off she ran, to tell Cook what a foul mood the master was in.

Rosemary was bitterly disappointed. 'Oh Edward, surely you haven't the need to go out again tonight? You've only just got back, for heaven's sakes!'

'Stop fussing, woman! I'm sure I won't be late. There are just a few loose ends to tie up.' He looked round the table. 'Where *is* everyone?'

'David is preparing his ledger for you to see . . . he's worked so hard in your absence, I think you'll be very proud of him. As for Sara-Jane, she's in the drawing room, practising the piano. Listen.'

Reluctantly, he cocked an ear and pursed his lips in frustration when he heard the piano softly playing. 'Hmh! She'll never make an accomplished pianist, that's for sure.'

'But she does so enjoy it, and that can sometimes be far more gratifying than playing for an audience.'

Just as well!'

Returning to the subject, she entreated, 'Couldn't you stay in tonight? I've been so looking forward to us spending the evening together.'

'Sorry, my dear.' He could think of nothing worse than spending the evening in his wife's dull company. 'Must go. Duty calls.'

Just then, Meg returned and he lost no time in polishing off the huge meal of roast potatoes, parsnips, baby carrots and a generous helping of steak and kidney pie. 'Excellent!' He mopped up the gravy with some bread, threw down his napkin and, getting out of his chair, came round to where Rosemary was sitting. 'I'll try not to be too late, my dear.' Giving her a dutiful peck on the cheek, he took his leave of her.

Some short time later he left the house, climbed into the waiting carriage, and gave the driver the address. 'As quick as you can,' he said self-importantly.

From her bedroom window, Pauline watched the carriage take him away. Quietly, she returned to her desk and sat for an age, thinking; hating; planning what she must do next.

It was almost twilight when Edward disembarked from the carriage some distance away from the address he was really visiting. 'Be back here in three hours,' he told the cab driver, with nary a please or a thank you. 'And mind you don't keep me waiting.'

The man tipped his cap respectfully, but as he went away he spat on the ground. 'Arrogant bugger, I'll be as late as I please.' It wasn't the first time he'd picked Edward up, and he was certain it would not be the last. Disgust flooded his face. 'Hmh! A married man, I'll be bound . . . having it away year after year with one floozie after another.' Chuckling, he had to admit, 'If only I had half the chance, I dare say I'd jump at it meself.'

Having walked the hundred or so yards to the apartment in the rather grand house on the corner that over the years had become his second home, Edward went discreetly up the steps. Taking the key from his pocket he turned it in the keyhole and let himself into the flat. 'Elaine? Where are you, my sweet?' He ventured into the living room; when she wasn't there he called again, almost falling over with shock when he turned to see her standing stark naked at the bedroom door. 'I've been waiting for you,' she murmured seductively.

'You're so incredibly beautiful!' He preferred his women to be long of limb, with slim, perfect curves and an appetite for sex to match his own. Elaine had not disappointed. Indeed, with her strikingly lovely face, large inviting green eyes and luscious thick, dark hair, she more than satisfied his every need.

Now as he went to hold her, she turned away. 'Not yet,' she purred. I've had my bath and now I'm about to get dressed.' Playing her finger against his lips she teased him until he could stand it no longer. Again he made a grab for her, and again she pushed him away. 'Not yet, you naughty boy! We've had three whole days and nights of romping about. It won't hurt you to wait a while longer.'

'Oh please, sweetie, it won't take long,' he pleaded ardently. 'Then I'll take you to the smartest restaurant in Bedfordshire, just as I promised.' Any other woman he would have just taken as he pleased, but Elaine was different. For the first time, he really believed he had fallen in love. With the 'love' came respect, and that was why he controlled himself. After all, it was only a short time to wait. 'You're a wicked woman,' he said huskily. 'You can't know how much I want you.'

She walked away, her narrow hips swinging and her hair falling loosely down her bare back. 'I'm hungry,' she said, pulling on her slip. 'I expect you've already eaten?'

He looked sheepish as he admitted, 'Well, yes, I did grab a snack on the way.'

'Liar!' She drew on her dress, lifted her hair from beneath the collar as the garment slithered over her perfect form, and gave him a knowing stare. 'I can always tell when you're lying.'

He laughed out loud. 'You know me too well,' he said. 'All right, I *did* have a meal at home, but how could I not, with my wife and family so pleased to see me?'

'That's because they don't know what a two-timing bastard you are.' A quick brush of her hair and a touch of rouge and she was ready. 'Will I do?' She did a half-twirl for his benefit.

He shook his head in admiration. 'You're exquisite,' he said huskily, and she purred like a kitten.

Grabbing the fur coat he'd bought her while in Paris, he draped it over her shoulders. 'I've booked us a table . . . "I want the very best", I told the manager. "I'm bringing a most important client here and I have need to impress her".'

Amused, she tickled him lovingly under the chin, 'I bet he knew all along you were bringing your fancy piece.'

When they arrived at the exclusive restaurant, the manager was there waiting, eager to show them to his best table; especially as Edward had placed a guinea in his hand on booking.

Edward ordered champagne, and the couple drank to each other. They ate a hearty meal and ordered another bottle of champagne. The orchestra played; they danced in each other's arms, and everyone was attentive to their needs. And when the time came for them to leave, Edward thought it had been the most perfect of evenings.

It was gone midnight when they finally left. 'Thank you for a wonderful time,' Elaine whispered as they stumbled on to the street.

'My pleasure,' he said, and swung her round right there, humming the tune they had danced to, and wanting the evening never to end.

As they walked along the darkened streets, they giggled and laughed like young sweethearts. Above them the moon shone down, and below them the trees shivered gently in the crisp night breeze, and he thought he could never be more content than he was tonight.

Walking through the narrow streets, where there were no lamps and few people, he felt the urge to make love. 'Let's do it here!' he suggested, and when she made no protest he pushed her into a shop doorway and sliding his hand up her leg, pulled her French knickers aside. 'Help me,' he panted. 'Open your legs so I can get in.'

Tiddly with champagne, she teased him for a while, but then, wanting it every bit as much as he did, she straddled her legs and left herself wide open for him. 'Come on then!' she urged. 'You've got me going now.'

Laughing, he put his two hands on her buttocks and entered her in great excitement. With eyes closed and every nerve in his body tuned to hers he was frantic in his lovemaking.

Behind them, the sound of music from a private party drowned out their cries of enjoyment, and from the main street the noise of passing revellers could be heard. But they didn't hear or care. They were too engrossed in each other.

When the soft footsteps drew closer, they were blissfully unaware. Then, with a sudden rush and a cry like some crazed beast, the stranger came at them. In that moment Edward turned, the fear knotted like a fist inside him, but it was dark and all he could see were moving shadows. The knife flashed in the moonlight, his throat was slashed across, and he didn't even feel it; instead he fell back, confused, blinded by his own blood.

The woman saw and was beside herself with terror, screaming uncontrollably, hands folded across her face as she was viciously set upon. There was nothing she could do to save herself and now, she, too, was swiftly silenced; the knife caught her across the face, then it sliced into her neck. A moment was all it took, before she slithered to the ground.

When, fatally wounded, Edward staggered to help, he was cut down yet again. As they fell, arms round each other, the walls pasted with their blood, they were brutally and repeatedly stabbed, until the gutter ran red with their blood.

'JESUS CHRIST!' a lone voice screamed out above them. 'POLICE! MURDER!' Suddenly all hell was let loose. The shrill sound of police whistles and running feet shattered the air; in minutes the area was alive, while in the midst of the confusion the attacker took flight, but then the cry went up, 'Look! There she is!'

Quickly surrounded, the murderess was manacled and led back to the waiting police wagon.

On passing the fallen bodies, she glanced down at her handiwork. In the gaslight, Edward opened his eyes to see the face of his assailant. 'I had to do it,' she said simply.

His eyes opened wide, his lips shaped her name disbelievingly as he gurgled it through his gaping throat. '*Rosemary!*'

It was the last word he ever uttered.

Chapter Twenty-two

It was Robert's first big assignment. 'I'm not sure I'm experienced enough for this.' Ever since he'd been told over a week ago that he was chosen to accompany Mortimer Jackson on this uniquely important trip, Robert had hardly slept a wink.

'Look, Sullivan, if you don't get out there and do it, how do you ever expect to *get* experience – tell me that!' Impatient and irritable, Mortimer was in no mood for small talk.

Robert had noticed how ratty the older man was, the minute he walked through the office door. 'We've a long journey ahead of us,' he pointed out good-naturedly. 'I hope I don't have to put up with your bad temper all the way there and back?'

'Oh, I'm sorry.' The big man scratched his tousled head and yawned for the umpteenth time. 'You'll have to forgive me, only I'm not used to getting up at four o'clock of a morning.'

Robert chuckled. 'If you must know, I feel the same myself. I was that excited when you said we were off to look at new vehicles, I hardly slept a wink up to midnight, then it was out o' bed at three and now I'm walking about like I'm half gone.'

'Aye, but you're not like a bear with a sore head though, are you? That's my trouble. If I don't get my proper sleep, I'm not fit to be with.' Gesturing to the spirit stove and the kettle on top, he begged, 'Go on, lad. We've a minute or two before we set off.

I might be more human after I've had a mug of tea. There's a drop o' milk in that jug.'

Robert made a pot of tea and the two of them sat for five minutes talking through the day's plans.

'Now then, like I explained yesterday, old man Carruthers is retiring, and his entire fleet of carriages is being sold off today,' Mortimer said. 'The auction starts at two o'clock this afternoon, and I want to be there a bit before, so's I can check the stock out proper. Oh, I know I've got the catalogue, but you can't see if a thing is rusted right through from a bunch of words on a paper. You've to get right under it and see for yourself, if you know what I mean?'

He took a long gulp of his tea before going on excitedly, 'That's one of the reasons I want you with me. Being younger and fitter, despite your gammy leg, you can get down on your knees and see what's going on, whereas I'd have a job to even bend my knees, never mind crawling about under the chassis of a carriage. Secondly, I know as how I promised to set you up with one carriage to start, but if I can secure the entire fleet, you'll be straightaway up and running, and we'll *both* benefit financially.'

Robert couldn't thank him enough. 'If it happens as you say, there'll be nobody more grateful than me,' he remarked sincerely. 'And 'I'll work my fingers to the bone to pay you back every penny as quick as I can.'

The big man laughed. 'With interest!'

Robert smiled. 'With interest,' he agreed. He had come to like and respect Mortimer Jackson, and that was *before* there had been any talk of setting him up.

'Right then, let's be off. By my reckoning, it's a good long journey. You start the first leg and I'll take over halfway. Agreed?'

'Fine by me.'

Robert had already tacked up the horses and carriage outside. 'I had half a mind to use one of my new motor-vehicles,' Mortimer chatted as they walked across the yard. 'Only I've found them to be a bit temperamental. There's a mile or so of isolated countryside we've to travel, and the last thing I want is to be stranded in the middle of nowhere.'

A thought struck him. 'Have you brought provisions for the journey? There'll be no time for stopping at inns and such, not if we're to get there before the sale starts.'

Robert nodded. 'There's hay and water for the horses. And for us, there's a hamper strapped to the back,' he said. 'We've ham rolls and cheese, and a jug of sarsaparilla between us.'

'Sarsaparilla!' The big man looked horrified. 'Couldn't we have had a jug of ale or summat more satisfying?'

'Not if the carriage and horses are to run in a straight line, no.'

'Aw, go on then. You're a hard taskmaster, but I'll make up for it when we get back. In fact, if we're fortunate enough to buy the entire fleet, I'll celebrate for a week!'

'What time do you think we'll be back?' Robert had other things on his mind just then.

'Oh, not too late. It all depends how long the sale goes on – though if I have my way, I'll corner Carruthers and tie up the deal before the auction even starts.' Curious, he peeked at Robert. 'Why do you ask?'

'Well, you recall me saying how I got an interview with the council official who is handling the case of Galloways Children's Home?'

'Yes, and you said he wouldn't give out any information until the investigation was done with.'

'That's right, but this morning when I got up, I found a note through my door from a woman called Alice Compton – her as used to work there some time back. The note said as how I should go and see this council official on Friday – the day after tomorrow, because she'd found out that the case was almost completed. The note said that I should be able to demand information about

Nancy and Jack, and their whereabouts, and that I wasn't to come away without having got it.'

'By! That's good news.' The big man was pleased that his search was almost at an end. 'It's as well we're going to this sale today then,' Mortimer realised. 'Because if it had been Friday I dare say I'd have been forced to take somebody else.'

'That you would, more's the pity,' Robert conceded. 'Because nothing on earth would keep me from the town hall on Friday.'

'No matter.' Mortimer would not have expected it any other way. 'Still, we'll be back in plenty of time,' he promised. 'But before then, you'd best try and keep your eye on what we're about. If it all comes off right, you'll be a man of business – a man to be reckoned with. A man of considerable means, who can take care of his family for the rest of their lives.'

A few minutes later, they set off.

With Mortimer in the back, and a blanket wrapped round his legs against the morning air, Robert climbed up front; he, too, had the good sense to cover his legs against the chilly breeze, though he wasn't a man to feel the cold. 'Gerrup there!' Tapping the reins across the horses' backs, he drove them gently on. With nothing on the streets at this time of morning they should make good headway, he thought.

They had hardly turned into the main street when Robert glanced round to speak with Mortimer, chuckling then to find the big man fast asleep. 'All right for some,' he said, and focused his attention on the journey ahead.

So much was happening to change his life, he thought wondrously. If he could only be reunited with Nancy and Jack, and be forgiven for what he did to them, he would be the happiest man on God's earth!

Over in Lytham St Annes, Mary Marshall was restless and unable to sleep, so she sneaked out of bed and went down to the kitchen.

After making herself a cup of tea, she sat at the table, mulling over the events of her life. 'I've ruined everything,' she murmured, 'and now I'm paying the price. It's only what I deserve.'

She almost leapt out of her skin when the door opened. 'What do you think you're doing?' Paul glanced at the wall clock. 'God Almighty! It's only half past four. Come back to bed.'

'It's no good,' she protested. 'I can't sleep.'

Crossing the room, he took her by the arm. 'Come on, sweetheart. You know I can't sleep without you beside me.'

'Please, Paul. I'll only lie there awake.'

'Nonsense! I'll cuddle you till you go back to sleep.' He gave her arm a tug. 'Come on, I'm lost without you.'

Sighing inside, she knew he would not go away until she went with him; or he would go and then sulk until being with him was even more unbearable. 'All right. You go up. I'll be along in a minute.'

'I'll be back down for you if you're not there in a minute or two,' he warned.

'I'll follow you up, I promise.'

Kissing the back of her head he told her softly, 'I think I'm in the mood for love now you've woken me. We'll see.' With that he turned and went; foolishly believing that he had left her thinking she was in for a treat.

With Paul out of the room, Mary began to breathe freely. It was as though a weight had been lifted off her shoulders. She hated it when he made love to her. Though there was nothing she was more thankful for, than the fact that since losing the baby, she had not conceived again. Whether it was because of something that happened when she lost him, or whether it was her own body that rejected carrying Paul's child, she would never know. But it was a great consolation to her, that he could make love and she did not have to pay the price.

Weary of spirit, she washed out her cup, turned it upside down on the draining board and reluctantly made her way back to bed and, just as she had feared, he was waiting for her, arms open, and ready to take her to himself yet again.

Afterwards, when her duty was done and he was snoring contentedly, she lay wide-awake, wanting to get out and go downstairs but not daring to, in case he followed her and took her back. It was a nightmare of a situation.

When at last the house was awake and she felt free to wash and dress and go down, she told Paul she had to go into town, making the excuse that she was in need of a new dress. 'For tomorrow evening,' she lied, 'when we entertain your hotelier friends.'

He never argued when it was to do with his precious hotel. 'Of course, sweetheart. But don't be gone too long, will you? And make sure it's not too gaudy – we don't want you looking more like a tart than the wife of a reputable hotelier. Oh, and it mustn't be too tight-fitting – not like the last one I had to throw away. I'd come and help choose it, only I promised Aunt Agatha I'd take her to see the flooring I've decided on for the new conservatory.'

'Of course.' Secretly delighted that she had escaped their company at least for a short time, she smiled sweetly. 'We wouldn't want to disappoint dear Aunt Aggie, would we?'

He grinned like a fat little boy given a bag of sweets. 'Exactly! That was my thinking, too.'

As she departed the house, he warned, 'Remember, the dress must be smart and fitting for the occasion. You won't make me cross now, will you, sweetheart?'

'Of course I won't.' As if I would, she thought angrily. What she would like to do was tear up everything in her closet that he had helped choose, and burn it in front of him and his 'darling' Aunt Agatha. Then she would like to storm out, with a smile and a wave, secure in the knowledge that she would never be back. One of these days, God willing, she would do exactly that.

* * *

Her only sanctuary was Emily, and that was where she headed now.

The dear woman was on the front doorstep, still in her dressing-gown, collecting her gill of milk and the early morning newspaper. 'Mary! Whatever brings you out so early?' She gave a wry little smile. 'The old woman's not chucked you out, has she?'

'Not yet.' Mary thought if she didn't have Emily to confide in, she would go completely out of her mind. 'I've managed to escape for an hour or so.'

Emily tutted. 'Come in, lass. I've got the kettle on. You can tell me all about it.' With the milk in one hand and the morning newspaper tucked under her arm, she led Mary down the passage to the sitting room, where she placed the newspaper on the dresser, before taking the milk through to the scullery and seating them both in the warm kitchen.

Neither of them saw the article on the front page, telling of the horrific murders . . . nor did they see the pictures of Nancy and her adopted family around her.

Instead, they chatted companionably, and when they were seated by the fire which was already blazing up the chimney, Mary told her of the way it was, and how things were getting worse by the day. 'Sometimes I feel no better than a prisoner,' she said. 'I'm not allowed to go out or have any friends, or even choose my own clothes. I don't know how long I can stand it, Emily. I feel trapped, I'm so unhappy.'

Being the straightforward woman she was, Emily could only suggest, 'You've got to have it out with him! He needs to know how unhappy you are. He has to see you're not his slave, or someone he owns, just because he put a ring on your finger.'

'I've tried that, and it only ends up with me being ostracised for days on end.' She sighed, wiping her hands across her face as if to shut him out of her mind. 'He doesn't mean to be selfish or unkind, and I know he loves me, though it's a suffocating kind of love. It's just that he's impossible to live with. Sometimes he's like a baby, always wanting to be reassured; always demanding attention. Then he behaves like a spoiled brat when he doesn't get his own way.'

Emily knew what was in Mary's mind, and her heart went out to her. 'You wish now that you'd never left Robert, don't you?'

'Oh yes, Emily! Every minute of every day.' For a moment it was all too much and she had to swallow hard to compose herself; though her eyes shone with tears of regret as she went on, 'I should have made more of an effort to befriend Jack. I should never have left them. To tell you the truth, Emily, I've never forgiven myself for what I did.'

'That's not being fair on yourself!' Emily was adamant. 'You tried your best and it wasn't enough. There's blame on the father, too, remember – *and* the boy. No doubt, wherever they are, they're probably feeling as bad as you are now.'

Mary doubted that. 'I shouldn't think they ever give me a second thought,' she confessed sadly. 'Although I think of them all the time, Robert and his children. I often wonder what they're doing now, and if they still live in the same house in Bedford. Hilltops, it was called.'

Suddenly she bent her head and the sobs could be held back no longer. 'I can't stay with Paul. I'm beginning to hate him. Agatha has him under her thumb and I play no real part in his life any more. I'm shut out, and in a way I'm grateful for that. But I feel I'm wasting my life. What can I do, Emily? What can I do to put it right?'

The older woman calmed her and they talked some more, at the end of which it was decided that Mary would have a heart-to-heart with Paul, and tell him exactly how she felt. 'I'll explain that I need to be released from our marriage,' Mary said. 'If he refuses, I'll take what's mine and leave. I'm still young. I can get a job, find a place to five and make a new life. However hard it might be, it can't be any worse than what I've got now.'

'It's time,' Emily agreed. 'And you don't have to find a place,' she chided, 'not while I've a spare room going – and if yon Aggie doesn't like it, she can damned well mind her own business, because I'm not her nephew, and I'm not so easily manipulated!'

Chuckling merrily, she suggested, 'Right – I'm ready for my breakfast now, and I suggest we celebrate with another cup of tea, and a plate of eggs, bacon and some of my homemade soda bread.'

Relieved and delighted that she had at last decided to confront Paul, Mary gladly offered, 'I'll make the breakfast. You sit there and relax.'

'All right.' Emily loved having Mary here. 'I'll go and get washed and dressed. I can't be sitting across the table from you, wearing my scruffy old robe.' She laughed. 'Besides, whatever would *Paul* have to say?'

While Mary went into the kitchen, Emily clambered out of the chair. 'I'll not be long,' she called.

A moment later, Mary almost dropped the frying pan when she heard Emily scream out, 'Oh, my God!'

Rushing into the sitting room, Mary found her staring at the paper. 'Whatever's wrong?'

Emily apologised. 'I'm sorry if I gave you a fright, but look at this. It's terrible!' She handed Mary the paper. This woman murdered her husband and his lover – cut them to ribbons, it says.' Clutching her throat, she had to sit down. 'Dear God, whatever is the world coming to?'

But Mary wasn't listening. Her attention was caught by the picture of that family, and in particular the girl at the front. 'Nancy?' Her voice was barely audible. 'It can't be. And yet I could never mistake your face, even all these years later . . .'

Seeing how the colour had drained from Mary's face and the way her hands trembled as she held the newspaper, Emily asked, 'Are you all right, dear?'

For a minute Mary remained silent, her gaze focused on Nancy's face. 'I can't be certain,' she whispered, 'but there's something about the eyes. Nancy had such beautiful blue eyes. She looks about the right age, too, but I can't be sure. And yet . . .'

'What is it, love?' Emily peered at the rather blurred photograph in the paper. 'Are you saying you think that girl is Nancy . . . Robert's daughter?'

Mary looked up, her eyes alight with excitement. 'Every instinct in my body tells me it's her,' she said. 'The eyes – unforgettably pretty, the way she shyly cocks her head to one side, the slim figure and long fair hair. And yet, how *can* it be? It's impossible! She doesn't belong to this Cornwell family. She's a Sullivan!'

Ever philosophical, Emily answered, 'You don't know what happened after you left,' she said. 'Happen that poor, crazed woman is the mother who deserted her, and she came back to take her away from Robert. That's possible, isn't it?'

Mary could not deny it, but she hoped for all their sakes it wasn't so. 'My God! It doesn't bear thinking about. If she did come and take Nancy away, it would have broken Robert's heart. He doted on those children. Oh, and what about Nancy? What will happen to her now?'

She made a decision there and then. 'I'm going back to Bedford, I *have* to see him. I have to be sure.'

Emily could not dissuade her and so she gave her blessing. 'What will you tell Paul?'

'That our marriage should never have happened and that it's best if we part.' Holding Emily in her arms, she told her, 'I'll keep in touch. Whatever happens I'll let you know.'

Emily was glad of that. 'Don't let Paul bully you,' she warned.

'And mind you tell him when that interfering old harridan is not about.'

'I don't care if she is – in fact, I'd prefer her to be there.' A great surge of courage welled up inside her. 'Take care of yourself,' she told her old friend; another hug and she was on her way.

Paul Marshall was shaken to his roots. 'What do you mean, you're leaving? You *can't* leave! You're my wife!'

'Not any more I'm not.' Addressing Agatha, she said, 'I hope you're satisfied with your handiwork. Who knows, we might well have had a chance to make it work, but you wouldn't let us alone. You've bullied and dictated until he's got just like you. You should be happy now. You've got him right where you want him, but you haven't got *me*, and you never will have. I hope to God I never set eyes on you again.'

'Get out then!' the old woman said spitefully. 'You were never a proper wife to him anyway.'

'Yes, go on,' Paul parroted. 'But you walk out that door and you'll not get a single penny from me, *ever*!'

At that point without even the tiniest of regrets, Mary walked away, leaving Paul blubbering like a baby, and his aunt talking to him as if he was a bairn in arms. 'It's all right,' she kept saying. 'You've still got me.'

As she boarded the tram, Mary allowed herself a little smile. She had the clothes on her back, and a fat wad of money in her purse – the money Paul had given her to buy the dress he wanted to show her off in that evening.

She had no home and no plans other than to see Robert and his children. But she was happier than she had been for years. It was as though she had just been released from prison.

Retracing the steps of the journey she had made ten long years ago was an arduous business. When Mary had fled from Bedford in 1895, she had scarcely known what she was doing, or where she was going. Now, with Robert at the forefront of her mind, and a hunger in her heart to see him, the tedious journey wore her out and, emerging from the station in Bedford, she made straight for a small hotel, where she slept twelve hours straight through.

The next morning, refreshed but apprehensive, she took the omnibus to the village where they had all lived together, and gathering up all of her courage, she knocked on the door of Hilltops. To her horror a young woman answered it. Was this Robert's new wife?

What she learned over the next few minutes left her gasping in shock. Never could she have imagined any of this!

The new tenant, for this was she, told her: 'I'm surprised you don't know about what went on. I thought the whole of Bedfordshire knew about the way he were torn to shreds under the wheels of a carriage and how they took away his children. Years he were in the hospitals, one after the other. At one time they thought he would never make it. Then when he came out they wouldn't tell him where the children had gone. It wasn't allowed, they said. "The children are fostered and you gave away your rights when you didn't come back".'

'Where is he now?' Mary could scarcely get the words out.

The woman shook her head. 'No idea. The last I heard, he were taken on by some carrier or other . . . ferrying passengers to and fro.'

Mary thanked the woman and took the omnibus back to the centre, where she booked herself in for another couple of nights at the hotel. That done, she set off to find out where Robert might be.

It was five o'clock on the following day, after visiting three carriers and various offices, that she arrived at the premises of Mortimer Jackson. Footsore and weary, she went into the office where the receptionist sat, scribbling into a ledger. 'Excuse me, I wonder if you could help me?' she asked.

At that moment, Robert and Mortimer were in the adjoining office, going through the details of the successful purchase he'd made. 'I told you, if I could only manage to corner Carruthers, I'd make him an offer he couldn't refuse,' the big man was saying jubilantly.

'It's a good job the other buyers weren't told why the sale had been cancelled,' Robert said wryly. 'If they knew how you'd robbed them of a chance to bid, they'd have strung you from the rafters.'

'Ah well, that's the name of the game,' Jackson crowed, tapping his nose artfully. 'It were the auctioneer I had to pay off, the rest was easy. Anyway, we got what we were after and once they're delivered, I'll have the vehicles stripped and serviced, then it's off with the old livery and on with a new one – the colour being your choice, I think.' He wrote on a piece of paper:

JACKSON & SULLIVAN
Carriers of Repute

Robert was astonished. 'I thought I'd be flying under *your* flag?' he remarked excitedly. 'I had no idea you were putting my name up there as well.'

'It's no more than you deserve,' the big man told him. 'Mind you, you've yet to earn first name first place, so think on that.'

Robert promised him he would. Then: 'You haven't forgotten I won't be in tomorrow morning?' he reminded him. 'I've to go to the council offices and depending what I manage to find out, I might not be in till Monday.'

'That's all right, I hope you find out where they are. Nothing would gladden my old heart more, than for you to find them children of yours.' He pointed to the door. 'Now, I know it's only three o'clock, but I reckon you've earned an early finish today, so be off with you, before I change my mind.'

At that precise moment the receptionist had ascertained Mary's business and was about to tell her that yes, they did have a Mr Robert Sullivan here, but he was ensconced in the office with the boss at the time – when the door swung open and Robert himself emerged, she told Mary, 'Here he is now.'

Mary turned; Robert stopped in his tracks, staring at her, wondering if he was seeing things. He came forward to see Mary's face, alight with love, the bright shiny tears hovering on her lashes, and he couldn't believe his eyes. '*Mary!*' His mouth fell open in a cry as he grabbed her to him. '*Oh, Mary!*' His voice shook with emotion.

After a moment he held her at arm's length. 'I can't believe it.' He laughed – a silly, nervous laugh that made her smile. 'Is it really you?'

Looking on, the receptionist thought she had never seen anything so romantic and wonderful, and even she had to fight back the tears.

With his arm round her and the feel of his strength holding her, Mary felt weak with joy. 'Come on,' he said, 'I'm taking you to a little café I know not far from here. I want to know everything! Where you've been. What you've been doing. Why you're here! *Everything!*'

In the café, with its private little corners and discreet waiters, they talked together. Over a pot of coffee, Robert told her of the tragic and unhappy events that had touched his life and that of his children, since she'd been gone. 'Tomorrow I should know what's happened to them,' he explained. 'I'm excited but worried all at the same time. They'd better not turn me away, not this time!'

'I think you should go *now*,' Mary advised. 'I don't think you should wait until tomorrow.'

He laughed. 'If only you knew how I've hounded them in that town hall, but they wouldn't give me any information and, because of what happened, the authorities were on their side, not mine. But now that Galloways is closed down and Ennington arrested, they're deciding on charges, but to do that they've had to examine each and every ledger and every entry that's been lodged over the years.'

'How long will that take?'

'Tomorrow is the day they should be done with their work, and that's when I'll demand to know where Nancy and Jack were taken.'

'No, Robert,' she insisted. 'I think you should go and see the officials *now*!'

'What are you getting at?' He sensed she was trying to tell him something. 'What is it?'

Taking out the newspaper cutting, she showed it to him. As he read it, she saw his face turn grey and when he put the paper aside, he didn't say a word. Instead he closed his eyes and groaned, as if all the pain in the world was oozing out of him.

Suddenly he was out of his seat and throwing money down on the table. 'Come on!' He took her by the hand. They went out of the café at a run, and didn't stop until they reached the town hall, where he demanded to see the officer in charge.

When the man arrived, Robert thrust the newspaper cutting under his nose. 'See that? That's my daughter – and you sent her to a bloody murderess! Now, unless you give me the exact address – *and* tell me where you sent my son – there'll be another newspaper article and you won't like what it says!'

The officer could see he would get no change out of this man, who had driven them almost crazy for too many years now. 'You'd best come in,' he said, and with hope in his heart and Mary by his side, Robert followed him into the office.

Chapter Twenty-three

Justin and Jack were coming back with the cart from across the fields, when they saw Lizzy running towards them; with her were three people, a man, a woman and a girl. '*Jack! Look who's here!*' Her voice sailed towards them.

The three people stopped while she ran on, waving her arms and calling out, 'Hurry, Jack! There's somebody to see you!' Excited and laughing, she ran alongside the cart.

'Get away from there, lass!' Justin was concerned she might get caught up in the shaft. 'What the devil's going on?'

As they drew nearer, Jack focused his eyes on the man – grey-haired and gaunt, he didn't seem to know him. The woman beside him was familiar, but he couldn't be certain. Oh, the girl though . . . his mind flashed back to the orphanage, to the images that had haunted him ever since. He saw Nancy being taken away, and he recalled how devastated he was when she didn't wave, and oh, how he had cried – then, and since.

Suddenly he knew, and his heart soared. 'NANCY!' His voice carried over the air and when she heard it she ran to him. As he leapt off the carriage he caught her to him, laughing and crying and thinking he must be dreaming.

He held her away and looked at her; he touched her face with trembling hands, and clasped her to him, sobbing like he'd never sobbed before. 'You didn't forget after all,' he wept. 'Oh Nancy, I thought I'd never see you again!'

Together they went to Robert. Strangely shy and unsure, they stood apart for a minute, then they were hugging, the pain and emotion of the past years spilling over. And then they embraced Mary, who was also quickly forgiven. 'I drove you away,' Jack confessed. 'I was bad to do such terrible things.'

Mary held him close. 'All water under the bridge,' she said. 'We've found each other now.'

At peace with each other, they walked back to the cottage – slowly, because Justin was not the man he used to be. 'I'm gerrin' old,' he told Robert. 'I need a man about the place.' He exchanged glances with Jack, and Jack knew exactly what was crossing his mind.

That night it was decided. Jack would stay with Lizzy and the old man, where he was happiest, while Nancy would go back to Bedford Town and live with her father and Mary.

It had been an emotional reunion and now it was time to leave. 'We'll be up here often to see you,' Nancy promised, and Jack told her the very same. '*We must never lose each other again.*'

Epilogue

In the years that followed, Lizzy and Nancy struck up the greatest of friendships and remained close for as long as they lived.

Justin lived to the ripe old age of ninety-two – long enough to see Lizzy and Jack married, with four lovely grandchildren to call him 'Gran'pa' and sit on his knee, while he told them stories of days gone by.

Robert thrived in business and became a very wealthy man. On the termination of her marriage to Paul, and of his own, long-dead marriage to Mathilde, he married Mary and a year later she gave birth to a son. 'He's the spitting image of you,' she told Robert, and everyone agreed.

Four years after his mother was hanged for the murder of her husband and three women, and with his sister Pauline put into an institution for the mentally ill, David was left a small fortune. He sold the family home and bought a house in the centre of Bedford, where he set up an accountancy practice.

Six months later, after a wonderful courtship, he and Nancy were married; in the following four years they had two beautiful daughters, Ruby and Lorna.

Pauline was treated and declared ready for release two years later. Throughout her time in the mental home, she had been visited by all the family, and in particular by the young man her father had approved of. Peter Carstairs was neither handsome nor brilliant, but he had loved her from the first. On the day she was released, they were married, and moved out to the countryside, where it was thought she might recuperate faster.

She and Peter were very happy together; being a man of means he could afford for someone to run the shipping business inherited from his father, while spending every minute with Pauline.

Little by little the truth emerged, as to how, after being the only girl, Sara-Jane was born. 'A mistake' her mother often claimed. After a time, she seemed to take an unnatural dislike to the child.

Possessive and protective of her mother, Pauline was always jealous of her little sister, yet on that day in the park when her mother had deliberately pushed Sara-Jane into the water, she had gone in to save her, but the icy river was fast-flowing and she lost her grip; a failure for which she had never forgiven herself.

Her mother had pleaded with her not to tell how the child had met her untimely end, and so the drowning was recorded as a terrible accident. It had been a crippling secret for her to keep for all those years.

Because of that, Pauline had been filled with hatred and distrust of everyone, hitting out whenever she felt threatened. Her mind slowly began to be affected.

Still manically protective of her mother, she had seen how her father was always seeking out other women. One day her mother confessed how she had killed and would kill again if it meant keeping her husband from leaving her. On seeing how Edward had seemed to become unusually fond of his last mistress, she had decided they must both be got out of the way.

So, the mother was the murderer, and the daughter an unwilling accomplice. It was the most terrible burden for anyone to carry, let alone a young girl. But, thanks to Peter and the support of her family, Pauline recovered.

In the park on this glorious summer's day, Robert and Mary sat watching their little boy and their grandchildren at play. 'Isn't it strange how it all came about?' Mary commented softly. 'But we're all safe now. We have each other.'

Robert kissed her tenderly. Glancing up at the blue skies, he smiled knowingly. 'Do you know what I believe?' he asked.

'I already know,' she replied, 'because I feel the same.' She wrapped her arms round him and held him tight. 'Somebody up there must have been looking over us,' she whispered.

The sun shone down, the skies were sapphire blue; the sound of the children's laughter was like a tonic.

This was the perfect day.

JOSEPHINE COX

The Woman Who Left

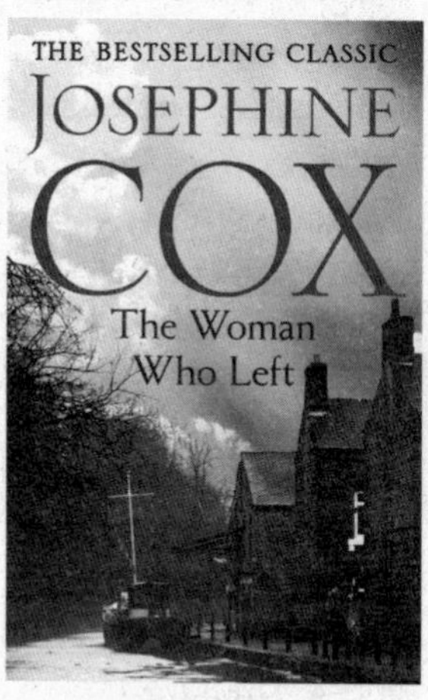

Louise and Ben Hunter's loving marriage is marred only by their unfulfilled longing for a child. Living and working with Ben's father, Ronnie, they are quietly contented. But when Ronnie dies, their whole world changes. Ben's lazy brother, Jacob, returns, convinced he stands to inherit Ronnie's small fortune. And he means to have his brother's wife; though just as she did years before, Louise warns him off. Jacob, however, is not so easily dismissed. When he realises Ben will inherit everything, Jacob is beside himself with rage, and commits a terrible deed, one that threatens to destroy everything his brother and Louise hold dear . . .